TWO PRISONERS

TWO PRISONERS

by

LAJOS ZILAHY

\
This edition published in 1999 by
Prion Books Limited, Imperial Works,
Perren Street, London NW3 3ED

ISBN 1-85375-318-1

Cover design by Bob Eames
Cover image courtesy of Images Colour Library
Printed and bound in Great Britain
by Creative Print & Design, Wales

CONTENTS

PART ONE: FAREWELL

PART ONE: FAREWELL

I

A young man, smoking a cigarette and leaning on a stick, stopped at a street corner to listen. A *tárogato*, an ancient wind instrument reminiscent of a giant oboe, lamented the flight of summer from the hills on the right bank of the Danube in Budapest.

It was six o'clock of an evening in September 1913.

Now that he was so near, he felt no desire to go up to the Vargas' apartment, where he had been invited to tea, and mingle with so many strangers to whom he would have nothing to say. Acquaintances thus formed serve only to embarrass you when you meet one of them in a trolley a fortnight later: Should you, or should you not greet that woman in the little velvet hat, sitting opposite, whom you met casually at some tea party? Not to greet her is bad, but to greet her is worse, for it is from such encounters that the most boring conversations may develop.

The young man listened to the lovely sound of the tárogato and felt it would certainly be more intelligent to spend the last beautiful hours of this September day taking a pleasant stroll through the silent little streets of Buda.

He swung round and went down the street, turning his back on the apartment building where Doctor Varga lived. He stopped in front of the large, dark, plate-glass window of a pharmacy and straightened his necktie. Then for a long moment he studied his face.

The first glance revealed it as attractive and pleasant. Summer had left it with a warm coat of tan, from which the gray eyes shone with an expression of serenity and good cheer. The features were grave and the chestnut hair, softly wavy, seemed to spring from beneath the wide-brimmed felt hat; the nose was straight, the neck long, the head carried rather proudly; the mouth with its clean, firm line, indicated reserve. After standing a moment longer in front of the dark panel as though posing for a photograph, he yawned and went on.

A light gray coat, somewhat worn, but still smart, clothed his lithe figure. If only by his calm and dignified gait, it was already possible to see what he would be like at sixty: an elderly man, slender and handsome, with the same measured tread, since he would doubtless be in mourning. He might have a title then—councillor, for instance—or be holding some high office, such as a membership in the House of Lords. Indeed, all of life lay before him; he had just taken his doctorate in law and was working, for the moment, in the claims department of a large bank.

With a flourish of his stick, Peter walked on. Occasionally a maid, dressed in starched and rustling muslin, passed him quickly and furtively in the empty street, and at the house doors the caretakers had settled to smoke their pipes. The warm boredom of the Sunday afternoon lay diffused, yellow and sad, in the length and breadth of the street.

Opposite the bridge, where a bathing establishment had once stood, a high wooden fence hid from the public gaze the construction of a new Gellert Hotel.

He raised his eyes and selected an empty spot, high up. There, perhaps, would be a room, a bed, and the head of a suicide hanging over its edge. There in the next room—a young married couple on their wedding night would seek each other in the darkness. How strange! What words and sighs, what voices and laughter, what life will assemble here in the near future—here where the wind now stirs only naked, empty air!

Tiring of his train of thought, he felt the bitterness of indifference stick in his gullet. But, turn where he might, no escape was possible.

With a shudder of trepidation, he suddenly saw life

stretching dull and aimless before him. While he was still in school he had looked forward with feverish impatience to passing his baccalaureate; and later, as a law student, he believed that once he had passed his final examination, mysterious and invisible doors would be opened to him —doors behind which light, warmth, women, and all unknown sensations waited.

And here he was now, in the street, without the energy or ambition even to light a cigarette. He stood motionless, scowling, looking vaguely ahead and wondering: "What will happen—what can life possibly have in store for me?"

Two days before he had kissed the Bunzes' German governess, Annie, pressing her hard against the wall on the staircase. He could still smell her exotic perfume, sweet and sickening. Then, abruptly, he abandoned those thoughts.

His mother wanted him to marry. She had been teasing him for months with her extravagant praises of the Vajnik girl, always pretending to be thinking of her quite casually. With naive caution and craftiness, she was trying to inoculate him, as it were, with Aranka—he already knew how many sheets she would have in her trousseau. Then he saw Aranka Vajnik's greasy skin and her inquisitive, suspicious glance.

His thoughts reverted to his mother and, as had happened so often before, his heart ached while he asked himself why he behaved so brutally to that sweet, lovely, little old lady. Only yesterday he had lost his temper with her because his collars had not been brought back from the laundry on time; and yet, poor woman, surely it was not her fault. He remembered distinctly the frightened, wretched look she had given him and, after she left the room without uttering a word, the dry, short little cough that held all her humiliation. He had promised himself once more that, from that very day, he would be most attentive and tender to his mother, whom he could hardly think of without tears when he was away from her. But would he be able to keep a promise that he had broken so often?

He beat the air several times with his stick, banishing these thoughts like a swarm of mosquitoes, and, whistling, he walked toward a poster showing the theatrical performances of the day. Suddenly, Paul Szücs came into view.

"Hello, old fellow!" Szücs cried, still some distance away. The two young men had met at an athletic club. Peter was accustomed to seeing Szücs in boxing tights— he was a clerk at Police Headquarters—and now he surveyed his Sunday elegance with an amused air, for Paul was dressed according to the custom of those uncouth devotees of the muscle when—rarely enough— they attire themselves for a social function.

Paul Szücs' derby—for obscure reasons at least three sizes too small—was worn over one ear and gave him an easy air of self-confidence. His thick bull's neck was squeezed into a high turned-down collar, whose rumpled appearance told of the young man's struggles to button it. Fresh little razor cuts adorned his countenance, and in each of these little scratches might be read, in cryptic crimson characters, all the vile curses Szücs had uttered while shaving. His loud, striped trousers were so short that the straps of his high boots were all but visible. His overcoat, too, was so tight that the powerful muscles of his shoulders threatened to burst through at any moment.

"Come along, old chap, we may as well go up now," said Szücs, who had also been invited to the doctor's and was waiting with obvious impatience for the moment when he might appear upon the scene.

"I was just thinking I wouldn't go," said Peter morosely.

"You won't go? There will be lovely girls, my dear fellow," said Szücs, who liked to use that form of address and whose speech was ordinarily very glib.

"And little Mme. Galamb will be there, too," he added, giving his friend a meaningful wink.

Peter smiled as he looked at Szücs, who, with his butchered face and impossible attire, was hastening with so much self-assurance to a gathering of strangers.

"We'll be bored to death," said Peter ill-humoredly.

"Don't you believe it," Szücs answered, taking his friend's arm. "We'll get into a corner and look at the women."

"Who'll be there?" asked Peter when they had started, thinking there would still be time to turn back before they reached the apartment.

"Don't ask me; I'm going there for the first time myself."

The two young men had met Dr. Varga at the athletic club, and his wife at a dinner at the same club. The doctor was a middle-aged man, a government adviser, and physician to several societies; he was a good man and, like most good men, an insufferable bore. The Vargas lived in great comfort, had no children, and liked to entertain. An impressive silver challenge cup had been presented to the club by the doctor. His wife was prominent in all the important charitable organizations.

After looking up the apartment number in the foyer, the young men went up. Szücs stopped at the first floor.

"Wait a moment, old fellow." Cautiously he removed his short overcoat and let down the tails of his morning coat, which he had pinned up so they would not show below the other.

The doctor's apartment was on the second floor. The hall was littered with an array of sticks, overcoats, parasols, hats, and officers' caps. Peter paused before the hall mirror, pulled a small comb from his pocket, and passed it twice through his fine auburn hair. Then he carefully arranged his handkerchief in the outside pocket of his coat. Meantime, Szücs was eyeing the parlor maid who was waiting to show them in.

"What's your name, little dove?" he asked the servant, who could have been taken for a guest if she had not been wearing a white apron.

"Rose," she answered smiling, pushing away Szücs' hand that sought to pinch her chin.

"By Jove, what a sweet little thing! I could eat her alive," he exclaimed, and his eyes devoured the pretty girl with her delicate hands and slender waist. Then, turning to Peter: "Do you see, my boy, that alone made it worth coming!"

They entered the circular living room, which was filled with tobacco smoke, the laughter of women, and the deeper tones of masculine voices.

The hostess came forward and, having greeted them, proceeded to introduce them. They grasped the gloved hands of women and masculine palms withdrawn from trouser pockets. They were of varying temperature and texture—cold or warm, dry or moist—and the manner of proffering the hand varied, too, from disgustingly lax to confidingly frank.

They shook about thirty hands, one after the other, without being able to distinguish a single face or remember a single name among the crowd.

When the introductions were over, Peter had lost Paul, who, with hands on his hips in accordance with his own ideas of elegance, was engaged in earnest conversation with a plump little woman. Surely that must be little Mme. Galamb. Peter, very uncomfortable, edged toward the wall.

"Do sit down, please," said the hostess as she quickly passed by.

But that was impossible; there weren't enough seats, and several people already were standing, their backs against the wall.

A frail, blond woman was seated in the center. She had been given the most prominent place and everyone addressed her in German; some called her *Graefin*, others *Frau Excellenz*. Her Excellency had hands as small and white as a twelve-year-old girl's, and these almost abnormally small hands were constantly and with nervous rapidity adjusting something in her hair, while she smiled mechanically at the person she was addressing. A slender man, whom she called Ivan, was standing beside her.

Two young girls sat by the piano. One had chestnut hair, verging on red; the other was a brunette. Hardly anything could be seen of their faces, hidden in the shadow of large hats. An elegant, blond young man, leaning against the piano, was talking with the reddish-haired girl. Peter saw immediately that he had a good tailor; he felt a slight twinge of envy, for he cherished a secret desire eventually to have his clothes made by the best tailor.

Many elderly women and spinsters were seated in little groups, leaning toward one another like reeds in the wind as they talked.

Surveying the assemblage, Peter got the impression that the women were more elegantly, more harmoniously dressed than the men. A pleasant-faced lad, in the uniform of a military school, brought him a chair, saying simply and frankly, as though he had known him a long time: "Take it, please." He could not have been more than nineteen.

"Oh, thanks," protested Peter, "but really I am not tired."

"Please do. I belong here," explained the cadet, "and it is my business to see that everyone has a seat."

Peter took the chair and carried it to a woman in a yellow dress, who was talking with a captain of the hussars.

The cadet, obviously tired of carrying chairs back and forth, stood leaning against the wall for a moment, and Peter learned from him that the blond countess seated in the large armchair was the wife of a brigadier general. The cadet whispered behind his hand to Peter: "I think there is something between them."

Then he proceeded to point out the most interesting persons present.

He indicated Sigismund Pán, professor of the Conservatory; the short, stubby one, with red hair, mustache, and beard was Dr. Schumeister, editor of a German newspaper. Some of them the cadet was not able to identify exactly. Peter had a vague impression of having read the names in the newspapers. The one who interested him most was the blond young man whose well-cut dark blue suit he had just been envying.

"That's Michael Ádám," the cadet volunteered, "Don't you know him? He has just got his lawyer's degree."

"And the two young girls by the piano?" Peter asked.

"Those—" the cadet began, but was unable to finish, as the hostess called him.

"Come along, Johnny!"

"I'll be back directly," he said to Peter and disappeared with Mme. Varga, who, holding his arm, whispered something in his ear. She was apparently sending him on some confidential errand.

Peter remained alone against the wall and surveyed the room, whose furnishings, second-rate and discordant, showed plainly that on working days this room served as a waiting room for patients. The hostess stood near a glass door and counted the number of guests on her fingers to determine how many cups of tea to serve. The eyes of pretty Rose, who stood beside her in her pert white apron, also went from guest to guest; finally, they agreed that thirty-two cups would be needed.

Mme. Varga fluttered from one group to another, sitting for a second at each place. Her face, her hands, and even her hair were heavily powdered. Her bulging waistline and large, flabby bosom were squeezed into a stiff corset. Her eyelashes were always sprinkled with powder, as those of a miller's apprentice with flour. She came and went about the room, feverishly restless, obviously uneasy and fearful lest everyone was being bored to death—a fear that was not without some foundation.

Her lifelong ambition had been to have a *salon* as soon as possible. But being typically lower middle class, she was incapable of developing into the guiding spirit of any gathering, and her guests, chosen for their social advantages, felt like animals of various breeds caged together in her house. They gazed at one another and sniffed the air suspiciously.

As early as eight o'clock, some of the guests began to make their escape. Peter noticed that the elegant Michael Ádám shook hands, somewhat stealthily, only with the red-haired girl who was sitting beside the piano with her friend.

"Please play something for us," Dr. Varga asked Professor Pán.

Pán sat at the piano. He placed his large pasty hands caressingly on the keys and played an easy piece by Mozart, which was applauded long and vigorously. Amiable words of congratulation mingled with rapturous sighs.

The wife of the German editor, Mrs. Schumeister, expressed a desire to hear the Ninth Symphony, but when the host sought to convey her request, it was discovered that the musician had slipped away in the interval.

Soon there remained hardly ten people in the room.

Mme. Galamb, who had gone on talking to Paul, was also getting ready to leave when an old lady in blue, Mme. Lénárt, declared she had come all the way from Szentlörinc, in the hope of hearing Yolanda—that is to say, Mme. Galamb—recite once more.

"Good heavens!" Mme. Galamb protested. "It is so long since I recited anything. Please, dear Aunt, don't ask it of me!" And her dark face, on which a number of velvety black moles were visible, flushed in anticipation of the ordeal; but she protested in vain; the company compelled her to yield, clamorously demanding the recitation. The cadet was most insistent of all, as if he had been appointed to the task. Finally, Mme. Galamb surrendered, and with an appealing smile walked to the center of the room.

Whispers of "Hush!" stopped the conversation, and an impressive silence fell at once. Her voice unsteady at first, she began to recite Endrody's poem, "Haidé."

She spoke the lines emotionally.

"And what the babbling sea-foam whispers . . ."

She closed her eyes and injected a sensual warmth into her words.

The dark young girl by the piano hid her mouth with her gloved hand, lest she burst into laughter. The other, with the red-brown hair, was indignant, nudging her friend with her elbow and turning her back. But she, too, was praying for the end of the poem, feeling threatened with hysterical laughter.

Mme. Lénárt was listening, her neck thrust forward, her eyes moist and blinking. Szücs stood staring at Yolanda Galamb, his legs wide apart, his arms hanging in front of him, the two big fists resting one atop the other.

Before the last verse, the pause seemed interminable. The distraught performer stared straight ahead, her eyes fixed on the floor. After a moment it was clear she had forgotten what followed. The atmosphere grew almost unbearable, the silence tense, painful, and uneasy.

Mme. Galamb continued to stand there in the center of the room, in a terrible predicament, the eyes of ten people focused upon her, suffering a horrible punishment for her boldness. But the hostess was even more embarrassed.

Szücs was trying to prompt her, but she stopped him with a reproachful glance, for the verse he was whispering was from another famous poem. Suddenly, when the unendurably long silence had become an agony, a resounding "Cock-a-doodle-do" rang out, providing a happy, noisy deliverance.

It was Johnny mimicking the cry of the cock, Johnny who could imitate any animal's cry. Mme. Galamb rushed at him and thumped him twice on the back; everyone laughed, and the situation was saved.

"You see, dear Aunt," said Mme. Galamb to Mme. Lénárt, "I told you it had been a long, long time since I had recited anything."

"Never mind, Yolanda dear," said Mme. Lénárt, wiping her eyes, "it was beautiful, just the same."

The doctor was looking about for some new form of entertainment to hold his departing guests a few moments longer, when his eyes fell on Peter.

"Come and demonstrate your science for us," he said, taking him by the arm and leading toward the writing desk.

"What science?" Peter objected. And suddenly he felt ill at ease, with everyone's attention fastened upon him.

"He's a graphologist," Varga explained to his guests; "he reads people's characters by their handwriting."

This was received with loud cheers. Peter was thrust into the armchair at the desk before he could utter a word of protest. The host made ready a sheet of white paper, pen, and ink.

Peter lent himself to the new game with good grace, and what was more, liked himself in his new role.

"This will be worth doing only if I can be quite frank and honest," he said, addressing the company. "So this is a warning to those who are oversensitive and cannot endure hard truths, to withdraw. I shall have no apology to make to anyone whose feelings may be hurt. But, since I know no one here, I shall be impartial."

This uncompromising statement was received with general approval. Of course, no one wanted to withdraw; they all crowded around the desk. Hands of varying shapes, one after another, rested on the sheet of paper. First, feminine hands, curious and impatient. The guests stood as they wrote their names, and Peter could not even see their faces, but only the hands that rested in turn on the paper. And he studied these hands in the brief instant while they wrote.

The first was old and willful; it grasped the pen almost fiercely. The forefinger made a half circle around the pen, holding it as in a vise. The joints formed clean-cut angles, like brass knuckles.

Peter examined the signature for a moment; then, the center of attention, he began to speak in a monotone: "Has traveled much abroad. In youth had a talent for painting; indeed, painted pictures of some merit. Willful nature, difficult to influence. Has children. Quarrels much with her husband. Inveterate smoker. Has no ear for music . . ."

"Oh!" Mme. Lénárt interrupted, for it was she who was at the bar. "I have never smoked in my life!"

She laughed a falsetto laugh and withdrew, quite

offended that her musical ignorance should have been made public. She was sorry she had been persuaded to participate in this game, and now considered it all a pack of nonsense. On the other hand, she racked her brain indignantly, wondering how this young man could have learned that she and her husband got along like cat and dog.

Another hand followed. A little, plump, white hand, in which the bones could scarcely be detected. It wrote in small letters, in a backhand slant: "Mme. Étienne Galamb."

"Madame, you are one of the happiest creatures in the world," said Peter, looking intently at the writing and not at her at all. "You have neither disturbing desires, nor artistic aspirations, and you are very religious. You had one year in high school . . ."

"Two," Yolanda Galamb corrected suddenly, behind his back.

"Only one," Peter insisted.

"I left at Easter time in the second year," she answered tremulously.

Everyone laughed.

Another hand followed. Lean, slender fingers, boyish.

"Madame, you are going to have a divorce soon, for your nature is very inconstant."

"What cheek!" the dark girl burst out. "Why, I am not even married yet."

"Then I have made a mistake," Peter said, without changing his tone.

Now it was a man's strong, hairy hand that appeared and wrote the name in vigorous rapid strokes, "Baron Camille Beszterczey."

Peter recognized Paul Szücs hand at once, but he pretended not to notice the fraud.

Frowning, he studied the writing for a long time, then spoke in a measured voice: "Unmarried; much given to sport. Self-sufficient nature. Believes himself shrewder than anybody else, and yet at the bottom is nothing but a mooncalf!"

Paul Szücs immediately dealt Peter's head such a blow from behind that it hung sideways for a full minute.

The doctor was laughing so uncontrollably that the tears trickled into his blond beard.

Then a white hand touched the paper. The fingers were marked with faint pink lines, because its owner had just removed her gloves. This hand was white, sweet, and meek, yet inspired respect. It was a strange flower, beautiful with that beauty that only human flesh and blood can achieve when they unite to form a faultless line. It was a petal untouched as yet by the coming of a breath of shadow. Fresh and delicate, yet possessing a steely strength, it was the body's perfect instrument. How beautiful it must be when it arranged the curls of her hair, how beautiful when it tied a ribbon or grasped the neck of a violin, or when its fingers were nimble flames, leaping among the strings of a harp; most woeful when waving a farewell, or lying languidly on a tablecloth; most beautiful and most sensuous when after a passionate kiss it rested on the lips of the boy with a melancholy movement of thanks. . .

Such were the thoughts, rapid and confused, that crossed Peter's mind as that beautiful hand wrote the name "Miette Almády." The three even strokes of the "M" fell stiffly; the loop at the top of the "l" formed almost a triangle, and the head of the "e" described a tiny but well-formed spiral.

Peter raised the sheet, studied it closely, then for the first time slowly turned his head. In the lamp's shadow stood the young girl with the duskily glowing hair who had been sitting with her dark friend near the piano and talking to Michael Ádám. She was already smoothing the glove on her lovely hand, her eyebrows raised high, her lids half lowered, a faint flush on her cheeks. Her lips were compressed and on those lips a smile had settled that held a faint but kindly contempt for all graphological science, and yet there might have been discerned in that smile something grave, humble, virginal, as though she would say: "And now—judge me."

Peter turned his eyes back to the paper. He fidgeted in his armchair, then looked once more at the girl and once more at the sheet of paper. Suddenly he was seized by the feeling that he could not pronounce judgment upon this girl. He was confused and nonplussed. The science he had been practicing simply for the company's entertainment and with which he would have had no success at all if he hadn't been able to guess right in two per cent of the cases—this science suddenly seemed to him a provoking piece of folly. Instead of answering, he questioned.

"Miette? What is the origin of that name?"

The young girl blushed slightly, and said in a soft voice: "Mary."

"And how does one get Miette from Mary?" Peter asked with the mock severity that the game demanded.

"From Mariette," she answered.

The hostess remarked sweetly but somewhat pedantically: "In French Miette means crumb."

Impatiently Johnny, the cadet, threw in: "Let's not bother about that; let's hear about her character." Peter smilingly scrutinized the girl for a moment more, then folding the paper slowly, put it into his pocket and said mysteriously to Miette: "Your handwriting is interesting, so interesting that it requires closer study. I feel that it will reveal many things that I couldn't tell you, except in private."

Miette's face grew very red, and she threw her head back in a whole-hearted laugh, in which there was also a touch of apprehension.

Everyone protested loudly. The cadet rumpled his hair, struck the table, and said: "I want my money back —this won't do—I want a refund on my ticket."

The doctor was weeping with mirth and wiping his eyes with his handkerchief.

Mme. Lénárt tapped Peter's shoulder with her fan.

"Suspicious—very suspicious. You staged this whole comedy in order to have a tête-à-tête with a pretty girl!" Then, turning to Miette, "Careful, my child, be careful!"

But Miette scarcely heard her, for she was already moving toward the hall.

Everyone was making ready to leave. Mme. Galamb was terrified to discover that it was already past nine.

"Oh, my dears, a nice reception I shall get at home!" she cried, hurriedly donning her short coat.

Paul Szücs forgot in his haste to lift and pin up the tails of his coat, and when he had put on the little yellow overcoat again, the two panels hung below like mourning draperies. He rushed after Mme. Galamb.

In the hallway Peter caught up with the two girls, who were apparently leaving together.

"If you will allow me," he said to Miette, "I'll accompany you home."

It was the dark girl who answered instead of Miette.

"Perfect! Indeed, we shall be delighted," said Olga, after they had taken leave of their hosts.

Peter gave a silver crown that he had kept ready in his waistcoat pocket to the servant who was standing near the door. Then they left.

Miette and Olga, their arms intertwined, walked down the hallway a few steps ahead of him. Peter joined them on the staircase, but there Olga stopped and, suddenly turning to him, held out her hand.

"Thank you so much," she said, "for having taken us home," and she shook his hand warmly, then threw her head back and laughed a gay, clear laugh that showed all her white, sharp teeth.

Peter looked at her, at a loss to know what she meant.

"I live here, on the fourth floor," she said, running up the stairs.

"And you live here, too?" Peter asked Miette.

"No . . ." said Miette, blushing—charming, apologetic, confusion in her voice.

Peter noticed that she blushed easily and often.

"Where do you live?"

"There," said Miette, pointing to a door on the other side of the landing.

"I'll take you home just the same," Peter insisted.

And together they walked the fifteen steps or so that lay between the two ends of the landing. Peter would have liked to say something to her, something witty or charming, but nothing occurred to him; it was as if he had suddenly grown dumb.

Miette pressed the electric button, and a moment later the foyer was illuminated.

She extended her hand to him.

"Goodbye," she said in the expressionless voice that a woman might use who had met a man for the first time, wasn't even quite sure of his name, and never expected to see him again.

"Goodbye, Miss Miette," he said quickly, almost rudely, suddenly irritated by the thought that this girl was about to disappear, perhaps forever, behind this door.

In the brief moment required for Miette to enter the apartment, he surveyed the hall.

At the end of a wide, spacious foyer, a door opened into the hall. There, several valuable pieces of furniture testified to the fact that the apartment was fitted out with luxury and taste. Through the hall, the dining room was visible, where the electric chandelier had been lowered over the table set for dinner. An elderly man in a linen summer jacket, with a snowy beard like a collar, sat at the table. The lamplight cast golden tones over his sleek, bald head and his beard. He wore spectacles and, holding the newspaper at some distance from his eyes, was reading absorbedly.

All this lasted only a brief moment, for the entrance to the apartment was immediately dark again. Peter remained motionless for a long time, eyeing the unfriendly door.

Before leaving the house he examined the roster of tenants below and found the name, "Francis Almády," without difficulty.

Once in the street, he raised his eyes again to the windows of the second story and tried to estimate the number of rooms in the Almády apartment.

Then he went down the avenue. He dined at Holfer's,

and during the meal the same question kept going through his head: Why had he not seen the two girls earlier in the evening? His thoughts reverted for a moment to Olga, and he saw distinctly again her long, well-shaped leg as she hurriedly climbed the steps, and he heard her gay laughter.

But then he thought of Miette, the girl with the beautiful hands, and he felt that a certain force, tender and mysterious, radiated from her to him. He had felt it from the first moment, even before he had seen her face, when only her white hand touched the paper, the hand that hung softly from the white grenadine cuff, tightly adjusted to her wrist.

Peter reviewed in his mind all the faces he had seen that afternoon. He could see the women plainly enough, but of the men he could recall hardly any but the cadet and Uncle Kramer, a member of the municipal council. And it was only toward the very end that he remembered Michael Ádám in the well-cut suit he had envied. And now he remembered, too, that Ádám had been talking to Miette, that he had left very early and had said goodbye only to her, Miette. He sought to establish some bond between the young man and the girl.

"Surely they are in love," he thought; "perhaps they even kiss each other in secret."

His thoughts fastened on Miette.

"Miette . . ." he tried it several times, with different inflections, tasting, as it were, each letter of the strange name that, pronounced this way, in the solitude of the Danube esplanade, sounded like the sensual voice of a little reed pipe.

"What senseless names women choose to call themselves," he thought at last when he got up, throwing away his cigarette, which described a huge arc before it fell.

He started for home, whistling; he was no longer thinking of Miette, nor even of the evening at all.

On the way he stopped at a café in Kossuth Lajos Street, where he generally met his friends and played billiards until midnight.

Then he went home and to bed. Lighting the electric lamp on his bedside table, he began to read, propped on his elbow.

He was reading Dickens' *David Copperfield*.

II

The autumn sun wove light golden veils over the Danube. It was a quarter of two by the landing place clock, and the pedestrians on the esplanade were few.

Here and there, among the leaves seared by the summer heat, September was already displaying her golden-brown hues.

A one-legged beggar was sitting under a tree. His face was emaciated, ravaged by tuberculosis. His head hung down in sleep, a shaft of sunshine pierced his bloodless hand; his cap, empty of the smallest coin, lay beside him on the dusty pavement.

The trees trembled under a light breath of wind that rose from the Danube. It was as if they had sighed; then one of the trees dropped a delicate gold coin, a golden leaf, into the beggar's cap.

A little fox terrier raced along the deserted river bank, as if he were late for an important dinner. High up in the heavy, bluish-gray sky, a hawk soared, chasing pigeons. A nursemaid, pushing a light perambulator, appeared from the direction of the Petöfi monument; it was evident that her afternoon walk was over.

Peter, leaving his office, reached the esplanade and sat down to read the afternoon paper. He was about to leave again and had already folded up his paper, when he noticed a young man and a girl approaching rapidly along the suspension bridge. The brown silk dress molded itself to the girl's figure as a sail molds itself to the mast under a soft, gentle breeze. She had thrown her shoulders back a little, and the outlines of her small breasts were delicately suggested. At each step, the soft skirt clung to her legs, and almost every line of her body was gloriously

revealed by her swift, rhythmic gait. Peter immediately
recognized Miette.

With an almost involuntarily movement, he seized his
newspaper again and to hide his confusion began reading
it. But his heart was beating fast.

The young man walking by Miette's side was Michael
Ádám. Peter waited for them to pass before scrutinizing
them stealthily. He would have liked to overhear something of their conversation, but as they walked side by
side in silence their steps accelerated as if they, too, were
late. Peter grimaced, thinking almost aloud: "Ah, those
two—I'll wager they understand each other."

He decided that Ádám and Miette had been tramping
along the river bank, or perhaps—who knows—had been
keeping an even more furtive morning tryst. One hears
so much of that kind of thing. Budapest was a corrupt
city, and even society girls lost their sense of decorum.

Suddenly, he began thinking of the life a society girl
leads. He had never even kissed one, though to do so
seemed to him more desirable than anything else. It
wouldn't be so easy, one couldn't simply push her against
the wall and without more ado kiss her mouth, as with
the Bunzes' German governess, for instance. Such a kiss
would doubtless have to be preceded by a long and
determined siege. There would be a lengthy, mysterious
road to travel, strewn with adroit, courteous words, with
half-whispered, unfinished sentences, with profound,
penetrating glances; such was the road that would lead
to that kiss as to a secret green bower. How would a
nice girl's kiss taste on the lips? Was it true that one
might go even further with her? Surely these two,
Miette and Ádám, had reached the kissing stage. But,
gathering together all his memories of Miette, remember-
ing her hand that radiated purity and delicacy as it lay
on the paper, and her attitude of reserve, he suddenly
felt that had anything taken place between her and
Ádám, it could have been nothing more than an innocent
exchange of kisses. And was he even certain they had
kissed? It might be that they had met accidentally, and

that Ádám had turned to accompany Miette . . . They might even be related—first cousins, perhaps.

All these questions remained unanswered as he crossed the Elisabeth Bridge, walking toward home, absorbed in his thoughts. His heart that had beaten faster when he saw Miette, though he didn't know why, was slow to calm itself.

He was in the habit of eating alone, for he reached home at irregular hours. His mother always served his meals herself. She was a widow, slight and small, who held her graying head a little to one side, and whose voice was rarely heard; when she happened to speak, it was in a light, birdlike voice. She was almost unbearably humble with her son, like a servant who is always in terror of being dismissed.

This humility had its origin in the fact that she had been an orphan and very poor when she had married Stefan Takács, a high-school teacher in the dusty little lowland town where her own father had taught in a Calvinist school. She had been a pretty girl then, with a figure supple as a reed and a soft, white skin; and even now, under her old lady's bonnet, she still had the same round, eager child's eyes, though they were dimmed by age, and the crow's feet were woven in delicate cobwebs about them.

Peter was irritable and sometimes rude to the silent little widow.

He was in the habit of resting for an hour or so after luncheon on the couch of the room that faced the court. That day he stretched himself out as usual, but sleep did not come to weigh down his lids. Five or six times he turned and re-turned the fresh little white pillow that he had crumpled beneath his head. He opened his eyes and from where he lay surveyed the black-and-green web of tapestry hanging on the wall a few feet away.

He felt that something had happened to him, something that his past experience could not help him explain satisfactorily. It was three days now since he had suddenly become infinitely, painfully sensitive. Passing through the streets, he would gaze attentively at windows whence the sound of a piano reached his ears, and the unknown melody made him sad—he who had no leanings toward poetic soulfulness and still less musical sense. When he regained his composure for a moment, he considered it foolish and pitiable to give himself over to such imaginative fancies.

If a woman passed, he would turn and look after her for a long time, though up to then this had never been his practice.

And since the party at the doctor's he would think, as he dreamed of Miette, that it must be a great thing to have such a woman in one's life, a source of infinite joy, exalting one to heaven, a marvelous adventure. How mysterious and fascinating a woman of the world must be!

"Am I by any chance in love?" he wondered. But this question seemed to him preposterous. No, this was not love. Up to now he had led a dull, monotonous life, and now suddenly his desires surged within him with all the force that had hitherto been restrained; the desire, not for Miette, not even for any particular young girl, but the desire for love itself.

In the morning, standing before his mirror, his face had assumed in turn the changing expressions of anger, astonishment, joy, sorrow, surprise, and exultation.

All this happened after he had finished shaving; then he would look toward the door, fearful lest someone might have been spying upon this strange game in which his solitude delighted. He grew melancholy and felt ashamed of himself.

At times, during these three days, Miette's face and voice were all confused in his memory. But sometimes they returned quite clearly and distinctly; now one, now the other, and occasionally he could plainly hear the expressionless, slightly sing-song tones of her voice saying, "Goodbye . . ." when she had dismissed him last Sunday at the illuminated door.

Closing his eyes, he examined every detail of Miette's face, to its finest subtleties. Her eyebrows were delicate and their arch was narrow. The left was marked by a small scar which, though plainly visible, did not mar the beauty; this was rather curious. The large eyes—he didn't know exactly whether they were blue or deep green—were shaded by long lashes. The mouth was large, but the lips were delicate, and the corners of her mouth were capable of expressing the sensitive play of her emotions in a thousand shades. Sometimes two different smiles appeared in the two corners of her mouth, which made her face very expressive and piquant. He had noticed that when she wanted to take a step forward she knitted her brows and looked first at the ground; she was, perhaps, somewhat nearsighted.

Her voice was melodious; if she sang, it must be in a contralto. But even though she only spoke in that voice, a velvety, sensual warmth lurked there.

Yes, now he remembered exactly. When he had said to Miette in the course of the game that he could communicate his findings to her only in private, the girl's face had flushed and, flinging back her head, she had suddenly exclaimed: "Oh . . . Oh!" in real alarm, though she had been laughing, too. Those two words of protest had suggested the warm tones of a delicate ocarina.

He was surprised at himself to find that he knew so much about this girl, remembered so many things connected with her, though he had seen her for only a few moments. He had met other girls who were as lovely as she—the dark-haired Olga was perhaps prettier—but in all his life no one had ever affected him as Miette did.

His mother entered the room, silent as a shadow, and looked for something on the dresser.

Peter, irritated, turned and said sharply: "Oh, my God! You never let me sleep!"

His mother went away silently.

He was alone again. He could not sleep, and his daydream had been dissipated. Nervousness and emotional excitement had mastered him, and they hurt. And suddenly he was saddened by the thought that he had been rude to his mother again. He would have liked to go to her and kiss her hand—but he hadn't the energy. He got up, lit a cigarette, went to the window and looked out.

For two or three weeks, almost all his days were spent in this fashion. He avoided the society of people; he liked to be alone and to wander through unknown streets. He loved billiards passionately, but now he played alone. He set himself problems—complicated multiple shots. He made the realization of a wish dependent upon the success of each shot. If the shots were successful he was happy for the day; if not, he wandered about all day disconsolate.

So the days passed.

At the beginning of October, the weather was still glorious. There were always large crowds on the tennis courts of St. Marguerite's Island, and the boat races below Buda streaked the dark-gold waters of the Danube with cheerful color.

At the club, Dr. Varga approached Peter. "We shall be very glad to have you come for tea next Sunday."

"Thanks very much," Peter answered, scarcely able to conceal his emotion. And immediately added: "Who will be there?"

"We've asked the same people as were there the other day," the doctor answered, already moving away, for someone had taken his arm.

Peter went home early that evening. He turned the whole apartment upside down, and went carefully over all his shirts and ties. For hours he sorted collars and cuffs, putting aside all those that were beginning to be frayed or worn.

His mother came and went, happy to be near him, hastening to obey without a word all of Peter's instructions.

His striped trousers had to be taken to the tailor's to be pressed; shoe polish and laces had to be bought; the laundress must be told that the collars must be ready for Friday.

Next morning Peter had his hair cut, so that it might grow a little before Sunday, lest people should think as they eyed his head: "That fellow's been shorn like a sheep today."

He made a number of purchases: a new hat, two very smart neckties, and a half-dozen pair of silk socks.

When he looked at himself in the mirror on Sunday morning, he fancied himself too pale. The feverish preparations of these last days had worn him out.

At a little past five he rang the doctor's bell. This time, too, the hall was crowded with all kinds of hats, sticks, and overcoats; and the pretty Rose stood in exactly the same place while she helped him out of his overcoat.

Peter looked about him somewhat uncertainly as he entered the living room.

At first glance, he saw not a single face that he knew.

He recognized a major, a pianist, and three of the ladies he had seen on that other Sunday, but to whom he had not spoken. There were more people here today than there had been four weeks earlier. His eyes wandered to the piano, but in the place where Miette and Olga had sat, two elderly women were chatting.

He discovered Yolanda Galamb in a corner of the room, flirting with an artillery lieutenant.

His glance kept returning to the piano, and he eyed the two old women with an inexplicable hatred.

Whenever anyone entered, he turned his head nervously, hoping that the two girls might still arrive.

But time passed and it was already half past six. Madame Varga poured him another cup of tea, which he accepted only for the opportunity it gave him to ask her: "Aren't the girls coming?"

"What girls?"

"Olga and Miette," said Peter, lowering his head over the cup of tea, so as not to betray his emotions.

"I don't know why Olga hasn't come; but Miette is ill, poor child!"

She had scarcely finished her sentence when she was off again, and Peter was left alone with the word "ill." She would not come; he would not see her today. He realized with horror that all his preparations, his feverish anxiety, his hopes had been in vain. At that moment, it was not of Miette's illness he was thinking; it was himself he pitied.

He hurried to the hall and donned his overcoat in great haste, but before going downstairs stopped on the landing. For a long time he eyed the opposite corner, where Miette's family lived. The dark door fascinated him.

Once in the street, he crossed to the other side, and there raised his eyes to the second-story windows. Only the farthest window of the Almády apartment emitted a feeble ray of light. From the doctor's apartment came the sound of the piano.

The street was dark. Peter had been standing on the opposite sidewalk for half an hour, leaning against the wall, while his breast heaved jerkily with stifled little sighs that were almost sobs.

"What has happened to me?" he asked himself in terror as, growing aware of them for the first time, he drove those little sighs back into his parched throat.

He was in a disagreeable mood when he went to the office the next day, but his ill humor was rather the result of fatigue than anything else.

His heart was cold and empty again, as dark as if a light in it had just been extinguished. He felt clearly this morning that it was not Miette he had lost, Miette who had not even entered his heart, but only that a flame had been suddenly kindled within him and then extinguished: a multicolored flame, an ardent desire for love for which he had waited for so long, for love that was to fill his life and soul, a desire in whose midst there had appeared to him, as if by the light of torches, the voluptuous figure of a beautiful girl with dark gold hair.

He was calm again, cool and ill-tempered, and he returned to the customary tedious routine of his life, from which the dreams of the last four weeks had torn him.

That week he did not think of Miette even once.

III

Summer had long since deserted the banks of the Danube. The autumn rain dripped from the bald little acacias, as if tears were falling from their lowered heads. On the square in front of the kiosk, the legs of the iron chairs had left a series of marks where they had sunk deep into the melted asphalt during the scorching days of summer. Similarly, a scattering of hoof-marks were the only traces left at dawn of the secret nocturnal passage of a herd of deer over the smooth, hard sand of the quiet river bank.

Where had it fled—the deer-colored summer?

Peter passed that way every day on his way home at noon. Sometimes the thought suddenly crossed his mind —what would happen if he should meet Miette unexpectedly? Would she recognize him? Would she acknowledge his greeting? Would he have the courage to approach her, to speak to her?

But these fancies passed vaguely and dimly through his mind, like the thousand insignificant fancies prompted at random by objects encountered, by human faces, by the clouds in the sky, and by shop windows.

He could no longer recall the girl's features. A month had elapsed since he had seen her; new desires, new faces, new forms rising from the dreams of his hours of solitude, had taken possession of his life.

During these last weeks he had seen Paul Szücs often. Paul had become seriously attached to Yolanda Galamb in the interval and lived in a dream of happiness. Occasionally he opened his heart frankly to Peter, who listened with secret envy. Szücs would stand before him, and raising his arm high above his head—one of his habitual gestures—would say to him, after having recounted some of the more intimate details: "You know, old fellow, I feel as if every hair of my head had been changed!"

He was like the poor man who, having won the grand lottery, didn't know what to do next. His eyes almost blazed, his very soul trembled, and he would have liked to initiate the whole world into his happy secret.

On a snowy November day, after a night spent carousing with Paul, Peter went directly home for lunch. On those occasions when he didn't come home to sleep, his mother never asked where he had spent the night, but she would prepare for him a sauerkraut soup. There was always a mute reproach in these plates of soup that were known as "hangover cures." After lunch Peter asked his mother: "Mama, wouldn't you like to go to the theater with me?" He did invite her sometimes.

"I am so sorry, my child, but I cannot go today." Mme. Takács said regretfully. "The Vajniks are coming." Then she added warily: "Aranka is coming, too. Wouldn't you like to stay home?"

Peter shook his head. "Never mind, I'll go alone."

He went out and from the placards on an advertising pillar chose a musical comedy at the People's Opera House.

The pit was half empty, and there were few people even in the boxes. After the first act he surveyed the house tranquilly through his opera glasses and discovered a group of three people in one of the balcony boxes. He could hardly believe his eyes. They were Miette and Olga, with the cadet seated beside them.

He rushed up to the balcony floor. There he stopped suddenly, half turned, then slowly descended the stairs. He could not make up his mind to open the door of the box. It was nearly two months since he had seen Miette. Their first encounter had been so casual that he felt it would be difficult to resume their acquaintance simply by entering the box. Furthermore, it was dark and the girls might not recognize him. He thought he would wait for them at the exit after the performance and pretend that the meeting was accidental. But he felt he could not sit through the two succeeding acts.

He returned to the balcony floor. First, he opened the doors of two other boxes. He was very nervous. Finally, at the third attempt, he found them. All his hopes lay in the cadet.

When he entered the box Miette was the first to turn, but of course she didn't recognize him in the darkness. Even when he drew nearer, the girls still eyed him as though he were a stranger. And the words, "My compliments, ladies!" from a dry throat did not help at all.

Now he was extremely sorry he had come.

Olga recognized him first.

"Good evening, kind sir," she cried gaily.

She held out her hand to Peter, and Miette's gaze also grew less remote. She gave him her hand too, suddenly blushing a little; but Peter knew that that meant nothing, for Miette's face flushed faintly when she was merely addressed, or when she herself spoke to someone.

"Don't give us away," said Olga.

"How?"

"Because we came without a chaperon. My aunt was to have come with us, but at the last moment she marched off."

"So I am the chaperon," said the cadet gravely.

Miette laughed but grew serious as she looked at Peter. It was evident that she did not know quite what attitude to take.

The house was darkened, the curtain rose, and Olga assumed an attitude of severity.

"And now, don't laugh so loud. Behave yourself or I shall have to take you home."

Johnny, the cadet, chose that moment to say something between his teeth; whereupon Olga buried her face in her gloved hands to keep herself from bursting into laughter, and from the house cries of "Hush!" were already being directed toward the box.

The cadet remained silent for a moment, then made another remark. It was enough that he should speak;

although the girls did not hear what he said, they burst out laughing just the same. An inextinguishable vitality and an infectious delight in life glowed within them.

Little by little, Peter regained his composure, and the palpitations he had suffered when he entered the box disappeared.

A sentimental love scene was being played on the stage when Johnny gave vent to a piercing "Cock-a-doodle-do!"

The girls jumped from their seats and rushed, stumbling, to the dark, far corner of the box; there, clinging to each other, they strove to repress the hysterical laughter that was choking them.

Johnny didn't stir. His arms folded across his chest, his eyes fixed gravely on the stage, he had assumed an expression as impassive as though his face were carved in wood. It was a necessary precaution, for as a result of that "Cock-a-doodle-do" everyone was looking nervously from one box to another; but fortunately no one knew exactly where the noise had come from, and the cadet's impassive countenance averted suspicion.

During the remainder of the act neither of the girls returned to the front of the box. When it had ended and the house was light again, they had completely regained their sobriety and assumed an air of offended hauteur.

"I give you warning, Johnny," said Miette to the cadet, "if you do anything like that again, I shall go straight home."

Peter was more disturbed by this threat than was Johnny, who placed a hand on his heart and said: "My word of honor as an officer, I shall not . . ."

Miette abruptly turned her head away, and Peter saw that she was struggling with laughter again. It was a joy to him to watch her and with his eyes to drink in greedily her slightest movement. The girl whom, since their first meeting, he had imagined under a thousand varying aspects was someone quite different—more ethereal, more abstract, more bodiless: femininity incarnate. Yet the girl who, pouting charmingly, was at that moment holding the doorknob and threatening to go home, whereas in reality nothing would have induced her to leave such a successful party—that girl was Miette, standing before him in a new guise, creating a fresher, more natural, more artless impression than at Dr. Varga's tea. Yes, this was the true Miette, and not at all unattainable, thought Peter.

Olga was still pretending to be seriously indignant. After lengthy negotiations and threats, the girls finally resumed their seats, and Johnny kept his word. He didn't stir through the whole of the third act until the final scene when, the audience being under an emotional strain, a deep silence reigned. At that moment Johnny pulled out his handkerchief and blew his nose with a sound that suggested a cavalry bugle sounding the call to battle.

The whole house, as one man, suddenly raised its eyes to the box.

In a single bound the two girls once more abandoned him. They hastily donned their coats at the back of the box and slipped swiftly outside.

Johnny, a little frightened himself, made his escape as quickly as possible. He did not overtake the girls till they had reached the street, where, arm in arm and pressed closely against each other, they were walking fast.

They would not have turned their heads for anything in the world, but they felt relieved when they heard the steps of the two young men directly behind them.

They put their heads close together; from the movement of their shoulders it was obvious that they were shaking with secret laughter.

A little farther on they stopped at a chestnut vendor's stand, and while the chestnuts were being bought Peter asked Olga: "What do I owe you for the seat in the box?"

"One florin, twenty-five kreutzers," answered Olga without a moment's hesitation.

Peter felt in his back pocket, drew out a horseshoe-shaped purse and counted one florin and twenty-five kreutzers into Olga's glove.

Miette gave one kreutzer back to him:

"That one is no good; it's too battered."

Peter changed it.

Olga clinked the money in her hand and ran ahead.

At the edge of the sidewalk a ragged old man was walking with faltering steps. He wore a yellow plush hat that didn't harmonize at all with his gray rags. With little thrusts of the stick in his hand, he was rummaging about among the street refuse, hunting for cigarette butts.

"Here," Olga cried to him. "We have found something for you."

And she poured the money into his hands. The old man gazed at her in alarm, and slowly raised his gout-gnarled hand as though someone had twitched it with a string. But he said nothing. He must have been dumb. The four young people continued on their way.

"Gracious, how cold it is!" Miette said, stamping her foot to warm it. With her free hand she drew her gray fur coat more closely about her, and all that could be seen of her was the tip of her nose and her large, laughing, shining green eyes. A bronze curl, escaped from beneath her dark leather cap, played on her forehead.

The girls linked arms and walked ahead again. They put their heads together, talking and laughing.

Peter watched their feet as they walked in front of him. Olga's were preposterously small. Miette's were long and slender, perfectly shaped and proportioned. Olga was wearing patent-leather shoes with cloth tops; Miette wore shoes of tan calfskin with low heels. Simple, flawless taste, quiet distinction, marked every detail of her costume. She wore a finely pleated dark green skirt of some British material in a large pattern, and her coat obviously had been made by a good tailor.

Darkness was setting in. The four slim-ankled feminine legs, the four feet, two clad in black, two in tan, preceded the young men with springy steps on the pavement where the shadows were beginning to gather. The girls were still laughing.

"Won't you tell me what makes you laugh?"

"Please don't be angry if I tell you," said Olga, with

delightful candor. "But we are laughing because we don't even know your name!"

Peter suddenly felt embarrassed.

"I am Dr. Peter Takács," he said abruptly.

Miette saw the painful embarrassment plainly apparent on Peter's face and felt sorry for him.

"Oh, yes . . . I remember . . ."

Of course it was not true. Olga began questioning Peter.

"You have taken your degree in law?"

"Yes, and I work in a bank."

"Have you a good position?"

"Fair. Why do you ask?"

"I want to marry," said Olga, with a quizzical little sigh. "Is there any hope for me?"

And she gazed at Peter in so comical a fashion that they all began to laugh.

"I should indeed be delighted," Peter answered, entering into the spirit of the game, and added: "It's a bargain. What dowry have you?"

"How much do you expect?"

"I would marry you if your dowry were only a crown."

"Why, that's just what I have. But on one condition—that you will never again wear a brown tie with a dark blue suit."

"Olga!" Miette laughed, in an effort to stop her, for she knew that when the little imp began teasing, she sometimes left a painful wound. She liked this slender, broad-shouldered, brown-faced young man, and wanted to protect him.

She turned to him with a smile and, to soothe his vanity, said: "When you were introduced, you spoke your name so low, that is why I forgot it."

"Why weren't you at the Vargas' the other day?" Peter asked Miette.

It was Olga who replied promptly.

"Because she gossiped about us."

"Don't attack my beloved aunt!" Johnny called Olga to order without conviction.

Just then Peter noticed a touch of lipstick on Olga's

lips. Then he examined Miette's face, but it was as unsullied as if it had been washed in the fresh water of a clear spring, while Olga's face was visibly powdered.

"Where are you going now?" Peter asked when they had reached Rakoczi Avenue.

"Home," Miette answered.

Then Olga added: "If you like, you may come up and have a cup of tea. Miette is inviting you."

Peter looked at Miette. "Are you inviting me?"

"Of course I am."

She said it simply and kindly, engaged meanwhile in thrusting back beneath her cap the curl that had escaped to her forehead.

They took the streetcar. There were only three seats inside, no room for Johnny. He attempted a spirited argument with the conductor, but the latter shook his head, pointing to the placard on which was written: "Standing inside the car is forbidden."

Johnny offered the conductor a cigarette.

"Don't bribe me." The conductor, who was fond of a joke, spoke in a loud voice, taking the cigarette, which he immediately thrust behind his ear. He took Johnny's arm. "I'm sorry, General. Do you mind staying on the platform?"

"Well—all right," said Johnny, quickly recapturing the cigarette from behind the conductor's ear.

Everyone in the car laughed, and the sparkling gaiety that these four had brought in with them communicated itself to all.

A man sitting next to Peter, who looked like a mechanic, rose and said to Johnny: "Here, General, take my seat."

Everyone burst out laughing.

Johnny made the obliging laborer sit down again. "Please sit still."

"Not at all," said the champion of politeness eagerly. "I am getting out here, at the Boulevard."

The attention of the passengers was fixed on them, and even those farthest away watched with smiling eyes the two pretty, gay young girls, the attractive young man opposite them, and especially the "general," who had suddenly won the hearts of these Budapest trolley patrons.

When they reached the apartment and rang the bell, a spare old woman opened the door. It was difficult to tell at first glance whether she was a servant or a poor relation. The most obvious thing about her was that she had no teeth, and from her expression it was immediately evident that she was deaf.

"Good day, Mili," Olga cried to the old woman, who blinked at the newcomers.

A Scotch terrier, detecting a strange scent, appeared at the dining-room door and barked fiercely at Peter.

"Quiet, Tomi," cried Miette, stamping her foot; then she said more gently: "Come here nicely and be introduced to the gentleman."

Tomi, growling low, eyed Peter suspiciously, but he sat up on his hind legs and offered a paw, rumbling: "Wah! Wah!"

Miette took Tomi on her lap and rested her nose for an instant on the dog's small one, cold and black and moist; then holding him close to her lips, yet without touching him, she blew him a kiss. She pressed him fiercely to her heart for a moment, then, without warning, tumbled him to the floor with a swift gesture that seemed habitual to her.

Peter helped her off with her coat. The little silk-lined garment exuded a warm fragrance that seemed to Peter to have acquired an almost glowing heat from contact with her body.

"Is Father in?" Miette asked the old servant.

"His Excellency is in his study, working," Mili answered.

When they entered the dining room Miette called in a melodious voice, each syllable distinct: "Good day . . . Pa-pa!"

The study opened off the dining room to the right. When the door was open, a big, old-fashioned, high-topped desk could be seen facing it. A tobacco jar stood on top of it, and a heavy cloud of tobacco smoke curled in the lamplight above the desk.

The same bald, white-bearded gentleman whom Peter had seen that day in September when he brought Miette home, rose from before the desk—the same old gentleman who had been sitting at the dining-room table in his summer coat reading the newspaper.

He was now wearing a dark brown house jacket and carried his long lighted Turkish pipe in his hand as he advanced toward them. Miette flew to him and, throwing her arms around his neck, kissed him on either cheek.

The old man gently patted Miette's face and asked: "Have you had a good time?"

He paid no attention to Peter who was standing near the door, suffering a little from stage fright. The old gentleman's head resembled that of General Arthur Görgei, painted by Philippe Lászlo—the bold head, the high forehead, the clear blue eyes, the small straight mustache, white as snow, and the same short little beard, also white as snow. But his face lacked the general's temples, those temples where the frontal bones projected at an almost savage angle; it lacked the indomitable chin, the air of profound meditation that marked every line of the face, and the melancholy expression that overcast the general's countenance like the shadow of Tragic History.

Francis Almády's face was gentle, and a tender mirthfulness lighted his blue eyes. When he saw Peter he turned a questioning glance on him. Peter bowed low and introduced himself. The old gentleman retained his hand and made him repeat his name.

"Are you the son of Gideon Takács?" he then asked.

"No sir; my father was a high school teacher; but he has been dead a long time."

The old gentleman scrutinized Peter closely, smiling, and it was evident that he liked this handsome dark youth, with his slender, well-built figure and his courtly manners.

"We met him at the Vargas'," Miette explained, and this time, too, her face reddened faintly.

"Well, have a good time," said the old gentleman, as he walked back to the study with his pipe.

Peter was delighted that the introduction had gone off so well. There was only one thing he couldn't understand —how was it possible that Miette's father could be so old? Surely, he was far past sixty, and he might easily have been Miette's grandfather, for she was certainly not more than twenty.

Another room opened off the dining room at the left; this was the living room. The furniture was simple, but old and handsome, the kind immediately suggesting that at any instant Grandmother's hands might appear to brush away the dust.

Peter looked about the apartment, expecting momentarily to see Miette's mother enter at one of the doors. And he was already imagining her appearance—he pictured her as a woman of aristocratic bearing, between forty and forty-five, a little distant at first, and with Miette's delicate features in a pretty, faded face.

Miette and Olga repaired to the room that opened out of the living room onto a court. On the threshold, Miette turned to say: "Please sit down and smoke. We shall be back directly; we are going to take off our hats."

Peter looked about the room. Above the piano there was a life-sized portrait in oils of a pretty young woman, hatless but wearing gloves. Her beautiful, luxuriant hair, braided in a wreath around her head, was reminiscent of Elisabeth, Empress of Austria, Queen of Hungary.

There are portraits, photographs even, in which the very carriage of the head is such that the eyes seem to be fixing with you with a gaze from beyond the grave, as if to say: "I am already dead."

This portrait was one of them.

"Who is it?" Peter asked.

"Miette's mother," Johnny answered.

"Isn't she living?"

"Not for many years. Miette never even knew her. She died in giving her birth."

Engrossed in their thoughts, they both looked long at

the woman in the portrait who, her gloved hands crossed and resting in her lap, really seemed to be gazing out over their heads with a look from beyond the grave.

"Who brought Miette up?" Peter inquired, with feigned indifference, for at bottom he was consumed with eagerness to learn as quickly as possible everything that concerned this girl.

"She was brought up by her grandparents in the country. Then she went to the convent at Sion."

"Where did you meet her?"

"My father was a judge, too, and old Almády's colleague."

"How old is he?"

"Sixty-five, I believe; I don't know exactly. He married late; he was about twenty years older than his wife."

"And how old is Miette?"

"Miette? Wait a minute . . . She is two years older than I, and I am nineteen."

Peter looked closely at the cadet. He studied him attentively, as if he wanted to discover whether Johnny was in love with Miette.

But the young man's face revealed nothing.

"They are extraordinary specimens, those two," continued Johnny without looking at Peter, but as if he felt that insistent, searching gaze fixed on his face; then he added: "Especially Olga."

But Peter wasn't interested in Olga now. Abruptly he turned the conversation into another channel. "Tell me . . . Michael—Michael Ádám? Is he courting Miette in earnest?"

"Who? Michael? Michael is courting Eve Torony."

Peter had to strain every nerve to keep his composure during this conversation. He called Ádám by his first name, though he had never spoken a word to him, merely so that this question and his curiosity might not arouse Johnny's suspicions.

The cadet had not responded immediately to Peter's remark, but after a moment, and without any special interest, he asked in his turn: "What made you think that?"

"Just an impression I had."

To keep his fingers occupied, Johnny played with the fringes of the tablecloth. Peter followed all his movements attentively, as if he were striving to learn the truth from Johnny, but the latter's remark made a moment later proved that he was as ignorant of the situation as Peter.

"After all, it's possible. Who knows?"

That was his cub's notion of a prank.

The girls came back. It was evident they had freshened themselves a little in the dressing room, especially Olga. For the first time Peter was seeing Miette without a hat. Her hair was twisted up in a heavy, luxuriant, golden-brown knot.

"Would you like tea or coffee?" Miette asked with the air of an experienced, self-possessed hostess.

"Thanks very much—tea, I believe."

"And you, Johnny?"

"I?... Both."

"Very well, if you don't drink them I'll pour them down your throat," cried Olga, and Peter was not surprised to hear her say: "Oh, you fathead!" or "Shame on you, Johnny!" It seemed to him that the girls addressed Johnny by his family name only in public.

For the rest, he could not keep his mind from dwelling on the thought: "How strange to be here, in Miette's home!" And how simply it had all come about!

From the next room, Tomi suddenly put in an appearance, wagging his short tail excitedly. Peter lifted him in his arms and kept him on his lap; then, just to say something he asked: "I wonder how old ...?"

"Miette?" Olga cut in quickly, pretending to misunderstand Peter's words.

"She's exactly ..." Johnny began, but Miette raised a warning finger at him:

"You! Don't give away all my secrets!"

Meantime Mili brought in the refreshments. There was

tea for everyone, and coffee besides for Johnny, who took the coffee and the tea and began to pour them together into his cup. "It was you," he said to Olga, "who told me that I had to drink them both."

"Fie!" said Olga grimacing.

"When I was a child," Johnny remarked with great gusto, "I swallowed a fat silkworm once for ten kreutzers."

"Aaaah, you filthy pig!" cried Olga.

"Why not?" Johnny asked, his face reserving his military dignity, "a silkworm is a very clean, appetizing animal compared to your favorite snack, Mademoiselle, the liverwurst, packed in the bowel of a pig." Miette rapped sternly on the table and said: "Johnny, take your cap and go home at once!"

"Leave you? Impossible!" said Johnny in a tragic tone, stirring the hideously colored mixture of tea and coffee. Even Miette couldn't keep from smiling.

Meantime, Peter was watching the movements of Miette's beautiful hands, with their pure, delicate lines, as she poured the tea. In his mind, he followed the movements of her body under her dress. The very dress revealed that that hand could not be but the extension of a flawless, naked masterpiece. He closed his eyes for a moment when the hot sensation flooded his thoughts that Miette might one day be his wife.

Olga threw a crumb of cake at his face.

"A penny for your thought, my Prince!"

As if she had divined Peter's thought, Miette turned her head away abruptly, and a scarcely perceptible blush spread rapidly over her face.

Miette's bedroom was visible from where Peter was sitting. The whole room was radiant with a foamy whiteness, and a large, shiny brass bed was pushed against the wall. He stole a furtive glance at that enviable bed.

There was a small bookcase in the living room, and after tea they began to talk about literature.

"We call it the Lily Library," Olga winked confidentially at Peter, "just because we were strictly supervised lest we should buy anything . . . anything improper, you know."

Peter happened on Strindberg's *Inferno*.

"Miss Almády," he turned to Miette, "will you be good enough to lend this to me for a few days?"

"Gladly," she answered sweetly, and Peter thought he could detect a soft surrender in the word.

As a matter of fact, Peter had no interest whatsoever in the book, and it was only vaguely that he knew who Strindberg was. But he realized at once how the borrowing of a book might affect his situation: When a book is borrowed, it must be returned. One might telephone after a few days, apologize for not having yet returned it. Yes, a Strindberg might be put to many uses.

"Wait, I'll wrap it up," said Olga, taking the book from him.

She carried it out and Miette soon followed her. Meanwhile Peter and Johnny investigated the bookcase.

When Miette and Olga returned, after a prolonged interval, the book was firmly wrapped and tied, and the package was equipped with a little wooden handle.

Johnny, who seemed to know the household routine, soon suggested that they go.

As he was taking leave, Peter asked Miette: "May I telephone you?"

Miette executed a little mock curtsy in token of assent. She was embarrassed and wanted to conceal it. She pirouetted away, seized Johnny's cap, and thrust it quickly on her own head.

Olga, about to go, said to Peter: "Be careful, don't lose that book."

Peter took the package.

"I will guard it like the apple of my eye."

"Goodnight, Miette darling." Olga said.

Peter mustered the courage to hold Miette's hand a second too long, squeezing it in his as he took his leave. She pretended not to notice, but Peter felt she must be aware of it.

As they went out, the hall door closed, and all was dark behind them.

Olga said goodbye quickly to the young men and ran up the stairs. Peter watched her going up: Her stockings were as taut over her pretty legs as they had been that September day after tea. Today, too, her legs were visible to the knee, and now and then her white petticoat gleamed.

She had already reached the third story when suddenly she broke into loud laughter.

The young men stopped and listened.

"What is she laughing at?" Peter asked.

"I haven't the least idea," answered Johnny, but at the same time he rummaged in his pockets to see if the girls had slipped something into them, for he was used to their playing tricks of this kind.

When they reached the street door Peter asked Johnny: "Which way are you going?"

"Toward the bridge."

"Well then, goodbye," said Peter.

Although that was his way, too, he wanted to be alone with his thoughts.

He made a detour to get home and, worn out from the evening, went to bed soon after dinner.

But before extinguishing the light, he opened the package to take out the book and read a few pages of Strindberg.

Much to his astonishment, he found only a little rectangular board in the package, pasted to it a slip of paper on which was written:

"It is a matter of principle with us never to lend our books to anyone.

Signed, THE OWNER OF THE LILY LIBRARY."

Peter, disconcerted, turned the little board over and over between his fingers. He understood now why Olga had burst out laughing on the stairs when she left them. It must have been her idea and Miette was only her accomplice.

He sat up in bed and thought of how he might reciprocate in kind.

Before falling asleep, he placed the little board under his pillow, and his heart felt light and tender.

IV

Miette's father spent the greater part of the day at his desk, appearing only rarely in society or at his club. But he often could be seen walking toward the hills of Buda, hatless, exposing to the air a scalp which the spring sun had strewn with ludicrous little freckles.

He stopped every child. His pocket always held sweets for the children, and he had convinced them that he owned an enormous house in Budapest, where he raised elephants and hippopotamuses. One of the elephants had already learned to talk, but the annoying thing about him was that he had such a very deep voice.

Since the old man's retirement he had been at work on a symposium of court decisions that progressed very slowly. He was convinced that "A History of Fiscal Jurisdiction in Hungary" would fill a void and was the answer to a real need in jurisprudence. He could not understand how streetcars continued to move and men to live and die, while any detail of these fundamental questions remained unsettled or unexplained.

He had married rather late, having passed forty. He maintained that it was the bachelor's best age. There was, however, a reason for the long delay. He had expected to finish his first book (a history of boundary-line lawsuits) in two years. Convinced that one could not hunt two hares at the same time, he determined not to marry until he had finished it.

But he struggled in vain; he made little headway. At the end of two years he had only plunged deeper and deeper into the study of sources. Imperceptibly the two years grew to five, and the five lengthened to ten and finally, to seventeen. He was a slow worker; he would labor for months over a short chapter. At last, when the fat little book appeared, he was already nearing his forty-second year. The very same day he said to himself: "Well, now I am going to get married!"

From that moment he was often seen in homes where there were young girls; he was a constant attendant at balls, and he never stopped to consider that the most important boundary-line lawsuits had robbed him of seventeen years of his life. Before two months had elapsed he had asked for the hand of Mariska Wild, who was not quite twenty. The girl's father was chief inspector of the forest and water supply of an episcopal estate; her mother was the Baroness Amalia Feder, descendant of a family of Austrian officers.

Miette, born of that marriage, was baptized Marianne, like her mother. Because of the difference in age between her parents, gossip did not predict a happy future for the marriage. But the young woman's sudden death cruelly silenced all prophets of ill omen.

Miette grew up in her grandparents' home. The servants in that lordly old Hungarian household walked softly, on tiptoe, among the stags' antlers, wild boars' heads, arms racks, and sacred images that decorated the lofty, vaulted chambers. It was in those clean, well-ventilated rooms that Miette learned to walk. The two old people surrounded her with a love so fanatical that when they looked at the child they seemed always to be weeping secretly for their lost daughter.

Miette was seven when her grandfather died after an illness of a few weeks. She saw him stretched on his death bed; she did not understand what death was, but a nameless terror clutched at her heart, and her grandfather's face—that face stamped with an impressive serenity—remained forever engraved on her memory. His forehead seemed higher, the shining skin stretched across it, and strange lines furrowed the length of his nose. It was the first dead face she had seen.

She remained with her grandmother four years longer. The old village schoolmaster taught her to read and write. She still remembered the gray flannel lining that was always coming out of his necktie, and his mustache that smelled of pomade.

Then a German governess was engaged for her. She saw her father only once a week; Almády took the train every Saturday and spent Sunday with them.

At eleven she had finished her elementary schooling and was placed in a girls' boarding school at Buda, but she continued to spend her holidays with her grandmother.

At fifteen she returned to her father. He experimented first with a distant relative, whom he brought from Transylvania to act as chaperon to Miette, but Aunt Prisca was so unbearably meddlesome that they were both happy, after several months, to be rid of her.

Since then Miette had been officially under the wing of Mme. Varga, whom she called "Mother Elvira," and she spent the greater part of each day in the doctor's apartment.

Miette was not very independent by nature, but she scarcely needed to be, for her life flowed smoothly and evenly between the tennis courts of Buda and family gatherings. Thanks to her father's prominent social position, she moved in the city's best society and felt quite at her ease, little girl though she was, in that distinguished, conservative atmosphere.

That evening, soon after the young people had left, Miette and Father, as was their habit, dined alone and in silence.

"What did you see at the theater?" Father asked.

"Nothing of any consequence," said Miette, who, having allowed her eyes to stray for a moment, fixed them on an invisible spot on the tablecloth, the pupils motionless as when the mind is a blank. Confused memories of the afternoon entered her consciousness by some wholly obscure and automatic process, without any voluntary effort of her own to recall them.

Father, too, was engrossed in his own thoughts. The room lay in deep silence, broken only from time to time by the sharp little noise of knives clicking against the porcelain plates, or the rustling of Miette's silk sleeve as she reached for a piece of bread; the fire crooned gently in the stove.

Tomi sat beside Miette on his hind legs, his eyes rolling, nervous and impatient, behind tufts of hair beneath shaggy, pendant brows, like an old man's.

After dinner Father returned to his study, while Miette busied herself with some fancy work in her own room.

A moment later there was a loud knock at her door. Olga walked in. She executed a military salute, clicked her heels together, then, taking a chair, went on with some work she had brought with her. She was wrapped in a thick, warm dressing gown which might have served equally well as a house dress. On her bare feet she wore patent-leather slippers. She was in the habit of coming down to Miette's apartment after dinner, in this state of deshabille, to have a chat.

"Is Father in bed?" she asked absentmindedly, while her left forefinger, straight and stiff, gleamed white as it followed rhythmically the movements of her crocheting.

"No . . . He is still working," Miette answered, absorbed meantime in her thoughts and in her work.

They remained silent for a long time, deep in their reflections. Occasionally Olga would pass the crochet needle cautiously through her hair, its tip just scratching her head.

"We had a good laugh today," she said.

Miette's only answer was a reflective smile.

"He's a nice boy, that Takács," Olga continued casually, without looking at Miette. Then she added: "He has fine eyes . . ."

Still Miette made no reply. Olga went on: "I noticed he took quite a fancy to you . . ."

Miette answered with a short, protesting little laugh: "On the contrary; *I* saw well enough that he was devouring *you* with his eyes on the sly." But she spoke without conviction.

Olga grimaced, a little vexed because she knew Miette

was not speaking the truth; but she didn't really take it to heart.

Once more they were silent for a moment, and again it was Olga who broke the silence: "I'm sure he must be reading Strindberg's *Inferno* this evening with great interest."

They both laughed.

Then Olga, seizing upon another topic, as if her mind had flung Peter to some remote distance, said: "Do you know whom I met this morning on the Boulevard?"

"Who?"

"Golgonszky."

"Who is he?"

"Ivan Golgonszky. Don't you know him? He comes to the tennis courts constantly. You *do* know: that attaché at the Embassy."

"No, I don't remember. I never saw him. Is he nice?"

"Very. *There's* a man with whom I could fall madly in love."

But Ivan Golonszky could not possibly interest Miette today, for involuntarily her thoughts were engaged with Peter. She straightened up and passed her hands along her sides; she ached a little from having been bent so long over her work.

"Listen," Olga went on after a moment. "Do you remember that little blond countess of whom Mme. Varga was so proud? They say that Golgonszky is having an affair with her."

At the word "affair" Miette felt a little inward leap. It conjured up for her a world of strange, wild pleasures, combined of terror and mysterious, guilty delights. A warm little shiver ran through her body. Olga, on the other hand, had uttered the word with airy assurance.

Even at boarding school, Miette had avoided those discussions carried on by her companions in whispers, their ears burning, or with the pedantic superiority of children, about love and sexual matters.

Very early she had acquired clear and precise notions of the life of adults, of the relations between men and women, seeing therein, with her lucid child's intelligence, as simple a manifestation of Nature as in the union of animals and of flowers, of which she had been a frequent witness in the country, in the poultry yard, in the orchard, and in the garden flower beds. The blossoming of the evidences of her own femininity, the development of her body—these for her were not soul-disturbing events, and she was satisfied with brief explanations. And when the call of her woman's body as it grew made itself manifest within her, she strove to reply quickly to those clamors, choked and incomprehensible as they seemed to her. She did not repress them but accepted them rather and hoarded them away. "This exists; it is mine; the rays of life are gathering within me."

But she did not like to talk about these things.

And so this evening she made no attempt to follow Olga's imagination, which was apparently on the lookout for the slightest titillating details of this amorous intrigue. She made no comment, but went calmly on with her work.

Olga continued: "I heard Mme. Sági say that they go to Vienna together and stop at the same hotel . . ." After a moment she added, without looking at Miette: "Would you like to have an affair with someone?"

These last words had the effect on Miette of a brutal blow. Again she straightened, eyeing Olga haughtily. But the pretty brunette went innocently on with her crocheting, as if she had said the most natural thing in the world. She didn't even look for the answer that was not forthcoming, so engrossed was she in her own thoughts.

Olga's eyes were glued upon her work and a scarcely perceptible smile played about her lips; her face, deep in reverie, clearly betrayed that her imagination was galloping gaily after the clattering Vienna Express that bore the handsome Golgonszky and the little blond countess, with her delicate hands, to their romantic trysts.

Once more silence lay upon the room, broken only now and then by the faint whisper of needle and hook against thimble or thread; from the outside only the insinuating strains of gypsy music from the café filtered in to them.

Olga rose and stood before the door of a wardrobe whose mirror reached to the floor.

"Do you ever do exercises at night?" she asked, and without waiting for an answer she flung off her heavy dressing gown with a swift movement.

To Miette's astonishment, she saw that Olga was naked.

Olga began doing rhythmic exercises in front of the mirror; she stretched and moved her arms in unison, bent and raised her delicate white body, completely absorbed in the easy play of her own movements.

Then she put her dressing gown back on.

"You'll take cold," said Miette, feigning unconcern, not wishing to betray the effect produced upon her by this scene.

"Oh, I'm used to it," Olga answered, and took leave of Miette quickly.

Miette, left alone, soon went to bed. She sat on the edge of her bed and pondered. She clasped her knee between her hands and bent her head forward; her russet hair, loosened, flowed over her shoulders. Eyebrows raised, eyes motionless, she looked straight ahead. Then, with a sudden movement, she thrust one of her hands out and spread the fingers apart; slowly she turned her wrist this way and that, gazing meanwhile at her fingers. Then she placed her hand against the wall. The contours of the white hand were better outlined against the wall's dark hangings. These were the privacies of her absolute solitude and her sense of security. Then, with a sudden jerk, she bent her head low, shook her thick hair out over her knees, and with a few energetic movements plaited a heavy braid, thick as an arm. She held it a little away and surveyed the compact, silky plait, whose color suggested that of polished cherry wood, very bright in spots, with loam-colored streaks.

Then she flung her hair back over her shoulder like one whose capricious curiosity has been satisfied. Holding her nightgown open with both her hands, she contemplated her pretty round breasts. But, immediately alarmed, she turned her head swiftly toward the window, for in a flash it had occurred to her that she might have forgotten to close the shutters and that someone might be peering into the room from the darkness outside. (No matter that her room was on the second floor.) But the shutters had been carefully closed. As a result of the same instinct, not only was she in the habit of looking each night under the bed, but of opening the wardrobe as well. And each time she felt a cold shiver run down her back at the thought of what might happen if an unknown man should stare out at her from the depths of that piece of furniture.

If she had no valid reason for being frightened, she would seek some secret source of fear, and fall asleep with a terrified little thrill, hugging her pillow close.

So now she thrust her white foot from under the blankets and climbed down cautiously, as if she were stepping into cold water. She went to the wardrobe and opened it, but it emitted only the faint sweet perfume of fresh linen, the perfume of a young girl's wardrobe.

When she had closed it again she suddenly saw herself in the mirror, just as she was, standing, clad only in a thin gown. She raised the gown and looked at her knees; then, swiftly, she removed it. Her heart beat faster as she saw herself naked in the mirror. Curiously, her eyes followed the lines of her body. The marked differences between Olga's contours and her own seemed strange to her. Everything was dissimilar, even the shape and color of their breasts. But she couldn't decide if this difference was in Olga's favor or her own.

Quickly she put on her gown again, as if concealing herself from strange, piercing eyes, and cuddled up once more in her bed. She stretched herself out, pulled the blankets up to her ears, yawned a little, more from habit than drowsiness, and tried to sleep. But sleep would not come. She had given much thought to herself today, more than usual. After the young men had left she had stood absentmindedly in front of the mirror, fingering for some time the pale scar from childhood, since that day in the orchard of Fehérpuszta when she had run after little Bertrand, the gardener's son, and fallen among the raspberry bushes that were supported by sharp laths.

Just as she was, stretched out in the bed, she listened, straining her ears in the silence, and began to take note of herself as of a stranger. She felt that something was being liberated within her this evening, that something was being set in motion; but she did not know how nor exactly what it was.

It was all so obscure, so incomprehensible, so sweetly pacifying, yet so disturbing.

V

The afternoons were beginning to grow dark early, and the little houses of Hadnagy Street seemed to huddle lower and lower in the gloomy autumn weather.

Peter was sitting at his writing table in the darkening room, carving letters with the point of his knife into the little pine board that the girls had given him instead of Strindberg's *Inferno*; as he worked, he whistled softly.

He was carving the words "I love you" into the little board. He wanted to send it to Miette with that inscription and without any other identification. She would be able to guess whence the message came. When the idea had occurred to him after luncheon, it had taken his fancy to such a degree as to drive away any thought of sleep, though he had never gone without a short nap in the afternoon.

But the task turned out to be much more difficult than it had seemed to him at first. At the first letter the little blade of the knife sank easily into the soft wood, but the work grew more difficult with each letter, as if the steel blade were growing duller and the wood harder at the same rate.

Finally, when with great difficulty he had finished the last letter, he threw himself on the couch and surveyed his work from there. The board stood upright, in plain view.

Now that it was done, Peter did not like it at all. Suddenly the idea seemed to him puerile, really altogether senseless. He jumped from the couch, strode nervously up and down the room several times, then, seizing the board, flung it among the books.

He lay down again on the couch and, propped on his elbow, stared into vacancy. He was recalling the previous afternoon, from the moment when he had entered the girls' box to the time when he had said goodbye to Miette in the hallway. Always he returned to the one point that remained obscure to him.

When he had asked Miette if he might telephone her he had received no definite answer. Her conduct might be explained in two ways: Either she did not wish or did not dare to evade the question. There was a certain reserve in Miette, a little coldness; Peter liked it, but at the same time it continued to torment him.

"I will marry her," he said to himself, but so loud that he started, as if a stranger had just spoken in the darkening room.

There was a ring at the outside door, and a moment later someone gently turned the doorknob and stuck his head into the opening. His hat was pulled deep down over his eyes, the collar of his coat turned up to his chin, so that only his nose was visible.

"Are you asleep, comrade?"

Peter immediately felt a premonition that it must be some great sentimental crisis that brought Szücs to his house at this unwonted hour. He had already been to Peter's office that morning and, clinging to his arm, had dragged him up and down the bank of the Danube several times, while he insisted on relating to him the whole story of his affair with little Yolanda Galamb, interrupting himself at every other sentence to demand Peter's word of honor that he would not repeat a word of this to a living soul. As a matter of fact, the whole tale was unfolded without revealing the least compromising sugges-

tion with regard to Mme. Galamb. When all was said
and done, she was sorry that Szücs should be in love with
her and behaved as far as possible in such a manner as to
persuade him that she was madly smitten with him as well.

Yolanda Galamb was in the habit of spending the
forenoon in bed, which time she occupied in telephoning
her various swains. It was from there that she controlled
the sentimental conflicts of several men in various sections
of the city, as a general controls the fate of battles from
headquarters. If such a thing as a telephone perversion
exists, Mme. Galamb was one of those who seek and find
in this compulsion a certain kind of amorous release. In
the morning, after her husband had left, she had her maid
bring her the instrument, and from her warm bed she
distilled her sweet, tender sensuality, like mild honey.
Half huddled beneath her blankets, she dared say everything to the black mouthpiece, feeling no responsibility
toward it. She had a peculiar gift for inventing her own
euphemisms for things she did not wish to utter, thus
allowing unspoken fancies to be divined and making
them all the more exciting to men.

She was one of those women, besieged by thousands of
contradictory desires, who do not step beyond the bounds
of curiosity; who would like to experiment with everything, but are disillusioned before they make the attempt.

There had been such a conversation this morning with
Szücs that had succeeded in unnerving the big, healthy
youth. For the third time now he was repeating to Peter
all its details, always the same, convinced that these cast
a clear light over the whole affair.

Under the influence of that day's conversation, Szücs
had made an irrevocable decision to marry Mme.
Galamb. There were, of course, at the moment a number
of obstacles; in the first place, Yolanda Galamb had no
idea of divorcing her husband. But for Szücs the matter
had suddenly grown very urgent. Sitting astride his chair,
he faced Peter, and as he talked, voluble and very excited,
the chair danced beneath him:

"The best thing would be for you to talk to her

husband, old man, and tell him to begin divorce proceedings at once; because if he doesn't, I'll kill him like a dog."

Peter, having taken in the whole situation, felt very sure there was more cynical levity on the part of Mme. Galamb than honest love for Szücs, and tried to make him understand that he was doing a stupid thing. But Szücs would listen to nothing.

He waved his hand wildly and galloped on his chair, in order to get closer to Peter.

"You don't know, old man, what's at stake. Listen . . ."

And he repeated to Peter what he had already told him three times.

Peter pretended to listen patiently till he had finished. But he was really not paying the slightest attention, so absorbed was he in his own thoughts.

The room now lay in total darkness. The two young men sat on; only the glowing ends of their cigarettes gleamed in the darkness, and a woman's white body lay outstretched in the imagination of each.

Szücs left soon after.

At six Peter went down to the café and telephoned the Almádys' apartment.

Mili answered.

"Shall I call Mr. Almády?" she shouted into the telephone.

"No, *Miss* Almády," Peter answered, and the receiver shook a little in his hand as he stood there in the dark booth.

After a moment he could hear Tomi's barking, as if from an infinite distance. And at once Miette's voice sounded so amazingly close that Peter could almost feel her breath.

"Hello!"

"Hello! Peter Takács speaking."

"Oh—good evening!"

"Good evening—how are you?"

"Very well, thanks."

"When am I going to see you?"

"When? . . . Really, I don't know . . ."

Peter was taken aback. "You are not coming . . . shan't I see you again?"

Peter, his throat dry, swallowed and, opening his eyes wide, stared at the mouthpiece on the wall.

"What did you say?" asked Miette's melodious voice.

"It's a bad connection . . ." Peter groaned. And he could not add another word. He was silent. The telephone, too, remained obstinately silent. It was as if his brain had been paralyzed; nothing, absolutely nothing, came to mind. He had had the same experience once before when, after the Vargas' tea, he had walked with Miette along the hallway to the door of her apartment. Now he keenly regretted having telephoned her.

He summoned up all his courage.

"Hello!" he shouted.

"Hello!" Miette answered, somewhat impatiently.

"Aren't you going to come to the Boulevard to-morrow?"

"Tomorrow? No, we're not going. We expect the dressmaker."

"When will you come, then?"

"When? I don't know, really."

Silence fell once more. Peter, whose nerves were stretched to the breaking point, had reached the end of his strength. Exhausted, he said softly: "Well, then . . . good night!"

"Good night!" Miette answered with the same melodious inflection as when she had first bid him good night in September before the door of her apartment.

Peter heard her replace the receiver, but he stayed where he was, his head buzzing, listening to the mute telephone. He did not have sufficient strength to hang up.

Then, suddenly realizing the unbelievable absurdity of the conversation he had just had with Miette, completely upset in the dark booth, he kicked the door open and rushed toward the café exit.

He was already at the door when the cashier pounced upon him like a hawk on its prey. She called to him politely but with cutting irony: "How many calls did you make, sir?"

"Oh! I beg your pardon—" Peter stammered, and paid the telephone charge.

This helped him recover his self-possession, and he walked slowly toward his house.

He felt that things could not go on in this way.

He must rid himself of this obsession. One way or another, he must put an end to this affair that daily was having a more disturbing effect on his heart and nerves.

He sat at his table and began to write to Miette. He did not rack his brains for what he wanted to say; he wrote what was throbbing painfully within him, threatening almost to overflow.

"I have decided after lengthy debates with myself to write this letter," he wrote without introduction, "without asking myself whether I have the right to break into your life with my own feelings; but I can no longer bear to be alone with my sorrow and my pain. Since the day I met you, the fact that you are alive has been a source of suffering to me. There have been days—even weeks, perhaps—when I have forgotten you completely, but now, as though forced by some fatality, I am once more under the sway of my feeling for you. I no longer have a moment's respite. It is as if my whole life were poisoned by it. I am unhappy.

"Don't take this letter for an ordinary declaration of love. Perhaps I do not know how to express myself, but what I feel is more than love; if there is a word to express it, it may be destiny or fate that drives me toward you; I think of you all the time, and in all my thoughts I am at your feet.

"If you have any feeling for me, not of love, but of pity or friendship, I beg you to help me, to give me the opportunity to tell you all this face to face; perhaps in that way I shall recover my tranquillity and my heart will not ache so.

"I shall be looking for you tomorrow, before luncheon, at about two, on the Boulevard in front of the kiosk.

"It is not necessary for me to sign this, is it? You will know, without that, who I am."

He slipped the letter hastily into an envelope, without rereading it, fearing he might change his mind.

In the street he looked at his watch. Eight o'clock.

They would not be at dinner yet. The old gentleman would be working in his study. There would be no guests. The time was most propitious.

In front of the café he gave the letter to a messenger, telling him to deliver it immediately; then he jumped into a streetcar.

"At least it's done now," he thought.

In the morning he went lightheartedly to the office. He did not prepare himself for the meeting with Miette, and when he thought it all over at breakfast he decided it was impossible that she would come to the Boulevard.

Toward eleven a quiet rain, like a mist, began to fall over the city. That comforted him, since at least there would now be a reason for Miette's not coming. The possibility that she might come still had been disturbing and exciting him a little.

When he left his office the rain had stopped, but a moist fog lingered, like rain passed through a sieve: Not a soul was to be seen along the Boulevard. It was seven minutes to two. He sought shelter under a tree.

He decided to wait those seven minutes and then go home. He was composed, and his expression was bored as he walked along the empty Boulevard.

Suddenly his heart leaped. A woman was approaching slowly along the suspension bridge. But his agitation lasted only a few seconds, for he saw almost at once that this woman could not be Miette. He waited for the unknown stroller, who was a head taller than Miette and must certainly have been forty, to pass him at her slow pace. Then he sent a malignant glance after her. Why should she have passed there at just that moment to make his anxious heart leap?

He looked at his watch. Only three more minutes to wait. He would have liked to have them behind him, those three minutes. But as he sauntered up the Boulevard again he was annoyed to see that by the clock at the boat station it still lacked five full minutes of two; he felt as if this idiotic, impatient, purposeless waiting in the shifting fog, of which he was secretly ashamed, had been deliberately prolonged by just those minutes.

"It can't be helped. I'll have to wait these five minutes more," he thought, calculating that if he walked slowly to the suspension bridge he would then be able to turn homeward.

As he walked along the deserted bank he tried to take up his thoughts at the point where he had left them that September afternoon, when he decided not to go to Dr. Varga's tea.

"Something might be done with this Annie," he mused, and now, suddenly, the Bunzes' German governess seemed very attractive to him. In his mind he noted the details of dark little Annie's dumpy figure, the neck sunk between the shoulders, the pink cheeks, the brown hair, and the two little dimples at the corners of her mouth; her gray cotton gloves, high-laced boots, her sharp little laughs, and her bad Hungarian that was, nevertheless, so charming.

He scarcely noticed when a young girl, walking swiftly, passed him like a flash of lightning. He did not see her face because she held her head very low, and looked neither to the right nor left. She wore a brown leather cap and a long leather coat, and carried a few parcels.

Nevertheless, Peter turned toward her.

Could it be Miette? The thought suddenly occurred to him, but the long raincoat covered the girl's figure completely. And everything about her seemed strange to him, the brown leather hat and the boots, too. She was walking rapidly, as if she were fleeing something.

Peter hurried after her, passed her, and looked her full in the face.

It was Miette.

Peter raised his hat.

"How do you do?"

Miette stopped short and raised her head abruptly as if in dismay. Peter noticed that she was unusually pale.

"Good morning," she whispered in a voice scarcely audible. Then, on an almost terrified note, she added: "Have you seen Olga anywhere around?"

She surveyed the length of the Boulevard so that she should not be compelled to look directly at Peter.

"I am looking for Olga," she said then, without waiting for Peter's answer. And she walked on, keeping her head lowered as far as possible so that her face could not be seen.

Peter was obliged to take long strides in order to keep pace with her. Miette's unexpected appearance had so upset him that the words emerged only with the greatest difficulty from his throat.

"Have you been shopping?"

"Yes, I bought some silk because the dressmaker is at the house today. I must hurry; I'm afraid I shall be late . . . What time is it?"

"Two o'clock."

Miette hastened her steps again and the conversation was broken.

"I finished reading the book last night," Peter said after a moment.

"What book?"

"The volume of Strindberg that you lent me."

"Oh, yes . . ." said Miette gaily, venturing for the first time to raise her eyes to Peter.

The thickness that had muffled her voice had almost disappeared when she added: "Olga is always playing tricks like that."

"What's Tomi doing?" Peter asked.

"Tomi? Waiting for the little bone he'll get at lunch. Have you a dog, too?"

"No, unfortunately."

"Wher do you live?"

"Hadnagy Street. The old section of Buda."

"Alone?"

"With my mother."

After a short silence Peter asked her: "Have you brothers or sisters?"

"None. Have you?"

"I have a sister, who is married and lives in Transylvania. She already has two little boys."

As they talked in this fashion, Peter was debating in his mind how he might begin to say what he wanted to say, as he had written to her the previous evening: " . . . the opportunity to tell you all this face to face . . ."

But the thoughts that had come to him last night under the influence of his violent emotion in the little well-heated room filled with cigarette smoke, and what he had confided to paper by the soft light of a lamp—all that seemed to him now, on the Danube esplanade, in the cold wind, in the moist, penetrating fog, in the midst of the irrelevant noises of this gray autumn morning, the harsh grinding of the streetcars on the wet rails, and the thundering of heavily laden trucks—a remote hallucination that filled his head with a confused murmur but never reached a point where he could find words to express it.

Arriving at the bridge, they boarded a trolley. Miette, encumbered by all her little packages, had difficulty in reaching her purse, but when Peter moved to pay for her ticket she protested vehemently. There were no seats, and so many more passengers got on at the other end of the bridge that Peter and Miette were pressed close against one another. Their legs touched and the crowd, like some invisible power, pushed Miette almost against Peter's breast. He clung to the strap with his right hand, and stiffened his legs so as to protect her from the crowd.

"It would have been better to walk," said Peter.

"Yes, but then I should have been late."

They could not say much more. Occasionally Miette made small, cautious efforts to free herself somewhat but, crushed in as she was on all sides, the only result was to squeeze her still closer against Peter. And in a few minutes he could feel through the raincoat and overcoat that the girl's body, crushed close to his, was beginning to glow.

But Miette, with a little shiver of cold, was thinking only how pleasant it would be to be delivered as quickly as possible from this disagreeable position.

Meanwhile Peter was wondering if Miette had come to the esplanade on his account—whether she had even received his letter, whether the messenger had given the letter to Mili, and Mili by mistake had given it to the old gentleman. Mili was hard of hearing, and nearsighted as well. Perhaps the letter had never even reached Miette. And besides, it was possible that the messenger hadn't delivered it; no answer had been requested, and Peter had paid in advance. Who could fathom the souls of these Budapest messengers? It had been dark, and Peter had not even made a note of his number. Recalling Miette's attitude, it seemed to him more and more likely that she had come to the Boulevard only by chance.

The girl was crushed so tightly against Peter that when he looked down at her he could see nothing but the brown leather hat. He examined attentively all of its smallest folds and seams. At one side the dark red hair showed a little, and when she made another movement to disengage herself, her silky hair brushed his mouth and its slight tickling sent a thrill through his whole body. A strange, delicate perfume was wafted to him from her hair.

"I'm sorry," Miette murmured and, smiling, raised her eyes for a moment to Peter's.

The trolley finally stopped before her door. In the doorway she held out her hand to Peter, and her voice was low and a little embarrassed as she said goodbye.

Peter clung to her hand and looked deep into her eyes. He had to muster all his strength to say from a constricted throat:

"Did you receive my letter?"

Miette did not answer. She only looked at Peter with great, frightened, imploring eyes. She first grew very pale, then suddenly blushed.

"Did you receive it?" he asked again.

Still Miette did not answer. Slowly she withdrew her hand, turned abruptly, and fled through the arched entry.

Peter ran after her, but Miette made good her escape. She was already on the stairs. At the first turning she stopped and, her cheeks flushed, looked down at Peter with an air of gay assurance in the carriage of her head, as of one who feels he has escaped from danger. Her face flushed still more deeply, and her expression was a blend of fear, excitement, and a little innocent, timid coquetry.

She smiled at Peter.

Peter stood below, his head raised, his neck outstretched, listening to the sound of her light heels hastily climbing the stairs. Between landings the sound of her receding steps came to him in distinct arpeggios, interrupted at each turning.

He stood there, motionless, till the dry, sharp little sound stopped.

Then he turned and went into the street. A strange feeling sang joyfully within him and his heart seemed to swell and fill his chest.

He walked faster, his hat slid backward, and he dashed on, his face so transfixed and his manner so dazed that people turned in the street to look after him.

VI

Inside the closed *konflis*, a hired carriage drawn by a single horse toiling up Arena Avenue, Olga sat with Elmer Koretz in the gathering twilight.

Their love affair was only ten days old, but was rushing feverishly toward the moment when Olga would give herself to Koretz.

Olga was herself aware of this. She sat huddled, shivering a little, in a corner of the carriage, waiting with chattering teeth, but with a kind of voluptuous anticipation, too, for those developments that she neither wished nor had the power to resist.

There was something wildly and beautifully romantic about sitting thus in a jogging old cab beside Koretz, while his powerful motor car waited in front of the

Terézváros Club, on the assumption that the director general was playing cards behind the yellow curtains.

Koretz was no longer a young man. He was at the head of an industrial organization. His corpulence alone would have betrayed his forty years, while his ruddy, wholesome face shone with an almost childlike simplicity and appetite for life.

For years he had been moving heaven and earth in an effort to divorce his wife, from whom he was separated, but neither money nor threats were of any avail.

During the last two years he had savored every variety of lip rouge, those of both theater and music-hall beauties, and of the elegant prostitutes in the big hotels along the Danube. This had cost him much money, but he gave generously. Yet his simple, healthy ego felt no repose in the boudoirs of these women, and their Budapest slang was alien to him, leaving on his palate a taste of rotten fruit. He was already repelled and even a little sickened by this life, when chance brought about a meeting with Olga.

They met at a supper party where they were neighbors at table. At first Koretz had paid no attention to the little society girl at his side from whom, he thought, he need hardly hope for anything. In the course of their conversation, however, he began to realize that there lurked in this dark girl, with her glowing eyes, a deep, eager thirst for life; not only from her glance did he divine this, but from various remarks she would now and then toss lightly into the conversation.

After supper he sat with her in a dark corner of the drawing room until very late—till the coming of dawn, in fact—and during that time they emptied between them a bottle of liqueur.

Koretz saw in Olga only a fashionable young woman who happened to be a little befuddled—flirtatious, very intelligent, and expressing herself with a freedom bordering on recklessness. He did not suspect the physical and moral revolution that was taking place within her as the result of deep underlying causes, whose first roots had been planted in her soul, tenacious as hair in the head, some years before. These causes had crystallized into a well-considered plan of life that was to drive this girl, with her frail, delicate body, unresisting into the arms of the first man she should meet.

Olga had early and accurately discerned how empty and purposeless was the fate in store for her. She had realized that her beauty and all her physical attributes would not suffice to find her a husband. It was she who managed her mother's money, and she knew that this money would hardly ensure them another year of the quiet existence they were leading, despite the fact that they had reduced their living expenses to the lowest possible figure. What might she expect? Perhaps, if she were to muster all her efforts and talents, of which she had no lack, and direct them all toward the achievement of this single goal, she might succeed in marrying some young man of her own class, a small-salaried employee. Yet among the marriageable young men whom she met at the tennis courts of Kelenföld in summer, or on the ice or at afternoon teas in winter, and who might have been in the running, there was not a single one on the horizon whose conquest would have been worth the effort.

She saw with wide-open eyes—perhaps sorrowfully open eyes—that the only domestic happiness she could hope for was in a three-room apartment—a happiness whose secrets she knew through the lives of her married friends; and when she studied love in these small, impecunious homes, her piercingly sharp eyes never failed to discover livid patches of monotony and boredom.

But perhaps, more than anything else, it was her sick mother's proximity that made her so irritable, so rebellious against her own lot. Her father, who had been a customs official, had been dead for five years. The year before, her mother had suffered a spinal paralysis which would prevent her ever leaving her bed again.

"So this is what one gets for living, for being honest, kind, a good mother," she often thought as she sat for hours by her mother's bedside, seeing in the pale, withered hand that lay on the quilt a kind of mute but terrible reproach to life.

"Take good care of yourself, little daughter," her mother said when she went out to a dinner or a party.

"I'll be careful, Mother dear," Olga would reply from habit, leaning over the bed and kissing her mother. And then, before going, she would always spray a light cloud of her perfume about the invalid's pillows, which emitted a slightly rancid, musty odor.

She always left the house with the idea that some day or other she would find the man of her choice and give him, without a qualm, her spirited, glowing young body. What did it matter, after all? Ivan Golgonszky's slender, elegant figure had possessed her imagination for weeks after the Vargas' tea in September, but the attractive attaché had disappeared completely.

When she had been placed next to Koretz at this supper she had no idea at first that he was the man for whom she had been waiting. But soon her eyes were attracted by his strong, well-kept hands, and she began to examine his features more closely, finding them very pleasant, even boyish. She was aware that his person exuded that harmony, that aroma that money alone can give. This man's dinner jacket was of a different fabric, his studs and cuff links were of a different kind—in a word, his whole appearance diffused a polished elegance and the self-possession born of it, everything that the young men of Buda, who had composed Olga's circle up to that time, lacked.

Koretz had a habit of bursting into loud laughter, showing two rows of healthy, perfect teeth.

"How beautiful his teeth are, too . . ." Olga noted mechanically, as her eyes sought and followed the smallest details of his face. She knew he was married, but that fact caused her not an instant's recoil, and when after supper she and Koretz sat together she already liked him extremely.

The conversation turned at first to the problem of marriage. It was only then Olga learned that Koretz was separated from his wife.

"Of course you have mistresses, then," she said simply.

Koretz swore by all his gods that he was leading the soberest kind of existence, but from there the conversation glided easily to the topic to which Olga wished to direct it—that of the virginity of girls who cannot or do not wish to marry. Olga discoursed on this theme with such poise and assurance that Koretz received the impression of a superior conception of life rather than of levity or corruption.

Which was, as a matter of fact, the case. Koretz listened with increasing pleasure to this slight, dark girl, whose intelligence delighted him, ascertaining meantime that the contours of her delicate figure were perfect and at the same time very provocative.

Meanwhile, they continued to drink. Conversation languished; the periods of silence and the exchange of long, deep glances grew more and more frequent. In the dark, half-hidden recess of the drawing room where they sat among the cushions of a corner sofa, protected from indiscreet eyes by a large armchair placed before them, it was a matter of course for Koretz soon to begin kissing Olga's shoulder. Already, as if by accident, he had lightly touched her firm little breast; and today, so soon after, Olga was sitting in the hired carriage that was taking her to his bachelor apartment.

During the past ten days Miette had seen nothing of Olga, and she concluded that events of importance must be taking place in her friend's life.

But since the previous evening, when she had received Peter's letter, she had completely forgotten Olga's affairs. After reading the letter, such a spasm of nervousness had seized her that all through dinner she had sat unwontedly stiff and straight on her chair, starting up every now and then with a frightened look, until even Father had asked: "What is the matter with you today, Michel?"—a name he sometimes used for Miette.

"I have a slight headache," she answered, affecting unconcern; she raised her eyebrows very high, restraining a little forced yawn, but her heart was filled with sweet, apprehensive emotion.

The next morning she had struggled with herself till she grew wan with the effort of deciding whether or not to go to the Boulevard, and in the end had made up her mind to go but to act as if she were there by accident.

After the meeting with Peter this feeling of restivenesss and uncertainty had completely disappeared, and in its place a gentle, pleasant sense of drowsiness came upon her; she spent the whole afternoon indolently on the couch, reviewing the most minute details of their encounter, every word and every shade of their conversation.

Outdoors the weather was disagreeable, windy and rainy. She pulled the robe over her shoulders and tried to doze, but sleep eluded her. Peter's voice and eyes haunted her, rising and passing before her in flashes with the striking accuracy of an apparition. She would have liked to know what was going on inside her. Her will had no part in her memories; her thoughts whirled of themselves, bringing her in disordered, haphazard fragments everything they had encountered during her short, sharp bursts of sight and hearing. Now it was the young man's pleasant face under his hat with its turned-down brim, dripping in the rain; now it was the little clatter of his shoes on the pavement as he hurried after her before he spoke; and then his eyes, fixed intently upon her; and then, when he greeted her, the huskiness of his voice, timid and tender at the same time, saying: "How do you do?"

There was something in that voice—its restrained emotion, perhaps, the pounding of the heart carefully masked by his words but apparent, nevertheless—something that made those words she had scarcely heard penetrate deep into her being.

She pulled the robe up to her ears, and cuddled beneath it.

She spent the whole day in a formless reverie. She expected Peter to telephone toward evening, but he did not. And she was glad of it, fearing lest something should happen to spoil her mood.

After dinner she went to her room and worked at her

embroidery, with that steady gaze behind which thousands and thousands of thoughts crowded "visibly" —thoughts whose subtle gradations quivered in the nervous little twitchings of her tightly compressed lips. So she sat, straightening up and moving her pretty neck now and then to ease the strain of her motionless position, when she heard a well-known knock at the door.

Olga came in. This time, too, she said nothing, stopped at the door, clicked her heels and executed a military salute, as was her custom. This time, too, she wore a dressing gown, but a warmer one than before.

She came without her work this evening and was smoking a cigarette. She was extraordinarily pale, her eyes seemed larger and deeper, and Miette felt that something unfathomable radiated from all her being.

"Good evening!" she cried with a gay little note of reproach in her voice for Olga, who had remained invisible all these days.

"Good evening!" answered Olga, contrite and rather mysterious, sitting down on the couch. Suddenly she raised her eyebrows very high, taking a deep pull at her cigarette.

"You must have discovered a very charming friend," said Miette, without taking her eyes from her work.

"Why?"

"It's been days since anyone's seen you."

Olga made a little grimace.

"My child!" she said, in a tone indicating that the rest of her sentence, though not uttered, would have been: "What do you know of what I am going through just now?"

She stretched herself full length on the couch, propped on her elbow. They exchanged a few inconsequential words, interrupted by long silences. Finally, Olga's abstraction and self-absorption grew so apparent that Miette dropped her work into her lap, looked at her friend, and asked in a tone of affectionate reproach: "What's wrong, Chouchette?" They had these little names for each other.

Scarcely had Miette uttered the words when she suddenly remembered that Father had asked her the same question at dinner that evening, and in the same tone. It occurred to her that if Olga should now elude her question by some evasive word and pretend unconcern she would be lying, just as Miette herself had lied to Father.

But Olga seemed to be expecting the question. She did not answer immediately, but again raised her brows very high and took a long pull at her cigarette; the thought that she had not yet put into words all but trembled on her face. She extended her arm calmly and slowly toward the little stand that held the ash tray. The sleeve of her robe slipped back, baring her firm, lovely white arm to the elbow. With three even little taps she struck the ash from her cigarette, never taking her motionless eyes, with their raised brows, from it. Miette noticed that an extreme but unnatural composure ruled all her movements. Her voice was quiet too, but it was this very calmness that frightened Miette when Olga began to speak.

"Listen—I have something to tell you."

All attention, Miette held her breath to stare at Olga. From the sound of her friend's voice, she felt intuitively that she was going to hear something dreadful. During the short pause that elapsed before Olga went on, her mind grew almost numb with foreboding. Olga continued with the same icy calm: "At seven this evening I ceased to be a virgin."

Hardly had she uttered the words when she stopped short, as though her breath had suddenly failed her.

She did not raise her eyes to Miette. Again she reached toward the ash tray and with the same three mechanical taps struck a nonexistent ash from her cigarette.

Miette gazed at her with wide-open, staring eyes. Her hands, which had been about to pick up her work from her lap, stopped in midair. If Olga had said to her, "Listen—I took poison half an hour ago and I am going to die here, before you, in a moment," or if she had said, "Listen—I have just killed my mother because I could no longer bear that bed, with its sickly smell," it would not have made so great an impression upon Miette.

She gazed at Olga and at the folds of Olga's robe, at her hair and her eyebrows, with the same queer, inexplicable feeling that had once seized her when, as a child, she had seen her grandfather's coachman, arrested for thieving, standing in front of the town hall, guarded by two policemen, with dangling steel handcuffs glistening white on his tanned wrists crossed in front of him. She looked at Olga not as one looks at a human being but as at some alien object.

Still Olga did not look at her. Her fixed stare seemed to cling convulsively to the memory of a certain moment that, for Miette, was mysterious and fearful. But her face retained the same strange, forced calm. Slowly Olga touched her lips with her finger, removing a small flake of tobacco that she contemplated thoughtfully for a moment. But a tempest was raging in her heart.

She felt herself horribly alone with the secret of what had taken place that evening between Koretz and herself. It was almost with the idea of escaping from herself that she had come down to Miette, because she was desperately seeking someone with whom to share this secret that weighed upon her with a strange and terrible heaviness. Her icy, disdainful manner concealed a little girl in tears who, when she had returned home and changed her clothes half an hour before, had stood in her short petticoat in the middle of the room, staring straight ahead of her with an overwhelming sense of desolation.

Now she was waiting; she would have liked Miette to come and cuddle beside her on the couch, to seize her hand eagerly, to whisper tenderly: "Tell me—what happened—how—what is it all about?" Pressed close against someone, she would have liked to relate and discuss the whole story in a whisper, like a passionate adventure, living again the burning memory of those moments. For alone and abandoned as she was, her conscience, innocent heretofore of any transgression, paralyzed her thoughts and made her hands cold and clammy. She would have liked to fling those icy hands far away from her, as if they had been foreign objects, and to dissolve into a confidential, glowing, fearful little whisper, to share with someone this secret under whose burden she now felt so terribly weary and forsaken.

But Miette did not stir. It was as if she had been turned to stone.

A few moments passed in this agonizing silence. Then Miette's hands trembled; with a rapid movement she raised her work to her eyes and resumed it where she had left off, but now she worked much more rapidly. The pounding of her heart almost pierced the silence.

Olga grimaced a little as if she were saying something to herself. Cautiously and furtively she raised her eyes for a moment to Miette. She felt that their souls were now withdrawing from each other forever, and she was sorry she had confided her secret.

She might have known that Miette was too sensitive, her spirit not yet sufficiently mature to see such things from the height she had achieved. For an instant she was very close to abandoning her simulated calm and bursting into sobs. But she conquered the momentary weakness.

Frowning, she gazed into space while all the afternoon's memories crowded together into her mind.

She still felt Koretz' heavy, labored panting on her forehead.

She forced herself to smile—a disdainful, wicked little smile—so as not to weep aloud in front of Miette.

Meantime Miette had recovered from her first emotion, but still she did not take her eyes from her work. She could not settle the question of what she should do now, of how she should act. She knew that something terrible had just happened, and had she followed her own impulse she would have called for help. But at the same time another thought, obscure and confused though it was, was dawning within her—perhaps after all, it was not such a tragic affair. Yet she dared not speak, and not a sound emerged from her tightened throat.

Olga began to stretch and, yawning, patted her mouth

with the palm of her hand; but this feigned indifference was so pathetic, and her eyes so clearly revealed its pretense, that Miette pitied her with all her heart.

Olga stood up and, still stretching, said only: "Well, I'll be going—"

She took Miette's chin, raised her face tenderly, and kissed her forehead.

Her hand was so cold and stiff that Miette shivered at its touch.

"Going already?" she murmured, frightened at the sound of her own voice. She, too, would have liked to cry.

When she was alone she sprang from her chair and listened feverishly. She remained in the same position long after the door had closed behind Olga.

She threw aside the work that had helped her through those difficult moments. Sitting down on the couch, she remained for a long time lost in thought without attaining any clarity of vision.

She undressed and slid quickly into bed, as if she wanted to escape from everything that had happened that day. Up to now her life had been composed of calm, serene, eventless days. She could not quite make up her mind whether what had happened was good or bad for Olga . . . whether she ought to envy or despise her, hate her or pity her.

She imagined the whole affair taking place in a dark bedroom that she saw as if in a dream; and Olga was there, naked, in the center of this dream room.

From these visions her imagination always returned to Peter's pleasant face for refreshment and purification. She saw again every word of his letter, which she had read and reread so often that she knew it by heart. She saw in Peter's eyes the sorrowful desire she had read there when he held her hand at the house door.

She was almost shivering under the blankets. A strange fear filled her, mingled, however, with an indescribable happiness; she would have liked to shed tears and she felt that everything that had happened to her yesterday and today was part of the glittering, reverberating whirlpool of life and love that had come to seize her and bear her away to unknown depths.

VII

It was already dusk. The snow sparkled, soft and white, in the street, dissolving all the shadows and absorbing them into itself. The heavy fall of snow muffled all the city, and the very clangor of the electric trolleys seemed to issue from beneath glass domes. In all this white purity the lamps, which had been lighted early, burned with a lemon-yellow radiance.

The room was filled with soft shadows that swarmed like strange creatures bereft of their bodies. Through the window the snow sparkled, and in a corner the stove spread its warm glow. Above the piano, half drowned in the shadow, the large portrait hung in its gilded frame. In her old-fashioned dress, with the crown of luxuriant hair about her young forehead, the girl held her head so that she seemed to be looking eagerly out over the soft, snowy roof tops.

Tómi lay in a corner of the couch, breathing deeply in his sleep. Then he extended his forepaws and stretched with the movements of a man.

Over the arm of the couch a large shawl of peasant embroidery had been thrown, its warm colors lost in the somber twilight.

The doors of the room were wide open, except for Father's door on the other side of the dining room, which was only half open; but even in the living room he could be heard, coughing slightly every now and then to clear his throat as he worked, and the creaking of his chair was audible when he moved.

Peter stood in front of the stove, his hands in his pockets, one shoulder against the wall.

Miette had just gone to the door with Mme. Lénárt, who had come from the Vargas' to pay her a short call.

Since their meeting on the Danube esplanade, already

more than a fortnight ago, Peter had not had a single opportunity to be alone with Miette, though they had met very often. The previous Sunday there had been a tea at the Vargas', and he had come here to Miette's apartment three times already, but their own affair had made not the least progress, except for the stealthy exchange of eloquent glances, with now and then a deep look into each other's eyes.

Peter gazed with turbulent eyes at the multicolored shawl, which Miette used as a scarf. He felt an indescribable emotion, a kind of tenderness for this shawl; as a matter of fact, everything that belonged to Miette inspired the same feeling in him.

He saw the dog on the couch.

"Tomi—" he called softly, snapping his fingers. "Little Tomi, come here."

Tomi, without moving his head, opened an eye and with quiet disdain regarded Peter through the thick bush formed by the tufted hair of his pendant eyebrows. Then, without stirring, he closed his eyes once more.

Peter looked around the room. He would have liked to touch and caress every piece of furniture. Bathed in this weird, mysterious light, everything seemed to him beautiful as a dream.

Miette returned.

Standing in front of the stove, she patted it with her palm, in that gesture used by women when they caress the neck of a horse with their pretty hands.

"Mme. Lénárt is really very sweet," said Miette, her voice retaining the animation of the conversation she had just been carrying on.

"Yes," Peter answered on a note that unconsciously betrayed his desire to be done with the subject.

After that they remained silent for a long time. Only the sound of Miette's hand could be heard, gently patting the wall of the stove.

Peter was carefully scratching a small bubble, the size of a pinhead, in the enamel of the stove, nor did he look at Miette when he said in a low voice, all his soul in his

words: "Why didn't you answer my question the other
day? Did you receive my letter?"

Miette was still patting the stove with her palm, but
more slowly than before.

"Don't you want to talk about it?" he asked, softly and
unhappily.

Still Miette made no answer, but she nodded her head
several times, to the same measure that her hand was
beating on the stove. Thus did she seek to conceal the
embarrassment and emotion that flamed in her cheeks.

"And how did you feel? Were you frightened? Angry?
Or pleased? Or sad?"

Miette finally stopped patting the stove. She lowered
her head, and looked at the floor, apparently completely
absorbed in the difficult task of placing the tips of both
her shoes with the most scrupulous accuracy exactly on
the line formed by the grooves of the parquet, where the
stove cast a flood of red light over the wood.

"I don't know," she said sweetly, raising her voice on
the last word; she was evading the question charmingly,
with virginal shyness, more and more engrossed in her
game, her body swaying with a scarcely perceptible
movement on the line of the parquet.

"I am in love with you," Peter said abruptly, as if he
had had time to take a sudden resolve in order to be
able to say the words at all. And when he had said them,
without waiting for an answer he leaned his forehead
against the stove's warm wall and closed his eyes.

There was a long silence. Nothing could be heard but
the tiny music of the flames. The room was growing
momentarily darker and the street noises, muffled in
snow, filtered so faintly through the window as to be
scarcely audible.

Miette raised her eyes slowly and cautiously to Peter,
but when their glances met she turned her head away
abruptly.

He seized her hand and, after a short struggle, held it
prisoner in his own. Then he carried it to his lips, and
pressed his mouth into the soft palm, his mouth that

burned her cool hand like a glowing coal. Shocked,
Miette turned her back but did not withdraw her hand.
The kisses burned her palm and their warmth invaded her
arm and her whole body.

At length she drew her hand away gently and said:
"Father might come in and box our ears."

The threat sounded so implausible that she smiled at
herself. She listened, however, her head bent, straining
her ears in the direction of the other room, but nothing
could be heard save the occasional short, automatic
cough of solitude.

Peter seized Miette's hand again; she resisted feebly.
He tried to draw her toward him, but Miette clung with
the other hand to the inside ledge of the stove, so that
she all but embraced it, and he could not draw her away.

"I am strong . . ." Miette said, her cheeks red and her
eyes brilliant, filled with enthusiasm for this new and
fascinating game.

Peter took advantage of the moment and tugged at
Miette with so sudden and sharp a jerk that she lost her
balance and all but fell on him. He held her in his two
strong arms, so that she could not move.

With her hands against Peter's chest, she summoned
all her strength to free herself. Agitated as she had never
been before, she was whispering: "You mustn't, you
mustn't!"

But now a strange, cloudy flame gleamed in Peter's
eyes.

"Let me go!" she whispered in scarcely audible tones.
But she could not defend herself; fright had robbed her of
her strength. Peter kissed her by force.

Miette held her lips as tightly closed as she could, to
protect herself against this first kiss that seemed to her
terrifying in its strangeness; and a plaintive little moan
came from behind her closed lips.

In the corner of the couch, Tomi opened an eye and
gazed at them quietly out of that single eye, but only for
a second. When he saw that nothing untoward was going
on, he closed his eye again and resumed his nap.

Miette pushed Peter away and, holding her hands to her temples, cried in horror: "What have you done?"

Peter did not answer. At that moment he could not have uttered a single word. He dropped his arms to his sides, and with closed eyes, very pale, leaned against the wall as if he were mortally weary.

Miette walked slowly to the couch and sat down on the arm, her head bent, her chin in her hand, as if she were deep in thought.

After a moment Peter approached her and silently took her hand.

The room was now in almost total darkness. Only the square of the window glimmered softly gray, the color of a wild pigeon, in the winter twilight. In the stove, the burning coals shot forth narrow little red-gold tongues.

"I love you!" said Peter, pressing Miette's hand against his face.

He said it quietly and simply, yet there was something in his voice that went to Miette's heart.

They remained thus for a long time, not daring to stir, fearful of dissipating the moment.

Suddenly they heard footsteps.

Peter threw himself quickly into an armchair, and Miette slid down from the arm to the couch itself.

Mili crossed the dining room with dragging steps, entered the living room, and, feeling her way along the wall, turned on the electric switch. Looking about and seeing two silent persons in the room, she started.

Miette was fanning herself in confusion with a postcard that she had snatched from the table, while Peter was carefully turning his seal ring round and round on his finger.

With a great clatter, Mili threw a few shovelfuls of coal on the stove, then left the room.

They were left together in the sudden, blazing light, and dared not look at each other. Still less did they dare to speak, knowing in advance how strange the sound of their own voices would be.

Thus a few heavy, difficult moments passed in a strained, fantastic silence that seemed to strip all the surrounding objects of any semblance of reality.

Tomi crawled down from the couch and stopped in the middle of the room. He began to yawn, and his white teeth gleamed like snow against his black palate. Then he sneezed so violently and furiously that his nose struck the floor with a thud. Finally, he waddled from the room like a duck, wagging his little clipped tail. It was impossible not to smile at the sight.

Miette and Peter looked at each other. Miette raised a cushion to her face to hide her smile.

Peter sat down next to her on the couch.

"Are you cross with me?" he asked, attempting in a faltering voice a new approach.

Miette did not answer but from behind the cushion raised her eyes to him. With unwilling curiosity, she was contemplating Peter's mouth.

Suddenly she tossed the cushion to an armchair, rose and walked toward her bedroom.

"Where are you going?" Peter asked, softly, tenderly.

"I'm going to fix my hair," answered Miette in the same tone, and her whispered murmur acknowledged their intimacy and confessed her consciousness of a share in his guilt.

She disappeared behind the door.

Peter followed her. He caught up with her in the middle of the room. He seized her hand and gazed at her with imploring eyes. He drew her toward him, and now Miette made scarcely any resistance. At first she closed her lips again to protect herself from the kiss, but soon her lips relaxed, melted, and for the first time she experienced the rapturous savor of a kiss. Now her hand clung tight to the nape of Peter's neck and her shoulders quivered with this fiery, new delight.

Peter held her, trembling, in his arms. He was acutely conscious of the contours of the body that pressed itself against him and its two tender, burning little breasts.

Miette, too, felt exhausted after that kiss, and rested

against Peter's breast, as if it were already her proper place.

And from that day they kissed every afternoon for hours at a time, tiring themselves to exhaustion at the game. In the wintry dusk they sat in the darkening room, clinging to each other in sweet, fierce torment.

VIII

Through the narrow open windows, the icy morning, cold like a sharp wedge of steel, pierced the warm little bedroom, where the night air still lay heavy.

Along the sidewalk of crooked, sloping Hadnagy Street children hurried with their sleds. The winter's morning, in its pale, silver radiance, was filled with shouts from young throats. The bells were pealing in the tower of Calvary Place, and their notes vanished, quivering, into the upper spaces.

Mme. Takács, a kerchief on her head and fingerless mittens on her hands, stood by Peter's bed, piling together the still warm pillows, at which the icy air, entering through the window, was already biting. She turned her head very sharply from side to side, as if she were in constant fear of something, and she hopped about the little room like a queer little bird in its cage. Under her arm she held a feather duster, at whose top fluttered brown and yellow cock's feathers, which made her look more than ever like a bird.

As she worked, she was thinking that Peter ought to marry the Vajnik girl. That would be the best solution.

"I can't understand Peter," she said to herself, carefully sweeping the crumbs of bread from the blanket with her hand, for she awakened him every morning with fresh rolls and hot coffee.

"I'll speak to him," she continued, resolving, as she had often done before, that this time the question should be settled. But she didn't really believe that she would ever talk to her son; she had never yet had the courage.

Because of this weakness she was angrier with Peter than with herself.

"Aranka is such a fine little girl," she pursued her train of thought as she shook out and folded Peter's nightgown and, suddenly discovering a small brown coffee stain near the collar, she examined it carefully.

"Her uncle is a lieutenant colonel! Charlotte is married to a police lieutenant. Obviously, the family is making its way in the world. And such nice people!—and they must have money, too; that's apparent from the way they live. Aranka must be told to reduce a little. Well, her mother will probably tell her. If only Peter weren't so obstinate!" How she would love to bring the coffee to their twin beds every morning! And how well she would manage the household! Aranka needn't move a finger. For the rest, she would make a fine little wife; she was her mother all over again.

She thought of fat Mme. Vajnik tenderly, affectionately, as, with an easy, accustomed movement, she opened the lower door of the night table and tossed in Peter's slippers.

Then she noticed, wedged in between the bedstead and the mattress, a brass collar button already covered with verdigris. She scratched her finger to get at the button, and felt herself engulfed in a sudden wave of misery when she remembered the scene Peter had made one morning because of the button.

"Dear Lord, how rude he can be!" she mused, sighing deeply. She scattered the pillows about and left the bed wide open.

It all came of his not wanting to marry. Let him live a quiet, regular life and his good humor would soon return. It was terrible that he should treat his own mother so. Never a kind word for her—always this gloomy, harsh expression when he was at home. From whom could he have inherited such a disposition? His father wasn't like that; he was very amiable—talkative, even. She remembered that when Peter had been a little boy she had imagined a future when, Peter a man, she would go everywhere on the arm of her tall son with his fine mustache.

And now never—but absolutely never—did he go anywhere with her; as if he were ashamed of his mother. And why did he shave his whole face like a priest? Such a stupid fashion. Why, even Aranka believed that if you were a man you should stay as God made you.

As she stood in front of the night table, wiping the nickel handle of the match holder, a snowball thrown through the window splashed against the wall near her head and scattered in a white spray. It left only a round, damp spot on the wall.

Mme. Takács went to the window and cautiously put out her head.

At the street corner a little boy of ten in a cotton cap was hugging the wall as he sneaked away.

"Just wait! I'll tell your mother! Aren't you ashamed?" she called to the child, all in one breath. Then, suddenly changing her tone, she bade good day to an elderly, rather stout gentleman who, arms raised, was trying to keep his balance on the slippery, sloping pavement opposite.

"Good morning! Where are you going in such cold weather?"

"Good morning, madame," cheerfully called Kaládi, who owned a small butcher shop at the corner, and he lifted a derby hat whose grease spots shone in the sun.

"Good and cold!" he said, carefully crossing the frozen street with short steps and stopping under her window for a little chat. "I must go to the Council Chamber."

Mme. Takács knew and gossiped with everyone in the neighborhood. It was at this narrow window that she spent the greater part of each day and followed with her reflective gaze each detail of the life about her.

She would cast a glance into the baskets of cooks returning from market, stop them and talk to them. Children came to her window for sweets or asked her to lend them her pepper pot; and old Karg himself, with his bushy mustache, a retired general and one-time judge in the military courts, whose habit it was to stroll along the street leaning on his cherry-wood stick, stopped to chat beneath her window as eagerly as did the little

widows of the neighborhood, who resembled Mme.
Takács in every particular.

Fate had allotted her a drab existence, but she did not
allow herself to be cast down. Only on Peter's account
was she a little unhappy, because she did not have over
him the influence she would have liked. This taciturn,
strong-willed boy went his own way, forged ahead
according to designs hidden from her; they filled her
heart with apprehension. It was absolutely impossible
for her to conceive that anything she had not planned
for Peter could have a good or happy outcome.

With repeated nods she took leave of the butcher and
went back to straightening the little bedroom. Two weeks
before, she had dismissed the servant, and had since been
doing all the work alone. While she was dusting the book
shelf, she suddenly came upon the little board that lay
behind the books.

When she saw what was carved on it she flung it
violently away, as if a red-hot iron had burned her hand.

On several earlier occasions, in putting the room to
rights, she had happened upon the young man's secrets
but had felt no inclination to dwell on them, even in her
thoughts.

Those few letters, that "I love you" carved with the
point of a knife, danced ceaselessly before her eyes;
though she could not guess what the board was for,
whence it came, or why it bore this strange inscription,
she felt nevertheless that it held a significant secret of
Peter's soul. She remembered that one afternoon, when
she had entered Peter's bedroom, he had been sitting at
his table and cutting into this board as he whistled.

She felt, as she fitted the trees into Peter's shoes, that
she hated that little board; she felt as if it might be
responsible for the fact that Peter's life did not conform
to the plan she had conceived for him, adorned in the
most brilliant colors.

It was Aranka whom she pitied most. Poor Aranka
was so madly in love with Peter that she would be capable
of killing herself if Peter should become interested in

someone else. The whole family was counting surely upon
Peter. It was true that this was a little her own fault.
Often, in front of Aranka, she had put into Peter's mouth
words he had never spoken—but only well-meant
exaggerations; these now weighed heavily on her conscience.

At lunch she said nothing to Peter, but studied his face
closely when he wasn't looking. She could hardly wait
for the afternoon to come, so that she might call on the
Vajniks.

When Peter's name was mentioned she sighed and with
a disheartened movement of her hand, said: "Oh,
heavens! Peter! I believe he gambles. Today he came in
at daybreak again—"

There wasn't a word of truth in all this, but she was
ready to sacrifice even her son's reputation, that the
stronghold of hope and illusion she had helped to build
might be laid low.

And from that day on she took to Aranka, as one takes
medicine to a beloved invalid, her lamentations and her
sighs.

IX

For the past two weeks Miette had not once seen Olga.
But she had been so engrossed in the events of her own life,
and love for Peter had so filled her every moment, that
she had not given much thought to her friend's fortunes.

Occasionally every detail of their last interview would
recur to her, but the thought of what had happened
always served to upset her. She kept Olga's story to
herself, as an oppressive secret, not daring to admit to
herself that she was conscious of a tender, forgiving
impulse toward her friend. It was true that for some days
she, too, had been feeling very different about certain
things. Now, as the winter afternoons wore away, she let
her head rest on Peter's shoulder for minutes at a time

in the darkening room—a thing she would hardly have dared imagine several weeks ago.

One afternoon Mme. Varga drew Miette with mysterious air into her bedroom and closed the door behind them. She looked deep into her eyes and asked: "Is it true?"

"Is what true?" asked Miette with a timid glance.

"That this Takács is paying you court."

"Me?" she stammered, and her face reddened.

For a moment Mme. Varga reveled in Miette's embarrassment, looking into her eyes and smiling with kindly malice.

"Why are you so secretive with me? Is the young man in love with you?"

"Well, he comes to the house often," said Miette evasively, "but I don't believe he's really in love with me."

Mme. Varga shook her head thoughtfully and was silent for a moment.

"I don't like your seeing this young man so often—and alone."

"What do you mean, alone?" Miette flared up suddenly ready to attack.

"Yes, yes, that's all right," said Mme. Varga placatingly. "I know very well that your father is in the next room, but just the same I don't approve of all this. I wouldn't meddle in your affairs for all the money in the world, but you're an inexperienced child and a little goose into the bargain, and if I'm really your Mother Elvira, then I have the right to call your attention to certain things. There are times when one must observe the conventions. You should have asked me to come each time this Takács called on you . . ."

And now she scrutinized Miette's face sharply.

Miette did not answer; supporting her weight on one foot, with the tip of her other shoe she carefully traced the pattern of a flower in the carpet. Now she was feeling again the happy, thrilling emotion of those half-dark afternoons, and she thought with a little throb of malicious joy that Mme. Varga had not interfered until today; and as for what had happened up to then, no one could take it away from her.

After a moment of silence she said: "Do you think that's what I ought to do?"

"Yes," interrupted Mme. Varga, "you needn't ponder the matter any further; it must be so from now on."

"Very well," said Miette, lingering on the words, while her most intimate thoughts were limned in delicate patterns on her face. She turned her eyes toward the window and looked out thoughtfully, vacantly, as if her imagination were seeking, in a small, faraway, provincial town, the years of Peter's childhood and the figure of his father, the Latin teacher, of whom he had spoken so often.

Mme. Varga took Miette by the shoulders and turned her around.

"And now, look me straight in the eyes and be honest. Do you like this young man?"

Miette raised her eyes in alarm and a thousand, thousand, thousand thoughts whirled in her mind. She would have liked to seize Mme. Varga's hand and say to her: "I am in love—I don't know what it is—oh! how wonderful it is—help me, advise me—"

That was what she would have liked to say, but she was restrained by the inexplicable chill that she always felt in Mme. Varga's vicinity, perhaps due to the heavily powdered eyebrows of the doctor's wife.

"Well?" Mme. Varga urged, waiting for her answer. Once more she looked long into Miette's eyes. "Do you kiss each other?"

And she raised her finger sharply, protesting in advance lest Miette should not tell her the truth.

But Miette did not answer. She lowered her head, and once more, with even greater absorption, the tip of her foot traced the small circles in the carpet.

"I shan't tell her, but I shan't deny it, either," she thought. "If I don't deny it, I shan't have a lie on my conscience; and if I don't admit it, I can always deny it in case any trouble should arise."

All this passed through her mind like a flash.

"I don't like this at all," said Mme. Varga, very gravely.

So emphatically did she speak that Miette quickly raised rebellious eyes.

"I shouldn't like you to hurry things, for such haste is bound to be punished, sooner or later," Mme. Varga continued more gently. "Has he proposed to you already?"

"He hasn't asked Father yet," Miette answered heedlessly.

"Good Lord! How difficult it is to watch over you girls!" Mme. Varga sighed maternally.

And after Miette had promised to send for her next day as soon as Peter should arrive, she covered her face with fervent, eloquent kisses and let her go.

When Miette left the Vargas' apartment, she would have liked to jump for joy. One thought leaped within her: Someone knew of her love—knew, too, that she and Peter had kissed each other, for those passionate kisses had never ceased to oppress her soul with a dull consciousness of guilt, like some physical distress. Now she considered that the affair had been, in a sense, legalized —which made her infinitely happy. At that moment she felt a warm affection for Mme. Varga—she loved in her the creature with whom she had shared her blissful secret, jealously guarded till then.

Next day she repeated the whole conversation to Peter, word for word, and from that day Mme. Varga, fully conscious of her importance, came every afternoon to sit between them, shedding a prosaic light about her, for now the electricity had to be switched on in good time. However, she was tactful enough not to stay till Peter left.

One morning Miette was sitting by the window, looking out into the street. Suddenly, extraordinary happenings attracted her attention.

An ambulance had stopped in front of the house, and soon after a stretcher was carried out the front door, upon which she recognized Olga's mother. And she saw

Olga too, apparently very much agitated, tenderly spreading the rugs over her mother's knees. Miette turned pale with apprehension, for her first thought was that Olga's mother had suddenly grown worse and that her illness had reached a fatal crisis. But the invalid was bidding the caretaker goodbye, cheerfully nodding her head, and when she had been settled in the ambulance her face radiated happiness. Olga sat beside her and the caretaker remained standing in the street, his head bared, until the vehicle had disappeared.

Miette could not imagine either where or why the sick woman was being removed. But the riddle was soon solved. Mili brought a letter. She immediately recognized Olga's slanting, angular handwriting. The letter read:

"My dear little Miette, I am heartbroken not to be able to say goodbye to you. But I did not want to embarrass you by contact with a woman whose conduct offends the prejudices of your world. You know perfectly well that many things have happened to me in the last few weeks. This man whom I love cannot marry me because his wife, from whom he has been separated for years, refuses, from motives of hatred and revenge, to divorce him. However, I cannot wait: chiefly because— I have never told you anything about this—in a very few moments poverty would have knocked at our door, and I felt myself too weak to struggle with everything that would have followed.

"So I have put my life and fate into the hands of this man who loves me with a genuine, honest love, who pampers me and surrounds me with all the comforts of life, with everything that I should never have been able to secure by my own efforts.

"I am moving into a new apartment which he has had furnished for me, and we are putting my darling mother into an excellent sanatorium.

"I am breaking with everyone I know; I have said goodbye to no one; only to you, Miette, my darling, because I love you very much—oh, very much. I know that you, too, despise me now; you believe I have become a bad woman; perhaps a time will come in your life, too, when you will forgive your Olga.

"P.S. I bequeath the Lily Library to you and beg you, when you read the books, to think sometimes of me."

Miette dropped the hand that had been holding the letter, and for a long time sat staring into space, her mind awhirl. New aspects of life were being revealed to her, new problems assailed her, and just now she could find no answer to those apparently inscrutable problems. She felt a searing pain at the thought that Olga had fled, that there would no longer be an Olga for her; and suddenly all the carefree hours of their long, happy friendship were vivid in her memory. And at the same time she pondered Olga's fate with a secret pity; she tried to draw in fancy the figure of this man, of whom Olga had said only: "This man whom I love . . ."

"Poor little Chouchette," she thought aloud, and she felt her eyes fill slowly with burning tears.

X

Paul Szücs had broken with Yolanda Galamb, but Peter knew nothing beyond the bare fact, for Paul wrapped himself about in mysterious silence. Peter had learned of the latest turn of affairs in this way. As he was turning home for lunch one day, Szücs had come up behind him and seized his arm; then, taking a deep breath, and without further preamble, he had said: "You know . . . I have broken with her."

His words were accompanied by a brisk, disdainful wave of the hand, whereby he intended to convey that the whole affair was no longer of any more moment to him than the cigarette he had just thrown away.

Peter saw at once, however, that it had been a terrible blow. Paul's eyes were encircled by deep rings, and his face was pathetically sunken, as if he had lain awake all night, seared and racked by his pain. Peter, happy and successful in love, proved rather insensitive to his friend's suffering. Anyone else in his place would doubtless have behaved in the same way.

"Really?" said he, looking into his face. "That must have been very hard on you."

Szücs winked at Peter, but the wink was forced and quite out of place. "Bah! Don't worry about me, old man!" After a moment he added: "I'm only sorry for her, poor little thing. You know, she cries when no one's there—heavens, how she cries!" And as he spoke he shook Peter's arm.

Then, breathing deeply, he filled his powerful chest with air and with a whistling sound exhaled it out of the corner of his mouth, like pipe smoke. His face showed plainly that he himself was the last to believe a single word of what he had just said.

He would have liked to make Peter think that after the break it was he who had preserved the advantage, but the effort made him appear more pathetic than ever.

"Brr! How cold it is!" he said, stamping on the ground to prove that at the moment he was concerned with nothing but the cold, though he wasn't really cold at all. The pale winter's sun warmed the soft snow, and the Danube, bathed in the brightness of midday, flowed between its snowy banks.

They began to talk of indifferent matters. Paul's face was that of a man who strives in vain to turn his mind from the tenacious, terrible thing that has buried itself, like a steel wedge, into his skull.

"Well, goodbye, old fellow," he said abruptly, cutting Peter short in the midst of a long sentence.

And so he left him, in the midst of his broken sentence, betraying the fact that he had been following Peter's speech with his eyes, but had heard not a single word.

One evening, Peter's mother greeted him smilingly: "You know, my son, your friend is such a delightful man!"

"What friend?"

"Paul Szücs."

"Why?"

"He was here all afternoon. I gave him coffee."

"Why did he come?"

"Simply to pay a call. He stayed nearly three hours, and we had a delightful talk."

And on several later occasions, entering his mother's room, Peter would find Paul sitting there, talking to her in a low voice of one thing or another. He could easily understand Paul's state of mind. Szücs now spent the greater part of his time in the most incongruous places, where he had never been seen before. He deliberately sought out those people who had heretofore been most remote from his life, resembling therein a wounded animal who retreats into the depths of the thicket.

Mme. Takács waited for Szücs every afternoon, as someone on whose coming she could firmly depend. To have found someone who valued her society so highly gave her extreme pleasure. Oh, if only Peter were like that! Szücs, the son of a village blacksmith, could gossip for hours with "dear little Aunt" of things of which he understood nothing, and could display the keenest interest in some such serious problem as this: Why had the chemist Sumiczky, at Kecskemét, divorced his wife twenty-two years ago and finally killed himself by drinking at least fifteen cups of black coffee every day? Or else: how gay it had been at the skating rink in those days when she had met the Latin assistant of the provincial college. She had still been Helen Farkas then, a slender girl who skated very well—she really did not say this just to boast; she had skated very well indeed. Who would have thought that this man would one day be her husband! How many things had come of that handclasp exchanged in front of the pavilion, when they had been introduced! Peter . . . and Charlotte's family at Brassó, where there were grandchildren now . . . It was all so complicated, dear Lord! so difficult to follow. Oh, how strange life was! She even remembered that the thaws had set in that day and the ice was beginning to melt.

In the course of these long conversations Szücs had

made the acquaintance of the Vajnik family in detail. And before long the idea of bringing Szücs and Aranka together sprouted in the mind of Mme. Takács. For some reason she considered it her personal duty to help Aranka find a husband. If Peter—oh how difficult it was to know where you were with him!—was unwilling at any price to accept the yoke, she must somehow lead this dear, good Szücs to the road of Aranka's destiny. And from that moment she invariably considered, watched, and judged Szücs from that point of view.

The days slipped slowly by, and Christmas was drawing near. One afternoon Peter and Miette went shopping together. For weeks Miette had been racking her brain about what to buy and for whom. She had a little private notebook where she had written down how much she wanted to spend on the Christmas gifts for Father, the Vargas, Grandmother, Mili, and the caretaker's little six-year-old daughter. Olga's name was in the little notebook, too. Her greatest concern was what surprise to give Peter.

Both in high spirits, they went from one shop to another through the snowy streets that were already growing dark.

"Find me a funny present," said Miette to Peter. "I want to give Johnny something, too, for Christmas. Last year he sent me an old cooking spoon, and Mili discovered that it was one of ours."

So they sauntered gaily from one shop window to the next, their hearts already overflowing with the pleasures and joys of the coming Christmas season. Peter had been unspeakably delighted at the opportunity of accompanying Miette into various shops whose owners he knew. It made him so happy that everyone should see them come in together, and he tried to view with the eyes of others this slender, shapely young girl—the clear colors of youth in her face that glowed with the cold—who, in the excitement of shopping, hopped buoyantly, almost dancing on her delicate feet, in front of each counter; and who knew so well how to combine charm, courtesy, and dignity in talking to the tradespeople.

Never had Peter found her so pretty or distinguished. Her coat, trimmed with brown fur, fell just below the knee; a scarf of soft green silk was twisted loosely about her neck, protecting it against the cold; the exquisite lines of her long, slender feet showed to advantage in high tan laced boots; the feather-trimmed hat, worn a little to one side and pulled far down, gave her head a curious shape, very distinctive.

She haggled earnestly for everything, but she was one of those customers who haggle without conviction, in whom the tradesman's wary instinct promptly recognizes a defenseless purchaser.

"What are you going to buy for me?" asked Peter, as they were leaving a shop.

"It's a secret," she replied, arching her eyebrows with an expression that clothed the words in significance.

Tiny flakes of snow whirled thickly in the yellow light of the street lamps.

Suddenly a young man in a dark green velour hat passed near them. Upon catching sight of Miette, he raised his hat smilingly and bowed low. Miette acknowledged his greeting with an answering smile of friendliness.

Peter immediately recognized Michael Ádám.

"Who is that?" he asked, pretending indifference.

"Michael Ádám. Don't you know him? He's a very nice boy."

Peter stole a glance at Miette's face. He had a feeling that behind that lovely face there flitted a secret thought that might remain a mystery to him forever and at the same time he remembered that at the Vargas' first tea in September, Ádám had spoken only to Miette and had said goodbye to no one but Miette. He remembered, too, having seen them walking together one day on the Danube esplanade. How strange that he should have forgotten the man completely during these last weeks.

Suddenly an inexplicable sadness overwhelmed him. Had there been something between them? Suppose they too had kissed—at this thought he was seized by so violent

a rage and so fierce a pain that he began to hate not only
Ádám but Miette as well. What would happen if he
should discover some fine day that Miette had already
had some sort of affair? And what would happen if he
discovered that she was having one at this very moment,
when he thought himself the happiest of lovers? Why
wasn't it possible that Miette should be having a telephone
conversation with someone every morning, and meeting
him too, perhaps? And what would happen in the future
if someone should come along who interested Miette?
Things like that happened all the time with women.

Dark fear laid hold of him as he considered these
possibilities, and he was unable to find comfort just then
in the thought that he and Miette would prove the
exception to the rule. He dwelt on that frantic pain, of
which he had just had a slight foretaste when Ádám's dark
green hat had been raised for a second among the snowflakes. He saw Paul Szücs before him; and his ludicrous,
pathetic attitude, his disdainful winks, his futile efforts
to put Peter off the scent, all to the accompaniment of a
feeble smile, grew suddenly clear to him. Pondering all
this, the whole of life appeared to him discouraging,
aimless, empty, and sad.

Miette did not immediately notice Peter's silence, for
the shop windows claimed all her attention. Having
reached a silks shop, she seized his arm without looking
at him, and dragged him inside.

"What is the matter with you?" she asked a little
later, when they were in the street again and she had
finally grown aware of his morose air.

"I have a slight headache," said Peter, trying to seem
livelier.

Their hands were already filled with all sorts of little
parcels, so that they could scarcely stir. They took a cab,
and as the vehicle was crossing a nearly deserted street
Miette closed her eyes and proffered her lips to Peter.

The moment was rapidly approaching when it would
be necessary to speak to Father. Peter had stayed at the
Almády's for dinner several times recently, and the old

gentleman, though he pretended to attach no importance to Peter's frequent visits, would often contemplate the clouds of pipe smoke thoughtfully as he sat alone in his room, trying to form an accurate judgment of Peter, reconstructing in his memory, with the help of all the impressions he had retained, an exact image of the young man's features, his voice, his manner of speech, his glance, his gestures.

After lengthy, urgent pleas on the part of Miette, Mme. Varga consented to speak to Father first. Though Miette was very close to her father, she could not make up her mind to be the first to broach the subject to him. A sense of modesty, virginal and childish, restrained her.

That afternoon, immediately after lunch, Mme. Varga talked to Father behind carefully—and, as it seemed to Miette, mysteriously—closed doors. Miette sat on the couch in the living room, her knees drawn up, her heart pounding so furiously that it frightened her. She gnawed her clenched fists in nervousness. The minutes passed slowly. At intervals she raised her eyes to her mother's portrait, as if to implore the help of this unknown creature. She started at the slightest noise.

At last the doors opened, and Father put his head through the aperture.

"Miette! Come here!"

Mme. Varga was about to leave, but before she went she exchanged a significant glance with Miette.

Very pale, Miette entered her father's room. She perceived in his face, too, traces of unaccustomed emotion. He coughed several times—a short little cough—to clear his throat, and this slight noise, in the silence that preceded their talk, filled the room with a strange disquiet.

"Your Aunt Elvira has told me everything," Father began, and his voice was more tender than usual. He did not look at Miette as he spoke.

"My little daughter," he continued, "my one wish is that you may be as happy as possible. If you love this young man, then"—he raised his eyes to Miette for the first time—"well, you may become his wife."

Motionless, Miette gazed at her father, her eyes burning with emotion, her hands twisting nervously.

"But don't hurry things too much!" Father continued calmly. "Watch yourself, be very sure of yourself before deciding definitely, because this is the most important act of your life. As far as I am concerned," he added, "I should prefer not to be asked for my opinion till to-morrow."

He gave Miette a long look and suddenly held out his hands to her. Miette, understanding the gesture, rose, went to him, and laid her hands slowly in her father's outstretched ones. Slowly her eyes filled with tears, and when Father drew her toward him to kiss her, she put her arms around his neck with the impulse of a child who needs protection.

Then they began to talk quietly. One thought, perceived by both behind their words, put a damper on their conversation—the thought that in drawing vivid pictures of Peter and of the contingencies of this proposed marriage, they were casting the plummet of their words into the obscure depths of an inscrutable future. Miette told her father in detail how they had met, of their subsequent encounters, of the impression Peter had made upon her, carefully refraining from any mention of the intimacies already accorded their love.

When she paused in her recital Father asked her questions. He asked her what town Peter came from, what his father had been, and in which bank he worked. It was apparent from his expression that he considered these dates and details of importance, and was making a note of them in his memory.

And next morning, at an unwonted hour for him, he took his stick and his top hat—which he wore only on special occasions—and went to the center of the city, whence he did not return till late.

He made no secret of the fact that he had been gathering exact information about Peter and his family at the only sources in which he reposed confidence. This information must have set his mind at rest, for he was cheerful when he returned home. He had bought a bottle of perfume for Miette on his way and a new collar for Tomi.

After lunch he finished the conversation by saying: "Well, now you may send me your young man!"

And that very afternoon Peter was sitting in Father's study on the same chair where Miette had sat the day before.

The interview was carried on in simple, quiet words. Here were two men confronting each other, each of whom loved Miette in his own way, gauging and examining the other's resources. They set forth and developed their plans to construct for Miette's life a serene and happy shelter.

"What is your salary?" Father asked very simply. He was smoking his pipe, blowing smoke from his mouth in thick rings.

And, having heard the answer, he also told exactly what his pension was and the amount of Miette's inheritance from her mother, which was deposited in the bank. This sum was considerably larger than Peter had judged from Miette's account.

That night Peter dined with them. In speaking to Francis Almády he carefully avoided any form of address, for he no longer wished to call Miette's father "Sir," and he did not yet venture to address him as "Father." When he took leave and kissed Miette's hand, she suddenly offered him her cheek in a gesture impossible to misunderstand, so that Peter, after a moment's hesitation, kissed her. It was the first time he had kissed Miette in the presence of a third person.

When he reached home, he found his mother still up. He went to her room and said to her, an unusual note in his voice: "Mother, I want to tell you something."

Mme. Takács, as though divining what was to come, followed her son, her eyelids fluttering with emotion. When they were alone in Peter's room he turned to her abruptly. He had meant to begin quite differently, and had been rehearsing the words in his mind, but he said simply, his wide-open eyes radiant with happiness: "I am engaged!"

"Oh, my God" Mme. Takács cried softly, and her eyes promptly filled with tears.

Peter held his mother silently in his arms. The tearful little old lady scarcely reached his chin as she stood there, resting her head on her son's breast. After a moment he lowered her tenderly into a chair.

He told her all that he thought would interest her. She listened attentively, a finger at her cheek, and as soon as she was able to form a picture of Miette from Peter's description, she promptly compared her in her thoughts with Aranka Vajnik.

She dared not admit, even to herself, that this comparison was not to Miette's advantage. First of all she did not like the name Miette. Then she learned, to her dismay, that she had grown up without a mother, from which fact she drew all sorts of conclusions concerning her character and morals. She dared not ask Peter, but she gathered from his words that Miette's dowry was not nearly so large as Aranka's. Nor could she take any pleasure in Francis Almády's high social position because, for some reason, she felt herself humbled by it.

But she allowed nothing of all this to be apparent.

Peter thought that his mother's introduction to Father and Miette would prove a very awkward business. He thought the cramped little apartment of Hadnagy Street too mean; the furniture was a little shabby, suited to the position and taste of a provincial professor and bearing traces of the intolerable German style that had been the fashion in furniture in his day. Charlotte had taken everything of value to Brassó with her when she had married. But the furniture of the Almády apartment, the little cherry-wood cupboards, the dressers, the curving wood of the armchairs, and the old frames of the mirrors, all spoke of a long past of comfort and distinction.

But it was his mother who troubled him most in connection with this meeting. He believed that she would seem in Miette's eyes too simple, ignorant, and provincial.

It was for that reason that he tried to exaggerate things to Father and Miette, and in speaking of his mother or the apartment he drew a lively picture that painted them in colors less attractive than the reality.

He deliberately arranged the visit for the late afternoon, because the apartment looked better then than in broad daylight. Mme. Takács in a black silk dress awaited her guests.

When Miette entered the room, her cheeks flushed, she enveloped her future mother-in-law in a single glance, surveying her with childlike, undisguised curiosity. Peter watched her face anxiously, and tears came to his eyes when Miette, bowing low, kissed his mother's hand.

He realized after a few moments that all his fears had been superfluous. His mother, in her simple little dress, with her light voice of which joy and emotion made a continuous, charming little plaint, with her provincialisms that sounded droll and amusing—of which Peter had tried in vain to rid her—had instantly found the way to Miette's heart and Father's. There she sat on the couch, timidly stroking Miette's arm now and then; suddenly, without the shadow of a reason, shedding a few tears; passing without the smallest pause or the slightest transition from one subject to another. It was all so charming, with the charm of simplicity, of spontaneity, of candor and innocence—everything that Peter, through the staleness of habit, had failed to discover in her.

She was already talking to Father as if they were old acquaintances.

They decided to celebrate the betrothal on New Year's Eve.

The visit was prolonged until almost dinner time.

Peter left with the Almádys, for recently he had been dining with them regularly.

After dinner Mme. Varga came in. Suddenly Peter asked her: "What has become of Olga?"

For some time he had been conscious of the fact that he never saw Olga anywhere, but it was only now that he took the opportunity of inquiring about her.

Mme. Varga, to whom he had addressed the question, maintained a resolute silence, avoiding Peter's eyes. There was a kind of cruel condemnation in her silence.

Miette answered instead.

"Oh, they left here some time ago. Her mother has been put into a sanatorium."

But she hid her face from Peter as she spoke, and quickly turned the conversation into other channels.

The Christmas holidays slipped by in an atmosphere of tranquil, innocent happiness. Miette had racked her brain for weeks, trying to decide what to give Peter. Finally, all her efforts to find something better having failed, she selected a silver cigarette case, in which she wrote simply, in her distinctive, angular script: "Miette—Christmas 1913."

Peter gave her a gold wristwatch.

The gift intended for Olga—a diary bound in fine leather—she hid among the books of the Lily Library, because she had no way of discovering Olga's address. She did not even know her friend's name, and she dared inquire only of the caretaker, who was unable to enlighten her.

There were nine at table for the betrothal dinner—Father and Miette, Mme. Takács and Peter, Dr. Varga and his wife, Paul Szücs and Johnny—and as the most important personage, the parish priest, who had ready, hidden in the pocket of his soutane, two engagement rings.

After the first course he rose and, resting both his hands on the cloth, leaned forward and began his speech in a low voice, almost a whisper. His subject was the meeting of two loving hearts. His old face, comically toothless, betrayed not the faintest feeling, and a careful observer might have noted the triteness of each sentence he pronounced, as they issued in turn from his flabby lips—always the same for thirty years and God alone knew how many more. On the faces about the table the most varied thoughts were reflected. Peter kept his eyes fixed on the priest and listened attentively, as a believer might listen to the true grace of a sermon. Mme. Takács bent her head low and played with a corner of the napkin on her lap. Miette sat very straight in her chair, and roses of excitement reddened her face; her head was quiet, but the delicate lines of her nostrils and of the corners of her mouth seemed painfully sensitive. The gleaming arch of her neck and shoulders rose fresh and white from her dark green velvet dress. Her young girl's face—still almost that of a child—was in strange contrast to the rich golden crown of her hair, suggesting the color of cherry wood, hair that seemed ripe, altogether the hair of a woman. Miette bloomed that evening, flowered in all the glory of her young beauty.

Peter was absorbed in arranging bread crumbs in very straight lines on the tablecloth with the help of a broken toothpick. He was happy and felt touched as well; but when the priest spoke directly to him, disagreeable sensations seized upon him, and he dared not raise his eyes.

Mme. Varga, winking her powdered lids, assumed an expression seeming to indicate that the priest was addressing his discourse to her. The doctor, on the other hand, strove vainly to banish the boredom from his countenance. Long a family physician in this neighborhood, he had attended almost all its betrothal dinners in the last twenty years, and had already listened to the priest's address innumerable times. He knew, too, that it was much longer than necessary. So he was the only one whose eyes wandered inattentively and remained fixed, from time to time, on the wooden figures of the chandelier.

Johnny would now and then cast a long, sad look at Miette.

Szücs sat with folded arms, his head a little to one side, and contemplated the middle of his plate.

Mili stood near the pantry, the salad bowl in her hand, evidently furious with the priest for, being deaf, she heard hardly a word of his low-toned speech.

Tomi looked here and there, from one spot to another. For a full minute he had been feeling uneasy because of the unusual size of the company; he could not fathom

why so many people should be gathered there. His restlessness could not but be aggravated when the emotion,
released by the priest's words penetrated to his dim,
canine soul.

For a time he endured this nervous tension silently;
then, unable any longer to contain himself, he began
howling mournfully.

Dr. Varga, whose thoughts were wandering far afield,
lowered his head and hid his smile in his blond beard.

Johnny arose noiselessly, took Tomi in his arms, and,
walking on tiptoe, carried him out of the room.

On the threshold Tomi squirmed in Johnny's arms and
growled in a muffled rumble at the priest.

Finally the priest finished his address. It was almost
eleven. They all remained seated around the table, and
amid quiet conversation and unaccustomed thoughts bade
the old year farewell. Thus the new year came upon them,
entering and greeting each one. Father, who was in the
habit of retiring early, was already lifting his napkin to
his mouth, stifling little yawns. The priest was quietly
making ready to go, and gradually the entire company
was on its way home.

Peter and his mother, Johnny and Szücs walked through
the cold, starry night. All along the street New Year's
lights gleamed behind the apartment-house windows.

At the end of the street they separated, Johnny and
Szücs going toward the bridge.

Johnny, contrary to his custom, was silent and sad.
Szücs did not know why and did not ask. He, too,
pursued his own thoughts.

Below them, drifting blocks of ice in the river crumpled
with a monotonous crash against the supports of the
bridge. High above them, in the star-studded winter sky,
invisible flocks of wild geese passed. The darkness and
silence up there deadened their plaintive cries.

From a café on the other side of the bridge strains of
music issued. Drunkards reeled here and there in the
blackness of the cold night. A hoarse song echoed—
whence no one knew—and the new year stood there,

mysterious in the shadows, like the policeman who silently watched from beneath the dark arch of a doorway the disturbers of the peace.

XI

Their formal engagement did away with the panic fear of stolen kisses that had always caused a sweet, wild fluttering of their hearts. They no longer had anything to fear from the unexpected opening of a door; Miette was no longer compelled to vanish to the bathroom every few moments to wash away from about her mouth the red marks of biting kisses. Now they could live, serene and free, in their love. They were often alone for long periods at a time. Their hours of solitude together, when no one came between them, filled them more and more with the fire of sensual desire, as ripening grapes beneath the heat of the sun feel the mysterious savor of maturity fermenting and spreading under their delicate skins. Thus did every cell and fiber of their bodies swell with the eagerly anticipated delights of their coming marriage. For hours they sat beside each other, scarcely speaking. When they were in company they looked at each other furtively, and sensual longing ran like a sweet narcotic through their blood.

Meantime the days passed, the snow gradually melted, and sometimes, toward noon, the rays of the sun fell warm on the windowpanes. Little ten-kreutzer bouquets of lilies-of-the-valley and violets were already on sale in front of the churches. Day by day spring was drawing nearer.

Visits at first occupied the greater part of their time. Peter was astonished to see what a large and distinguished circle of relatives and friends Miette had.

Then shopping and the completion of Miette's trousseau helped to speed the time. So a second month passed almost unnoticed.

They had agreed not to take a new apartment but to live with Father.

They still needed another wardrobe and a little desk to complete the furnishing of Peter's room. Peter had been given the room at the end of the apartment, which up to then had been the guest room, and was separated from Miette's only by the bathroom. It was Miette's wish that each of them should have a room.

Peter had selected a wardrobe and desk in a shop, but Mme. Varga—who concerned herself benevolently in all their affairs, examined everything and offered her opinion on everything—suggested to them that they look through her villa at Mount Gellért, where there was a mass of furniture of no use to her. Miette gladly consented to go out with Peter to look at the furniture.

"Be careful to lock the doors before you leave," said Mme. Varga, giving them the keys.

"And tell Mme. Hilka I shall be coming in some day next week, to see how things are going," she called after them.

Mme. Hilka was the caretaker and lived on the villa grounds with her husband throughout the year.

They started out on foot toward the farther side of Mount Gellért. Miette was well acquainted with the road to the villa that stood alone on the slope of the hill, surrounded by a few puny fruit trees.

It was four in the afternoon and the sun was shining bright. It was as if the rays of this late March sun had passed through a sky of glass, diffusing an unusual warmth that penetrated their clothing and entered their very hearts. The yellow clods of earth, bathed in the warm, gentle sunlight, crumbled away beneath their feet. All along the slope of the hill, in the fresh green of the grass, in the buds ready to burst from the still-leafless trees, spring was now straining in an effort to reach the heights of her sovereignty. Higher up, on the level land, blossoming trees seemed to be wearing white and rosy wigs.

Higher still, a light breeze bore through the air the sweet, soft cries of the birds. In the distance a train passed noisily. It was crossing the steel bridge over the Danube and sounded from far off like a gigantic steel chain being unrolled. Low on the horizon over Pest floated a cloud of thick lavender smoke.

"Do you know what sweet peas are?" asked Miette.

She bent down and her white hand disappeared in the green grass to pluck a wildflower whose delicate, warm perfume breathed all the enchantment of spring. She put it into Peter's buttonhole, and the little flower seemed a tiny drop of blood on the lapel of his tobacco-colored coat.

They went on arm in arm, walking slowly, as if it were difficult for them to bear the burden of happiness that weighed heavily on their hearts.

At a turn in the road they paused and surveyed the nearby heights, gray and solitary, but resplendent this afternoon in the glorious radiance of spring. The brass ball on the tower of a villa sparkled in exultant joy, and continuous lines of long, slender, golden arrows seemed to be darting from it in all directions.

They walked alongside the palings of an estate. The sun shone through the bars and the blinding light struck them full in the eyes. On a rubbish heap by the wayside fragments of broken glass shot forth white flame, as if the light that flooded everything wanted to burst not from the sky alone, but from the gloomy depths of earth as well.

A little boy passed near them. He was eating an orange and the juice ran down his dirty hand. The pungent odor of the orange filled the air. From an old garden a few steps farther on there came to them the scent of hyacinths that were beginning to bloom. Somewhere a gate was being varnished, and the penetrating smell of turpentine clutched at their throats. Everywhere along their road heavy, warm smells eddied.

Miette blinked at the sun, then raised her eyes to an invisible point on the horizon.

"Ten days more, and I shall be your wife!" she said in a low voice.

Peter did not answer. There were words on the tip of his tongue, but Miette had spoken so tenderly—as if her soul had been listening to the words—that he was silenced.

Ascending the hill, Miette bent her head against Peter's shoulder, and rested all the weight of her body on his arm. The burden seemed to Peter infinitely soft and sweet. He had the feeling that unknown powers, never before realized, were being freed within him, coursing through his muscles and swelling them. He felt buoyant and elastic and was seized by an irresistible desire to clear at a single bound the high wall beside which they were walking. Then he measured with his eyes a stone as large as a man's head, and it seemed to him that if he should hurl that heavy stone it would leap from one hilltop to another.

A moment later, before Miette could prevent him, he had swept her into his arms and was carrying her up the hill.

"Be careful, idiot—someone might see us!" Miette murmured, clasping Peter's neck tight in her first trepidation.

But there was no one up there.

Her skirt was lifted to the knee and her long, slender feet, shod in low ties, and her legs, taut in their gray silk stockings, dangled free of Peter's arms, exquisite and provocative.

"Let me go!" she begged, imploring and reproachful, clutching his neck yet more tightly in her dismay.

"Let me go—don't you see my skirt is all up—" she repeated, trying vainly to cover her round knees that peeped impudently from beneath her skirt; above the stocking a bit of rosy flesh was visible.

Peter began to pant a little with fatigue; he stopped and let her slide carefully to the ground.

Once liberated, Miette ran ahead to the villa and called over the low hedge to an old woman who was raking the newly turned earth in front of the house.

"Mme. Hilka, we are coming to look at the furniture."

Her voice was melodious and childish.

The old woman put down her rake, surveyed them, frowning, and opened the gate suspiciously.

"Ah, yes—I didn't recognize the young lady at first!" she cried, beaming suddenly as she looked more closely at Miette, and greeting Peter with a smiling "Good day!" and a keen glance.

They stopped for a moment in the newly spaded garden. A warm, fresh, earthy aroma rose to their nostrils like the mighty, magic breath of spring. The earth lay spread about them in a dense mass of gigantic brown hummocks, its ridges glistening like oily chunks of bacon, exhaling a cool, moist perfume that included everything —the growing grass; the bulbs bursting into flower; the woods sown with violets; the billowing, flowing waters of the river; the clouds, light, snowy clusters of fleece skimming aloft through the heavens; and the perfume, the strength, the fever, the music of the March wind making the whole arch of the firmament resound, stretched apart, cleft asunder by its mighty blows.

"Have you the keys?" asked the old lady, taking up her rake and resuming her work.

"Yes, we brought them," Miette cried, jingling them gaily in her hand.

"Madame sent word," she said, turning as she went up the steps with Peter, "that they are coming out themselves some day next week."

"I have been waiting impatiently for them," Mme. Hilka answered, moving her arms and hips to the rhythm of the rake. The brilliant sun cast a long, dark, purple shadow at her side.

When they reached the landing Miette tried to open the hall door, but the key would not turn in the lock. She rose on tiptoe and, arching her shoulder, pushed against the door, but that was of no avail either.

Peter pushed her gently aside and turned the key in the lock with a single easy movement of the hand, winking at Miette, as if to say: "You see, little one, that is how it works!"

Miette burst out laughing.

They crossed the hall, but there was nothing interesting there. Then they entered the first room. Miette opened the shutters with a practiced hand, as if she were in her own home. Like water rushing through the breach of a broken dam, the sunlight flooded the dark room, redolent of camphor and mustiness, where for months darkness and winter had been sleeping.

The orange-yellow and blue of an embroidered table cover flamed suddenly, and the mirrors burst into laughter in the brilliant daylight.

Miette examined the room, well lighted now, with quick, sharp eyes. Her face gave evidence of nothing at the moment beyond a lively interest in the shapes of the furniture assembled there. She was searching for those pieces that Elvira had described and recommended to her attention.

Suddenly she disappeared behind a wardrobe and called out to Peter: "Come along! We'll push this one aside!"

Behind the wardrobe they discovered the little desk for which they had been looking. In the fine dust that covered its polished top Miette traced a few fanciful flourishes, then, with a swift, inimitable gesture, wiped the dust from the end of her finger on Peter's nose.

Peter tried to catch her about the waist but, twisting, she escaped him with a gay cry.

"Come on! Let's look for the wardrobe!" she cried from the door of the other room.

This room reeked not only of camphor, but of some other sweet, heavy, unfamiliar odor. Through chinks in the shutters the sun shot sharp rays of light into the room, aslant and blinding. One could hear the crackling of the shabby coat of paint on the heated window frames that were opening their pores to the first warm rays of the sun.

Near the wall there was a large couch, strewn with cushions. When they entered, the dark cushions seemed to stir like strange cavern-dwelling creatures disturbed in their slumber.

It was difficult for the eyes to accustom themselves to this warm, brown darkness. Miette went uncertainly toward the window to open the shutters, but Peter seized her hand and drew her toward him.

Never before had she felt his kisses so fierce and burning. Their flame spread through all her body, and she clasped her arms about his neck, holding him with all her strength. Dizzy, her passion unrestrained, she felt all her nerves and all her fibers melting in that kiss.

But a moment later she was thrusting him away in dismay.

"Leave me alone!" she cried resentfully, her face aglow, trying to free herself from his arms.

But Peter caught her again, and buried his burning face in her neck.

"You're mine—you belong to me!" His voice was strangled as if by a frenzy of madness, and each word burst graspingly from his chest.

So far as she was capable of judging, Miette felt pity for Peter in his terrible excitement and, to soothe him, whispering tenderly into his ear, though in a voice muffled by fear, repeating the same words mechanically: "Peter, enough . . . enough, Peter!"

But suddenly she knew only that Peter, with one movement, had pulled her clothes from her shoulders, tearing even her chemise, and that his brutal action had stripped her nearly to the hips. She hadn't even time to cover her breasts with her crossed arms, though instinctively she made the gesture; she felt only that she was being raised from the ground, and found herself suddenly half lying on the couch. Peter's mouth ran over her like a flame, while she tried in vain to protect her breasts from his kisses.

In a voice suffocated by alarm and despair, she kept whispering, and the smothered words could hardly force their way from her tight throat: "Peter, let me go! Leave me alone! What are you doing? In the name of heaven, are you mad?"

With all her strength she stiffened the side of her arm against Peter's neck, which movement freed her for a moment.

Peter knelt before her and seemed to be calmed. His voice sounded quiet; but he still kept Miette nailed to the couch with both hands, and in this position their bodies were strained against each other like two adversaries.

"Listen to me, Miette—you are mine, anyway—in a few days you will be my wife—What difference can it make? Don't be stupid, dear little Miette."

Miette did not answer. Her brows were arched in fury —her blazing, frightened eyes fastened upon him.

The flash of a moment and again it was body against body, the one attacking, the other defending. Feeling a current of fresh air, Miette realized that her legs were uncovered, but it was in vain that she struggled to move. Peter's arm held her so firmly that it seemed as if her body were clasped by burning bars of steel. The frantic cry of terror and disgust was already at her throat when the thought suddenly crossed her mind that Mme. Hilka in the garden below would hear that cry. And only a weak, plaintive sound, stifled in tears, escaped her lips. She felt that she was lost, and as if yielding, fell backward helpless; but the next moment she summoned all her strength and, stiffening her body and arching her back, with a single lunge she thrust Peter aside, who, losing his balance, fell heavily to the ground with a resounding, ludicrous thud.

Miette leapt up. She ran to the other end of the room and sought refuge behind a table.

She stood there, panting, gazing with staring pupils straight into Peter's eyes. Her hair had come down in the struggle, and a golden curl fell in disorder on her bare shoulder. With both hands she held together her dress that was torn at the breast.

So she stood, motionless, and in the silence that had suddenly fallen between them her rapid breathing was clearly audible.

The room was filling with a fine, golden-brown dust, and seemed to be growing lighter.

Peter rose slowly and staggered to the other room.

There he smoothed his hair hastily in front of the mirror, and adjusted his necktie with a jerk. Then he went down to the garden under the fruit trees. With one hand he supported himself against the lime-whitened trunk of an apple-tree and stared into the distance where the fading disk of the sun was sinking, red and orange, into soft, kindling mists of twilight.

A faint breeze sprang up from nowhere, and its light breath seemed to cast a shadow over all things, gradually, imperceptibly obscuring their colors.

The blood slowly began to leave his head, and the trembling of his knees abated. He let go of the apple tree and brushed from his hands the dry white lime dust that had collected there. Slowly he walked to the end of the garden and sat down on an old bench.

He lit a cigarette, inhaling the smoke in deep, greedy draughts.

He was unable at the moment to find his way through the maze of his own sensations. When he had left the living room he had been so angry with Miette that he would have felt no shame in striking her. Why had she been so silly?

But during his pause under the apple tree his anger had completely disappeared, giving place to hot pity for Miette. He reproached himself for the terrible situation in which he had placed her and the brutality with which he had behaved.

And suddenly it was with himself that he was furious. What had happened filled him with an overwhelming sense of shame before Miette; he wished he could live that afternoon over again from the moment when they had passed through the door of the house.

But soon he put his distress from him, finding comfort in the thought that after all he had done no harm, since Miette already belonged to him by right and by law; it was Miette who had been foolish. And he lived over that moment when Miette's shoulder had gleamed white and naked in the dark room, when she had crossed her arms in fright before her breast to hide it, and he could smell again the distracting feminine perfume of her skin. Then a new passion swelled through his veins, and he would not have given the moment through which he had just lived for all the treasures of the world.

In the valley below a train passed swiftly, its shrill whistle suddenly rending the silence. Hearing it, he instantly regained control of himself and started up. His thoughts began circling again, from anger to shame, and he was unable to stay them at any point.

He turned his steps slowly toward the villa. His heart was beating somewhat nervously, and he decided to say nothing when he should find himself again in Miette's presence. For some inexplicable reason, he was returning to the villa with a feeling of dull antagonism. He assumed a stern expression, resolved, if Miette should prove offended or rude, not to beg her pardon, for that would be an open acknowledgment that he had behaved badly.

Miette was sitting beside the open window in the first room that was already shadowed with dusk and very nearly drained of daylight. She had found a needle and thread somewhere and was sewing a button, torn off in the course of the struggle, to her dress.

She had an end of thread in her mouth, and was on the point of snapping it with her teeth when she caught sight of Peter entering.

This movement of her lips hid her smile, and she shook her head reprovingly. But she could not hide the smile in her eyes, the little mischievous smile acknowledging a share in his guilt. The expression of her eyes was innocent and tender, radiating such love that Peter went to her, sat down at her feet on the sun-warmed carpet, and buried his head, weary with the confusion of his thoughts, in her lap. It was a gesture that told everything—the shame that stabbed him, the remorse, and now, not his humiliation, but his humility, for he felt at that moment a gratitude and love for Miette that could not be put into words.

He thought how sweet it was to be vanquished by her, to kneel before her and to rest his head in her innocent lap. What dark accusations he would have made against Miette if she had weakened, what torturing doubts would have tormented him if he had known her to be a mere frail woman like the others, like those who allow themselves to be swept away by the whirlwind of a passionate moment.

Meantime Miette had finished sewing on the button. With her thimbled finger she gaily tapped Peter's head that rested against her as heavily as if he had fallen asleep.

"Well, my accomplice! Don't you think it's time to be going home?"

Peter raised his head and looked long at Miette, who nipped his cheek softly between her fingers.

They closed the house, said goodbye to Mme. Hilka, and arm in arm went down the hill.

On the way home they were seized by a kind of delirious gaiety. They jumped in unison, pulled each other about and sang happily. When someone came along they stopped abruptly and drew long faces, only to break out afresh. They were transported by an irresistible joy.

The sun had set and twilight, with all its ineffable voices, murmured about them. In the valley below, the slate-blue spring evening was sprayed with golden lamplight. On the hill the March wind soughed softly.

Turning their corner, they saw Father standing in front of the house. Spring had called him outdoors too, and Peter and Miette stopped, watching him from where they stood.

He had Tomi on a leash and was walking with him slowly, gravely, explaining something to him, as if he were talking to a child. Tomi wore a listening air, but when another dog approached he shot forward like a flash and fell upon him like a tempest.

Father stayed out a little longer for a walk, but Peter and Miette went on ahead.

They stopped in the dark living room. Mili in the dining room adjoining was setting the table for dinner. The door was ajar and the rattling of the dishes was distinctly audible.

Peter sat on the arm of the couch and drew Miette toward him. He held her close, pressing his face against her breast.

Miette shivered feverishly. For a moment it seemed as if she were struggling with a desire to slip her dress from her shoulders and to offer her breast, thus bared, to Peter.

But suddenly she escaped from his arms, and disappeared into the bathroom.

In those days preceding their marriage, passion consumed them with an intolerably torturing thirst.

XII

Miette opened her eyes after a long, deep sleep. Lazily, voluptuously, she stretched her body, still warm with slumber, under the blankets.

The room around her was already light. She raised puzzled eyes to the ceiling, thinking at first that she was at home. But after a few seconds, the mists of sleep having dissolved, the spot on the ceiling at which she was staring seemed to her strange and alien.

Slowly, automatically, she turned her eyes from side to side, not daring to take in the whole room at a single glance.

"Where am I?" she wondered in alarm.

Her eyes fell on the wall opposite; there, above a dresser covered with a lace runner, hung a gilt-framed mirror and in its sloping surface she saw the tilted image of the bed in which she was lying. Crimson double curtains hung in soft folds at the windows; outside, startlingly close, swift clouds scudding across it, the sky appeared lowering and overcast.

The bed was unusually high and everything in the narrow little room seemed terribly strange. The shape of the chair arms, the design of the brass locks on the wardrobe, the color of the carpet beside the bed, the glasses on the dresser, and the very shape of the carafe—everything, yes, everything, appeared dreamlike and bizarre.

Then she became aware of a man's clothes on one of the chairs. The gray coat and vest carefully hung over the back of a chair looked like a man's torso, hollow-chested and headless.

And in the bed next to hers a man was sleeping—a stranger!

Then, before her wide-open eyes appeared a chaotic reflection of everything that had eluded her mind while she lay in deep slumber.

Little by little she remembered that this night just passed had been her first as a wife. She knew now where she was; she knew it was Peter who slept there beyond her. She cast her eyes toward the other bed in which, his face turned away from her, his head buried deep in the pillow, her young bridegroom lay asleep, breathing quietly.

His head stood out, darkly outlined against the pillow. The collar of his snowy nightshirt contrasted sharply with his tanned neck, whose nape, as he lay there, looked deliciously young. A few dark brown locks of hair, glistening with sweat, tumbled from his forehead to the pillow.

Miette's thoughts were slowly and wearily taking shape. Her head felt heavy and numb. They had drunk some unfamiliar dark wine the night before, sweet and thick, and now a dull headache gripped her temples in a hoop of iron.

She felt her throat burning with a feverish thirst, and sat up in bed to reach for the carafe; as she did so, a violent pain, like a fiery arrow, stabbed her flesh where, in the course of the night, the seal of her virginity had been breached. So acute was this strange pain that she stopped short, biting her upper lip, making a little hissing sound.

Her thirst had suddenly vanished. She fell back on the pillow, reflecting in dismay on her situation. Her mind began to grow clearer; her memories emerged, one after the other, in silent flight, like birds, heavy with sleep, from beneath the dark eaves of a roof.

Yes, now she remembered, bits at a time. They had dined in the hotel dining room; opposite them had sat a rather stout woman in a blue dress and a man with a high forehead who, when he laughed, showed a whole set of enormous yellow teeth.

How confused everything was as she strove to remember! After dinner she had gone upstairs, supported on Peter's arm and leaning against him; she could hardly drag herself along, for the sweet, thick wine had filled her head with a red and fiery roar.

A man in dress clothes passed them on the stairs, whistling. She took up the tune and began whistling very loud.

"Be quiet, my angel," Peter murmured tenderly.

Where the stairway turned, there was a bronze figure holding aloft a torch. She recalled precisely the position of the arm, on whose muscles the lamp's reflection gleamed. And she heard, clear and sharp, the wheezy grating of the lift descending close by. But she was no longer in a condition to tell at exactly what floor they stopped. She thought again of the whistling man they had met; saw distinctly the shape of his diamond studs; but what his face was like, whether large or small, fat or thin, she did not know.

Insignificant details remained precisely, accurately in her memory, but she didn't remember any important things at all, and some of them she wasn't sure whether she had dreamed or actually experienced.

And the corridor! She saw again, on the short trip upstairs, the long, seemingly endless hotel corridor and, dark against the doors, the shoes sitting like living creatures; there they huddled, guarding the doors, it seemed, with a stubborn passion, and if anyone passed in front of them, they would certainly yelp after him.

She remembered that she had stopped and leaned her head on Peter's shoulder.

"Why did you make me drink so much wine?"

"I'll put you right to bed and you'll see—it will pass quickly."

"Do you love me?"

"Of course I love you!"

And then in the corridor she had put her arms around Peter's neck.

"Do you love me very much?"

"I love you very much."

She remembered, too, their entering the room and Peter's locking the door from the inside.

The room was lighted only by a shaded lamp on the dresser. Dull, colored lights, and warm, deep shadows lay in vague confusion on the furniture.

She remembered she was smiling then. That fixed smile tugged painfully at the corners of her mouth, and she couldn't erase it from her lips; it was as if some foreign object had come and glued itself there. She was drunk.

She was sitting on the edge of the bed, her head bent, her legs dangling. Peter knelt on the floor in front of her and unlaced her shoes.

She could still hear his voice: "Give me your little foot. Not that one—the other!"

Fully dressed as she was, she stretched herself out on the bed that had been turned down for the night. She lay on her back, waving an arm, and singing a dance tune.

"Get up—please! I want to unfasten your blouse—"

"Why don't you love me?"

"I do love you—but get up!"

And since she didn't stir, Peter gently rolled her over on the bed so that he could undress her.

"But now—you are going to see me?"

"No, I'm not going to see you; I'll close my eyes. I'm not looking. There, get up like a good girl!"

Oh, how chaotic and confused everything was, now that she was recalling it, sobered. in this pallid morning light. Nausea clutched at her throat and she felt disgusted with herself.

Terrified, she sat up in bed at the thought of what. had come after.

Oh, God, how appalling it was!

She saw herself in the tilted mirror, sitting up, disheveled, in bed, her face wan and her hair tangled. The frail silk gown had slipped from one of her shoulders and was crumpled like paper. And an angry bruise the size of a nut, whose origin she did not know, reddened the soft round curve of her shoulder.

Looking about her, she saw in the tumbled bed traces of the stormy night. The sheet was crumpled and wrinkled beneath her; the old beet-red mattress was exposed, and loathsome bits of horsehair showed here and there through the holes of its torn cloth.

Her eyes fell on the frame of the mirror, where a blue-winged dragonfly was poised, as if on the trunk of a golden tree. Perhaps it had come into the room yesterday to be taken captive there.

And then she noticed in the other bed one of Peter's feet thrust out from beneath the blankets as far as the ankle, and that strange foot, extended on the sheet, seemed lifeless, belonging to no one.

And all this in the cruel, gray light of morning that pointed an uncompromising finger at each object, saying: "Look! there is reality!"

She fell back on the pillows and wept softly. With the dull headache tight about her forehead, and this strange little darting pain in her body, she felt all that had happened to her as a nameless horror.

Why was she here now? In a strange country, in a strange hotel—and with this strange man sleeping in the other bed! A stranger, yes, a stranger! For at that moment Peter seemed not only a stranger, but an odious one.

Who was this man who had taken possession of her in this fashion, as if by right? Who was this man whom she had not even known a year ago, and what was more, of whose very existence she had been ignorant?

She hated him then with a heart sickened by misery, with the hereditary, instinctual hatred of the female, with the piteously shocked protest against the male who, in the frenzy of his desire, has for the first time entered her chaste body, rent the delicate veil of her virginity, broken within her the untouched seal of her womanhood.

"Who is this man?" she repeated to herself, feeling that all the blood was being drained from her heart.

What hidden faults, what physical and moral stains would come to light, when time would have stripped their lives of that outward cloak that today went by the name of love, tenderness, restraint, courtesy? What dark serpents of passion were coiled within this heart, whence they would emerge one day, writhing and hissing? Suppose he should turn out to be uncouth, unbearable? Suppose he had sickening, disgusting habits, successfully concealed up to now? How was it that most novels she had read showed human life stripped to its very skeleton, seeking always beneath the fine garments and the beautiful words the coarse, bestial human soul?

Who was this man there beside her? Where had he taken his body in other days, in what mud had he wallowed before coming to her? She knew nothing of all these things. What lay in store for her in the days, the months, the years to come? What unknown pains would come to lacerate her body again and cover it with blood, when she must give birth to a child? What paralyzing deceptions, what reunions, compromises, what crushing renunciations would still come to freeze, to lay waste, to mutilate her heart?

To know all this and to see it coming with open eyes! That was life, and there was no hope that her life would be an exception to these dark laws.

She looked at her watch: it was five in the morning. Through the window, open at the top, a strange, monotonous roar entered the room, like the noise of mill wheels. Somewhere in the vicinity great masses of water were rushing, but she didn't know where or why; the powerful roar was overwhelming. Besides, the city, scarcely awake, was still silent. From a neighboring roof could be heard the shrill chirping of birds, and now and then in the street below, the bell of a bicycle gliding easily, if sleepily, on its way, and from somewhere far off the rumble of a heavily laden lorry. The invisible waters rumbled, monotonous and melancholy, and clouds pursued and overtook each other in the lowering sky.

Here she lay in the bedroom of a strange hotel, whose walls her imagination could not pierce. She had no idea of the city that surrounded her, for night had already

fallen when they arrived, and she didn't even know what
the street below looked like, whose awakening sounds
were beginning to reach her ears.

"Why haven't I a mother?" Her pain groaned within
her, for she was suddenly discovering how tragic it was
that she had never known her mother. When the flood-
gates of grief and despair begin to burst, those things
that have lain buried in the heart's dark depths rise to
the surface. Now the thought that she was motherless—a
thought that had occurred to her only during her in-
frequent hours of suffering—was an excruciating agony.

Suddenly she remembered Olga. She reproached herself
bitterly for not having understood little Chouchette when
she had come to her with her unhappy secret for solace.
Now she suddenly saw clearly into Olga's soul, and her
heart was filled with hot pity for her. How terrible it was
even this way, under the protection and with the sanction
of society and the law, and how far worse it must have
been for Olga, in the secret torment of the consciousness
of her sin! To be defiled and wounded, cruelly ravaged
in body and soul—Oh, poor little Chouchette!

She could see her clearly now, her face deathly pale,
stretched out on the couch, supported on her elbow, her
eyebrows raised and her eyes staring straight ahead. How
deeply Miette must have wounded her in closing her
heart! And how desolate she must have been left—she
who had come for comfort and understanding, seeking a
little human pity.

And as she thought of Olga, her own fate seemed to
her a little kinder.

Slowly she began retracing in her mind the progress of
events; suddenly she saw herself in the compartment of
the train. She was seated beside the window, and the
Carinthian countryside was flying past.

The gigantic mountains turned slowly and majestically
before her eyes. Their snowy tops glittered under the rays
of the sun and sank slowly into the distance. Here and
there factories appeared, their chimneys smoking; signs
of life were thick on the upland slopes. Elsewhere lower

on the heights, a forest that was being cleared looked, with its tall white trunks, as if its dark green had been strewn with bunches of toothpicks. Then once more they were following perpendicular walls of rock, whence fell the straight silver curtain of a waterfall. The train passed over a precipice on an iron bridge, thundering, singing, and groaning with a deafening clatter, as if it were suddenly hurling itself headlong upon the bars of a giant xylophone.

The framework of the bridge passed swiftly in black zigzags before the window, like huge black sabers slashing at one another. Once the bridge was passed, the singing, shrieking, thundering rails suddenly fell silent, and almost noiselessly the train sped on along the brink of a mountain slope, nearly as high as the clouds, as if it were flying through celestial regions. Far below in the deep valley nestled gentle little Alpine villages, red-roofed towers and house walls brilliantly white. And again they were passing barren, rust-colored rock and blue-green firs, through whose vistas grazing flocks of parti-colored goats were visible. Then the train plunged into a tunnel, dragging the sky with it into the darkness. Clouds and mountains! They remained in the heavy, burning darkness for a few seconds, their hearts tightening, while an acrid smell of smoke clutched at their throats, suffocating them; then the sun again, the sky again, again the clouds and the ever-changing landscape, where the eye found no repose. Little railway stations, always the same, marked their progress, where oranges, chocolate, drinking water, beer, and sausages might be bought, and life beat always to the same rhythm. Men, women, and children ran toward the train, or alighted from it, and with the blowing of the signals were mingled the loving words and laughter of those who were parting or meeting each other again. The looks and speech of the people permitted a glimpse into the town's hidden personality. Here a town and there another town! Strange, fantastic human ant hills! What a multitude of people everywhere!

Gardens, houses, glamorous marketplaces, shops, and

little confectionery stores with sweet, warm odors; bed-
rooms where people kissed and suffered, made merry and
quarreled . . .

Life was the same everywhere!

Recalling all this, she could feel the train rocking her
to sleep once more, and hear the monotonous din of the
wheels; behind her closed eyes the telegraph poles began
flying past again, an unbroken, skipping line. Once more
she saw the traveling companions with whom the journey
had so long imprisoned them, and from whose faces it was
so difficult to tear one's eyes. A man wearing glasses,
whose round head was so closely shaven that his skull
seemed blue, while a glossy black beard spread itself over
his coat and his whole face. A man with a blue head!
An old lady with a long neck, whom she privately named
the woman with a man's face. Strange specimens, whose
like one meets only in railway trains.

And she saw Peter before her in his brown traveling
suit. She remembered how becoming his knickers had
been and that the traveling cap gave his head a fantastic
shape. Many details of the journey returned to her
memory, and, thinking of them, her heart was filled with
warm gratitude to Peter. How tender and thoughtful he
had been during the trip! What feeling and what deep
consideration were reflected on his fine, serious face, what
humble love shone in his eyes! And what a sweet, strange
sensation it had been when, on leaving Vienna, she had
felt sleepy and put her head in Peter's lap and fallen
asleep. Dozing, she felt his hand touch her back and feet
gently, as he kept adjusting the robe about her.

And the departure, and the goodbyes at the station!
They were already in the train and from the compartment
window were chatting with Father and Peter's mother,
with the Vargas and Johnny and Szücs, all of whom had
accompanied them to the train. What animation, what a
whirl and buzz about them, multiplied by the echo of
the huge, resonant, glass-domed vault. The locomotive
whistled, the metal discs of the buffers clanged, the car
wheels grated, the porters called. "Watch out!"; the

newspaper and candy vendors shouted; at the doors of the waiting rooms announcers of departing trains seemed to be chanting strange melodies; people rushed along, clinging to their luggage, the thronging words that always remain to be said at the last moment crowding to their lips. The fever of life burst over them in towering waves.

Father was holding Tomi and pacifying him, because Tomi wanted to bark at every passerby. But the crowd flowed and billowed before them like a river, and Tomi finally realized, not without a low, wrathful growl, that his was a hopeless endeavor. Yet every now and then he would attempt the impossible task once more.

"When you get back, the rooms will be redecorated," said Elvira, her head on a level with the carriage window. She could never refrain from displaying her concern for the welfare of others.

Szücs teased Miette.

"Look here, little lady, you can still get off. I advise you to consider it seriously."

Then he offered to accompany them on any terms.

"Be careful not to take cold on the journey, children," sighed Mme. Takács in her thin, birdlike voice, caressing them with her brimming eyes.

"Don't forget to stop at Bologna on the way back!" advised Dr. Varga, who had planned the trip.

"If you are short of money, telegraph," said Father.

She was silent, only nodding her head and trying to smile. She was afraid of bursting into tears. The sobs clutched at her throat.

Then the train got under way with a jerk and began to move. They all waved goodbye with hands and handkerchiefs.

Johnny was there, too, in uniform, his left thumb thrust through the buckle of his sword belt; he saluted in silence.

How strange that of all that had gone on at the station —the moment of farewell, the departure of the train— what stood out was Johnny's pallor; his glance had pierced her heart.

"That boy is smitten with me," she thought. Stretched out on the bed with closed eyes, reviewing her memories of the last few days, she tried to fathom the young man's expression. She would have liked to stroke his face, grateful to him for his silent love.

"Oh, how good it is to be loved!"

The thought of Johnny had cheered her.

Now she saw herself during the marriage ceremony, in the cool church, the kindling rays of the sun lying athwart the semi-darkness.

At the beginning of the ceremony she could think of nothing save whether she had put her sewing box into the big trunk. That question occupied her completely and for a long time she could give her attention to nothing else.

Then the organ pealed. Immediately her heart tightened and she wanted to sob aloud. Her soul was filled with the stirring power of that moment, with the wondrous might of God and the awe that forced them to their knees.

As if the ineffable essence of God had come to lean over her, the sublime import of human destiny was revealing itself in all its radiance and purity.

"Life is beautiful," sang the mighty chords of the organ, "life is beautiful and death is far away! Life is beautiful and love is infinite as the heavens. I, the Lord, I take you into My hand and lift you, gently, to the heights; live, rejoice, love one another! Stand naked on the palm of My hand, that new life may issue from your kiss! Delight in the savor of your bodies, wherein burns the glowing flame of My spirit, that pierces your marrow and creates life! Love each other and you will vanquish death; for the sap of your bodies, issuing in love, flows out into that infinite life in which you will renew yourselves. It is an eternal, fiery river that bears on its seething waves millions and millions of life bubbles and goes roaring on its way into Time!"

These thoughts made her feel quite drowsy. She opened her eyes and her glance fell again on the window. Dark clouds were still rolling across the sky, and very close, the invisible masses of water continued to roar. It may have been that roaring which had just brought to her mind all those confused thoughts of God and the Church that vaguely oppressed her.

She began to seek refuge in clearer, simpler memories.

At the door of the church Peter's face had been pale, as if transfigured by all that was going on within him. Oh, what unutterable gratitude, what humble love she had felt for Peter at that moment!

Everyone was weeping; hands pressed hers, and in the crowd that thronged about her she didn't know whose they were.

Thinking of all this, a feeling of warmth filled her heart. There remained no trace of the despair and misery that had overwhelmed her a few moments before.

"I am a woman," she thought, "a woman—and that is the most beautiful fate in the world. Yes, I'm a woman and I shall bring children into the world; if things weren't like this, and if all that has happened hadn't been, I shouldn't be on this earth myself. I was born of a night like this one, and I was launched into life on sheets as rumpled as these. Yes, that is how things must be!"

Her mind was now growing calm, relaxed, all but exhausted.

Her gaze rested on the chandelier of carved and gilded wood. It was a delicate, curious piece of work.

"I must buy one like that for the drawing room," she thought, examining it with an expert eye.

She thought about how she would rearrange the apartment when she returned, for Mme. Varga, with her mania for wanting to teach everyone, would surely have spoiled it all with her meddling.

And in her imagination she built the soft nest for the days when they would be "at home."

She thought back to the time that had preceded her marriage; the scene in the villa at Mount Gellért; and the moment that evening when at the strange instigation of she knew not what ardent desire, she had been moved to offer her young breast to Peter, the divine temptation of unchastity pervading all her being.

As these thoughts recurred to her, a secret fire, sweet as sun-warmed honey, ran through her body.

Then Peter awoke. He sat up suddenly and, propped on an elbow, turned to her.

"Awake already?"

Miette did not answer. She hid her face in the pillow; but when she felt his kisses on her neck, the fire of sensuality overpowered her, and she gave herself to him once more, feeling through all her body the frenzied delights of love in the early dawn.

Then she fell into a deep, sweet sleep.

She didn't awaken till noon. The sun was shining and new noises came up from the street. The hooting of auto horns, the ringing of streetcars—uproarious, urgent mid-day noises. But the invisible masses of water, dominating everything, continued to roar.

She went to the bathroom and splashed in the water. She opened the faucets wide, yielding her body to their fresh, plashing streams that hailed the exquisite nudity of her flawless feminine body with happy laughter.

She felt clean, healthy, and happy.

When Miette and Peter went out after lunch their first concern was to discover the cause of the mysterious roaring.

The waters of the Arno were thundering by, not far from the Alle Grazie Bridge, where their course had been dammed.

And this was Florence, the city of flower perfumes!

The waters of the Arno were swollen by the night's rain, and its yellow waves rolled, almost orange, under the brilliant sunlight. Old black tree stumps tossed in the current.

Above Fiesole, where silvery olive trees bloomed on the slope of the hill and a cascade of perfume descended into the valley, spring drove the last clouds of the night's storm toward the Apennines.

They lingered on the bank. Miette hung on Peter's

arm, dropped her head against his shoulder, and felt faint with happiness.

XIII

Behind the hills of Buda, a spring storm was brewing. The swallows were flying very low in the streets, grazing the walls with their pointed wings. The wind shuddered in the foliage, as if caught in the branches and trying vainly to free itself. The windows of the little houses were being hastily closed against the eddying clouds of dust.

Mme. Takács was standing at the window, gazing thoughtfully into the darkening street, where a hat that had just been blown from a little boy's head was leaping high in the wind.

She looked melancholy, and this melancholy lay on her face like one of those spiders that glide out of their hiding places but disappear again at the faintest sound. She hid her sadness from everyone, but when she was alone the folds deepened about her eyes and nose, and sometimes she even wept. She had always imagined, in thinking of Peter's marriage, that she would keep house for him, that she would go padding about through all the rooms, and always be where there was something that needed doing. She liked Miette, but she could not admit her into the core of her heart, for it was Miette who had robbed her of her long-cherished dream.

Paul Szücs had taken Peter's room as a lodger. He had arrived with a shabby trunk containing so little linen that even Mme. Takács, the foe of all extravagance, was appalled when she opened his wardrobe one day.

She was sorry for this great, uncouth boy who couldn't take care of himself, and she continued to view him secretly from a single angle: Would he make a suitable husband for Aranka?

Szücs enlivened the dreary little house. He was cheerful and animated, banged the doors, always had something to tell Mme. Takács, and very often they lunched together. He always went out for dinner and returned late at night. Through a sense of delicacy, lest Mme. Takács should discover his late hours, he walked on tiptoe and never switched on the light. Regularly he overturned an armchair that stood near the dining-room door, for he always came back a little tipsy. When the heavy chair fell with a racket to the floor, he would stand motionless, his tongue thrust out, straining his ears fearfully for a long time in the darkness.

Otherwise he gave no trouble. Only on one occasion did he bring home with him a large-hipped woman in a red hat, but he insisted that she was his cousin, a provincial school teacher.

After three weeks the young people returned from their honeymoon. They were both tanned by the sun and Miette had gained eight pounds. Her body was a little fuller, her color fresher, like garden flowers in summer after a shower. Yet her exquisitely slender figure remained unchanged.

Peter had gone back to work, and all of Miette's time was occupied with the changes she was making in the apartment. She overturned every room from end to end and changed the position of every piece of furniture in her desire to indicate thereby the beginning of a new life.

She spent all her morning running about from department stores to antique dealers and upholsterers. She would always come back with lampshades, little statues, linens, cushions, or curtains—like a bird carrying twigs to build its nest. Mme. Varga frequently accompanied her on these expeditions.

One morning, just as they were coming out of a shop in the center of the city, they saw Olga in an open car. It was a small, dark blue machine, glitteringly new, and Olga was alone in it. In the crowded traffic of the Váciucca, the car stood close to them for a moment.

Their eyes met. Olga smiled an embarrassed smile and bowed slightly.

"Don't notice her," whispered Mme. Varga rapidly

between her teeth, and her powdered face flushed in agitation.

Miette, startled, stared at Olga wide-eyed, but when she would have greeted her it was too late, for the car was already gone.

"You mustn't speak to her," said Mme. Varga, still very red, buttoning and unbuttoning her glove with a trembling hand.

"Was it réally Olga?" asked Miette, with pretended indifference, and only to give herself the opportunity of turning her head once more, in the hope that she might still be able to make a sign. But Olga did not look around.

Meantime the flush of excitement was fading from Mme. Varga's face. Miette, on the verge of tears, hated this woman just then with an impotent violence.

At home she awaited Peter's return impatiently. She had determined to tell him what had happened, and if Peter took Mme. Varga's part she would be very angry with him.

The luncheon table was already laid, a little basket in the center smelling deliciously of fresh bread. When he came in from the office Peter was in the habit of breaking off a piece of the crust and throwing himself on the couch to munch it, reading the noon edition of the newspaper while he waited for the soup to be served.

Miette, sitting beside him, all rosy with excitement, told him of the morning's encounter.

Peter, who was already acquainted with the details of Olga's story, followed the recital attentively to its conclusion; then, as if the whole affair was unimportant, said merely: "Well, why didn't you speak to her?"—and went on reading.

"That's what I thought," said Miette, scarcely able to conceal her joy as she gazed gratefully at Peter. To know that next time she might greet Olga, stop and speak to her, not only dispelled her ill humor but appeased her conscience as well.

Next day she received a letter in the morning's mail,

on whose envelope she immediately recognized Olga's handwriting.

The letter, without salutation or signature, read:

"I am not angry with you, because I am very, oh very happy."

Miette could read many things into this short note. It was an expression of Olga's innate kindness, for in that brief encounter she had seen in Miette's startled glance the desire to greet her, and knew that she was now being tortured by remorse. But her wounded pride was there too, striving, after humiliation, to gain the upper hand.

"Is she really happy?" Miette pondered, reading and rereading the one line, and deciding that she really was. Perhaps it was the letter itself that gave her that impression—the fine, perfumed mauve paper, the dusk of the purple ink gleaming lambent on the letters that breathed vitality, thrown together on the wing, as it were, a little space between each.

"If she had any sense she'd phone me," Miette thought, imagining how pleasant it would be to snuggle side by side on the couch, their legs folded under them, and tell each other the history of these past months. To repeat everything, to the smallest detail, the most delicate shading, living it all over again. Details as yet unperceived would come to the surface for, in communion with one to whom we may open wide our hearts, circumstances and memories appear in a new light. After such an unreserved outpouring, our memories either die or, buried in the depths of our hearts, they go on living with renewed vitality.

But Olga did not telephone. Often Miette tried to picture the face and figure of this man who had drawn Olga with him into some dark, mysterious fog, but her imagination always stopped short at the same point, as if she were dashing herself against an invisible wall.

Peter was gradually settling himself into the apartment, not just his clothing and desk, but all his little habits as well. Each evening after dinner, when Mili had cleared the table, he played cards with Father for an hour on its polished surface, not out of politeness nor in a spirit of sacrifice, but for his own amusement. They took the game so seriously as to become involved now and then in spirited argument. Indeed, after one such discussion, the old gentleman withdrew in dudgeon to his room; but next day they were seated opposite each other again, looking important, holding the cards that were already a little worn from having been slapped down so often, their chairs creaking beneath the difficult process of reflection.

During that hour Miette sat silently beside them with her work. She was often compelled to remonstrate with Peter: "For heaven's sake, don't shout so!" Peter would lower his voice immediately, but continue the argument.

So far there had been no serious differences between them. Peter was of a hasty and violent temperament, but his emotions were all on the surface and, once pacified, no trace of the outburst remained. Miette loved even these impassioned rages of his.

One morning, however, they nearly quarreled over the bathroom. Peter was in a hurry to shave and couldn't get in because Miette was still in the tub.

He rattled the doorknob impatiently. He sounded sharp and fretful as he hurried Miette, who answered sharply too: "Oh, but you *are* peculiar! Can't you wait a minute?"

Finally she opened the door. Shivering, she stood there in her little slippers, wrapped in the bathrobe she had thrown around her; drops of water beaded her face, and with her hair pushed back and knotted behind she looked so funny that Peter's anger vanished instantly. He burst out laughing and kissed the warm little drops on her face.

Thus they spent two months of their married life. Each slept in his own room, but when Miette opened her eyes in the morning she went, still half asleep, her hair disheveled, into Peter's room, dragging one of her pillows after her, and settled herself beside him in the bed. Peter generally awoke to feel this warm presence stirring gently at his side. They called this sleepy morning installation of

Miette's "the nestling," and they used similar words that rose spontaneously to their lips—the early flowering of the warm earth of their love—to describe other phases of their love life.

One morning Peter phoned the apartment. He wanted to ask Miette to send him his portfolio, which he had forgotten. But the line was busy.

Immediately he was seized by an inexplicable, oppressive sense of uneasiness. In a few minutes he called Miette again. The number was still busy. Enraged, he shouted at the operator: "Please be good enough to give me my number. I wish to speak to my apartment!"

"Sorry, sir; impossible!" was the curt rejoinder.

Peter replaced the receiver in a fury. He paced up and down the room, and such passion seethed within him that his teeth chattered. He was almost terrified—as if he had exposed himself to some unknown malady, for he could neither stifle this poignant emotion nor find a valid explanation for it.

Composing himself somewhat, he sat down at his desk and began pricking its surface with the point of a paper knife, keeping a tight rein on himself. He pondered this strange sensation that had just overpowered him.

"How stupid I am . . . she is probably talking to some shop; or perhaps to a friend, Mme. Galamb or Mme. Lénárt; and suppose it isn't even she on the telephone, but Father—"

However, he could not achieve complete serenity. He was suffering a foretaste of the torments of jealousy, and he thought with horror that a day might come when he would have reason to be jealous. He felt a presentiment of the agony of such sensations, for already they were gnawing at his heart with an effect of almost physical pain.

Again he called the apartment. This time he heard the click of the connection being established, and broke in on a conversation.

Miette was speaking. Peter heard the end of a sentence:

" . . . if you don't want to send it back, it doesn't matter. I'm not afraid! Keep it!"

He heard her pretty laughter through the words.

A moment later came the sound of a man's voice: "I don't want to blackmail you. All I said was that I still have it and am preserving it carefully."

"I should hope so," Miette cried mockingly.

Just then he heard the click of the connection again, withdrawn this time, and the operator, cutting him off, said only: "Still busy!"

Peter hung up the receiver. He leaped from his chair and glared furiously for a moment at the silent instrument. Then, just as he was, hatless, he bolted from the room, ran down the stairs, and found himself in the street below without knowing why he was there or where he wanted to go. He realized, appalled, that he had become a weak, witless puppet in the power of this passion that had driven him, within the space of a few seconds, from his office on the fourth floor into the street, exactly as if some huge and violent hand had hurled him down. Here he was in front of the bank, with a dreadful gnawing at his heart; here he was, hatless, the pallor of death on his face, gazing with stormy eyes into the eyes of a man whose name and identity he could not recall, and whose hand had just been placed upon his shoulder.

"Good morning, Peter! Where are you off to?"

"The tobacco shop," he said hastily, afraid of his own voice, and turned somewhat more quietly in that direction.

He was shivering as if all the warm blood had ebbed from his veins. He bought a package of cigarettes that he didn't want, returned to the bank and, once upstairs, began walking up and down the cool, echoing corridor.

Those few words, intercepted by chance, had buried themselves like spears in his flesh.

He tried to arrange his thoughts. The voice had been Michael Ádám's. Those few sentences, overheard by chance, were a searing torment, an unendurable agony. The first fact that emerged clearly, paralyzing all his

thoughts, was that Miette carried on telephone conversations with someone in the morning while he was at
the bank. In the third month of their married life! This
knowledge seemed to him so appalling that he felt
himself on the verge of collapse. He went to the window
recess, leaned against the wall and stared blankly into
space. He repeated to himself, word for word, the conversation he had overheard, trying to unravel its meaning.
The only thing of which he could be certain was that
Ádám was witholding something that Miette would like
him to return to her, but what was it? His sensitive
imagination, shuddering in its first apprehension, was
assailed by vulgar suspicions. He thought of the feminine
garment or hairpin that Miette might have forgotten at
Ádám's apartment after some secret rendezvous. His
imagination, writhing in 'torment, pictured Miette in
Ádám's arms and so piercing was his vision of her during
the breathless moments of that forbidden embrace that
it became an excruciating pain. Stupid, meaningless
sentences rose to his mind: A woman is the curse of man—
there is no woman who cannot be led into temptation—
Eve and the forbidden fruit. These words arrayed themselves before him like terrible, inevitable laws of life.
Even in his happiest moments, he had carried in the
depths of his soul an obscure little whispering fear that
things could not always be the same, that a day would
come when Miette would deceive him; but now that he
had just discovered, or at least believed he had discovered, her infidelity, he felt suddenly like a man lost.

He left the window recess and began pacing the
corridor again. One of his colleagues, chancing by with
some files under his arm, stopped to exchange a few
casual words with him. He had to muster all his strength
lest he betray the fact that his soul was beset by the raging
billows of an inward storm. This effort restored him somewhat and he began to deliberate more calmly. He
examined his life with Miette, almost second by second,
as if, with sensitive fingers, he were probing a naked,
sleeping body in a feverish search for some flaw or

hidden wound. But he found nothing. Miette was innocent. From all he knew and felt about her, she had given herself to him utterly, without reservation. Since they had been living together she had not left him for a single moment. If she were having an affair with Ádám, the only imaginable possibility was that they were meeting somewhere in the mornings while he was at his office. And he himself realized that such a supposition was senseless. And yet there was something that dragged him back to this torment, that would not let him proceed along the path on which his mind, shaken by suspicions, might have achieved a degree of composure. Suddenly he remembered Miette's impassioned account of her meeting with Olga, and how fervently she had taken Olga's part. What secret precepts of love and marriage did she harbor in her soul, and what value did she place on her own body, that might be a glorious gift and a transfiguration of any man, without the surrender of her inmost self? And, desperately, he began to plumb the soul of Miette and realized wearily that he could not penetrate its mysteries.

Then this tearing pain was eased for a moment. Considering all things, once more he found it impossible that Miette should have allowed herself to be seduced. There might have been a love passage between her and Ádám a few years before, more or less serious or innocent, he did not know. Ah, now he remembered their first meeting at the Vargas' tea in September; then he saw them again walking along the bank of the Danube; then that moment before Christmas was revived when, among the snowflakes, in the light of the street lamps, Ádám's dark velour hat had suddenly been lifted to them. The thoughts that had made him tremble then made him tremble anew, and he could not but suppose that the mysterious object under discussion in the telephone conversation between Miette and Ádám must be a love letter, dating from before her marriage.

Having reached this point, to which his spasmodic thoughts clung, he grew calm and succeeded in extinguishing the flames of suspicion that had been consuming him. By the time he reached home he had regained complete control of himself and carried his discovery, like a strange, oppressive object, in the very depths of his heart.

He said nothing to Miette. He was terrified by the thought that, confronted with a direct question, she might turn pale and entangle herself in lies. What he knew, and his own explanation of the secret, although his solution of the problem seemed to him dubious, still appeared preferable for the time being to the possibility of losing his faith in Miette forever.

Now that his jealousy was aroused, he had need of all his strength to conceal from Miette this crisis of his soul. But he studied and watched her with keen eyes. Each of her gestures, each of her words, each of her glances, he weighed on the painfully sensitive scale of his tortured soul.

But despite the most careful observation, he could discover nothing to give him fresh food for suspicion. Luncheon passed off as usual. Father sat at the table in his summer coat of linen and complained of the heat. Miette wore a light housedress with nothing underneath and her bare feet were thrust into an old pair of dancing slippers.

Peter saw that she was in good spirits, her attention concentrated unreservedly and ingenuously on all sorts of details—on the necessity, for example, of having the living-room floor covered by a felt matting and what the upholsterer thought of it; in all of which Peter found fresh grounds for reassurance. If there were anything hidden in her heart, wouldn't her glance occasionally wander, and would she be able to display so keen an interest in trifles?

After luncheon they darkened the rooms because the sun was beating in upon them. It was a warm day at the end of May, already diffusing the heat of summer. From the trees in the street came the plaintive, sleepy chirping of sparrows. The acacia in front of the house, whose crest was on a level with their window, cast into the room the warm, lacy shadow of its dusty green leaves.

It was their habit every afternoon to sleep side by side on the couch in the cool living room. Today Peter pleaded a headache and refused to be cajoled out of his sulkiness by Miette's playful spirits. Though he was in a state of spiritual perturbation, he was not yet ready to display his anger and make a scene, for he didn't know how to go about it. He was waiting for the propitious moment.

Miette had invited Peter's mother, the Vargas, Paul Szücs and Johnny to dinner the following Saturday. Saturday was only two days away and during those two days no one could speak to Miette. She never left the kitchen; she wore on her head a little kerchief, knotted at the back like a young peasant woman's, and whipped cream and made delicious little cakes. Her arm, bare to the elbow, resting on the pastry board, became unrecognizable beneath its coating of the soft dough into which she was mixing honey, eggs, and butter. With childish, touching excitement, her heart throbbing with trepidation, she set about baking her first tart, as if her whole life and her reputation as a housewife depended on its success. She carried on long telephone conversations with her friends, and asked each one for her tart recipe several times over, feeling less and less confidence in herself after each explanation.

Peter, who, ever since the intercepted telephone conversation, had been spying with sharp eyes and a keen watchful mind on the very tremors of Miette's soul, saw her unfolding before him in colors entirely new.

Finally the long-awaited Saturday arrived.

"How many to dinner?" Father asked at luncheon.

"Only six," Miette answered, "because Johnny can't come."

"Why not?"

"I don't know. He wrote me a letter apologizing for not being able to come."

After luncheon Peter and Father stayed at the table talking. Miette, who was obviously waiting impatiently for Peter, signaled to him to come to the other room.

"Read this letter!" she said when they were alone—

Johnny's letter, apologizing courteously for not being able to come to dinner.

The last sentence of the letter read: "And please, don't ever invite me to your house again—"

"Well, what do you think of the cub?" Miette asked, one hand on her hip, when Peter had finished reading, she having watched with lively interest his perusal of the lines already familiar to her. "You must go to his house, give him a couple of sound cuffs, and drag him here by the ears. There is no doubt about it—he's smitten with me. Ah, well! I'll cure him of that!"

Peter smiled. He folded up the letter reflectively and returned it to Miette. He could not analyze the cleansing, comforting sensation that filled his heart at the thought of Johnny.

"Don't be angry with the poor boy," said Peter, taking her hand tenderly into his and retaining it as if there were something more he wanted to say. He looked deep into her eyes.

"Have many men been in love with you?"

Miette dropped the corners of her mouth, a little mischievous and roguish. She didn't look at Peter; she was busy returning Johnny's letter to the envelope, which wasn't easy, for the lavender tissue lining was crumpled.

"Of course! Several! Do you think no one noticed me before you?"

She brushed Peter's face with Johnny's letter and was about to depart when he seized her hand and made her sit down beside him.

"Don't be in such a hurry! First tell me something else. With whom were you in love before you knew me?"

Miette looked at him out of the corner of her eye, coquettish and mocking.

"Well?" Peter insisted.

Still mockingly she replied: "With whom? With several, perhaps—"

"Really!" said Peter in feigned concern, and with a pretense at pleasantry, but his fingers tightened on Miette's hand, and the sound of his voice changed suddenly when he asked her, without any transition, the blood of the painful wound he had been staunching for the last two days filtering drop by drop through his muffled voice: "To whom were you speaking on the telephone the day before yesterday?"

He was very pale and stared wildly at Miette.

"When?" she asked, dragging out the word.

"Day before yesterday! About noon. You were speaking to a man—"

She opened her eyes wide, a trick that suddenly gave her face a strange expression. Astonished and indignant, she protested: "I?"

Yet at the same time a scarcely perceptible shadow of fear crossed her eyes, as if she were already regretting this lie she had blurted out. But now there was no getting out of it. They remained thus for a moment, their glances locked, with Miette striving vainly to cast off the spell of those eyes that pierced her very soul. She arose and went toward the door.

"How silly you are!" she said, with a wan, strained smile on her lips.

She crossed the dining room, whistling—she who had never been in the habit of whistling.

When she had closed the door behind her, Peter threw himself on the couch and buried his face in the cushions. He wanted to die.

Miette soon came back. She stretched herself out as usual beside Peter as if nothing had happened, and sought a place for her hand at the back of his neck, burying her fingers childishly, sleepily, in his hair—a gesture habitual with her.

At her touch Peter arose and, without looking at her, left the room. Miette, in a whirl of emotion, sat up on the couch and followed him with terror-stricken eyes.

Peter went down to the street. He sat on the terrace of a nearby café and stared at the letters of a newspaper that the waiter had brought him in its wooden holder. His steaming black coffee stood before him untouched.

He remained there a long while, but he paid no

attention to the passage of time, for his mind seemed paralyzed, and his heartsick thoughts fastened themselves on Miette's lie, like flies on a paper coated with deadly glue. They buzzed, stirred, but could not escape. Sometimes they fell silent and remained poised, weary and motionless. He saw one thing clearly—that he would divorce Miette. But how would he break the news to his mother, to Szücs, to his friends? What would his relatives and his colleagues say? What would they do about the dinner this evening that couldn't be countermanded? And thinking of these things, pain, shame, and humiliation rent his heart.

He might have been there an hour when someone stopped at the terrace and laid a hand on his shoulder.

It was Father.

"What's happened between you?" he asked, looking into Peter's eyes with a kindly smile.

Peter blushed. He was terribly ashamed.

"Nothing—" he said, embarrassed, turning the paper mechanically to avoid the direct glance of Father's eyes.

Father shook his head silently as if to say: "Oh, what children you are!" But his face immediately clouded and after a brief moment's silence he said to Peter: "Go up to her; she is crying her eyes out." Hearing these words, a sensation of warmth pervaded the depths of Peter's being.

Father continued on his way, his hands, one laid carefully over the other, behind his back, bending a little forward as old people do.

Peter went home. Miette, her shoulders hunched, was sitting near the stove. She held her little tear-drenched handkerchief to her mouth. There was obstinacy in her bearing and the rancor born of an injury. She did not raise her eyes when Peter came in, but a moment later closed them in wretchedness, almost in contempt.

Peter stood beside her in silence for a long interval. They were both suffering. Then he asked with wistful tenderness: "Why did you lie?"

Miette did not answer.

"Who was the man you were talking to?"

Miette spoke chokingly through her handkerchief:
"Michael Ádám..."

"And what is it that he doesn't want to return to you?"
Peter asked, a warning note in his voice.

"Once—I was still a little girl—I wrote him a stupid
love letter. I don't know any longer what was in it.
And now he telephoned and told me he had happened
to find the letter, and he jokingly offered to return it to
me if I would pay him a hundred crowns—"

After a moment she added: "Ask him, if you don't
believe me."

Peter scrutinized Miette's face long and attentively.
"Then why did you deny it to me?"

"Why? Because of the way you asked me. And besides,
I was stupid—"

Suddenly she glared at Peter, enveloped him in a
blazing glance and cried passionately: "You can be sure
that I have nothing to hide!"

And moving away from him, she turned to the wall.

Peter thoughtfully contemplated the elbow that seemed
carved in marble, resting on the arm of the chair, at right
angles with it. That bare elbow suddenly recalled to him
Miette's arm above the pastry board with its ludicrous
coating of dough. He thought of her passionate, childish joy
in the preparation of that evening's dinner, and suddenly
his heart was filled with warm compassion for her.

He saw how senselessly he had behaved through this
whole affair. Miette was right. He had put the question
in such a tone—he remembered distinctly—as to cause
himself a slight shudder.

Miette rose to leave the room. Peter seized her arm and
drew her to him. But she resisted. After a brief struggle
he was holding her by both arms and pressing his face
against her cheek. Soon they found each other's lips.
Miette remained a long time in Peter's embrace, savoring
the new rapture of the first reconciliation.

Mme. Takács and Szücs were the first of the guests to
arrive. Szücs had escorted Peter's mother and began

creating a disturbance as soon as he arrived in the ante-room.

During dinner Peter whispered to Paul behind his napkin: "Say something nice about the tart; my wife made it herself!"

Szücs made a cautious sign of understanding. When they had reached the dessert he asked: "Did this tart come from the bakery?"

Miette was standing by the serving table, obviously apprehensive.

"Why?"

"Because it's heavenly!" said Szücs, with exaggerated emphasis, scraping the chocolate cream from his plate with a knife.

Peter watched Miette, and though only her back was visible, he could see that she was blushing to her very ears. She didn't dare turn away from the serving table.

At that moment Peter loved Miette so that the tears started to his eyes.

XIV

It was ten o'clock in the morning. Under the lash of the wind, the waves had flecked the apple-green waters of Lake Balaton with their silvery crests. Those little white curling waves came from the Tihany side and, like a driven flock, sought endless refuge on the hither shore. The wind that harassed them rattled gaily through the snowy sails of a boat that was dragging at anchor.

Peter and Miette were walking along the shore. They wore bathrobes and after ten days of country life at Balaton were as brown as if they had just returned from Africa. They paused before a villa, and Peter shouted toward an open window on the second floor. His cry remaining unanswered, he made a trumpet of his hands before his mouth and shouted louder. But nothing stirred up above.

Then Miette called, her sweet voice soaring to the window, "Zsigaa-a!"

And sure enough, a moment later the soap-smeared face of Sigismund Pán, who was shaving, appeared at the window.

"May we take the *Neptune*?" Peter asked.

"Of course! Please do!" he said, continuing to lather his chin.

Miette, her head cocked, raised her eyes to the window, squinting in the sunlight.

"Are you getting ready to go somewhere?"

"I'm going to Budapest, but I'll be back tomorrow."

"Would you be kind enough to bring me a little package from the house?"

"With pleasure!"

Miette remained for a moment under the window, charging Pán with various commissions, as the sojourners at this seaside resort had a habit of doing when their friends went to Budapest.

Meantime, Peter had gone down to the water's edge and was unfastening the *Neptune* from its mooring.

He threw off his bathrobe and waded in up to his knees.

The *Neptune* was an old, heavily timbered craft; dirty pale-green moss hung from between its slippery planks. It was a primitive affair, equipped with a mast and sail, but not really adapted for long trips on Lake Balaton. Storms lurk even on sunny days behind the Badacsony hills, and when the fancy takes them, they draw black curtains over the sky as if by the sudden jerk of a hidden cord, and pour in torrents down upon the lake.

The *Neptune* was a coast craft, and proved very useful to seekers after solitude or those who liked to take sun-baths stretched naked on its wide bottom that was covered with soft mats. Now it was taking its ease, swinging its ample haunches in the water.

Peter loosened the sail ropes.

At the end of the ropes the unfurled sail began waving, yielding itself in exultant joy and with an almost virginal

shudder to the light breeze. Peter held the main rope
in a firm grip, and as he leaned all his weight on his feet,
planted in the thick mire of the low waters, the muscles
that covered the back and bronzed arms of his sturdy
young body rippled undulant and strong. His black
bathing suit had slipped from his shoulders, and as he
exerted all his strength to pull the rope, bending to an
angle almost acute, his half-naked, athletic body strove
with powerful, splendid movements against the open sail
that sought to escape him.

Miette came down to the shore. She removed her light
sandals and stepped, barefoot, into the water, her white
feet testing its coolness gingerly. Carefully she lifted the
ends of her lavender robe and advanced cautiously
toward the *Neptune*, which Peter had already moved away
from the shore.

He reached his hand to Miette and helped her into the
boat.

"Where are we going?"

"Nowhere. When we're a little way out I'll clew the
sail. Perhaps you'd like to go to sleep?"

Miette, sitting in the prow, nodded her head,
yawning.

The night before they had all stayed up late on the
terrace of the Grand Hotel, and it was four in the morning
before they had gone to bed. Miette, elbows on knees,
looked ahead with sleepy eyes and imagined she was still
hearing the soft murmur of the violins. They had drunk a
little champagne too, just enough to make their eyes
sparkle and the blood flow warmer through their veins.
And when they had reached home at dawn, as the first
rosy rays of the sun were playing over the lake's surface,
and had gone to bed in the little hotel room whose
blinds they had drawn against the inquisitive sunlight,
there on the bed, intoxicated by wine and music, they
had thrown themselves into each other's arms.

Now, an unutterably sweet languor took possession of
Miette. Her body seemed empty and light in the morning
freshness. For a long time she sat motionless in the prow

of the boat, her eyes half closed. A loose knot of hair had fallen to her shoulders, and the wind caressed it with what seemed an almost sensual impulse.

Peter toiled over the oars. The sail, too, was spread to the wind, and the *Neptune* plowed slowly through the water, moving farther and farther away from the shore. But soon after, as if weary, the sail ceased to draw the boat and sank alongside the mast. Peter raised his dripping oars from the water and withdrew them.

The wind had died down completely. The multitude of tiny waves that had been jostling one another on the surface of the lake plunged down and disappeared. The water grew smooth as a mirror, and a few minutes later the downy, silky little thistle balls that had been flying in the wind came to rest on its quiet surface.

The air was constantly growing hotter. But it was not an oppressive heat for it had rained in the night, and the ground everywhere exuded a clean, fresh smell of earth. From various directions came the Sabbath sound of faraway bells, surmised rather than heard somewhere beyond the shores of the lake. Now and then a little fish would dart from the water and gleam white and silver for the flash of an instant. The water made a soft *plop*! when he fell back, then all was quiet again.

The *Neptune* lay motionless, so far from the shore that no one could be descried. They were alone beneath the sky, with the silence and the wide waters. Miette stood up and with a lazy movement discarded her robe, which had grown too warm for her.

She wore no bathing suit and stood there for a second, stark naked. One hand on the mast, she unbound her hair and shook out the luxuriant red-gold locks, as if their weight were too heavy. As she stood with flowing tresses at the front of the boat, against the background of green waters, she seemed a nymph, white-skinned and tawny-haired. With slow, tranquil movements she spread her hair over her shoulders and, divinely shameless, uncovered her nakedness before Peter, who was busy with a knot in the rope and paid no attention to her. They had

long grown so accustomed to their bodies that they held
no secrets each for the other.

With lovely, lazy movements Miette stretched herself
full length on the mat at the bottom of the boat, closed
her eyes, and abandoned her body, now honey colored,
to the warm, golden rays of the sun.

Peter began to feel drowsy, too. He yawned prodi-
giously, but beneath his torpor his mind eluded sleep. The
clear Sabbath serenity that enfolded them almost palpably
induced meditation. He contemplated Miette, who lay
stretched out, arms crossed behind her head like a great
wondrous cross of gold. He tried to imagine what the
future held in store for him. He saw himself and Miette
under the most divers physical and spiritual conditions.

What he had most dreaded, the torment of the gnawing
agony of jealousy of this glorious woman—like that which
he had already suffered because of a stupid telephone
conversation—on that score he was entirely easy. Since,
guardedly but vigilantly, he had been watching Miette's
every movement, since he had been trying to draw her
soul toward artfully and cleverly barbed traps, laying
snares for her, all for the purpose of acquiring more
complete dominion over her thoughts, he had felt completely reassured. Miette's soul was pure.

The more unrestrainedly and unreservedly she gave
herself to him in love, the more she displayed an almost
virginal reserve with others. She had none of that
coquetry that Peter hated so in other women and that
would have made him so miserable in her.

He thought, too, that if Miette were to have a child it
would draw them still closer together. But would she
have one? Yes, of course she would; they had agreed
not to have a child in the first year of their married life.
They wanted to consecrate the first year to their love
alone, and this was right, for what a pity it was when the
shadow of a child fell between two young people in love,
during the first months of their union! As he gazed at
Miette, it occurred to him that pregnancy would mar the
perfect lines of her body. And as the child developed in

her womb, the house would be filled in advance with an atmosphere of anxiety, and even before its arrival the little tyrant would engage all his mother's thoughts, monopolize all her love, as her heart unfolded and ripened to motherhood. The layette must be prepared, the doctor consulted, and terrors suffered in advance at the thought of the agony of confinement and its unpredictable contingencies. Pregnancy is an unwieldy burden on the path of love.

But he heard, too, in his imagination, the shrill little voice and the piercing shriek of the child, and saw Miette giving it the breast. He saw the movement of her hand, the carriage of her head, and her fashion of offering the divine chalice of her maternal breast—whose nipple she held gently between her pretty fingers—to a child's small, greedy, famished mouth, all beaded with milk.

His imagination wandered along the faraway roads of future days. He saw himself, after a few years, with two children—a little boy and a little girl, in their small, clean, white clothes, whose every fold and knot and ribbon testified to Miette's taste and to the cleverness of her fingers. The little boy would be called Peter and the little girl Marianne. He saw the two children sitting on Father's knee, and he saw them in the bedroom of the little house in Hadnagy Street, where his mother was making them sip eggnogs.

"My son shall learn languages," he thought, his attention distracted for a moment by a gray heron that hovered on silent, motionless wings just above the boat.

He recalled the conversation of the night before when one of the members of their little group, Professor Rivolsky, had produced some very convincing arguments to the effect that, if the Hungarian middle class wished to survive, they would have to adopt more practical careers. Peter was in complete agreement with him.

"I shall have my son trained for a commercial career," he thought as he gazed frowning beyond the sunlit mirror of the lake toward the hills of Tihany.

He saw his son at four, on a wooden rocking horse;
he saw him as a schoolboy with ink-stained fingers, and
he endowed him with his own features as they had once
been. He saw him in his first long trousers, he imagined
all sorts of situations, and subjected him to the discipline
of paternal authority. He would love the little rascal, he
would be severe with him, unsparing at times, but he
would love him dearly all the while; still, the little girl
would be his favorite. Her mother would bring her up.
There was no doubt that the little chit would be a sweet
treasure! Of course she would look like her mother. It
would be a new Miette who would still not be exactly
like the other, for subtle, mysterious differences would
appear in her body and mind, according to Nature's
custom of perpetuating her creatures from generation to
generation.

A gull drew near the boat with piercing cries, but
wheeled suddenly and flew northward, as if it felt the
presence of someone whose meditations must not be
disturbed.

"Life will have its dark moments, too," he thought,
pursuing his reflections, "but are they worth thinking
about now? God in His wisdom has created the human
mind so that we can enjoy everything in anticipation; our
imaginations may enter wherever pleasure and happiness
await us, while the hours of suffering and agony remain
concealed. . . . And if Miette were to die suddenly? If
some unforeseen malady should slowly drain her strength?
If her body were to be mutilated by some accident? Or
if she should fall in love with another man? But all that
seemed impossible to him just then.

His gaze fell on Miette, stretched before him in the
perfect nudity of a Venus. Her head, a little bent, rested
on the golden pillow of her loosened hair. A faint,
enigmatic smile played about her lips and her closed eyes.
One of her hands had strayed, in her sleep, to her hip,
and lay there in a curious position as if she were about to
strike the cords of a harp.

The thistledown began fluttering again, and a silky

fragment dropped upon Miette, rolling slowly over her stomach and thighs, as if kissing the slumbering body.

As he resumed his contemplation of Miette, sensual thoughts stirred within him, their slow waves making him quiver from head to foot; he tried to stifle these thoughts for he didn't want to waken Miette, whose sleep was quiet and deep. Her breast rose and fell in rhythm with her tranquil breathing. But it was useless to turn his head away, useless to try to lose himself in contemplation of the misty remoteness of the violet hills; his eyes kept returning to Miette and his desire mastered him.

A second later she awoke and, still only half awake, cuddled into a new position on the mat. As if it were simply the continuation of her dream, she showed no surprise when she felt the touch of Peter's burning kisses. Then, after a long embrace, they stretched out side by side in the warm radiance of the sun and slept heavily. But before going to sleep, Miette covered herself with her bathrobe, lest some boat should pass by as they slept.

The water rocked the *Neptune* gently, with a hardly perceptible motion. The sun was high, having crossed the zenith, when they awoke.

"Come, let's bathe!" said Miette, walking to the edge of the boat.

"Wait! I'll go first. I think the water's very deep here."

Peter discarded his suit too, and slipped into the pearly water. Miette put up her hair, covered it with a rubber cap, and entered the water. They couldn't touch bottom, and swam with sure, quiet strokes around the boat, feeling the cool, mysterious sense of watery depths below them. Their bodies felt refreshed and invigorated and as they frolicked in the water they reveled in the sensation of swimming nude in this absolute solitude, the soft, silken water boldly caressing every inch of their bodies.

The wind had died down altogether, and the sail was useless when, after the bath, they saw by the position of the sun that the lunch hour was long past. Peter had to row vigorously in order to bring the heavy boat to shore. Having moored it there, they walked past the bathhouses to the hotel, for they were in the habit of lunching on the terrace.

It was already three in the afternoon.

Much to their surprise, the bathers were gathered in groups in front of the terrace, talking excitedly. They hurried toward one of these groups. The Countess Rengard, who up to then had consorted with no one, was the center of it.

"It's horrible! It's horrible!" she kept repeating, her face streaming with tears, as she nervously pressed her handkerchief to her mouth. There were five or six persons in this group and the face of each reflected helpless stupefaction or burning curiosity. Two gentlemen had interrupted their afternoon card game to run down to the terrace, and one of them, a big man with short arms, was still holding his cards spread fanlike between his fingers.

"What's happened?" Peter asked a woman next to him, a complete stranger.

His first thought was that someone had drowned in the lake.

Miette had pushed her way forward too, and thrust her terrified face between the shoulders of two men.

"What's happened?" Peter asked again, impatiently.

The stranger looked at him then and answered in a low voice: "The heir apparent and his wife were killed at Sarajevo this afternoon!"

One of the group, a barefoot man in a bathrobe, was holding his dripping bathing suit in his hand.

For a time there reigned a profound silence in which the only sound was the dripping of the water, drop by drop, onto the ground.

XV

It was eight days since he had been mobilized. Former comrades, one-year volunteers like himself, kept turning up, some already bald, others wearing mustaches. The four or five years that had elapsed since their last meeting had brought many changes. They soon discarded the black, gold-ornamented caps, whose threads had been tarnished in the long interval spent in lofty garrets during the years of civilian life. Now they were dressed in uniforms of rough field gray, reeking of camphor, that the commissariat issued by hundreds of thousands.

During the first few days of training they were high-spirited as students. They all knew it would be an affair of a few weeks at the most and were making their plans accordingly. Peter, nevertheless, meant to take a flying trip to Budapest the following Sunday, having already obtained his captain's permission and written to Miette.

But one afternoon—it was Wednesday—his orderly arrived, breathless, at the café of the little city, where Peter was playing billiards with an artillery officer.

"Lieutenant, you are wanted at headquarters immediately."

When he reached the barracks yard the entire battalion was drawn up, having received orders to leave at once for the front. He had only enough time to throw his things together before joining the march to the depot.

At eight that evening the train reached Kelenföld, where they received their marching orders and learned that their train would not leave for an hour and a half.

Peter ran to the train station and jumped into an already moving streetcar. The short trip to the house seemed endless. In the warm August gloaming, already darkening to night, the sound of gypsy music, thin as spider threads, floated to him from the direction of the Salt Bath, and the white trousers of a few persistent players still flashed on the Kelenföld tennis court. The water of the little lake reflected wanly the dark red of the sky.

Peter reached the house and looked up at the apartment windows. There was a light in the dining room. In a transport of happy impatience he shouted toward the open window: "Miette, are you there?"

Without waiting for an answer he disappeared into the

vestibule. He ran into Varga on the stairway but, unwilling to stop, passed him like a hurricane. The doctor,
recognizing Peter with difficulty in his gray uniform,
shouted: "Peter! Is that you?"

But Peter did not stop, only shouted as he mounted the
stairs: "I haven't time; just came from the train!"

The doctor, a little offended, looked after him.

Finally he reached the hall door and rang long and
impatiently.

"Are they at home?" he demanded of Mili.

"Only the master," she answered, gazing in awe at
Peter in his strange costume.

Breathless from having run so fast, he panted: "Where
is my wife?"

"She just went down to take Tomi for a walk."

"Run after her quickly!"

Sword at his side, Peter entered Father's room. The old
gentleman stared at him over his spectacles in amazement.
Peter held his cap in his hand; above his tanned face his
skull gleamed white, for his hair had been shorn close,
giving his head an entirely new shape. They were
delighted to see each other again. In a single breath
Peter revealed that he was not on leave; that he had a
scant half hour, and that the train was waiting at Kelenföld. As he talked he still panted a little from his hasty
flight up the stairs.

Father's expression grew grave. He carefully removed
his glasses from his nose and returned them slowly to
their case, coughing a little meantime to clear his throat.
That short little cough summed up all that he was
thinking, but he said nothing, never raised his eyes to
Peter's face, only got up and moved the tobacco jar from
one end of the table to the other, absentmindedly,
without the shadow of a reason.

Peter understood that this unexpected news had made
a deeper impression on Father than he would have
believed, that it had upset him thoroughly. Impatiently
he looked at his watch. "It would make me very unhappy
if I could not see Miette!" Then he added: "I shan't be

able to say goodbye to my poor mother." The next moment Miette ran into the room. She was flushed from hurrying and her eyes were radiant with joyful emotion. When she saw Peter's bald head she clapped her hands and burst into laughter.

"Good heavens, your head! How funny you look!"

She rushed to him and began rubbing his newly shaven head, like rough velvet to the touch.

It was only then that they kissed.

"How long can you stay?"

"At least another thirty minutes," Peter answered as if it were a joke, but he felt his voice tremble a little. Once more he related in a few words what had happened. Miette stared at him wide eyed, appearing not to understand.

"And when are you coming back?"

It was evident from her eyes that she still failed to grasp the significance of the situation.

Peter shrugged his shoulders smilingly, and made a gesture expressive of his total ignorance.

Miette closed her eyes slowly and laid her hand on the table for support. For a full minute complete silence reigned. Through the open dining-room window rose the grinding of trolley wheels and the noise of a passing motor. Meantime Tomi was excitedly sniffing the strong odor of camphor on Peter's trousers.

After a moment Miette left the room without having uttered a word. This silent, unexpected exit was so affecting that they both looked after her in alarm. Such an exit indicates the taking of a portentous resolve, and something of the soul remains hovering behind in the air.

Peter followed her and found her in front of the wardrobe in her bedroom. She was turning everything upside down in her feverish search for something hidden among the sweet-smelling, pink-ribboned lingerie.

"What are you looking for?"

She did not answer, but continued her search.

Peter stood watching her. She was wearing a thin, pale blue dress that she had had made for the summer holidays and that brought back to Peter's mind all his memories of Balaton. She stood there, stooping a little, in front of the wardrobe, her slender body gracefully arched. Her tawny hair, disarranged by the hasty removal of her hat, lay in disordered tendrils on her delicate neck. Thus a few seconds passed as she continued her search. They sufficed for the passage of an infinite number of thoughts, like tiny, sensitive darts, through Peter's mind. During those few seconds all the memories of his life with Miette seemed to assail him in a clamorous throng, their significance immeasurably heightened; his nostrils dilated, he inhaled the sweet, subtle odors of the room; the faint, scarcely perceptible perfume of Miette's garments and, above all, the delicate odor of her fresh body. His senses caught the slightest sounds—Miette's hands, feeling here and there beneath the piles of linen, and the soft rustle of her dress. His glance swiftly embraced the room, already half dark, and all it contained—the shapes, the smells, the quiet little sounds, the colors fading in the twilight—all clamped themselves upon his nerves, piercing them to a state of painful sensitiveness. And from the depths of his consciousness rose a great uneasiness that spread through all his being.

Miette had found what she was looking for. She held in her hand a little leather case, from which she drew a medal of the Virgin Mary at the end of a thin gold chain. Peter knew that it had come to her from her mother and was a treasure reverently preserved.

"Here, take it," she said, her voice so faint it could barely be heard, her eyes suddenly filled with tears. The next second she was in Peter's arms. Thus they remained for a moment, Miette shaken by sobs, leaning against Peter's breast, he the prey of a mighty, speechless emotion. As he held Miette tight in his embrace, he kept the little chain clasped in his right hand. He felt the tears rise in his throat, burning tears that started to his eyes. At first he tried to restrain them by blinking, then he raised his head to prevent them from falling. Warily he lifted his left hand and pressed the tears quickly back.

"Don't cry," he whispered, smoothing Miette's hair.

He leaned over her and kissed her mouth, salty from the warm tears she had shed. And kissing her, he suddenly felt through the taste of tears the sweet, familiar flavor of Miette's mouth. Her cool arms clasped his neck in limp misery, her voice was still choked with tears, but Peter was holding her tighter and their kisses were growing more and more passionate. As if some invisible power impelled them, their youth rose up to defy the world that held them in thrall, and their dark fear of the future—the shadow of terror hovering over their hearts, importunate time doled out in miserly minutes, everything about them—was devoured for the moment by this flame that had just burst through the tear-wet kiss of farewell and consumed every other thought. Their embrace grew more and more desperate. Once before, in the same place, they had clasped one another thus, in the pearly darkness of a winter's twilight with the snow sparkling outside, and had kissed for the first time.

Peter freed one of his arms and turned the key in the lock.

It had all come about so wildly and spontaneously, at the dictate almost of powers outside themselves, that Peter didn't even remove his sword that clanked against the edge of the brass bedstead.

"I must go!" he said later, his breast heaving.

Miette lay stretched on the couch, her eyes closed, and rolled her head from side to side with a sobbing little moan in the sweet, burning torment of her unappeased womanhood. She had herself so little under control that she had not even put her clothing in order.

Peter touched her gently as if he wanted to wake her.

"Miette, I must go—Miette!"

He looked at his watch in alarm. At once, without waiting for her to get up, he turned the key softly in the lock and went into the dining room. He had only twenty-five minutes before the train left.

He entered Father's room. Father was still standing thoughtfully in the same position before the stove. Peter went to him and extended his hand as simply and casually as possible.

They embraced and Peter bent to kiss Father's hand; then he left the room quickly. He stopped in the foyer and called, "Miette!" She answered from the bathroom: "I'm going with you; I'll take you there."

"Can't be done; I haven't any time, I must run!"

But the door was already opening and Miette, her hat on, came out. Mili, too, had emerged from the kitchen and was standing in silent apprehension near the door. Father stood by the door connecting the dining room with the foyer. As they were about to leave, Tomi began whimpering so that Miette seized his leash that had not yet been removed, saying, "All right. You may come, too!"

Peter cast a glance around the foyer, raised his right hand to his cap, saluted, and went out without saying a word.

He descended the stairs first, hurriedly, and Miette overtook him only at the door.

Involuntarily Peter raised his eyes to the windows. Father was leaning out and waving. Peter saluted once more and kept turning his head again and again to wave goodbye.

The car they took was crowded with civilians and soldiers. They stood on the rear platform and Peter took Tomi from Miette's arms. Tomi was still sniffing suspiciously at Peter's new coat and sneezing violently because of the camphor, forcing a smile from Miette, whose eyes were red with weeping. At the next stop more passengers got aboard, squeezing into the already jammed space, and Peter and Miette were jostled apart a little. Through the crowd of tightly packed bodies they sought each other's hands, and interlacing their fingers, held them tight. They both remembered just then that once before they had traveled this way on the tram's platform, squeezed in among the passengers and amid the stifling odor of damp clothes—on that November morning when they had met on the Danube esplanade.

It was nearly nine o'clock when they reached the station. It was almost dark, and in the cattle cars of the long military train sharply outlined shadows moved in the light of tiny candle flames. A few soldiers, stumbling over the rails, were running alongside the train, their arms heaped with plates, rolls, and postcards. Others vaulted the closed gates and leapt at a single bound, one after the other, into the candlelit carriages. Soldiers were singing in all the cars, different songs in each one. The dragging, plaintive songs of the peasants, blending with one another, melted in a confused dissonance, like the mournful howling of human cattle caged in a fantastic zoo. The crowded cars exuded a heavy, warm odor.

Peter and Miette walked back and forth in front of the train. They could scarcely hear each other through the clamor.

"When will you write?" asked Miette.

"I will write you from every station."

"Where do you go first?"

"None of us knows."

Miette pressed close to Peter and squeezed his arm. "Aren't you afraid?"

Peter laughed. "What should I be afraid of?"

They took a few more steps in silence. Their hearts were so heavy that every word was too much for them. Their tired thoughts circled sluggishly and they were both secretly wishing that this moment, which held them together, yet gave them no joy in each other's presence, would pass as quickly as possible. The poignancy of the farewell was over for them, and as if in a stupor, they walked slowly side by side, trying to appear gloomier than they really were. They could not, dared not express what was weighing, dark and heavy, on their hearts, for they dreaded oversentimentality. It was better to walk back and forth side by side, in silence.

It was nine o'clock and bugles began to sound at the back of the train. They were sounding the tattoo and their music rose high above the tumult, the long notes reverberating solemnly in space. That magnificent brass voice, leaping almost visibly into the air, shook them instantly from their lethargy.

Miette stood still, her lips trembling, clinging to Peter, and under the influence of the bugle notes she began to sob aloud like a child whom something has just frightened. Tomi stood motionless, his ears pricked, and stared belligerently in the direction of that piercing voice.

A noncommissioned officer ran to them, saluted, said to Peter, "Please step in, Lieutenant. We are leaving," then ran on.

Peter took Miette in his arms. His own voice was so choked that it frightened him.

"Goodbye, my love. God keep you." Then he added: "You'll go to my mother, won't you, and tell her how unhappy I was to leave without saying goodbye to her."

As they clung together their mouths melted beneath the kiss, seared as if by exquisite pain. Thus they remained in a long, close embrace, separating abruptly only when the train buffers clashed suddenly with a terrific clamor, making a noise like thunder, and their wide, resounding surfaces clanged one upon the other in hideous din.

The train got under way, drawing its vast burden slowly. The bugle was still playing and the howling of the songs grew louder and louder, leaping like a flame in a draft of air as the train pulled out.

Peter jumped to the step of the officers' car. He was very pale and his face was contorted with emotion. He waved to Miette in silence. Miette waved in response, feebly—very feebly. Then, seeing that the train was not going so fast that she couldn't follow it, she ran alongside, lifting her hand to Peter.

He leaned forward: "Be careful. You might stumble . . ."

Tenderly he took the tips of the fingers she offered him and kept them for a moment in his. But Miette had to run faster and faster, the train was gathering speed every second, and reluctantly the two hands parted. But still they held them aloft, each feeling the pressure of the other's fingers on his own.

Miette stood still, took Tomi into her arms, and waved her handkerchief to Peter. and Peter's handkerchief fluttered white at the car's gate till the darkness swallowed it.

The dimly lit cars, noisy with song and crowded with moving shadows, passed clattering by Miette like a hideous nightmare. The earth, shaken by the heavy train, trembled beneath her feet, and this tremor of the earth communicated itself to all her nerves.

The bugle was still being blown in the last carriage, and the train bore away with it that metallic voice, ringing aloft in the darkness, like a huge, invisible golden banner raised at the end of the singing train, fluttering and beating the air for mile upon mile.

The songs, which had come clearly to Miette as each carriage passed, were dissolved into discord again as the train receded, and sounded once more like the faraway, fantastic howling of thousands of fabulous beasts.

Then all was silent. First the songs, then the bugle, then the squeaking of the rails, and finally the muffled rumble of the train receded into the night.

Suddenly the station was enveloped in a silence so deep that the faint, doleful trickling of a faucet could be heard, and through the open window of the telegraph office, the monotonous click of keys.

For a long time Miette remained standing in the darkness and the silence. Then she turned homeward.

Once at home, she went directly to her room and sank, very weary, onto the couch, her hat still on her head. One of the rumpled cushions beside her still bore distinct traces of the last frenzy of their love, where Peter had unconsciously seized it with madly clutching fingers in the final moment of their embrace.

Mili opened the dining-room door and, on this evening as on every other, called toward Father's room in her mournful voice, "Dinner is served." The distant whistle of a train passing through the sultry August night entered at the window. It rose like a cry of terror, freezing the very marrow, then subsided in a flash, with that airy resilience characteristic of train whistles on silent nights, its volume gradually abating as it leaped from one faraway mountain peak to the next. . . .

Miette sat down to dinner, her soul transformed.

PART TWO: SIBERIA

PART TWO: SIBERIA

I

Lemberg is in the heart of Galicia, and the main road that leads to it, rising in places to an embankment thirty to forty-five feet high, seems with its vast proportions like a swollen artery in the body of the country. It is by way of this artery that the blood of Galicia circulates through the exchange of factory products: machines, matches, candles, chocolate, leather, chemical stuffs, and beer. It is not very long since this Appian Way of the Polish Jews was heavily traveled. The rows of passing carriages covered one another with clouds of dust, trucks clattered noisily, whips cracked, and drivers, all of them long-haired, shouted to one another at the top of their lungs. But since the beginning of the war this immense highway had been the hub of battles. Deserted, desolate, time seemed to have rolled back many centuries. At long intervals a solitary, belated horseman would pass at a trot, riding, it would seem, along the ridge of a tremendously high wall that extended into infinity. His figure might be seen clearly outlined, high and black against the summer sky, a dark, slanting line—the tightly strapped hussar's rifle—across his back.

Scout patrols also galloped across this road.

Having abandoned their defense positions on the main highway, the Russians had retreated from this shelter toward the Northeast.

Now, again, as far as the eye could see, the road was deserted.

Peter's regiment was encamped not far from the main road, near a miserable little Galician village. The light morning breeze stirred the canvas of the tents. It was the end of August, and the days were beginning to grow cooler. Fully dressed and wrapped in his coat, Peter lay stretched on a bed of straw, just waking from a deep sleep.

He sat up, his face crumpled with sleep, his eyes red, and, propped on the rolled-up blanket that served him as pillow, he tried to collect his thoughts. They had detrained at noon yesterday and after eight long hours of marching had reached this village, where after dinner they had gone to sleep exhausted. They had been in the train for two days and a half. Today was Thursday and he had said goodbye to Miette on Sunday night.

After having released Miette's hand, he had remained standing for a long time on the car step, holding on by one hand, powerless to turn his back on all he was leaving. Leaning forward, he waved his handkerchief. He could see Miette standing down there among the rails in the light of the station lamps, in her light blue dress and white felt hat, trimmed with an English black ribbon. She was holding Tomi in her arms and waving goodbye.

The train, gathering momentum, plunged beneath a viaduct and suddenly he lost sight of her. He remained standing in the dark passage, closed his eyes, and leaned his burning forehead against the cool windowpane. He was seized by a confused impulse; he wanted to tear the car door off its hinges and jump off the train, which was not yet running at full speed, to return across the wheat fields, stumbling through the plowed earth, to Miette. He stayed for a long time in the dark passage, as if mortally wounded, the spear of anguish buried deep within him.

A soft, meek voice suddenly spoke at his side: "Please, Lieutenant, won't you lie down? I have made your bed."

It was Michael Racz, who had been appointed his orderly.

Racz was no longer young. A thick, sun-bleached mustache and eyebrows of the same color adorned his brown, earth-colored face. Beneath his uniform he was still a small colorless peasant, and it would have been difficult to decide from his appearance whether he was thirty years old or more than forty.

In the officers' car half of a second-class compartment had been assigned to Peter, and it was there that Racz had prepared his bed; in reality he had simply spread two blankets over the cushions of the seat. For himself, he would lie stretched out in front of the door with the other orderlies like a watchdog in the hallway of a house.

Peter gave Racz a cigarette, which the latter held awkwardly between his blackened, calloused fingers as he lit it. He turned up the two ends of his mustache with his thumb and began smoking with evident relish.

"Where do you come from?" Peter asked, in an effort to escape his own thoughts for a moment.

"From Gúta, Lieutenant—in the Csallóköz."

"Have you a family?"

"Surely; I have two children."

"Boys?"

"No, both little girls. Vera is twelve and Mari fifteen."

"Have you a bit of land, too?"

"Yes, Lieutenant. Not much, to be sure—thirteen acres altogether; a few beasts, too, of course—two horses and a little cow. I'm sorry the war broke out just now; I would have liked to wait for the red cow to calf."

As he stood there in the doorway, holding the cigarette delicately between his fingers, he would turn occasionally and shoot a long, pointed jet of saliva into the darkness.

"And—excuse the question—I don't want to be impertinent—is the lieutenant married?"

"Yes," said Pater in a low voice.

"Is there a family at home?"

"No."

"Ah, well—" said Racz, and daintily, with the tip of his finger, knocked the ashes from his cigarette.

They chatted for a while longer, then Peter stretched himself out on his makeshift bed.

He tossed restlessly, turning this way and that, unable to summon sleep, the vibrations of the train bruising and tearing not only his soul but his flesh as well.

Those two days on the train were spent in a state of heavy torpor. They began in the morning with stiff draughts of cognac, followed by beer; at luncheon they drank heavy wines, and after meals there were always liqueurs with the coffee.

As Peter lay stretched under his tent, leaning on his elbow, recalling all that had happened to him in the last three days, he suddenly heard a strange noise; as if far away—it was hard to say where—the corks of gigantic bottles were popping, filling the distant horizon with the muffled sound of their reports.

He heard someone shout outside his tent, "Do you hear the cannon?"

Yes, it was the cannon, already.

The Austro-Hungarian army had overtaken the retreating Russian army at this point on the main road to Lemberg. The Russians had taken positions somewhere farther north. They occupied hills whence they dominated the whole country, and they were bombarding the road from there.

A moment later came the order to advance.

The Hungarian infantry deployed along the high embankment, which formed an excellent shelter. Soon the air resounded again with mighty voices. The Russians were beginning to pound the great Lemberg road with heavy shells, sending echoing shudders through its huge body.

Suddenly, at the rear of Peter's squad, hardly three hundred feet away, the Hungarian cannon, hidden behind bushes and embankments, answered. This unexpected thundering was as fearful as if the whole blue vault had collapsed with a tremendous din. Cannon rumbled, roared, thundered, in the dread fortissimo of an infernal tornado.

Peter's company hurried to the shelter formed by the high embankment of the road. After a half hour's march they halted. Peter, terribly excited, climbed to the top of the embankment and, lying flat on his stomach, surveyed the Russian trenches, eight hundred yards away, through his field glasses. The Russian positions were clearly visible high on the hill.

The newly dug trenches meandered down the side like long yellow caterpillars, pricked by the barbed wire as by sparse, disgusting black hairs.

The glasses trembled in Peter's fingers. Twenty, thirty shells burst suddenly, one after the other, in a thick, uninterrupted hailstorm. New ones kept coming all the time, plowing in all directions through the flower-covered hills and raising dark eddying clouds of dust and smoke. Men in flat caps could be seen up there, fleeing as if from the judgment of God, their arms before their faces in an instinctive gesture of protection. They were retreating in groups of ten or twenty. Just then a shell burst in the midst of one of these groups, and some of the men, torn from the ground as they ran, were hurled high in the air, then fell heavily to earth, their limbs sprawling in every direction.

That was the moment for action on the part of the pursuing army. A noncommissioned officer was already running toward them, panting and excited, bringing the order to advance. The men leaped from behind the road embankment and charged the hill.

They were met by a barrage of infantry in a sudden furious burst.

From somewhere above, the rattling tac-tac-tac of two Russian machine guns, operating at top speed, was turned against them.

But they kept on running, running, their eyes bursting from their sockets. The enemy's bullets caught more than one in full flight and they fell, cursing.

Peter was conscious of running forward across a potato field, but where he was going or why he did not know. All about him the air was filled with strange sounds: the whine of bullets whizzing past their ears in rapid flight. And above their heads the shells, like huge, invisible telegraph wires, went their way, roaring.

A tremendous battle was going on all along the line of combat. They had already reached the hill, and to their right the famous Székely regiment, its ranks thinned, was leaping over the mounds that splotched the overturned field with yellow here and there. The Russian front had been broken at several points; at other points the two armies were still grappling, and in the hand-to-hand encounters the spades of the Székelys—long-handled and keen-edged—were getting in their terrible work.

One or two hours perhaps were spent in this inferno, racing beneath the thunder and crackle of the gunfire; it produced the effect of a strange storm in bright sunlight, for it was a sultry day and the sun beat down, burning their necks.

By the end of the day the Russians had abandoned all their positions. The Hungarians held their trenches, and Peter saw, sticking out among the shell-battered trench walls, here the hand, rusty-brown from blood, of a dead Russian; there a boot, sole up, in a grotesque position; farther on, at the bottom of the demolished trench, a flat, ownerless cap, soaked in the dark red of clotted blood and covered with tufts of bloody hair.

It was quite dark when the last shot was fired. The moon rose, clear and round, above a distant forest that seemed to crouch, sinister and hostile, beneath its light. It is strange—and perhaps only martyred ears can really know it—that after-battle silence that seems to stretch into infinity. At that instant the whole countryside, lying stiff and frozen in the silence of death, seems bewitched by the icy, venomous magic of the full moon.

Orange-colored fires began to dot the underbrush everywhere; huge wads of cotton were thrown here and there in the grass; and in the bushes men, stretched on litters, their hands crossed over their chests, waited their turn to be carried away and perhaps saved. Other small flames were not slow to make their appearance—the fires, the tiny fires, of the field kitchens, where dry wood burned with a happy crackle and, when the cooks stirred the pots with their long ladles, the spicy odor of steaming soup filled the air all around and taunted the nostrils.

After dinner the day's mail was distributed. The

sergeant gave Peter two letters: one was for him, from Miette; the other was addressed to Racz, his orderly.

They were encamped once more in the shelter of the huge embankment; they had dug little holes in the clay wall with their spades, and soon the light of candles was shining from each one of these tiny niches. Peter read Miette's letter by candlelight.

"My darling Peter: I do not know whether you have received my first letter, which I wrote the very night you left. I sent it early Monday morning and now, Monday evening, I am writing to you again. This afternoon Elvira and Dr. Varga came in and tried to comfort me; I feel terribly lonely and sad. Then Sigismund Pán came, too, this afternoon, and I went out to play tennis with him for a little while. I asked him to dine with us, because it gave me such an awful sensation to see your place empty at noon, but he couldn't accept. . . ."

Thus Miette went on, giving vent over two long pagse to her childish expressions of misery. Peter felt he could hear issuing from those long, angular strokes the moan of love's desire, its voice mournful and veiled in tears. Miette was saying in words what her arms said so well when they clasped Peter's neck in an indescribable gesture of confidence and abandon.

"Father sends you much love, too (Miette ended her letter), and wants me to tell you he will send you some tobacco, the kind you like best, because he expects friends on Saturday. Write to us, Peter darling, and tell us if you need anything, no matter what it is; send me a list of everything you want, and I will forward it immediately. Anyway, you cannot possibly remember everything you ought to have and I have had a long conference with Elvira and decided to get ready for you: a large bottle of toilet water, some menthol, an electric flashlight, one of those little traveling dinner sets that come from England, some good preserves, a fountain pen, a light camel's-hair blanket, and any other thing that might occur to me whilst I'm shopping. Please write me, my dearest Peter, because I am terribly anxious, and I can hardly endure the uncertainty of not knowing how long you will be absent from me."

Peter dropped the letter and gazed attentively at a rust-colored blade of grass lying across a clod of earth that the candlelight illuminated. The evening breeze overhead brought him the fresh breath of the forest, though the acrid smell of powder persisted in the air, and the pots of the field kitchens nearby diffused a heavy, greasy odor. But through the confusion of those wild, strong, strange scents, Peter distinctly smelt the sweet perfume that rose from Miette's hair and neck. His eyes fixed on the blade of grass, he saw Miette clearly, swaying before him in various attitudes; saw the delicate smile, mysterious and sensitive, that played about the corners of her mouth; the easy, graceful movements of her hand.

Then he suddenly remembered that he had received another letter, addressed to Racz. He got up and let his eyes travel down the long row of men resting, and smoking in the moonlight.

"Racz," he called, at least three times in succession.

But Racz was nowhere. Up and down he surveyed the long line, calling the name over and over again. At the top of his voice and in every direction he trumpeted through his hands: "Michael Racz."

Suddenly a man appeared before him—but it was the sergeant.

"Excuse me, Lieutenant, whom do you want?"

"Michael Racz, my orderly."

"He has fallen, Lieutenant," said the sergeant.

"What has he done?" Peter asked, not altogether sure of the significance of the word.

"He is dead," said the sergeant. "Tomorrow morning you shall have another orderly, Lieutenant."

"I have a letter for him," mumbled Peter, stubborn, uncomprehending.

The sergeant did not answer; he stood there motionless, as if waiting for an order or a sign. Peter turned and went back to his place. He felt as if he had been wounded himself. He put his hand to his neck as if he expected to feel a gaping wound.

"Is it possible?" he wondered. He knew that a great number of men had fallen that day on the hills and in the potato fields; the stretcher-bearers were still at work, and the stretchers were being borne in a never-ending line down the gentle slopes of the hill; but those were not men, nothing but corpses, strangers, people he did not know. But Racz . . . this very afternoon, even, he had . . . could it really be true?

He still held the letter in his hand. He felt rising within him an irresistible desire to tear open the envelope, which the censor had already opened in any case. He stretched himself out on the ground, lit the candle in the little hole again, and began to read.

This is what it said:

"I am writing this letter on the 10th day of August, my dear husband, and I hope that these few lines will find you in good health. God be praised we are also well dear husband, I am letting you know that the red cow has calved and everything went well the pains began at midnight and at three in the morning the calf was born and I was alone there with poor Mari so you can imagine what difficulties we had but the Lord helped us and he is a fine little calf and his legs are as fat as the big calves so write to me, my dear husband, if I should sell the big or the little one I would rather sell the big and with the one we have now I would like to buy a good pair but it is not yet certain that there will be a fair and I am also letting you know that I sent you a package. Vera took it to the post-office and if you receive it let me know there were onions and garlic in it and also brandy wine two boxes of cigarettes a penknife some salt cakes, and also others three shortcakes a pencil a pipe green pepper salt and red powdered pepper chocolate white sugar ham cigars and other things besides I can't write it all down now I am letting you know that the hay is cut your brother Pista cut it a letter came from Gyuri he says poor fellow that he is in the regiment that is going and he is with Gyuri Sós and dear husband I have bought rye and wheat for sowing but everything is so dear and when I have paid the tax and the rent I will have nothing left but if I can sell the cow and the pigs get fat then that will bring some money again dear husband write me where you are and if you are in the battle. I am letting you know that there will be a new examining board here on the 25th so instead of the war ending perhaps all the men will be taken now. Dear husband I have written so many things that my hand hurts me write me everything about yourself too so I will have a lot to read but the letters do not come quickly and we have no good news of you take care of yourself so that we may see each other again in this life and so I end my letter. I remain your faithful wife and your two little girls and may God protect you we kiss you a hundred thousand thousand times and may God bless you your faithful wife who loves you

"Erzsi Fejér."

On the envelope was written: "I expect an answer to this letter. I expect an answer without fail and that happy days will dawn for us again."

Peter touched the letter to the candle flame. The paper burned with a great yellow flame and fell in crumbling black ashes on the clod of earth. He felt a painful tightening of his heart during the instant it took for the paper to burn.

Then he pulled the blanket over his head. It wasn't long before complete physical exhaustion blotted out his sad thoughts and there on the bare ground he fell into a deep sleep.

He couldn't tell how long he had been sleeping thus. Had it lasted ten minutes or two hours—this overpowering slumber—when someone shook him by the shoulder? He sat up, startled; all about him men were moving, running in all directions.

The moon rode high in the heavens and its light was as bright as a magnesium flare. A faint night breeze was stirring, its gentle breath pervading all the atmosphere. It was a ghastly spectacle—the sight of these men running to and fro, uttering not a sound, as if some mysterious calamity had suddenly struck them all dumb.

"What's happened?" Peter asked a soldier near him who was hastily gathering his belongings together and stuffing them into his kit.

"We are prisoners . . . The Russians have surrounded us!"

Peter considered these words for a moment without understanding their meaning. His head was still numb with sleep, and all that was going on around him seemed like the continuation of his dream.

A sergeant arrived with orders for the third detachment to advance. The soldiers finished their preparations and fell into line—all amidst a fantastic silence. No sound of a human voice was heard—only the occasional clinking of tin plates as they struck one another, or of spades knocking against the soldiers' knapsacks.

The third detachment marched away under the command of the sergeant. They had gone northward along the bottom of the high embankment for about two miles when they met the other companies of the regiment, formed into huge squares under the bright moonlight and already disarmed.

In front of the troops stood several Russian officers of high rank, whose figures, topped by the flat caps, gave Peter a sense of unreality. One of them was nonchalantly smoking a cigarette, his gloved right hand that held a riding crop resting on his hip. His fine patent-leather boots and gilded epaulets shone brightly in the moonlight. Near him a little spotted fox terrier was jumping nervously about.

After Peter's detachment had also been disarmed, the whole captive regiment advanced under the guard of the Russian infantry, their bayonets fixed, and, crossing the embankment, they moved toward the hills behind which, invisible and mysterious, the Russian army lay hidden. On the broad highway an affecting sight met their eyes. The long road was strewn with dead bodies that the stretcher-bearers had not had time to remove.

There they lay, some with arms extended, looking crucified; others crumpled up in strange positions. They all belonged to the Székely regiment, and their faces, young or mature, gleamed waxen yellow beneath the moon.

They marched for about two hours, climbing up and down the slopes of low hills. The moon was still high, but at the horizon line the sky was already showing a faint rosy tinge. It was then, from the top of a hill, that they saw before them the huge masses of the Russian troops, which, with their vast army of trucks and their thousands of tents, lay spread out like a silent, antediluvian, ghostly community. And nowhere the faintest glimmer of lamp or candle!

Peter stood still and looked back for a moment in the direction from which they had come. Somewhere down there in the distance, behind the wooded hills, the life that had been his up to then was sinking, pale and mysterious, into the moonlight.

II

Miette did not keep a regular diary, but in a memorandum book she made a little note, with the date, of every event in her life that seemed important. So when she came upon the book occasionally and began turning its leaves she would always find something new and astonishing there. There were dates she had thought would have a decisive influence on her life, but after a few months they had lost all significance; on the other hand, there were ten others that she had put down only for the sake of system, without attaching any special significance to them at the moment. And like the tiny spark destined to consume everything, these were the very dates that had gained in importance, grown in size, and were now all but engulfing her personal life. Thus it was, for example, that she found this entry in the little book one evening:

"Sunday, September 11th. Tea at the Vargas'. A few people I knew and many strangers. Rather amusing. Mme. Galamb recited. Sigismund Pán played the piano, and a young man whose name I don't know read our handwriting."

That was the afternoon she had first met Peter. Beneath those few penciled words she now saw the mysterious depths of her life and destiny opening before her. What a great variety of things lay hidden—all living, whirling, flaming, murmuring, echoing—beneath those carelessly written words. Just one year had passed since that pleasant afternoon. And she had lived more in that last year than in all the first twenty of her life.

Since she had learned that Peter had been taken prisoner, she hovered uncertainly among thoughts that sometimes reassured her, only to weigh her down at other times with apprehension. All her friends tried to console her, telling her it was the best thing that could have happened. The war had already lasted six weeks and those who had said at the outset that this tremendous mobilization would be over in a fortnight were now disconcerted by developments. They sought new arguments for a speedy conclusion of the war, but these arguments grew weaker from day to day, like a sick man marked by death, for whom every hope of recovery has been abandoned. There were even skeptics who believed the soldiers could scarcely be home before Christmas.

That was what Miette believed. She could not hope to see Peter before Christmas, and those few months stretched interminably ahead of her. But since news of the first fatality had taken them unaware, they had suddenly begun to view the war with mute horror. Other messages followed, announcing, one after another, the death of Sanyi Galamb, Yolanda Galamb's young brother, whose kind, chubby red face Miette remembered very well; Alex Lénárt, an artillery lieutenant; Stephan Kramer, and Balogh, the groceryman, whose shop was at the corner of the street. This tall, gaunt, solemn fellow, his neck buried in his shoulders, had fallen as a private.

Miette learned of his widow's loss when she went to the shop one morning. Those tidings of sorrow burst wherever they were heard—in the streets of Pest, in the trolleys, or at social gatherings—with the explosive force of terrible shellfire. War was being waged far from the city but was bombarding it incessantly—with messages of death.

Since each new day brought with it some fresh horror, and since the number of dead and wounded among their acquaintances increased daily, the knowledge that Peter was no longer on the firing line did comfort Miette. She was told that his rank assured him of courteous treatment, even though he was a prisoner of war, and that he was in effect the guest of the great, powerful empire of Russia.

Ten days had passed since Peter had been taken captive, but no news of him had yet arrived. Nothing beyond the brief, official communication sent by the commander. This was terribly disquieting. There were days when it was useless to try to point out to her that the mail didn't travel through the regular peacetime channels and that it would be three or four weeks before she could receive her first letter. Every morning she waited for the postman in a state of distracted excitement. In her impatience she even went so far as to wait for him in the street, always returning to her room in bitter disappointment and despair.

Since Peter's departure—except for a few postcards sent en route that, in the agony of his grief and desire, he had covered with burning words of love—there had come from the front only a single card. All it said was:

"My dear little angel! I am in excellent spirits and, thank God, in perfect health. This whole business is extraordinarily interesting. How many things I shall have to tell you when I come home! My thoughts are always with you, my darling, my little Miette. My love to Father. Tomorrow I shall write more, and meantime I kiss you millions and millions of times. Your Peter who loves you very, very much."

Miette carried this card always with her. She knew

every line by heart and the formation of every letter. It must have been written on the day when he was taken prisoner, for the letter he promised for the following day had never arrived.

During the first weeks Miette felt in every fiber, in every nerve, a burning, intolerable pain. Her union with Peter had become in that brief period a physical and psychic habit so natural that now that their life together had been interrupted, presumably for a long period, she could endure his absence only at the cost of terrible suffering.

On several occasions it happened that when she opened her eyes in the morning she would take her little pillow and, still half asleep, go as far as Peter's bed. Only when confronted by the cold, empty sheets into which she had been about to slip, would she start suddenly awake. Then she would take refuge hastily in her own bed, carrying with her a vague terror, like that of a child who has accidentally touched a corpse. Gradually the impression faded from her heart, but there remained a dull despondency and an unalterable sorrow. Habit played strange tricks upon her. Often when she came home at lunch time and entered the dining room she thought she saw Peter stretched on the couch, propped on an elbow, munching a crust of bread and absorbed in his newspaper.

Naturally the illusion never lasted more than a flash of a second, vanishing as quickly as it came, to leave the couch still emptier, it seemed. Habit was probably responsible, too, for the fact that Peter's figure, with all its familiar gestures, haunted the rooms so strangely, the very furniture even, so that it became one with them. Often in front of his empty chair at luncheon, she saw his hand resting on the tablecloth, breaking up toothpicks. The ghostly hand would even take a piece of bread from the basket. And when she worked at a piece of embroidery in her room, she had the feeling that Peter was sitting or standing behind her, in the attitude she had seen so often. The suggestive power of this hallucination was such that she would turn her head involuntarily, and it seemed to her absolutely preposterous that there should be no one there.

Then, too, she would suddenly think that she had recognized his voice distinctly. Jumping up, her heart pounding, she would turn her head toward the hallway to listen, only to hear the janitor's voice or that of some workman come to fix the electric meter. In the street she would suddenly hasten her step, mistaking some stranger for Peter. It was enough if a hat was the same color, a figure somewhat similar, to make her heart beat faster in the belief that she was seeing Peter. Disappointed, she would always think disconsolately how far off Christmas was, for that was the date on which she counted surely for his return, and she would feel poignantly in the very marrow of her bones, in the deepest and most intimate reaches of her own being, every characteristic of the soul and body of Peter.

One afternoon she went to visit her mother-in-law, only out of a sense of duty and propriety, for she would not voluntarily have sought the society of people even sadder than herself.

Peter's mother, who had hitherto been obliged to conceal her unhappiness, gave it free rein now that she had a legitimate reason for it and wept continuously. By virtue of obscure, unfathomable arguments that she buried at the bottom of her soul, she regarded Peter's marriage and, for some unknown reason, Miette herself, as entirely responsible for the war. Her intelligence and imagination were far too superficial to disencumber themselves of her stubborn maternal instinct.

Szücs, who had been assigned to home duty temporarily and was still in Budapest, displayed great affection for Mme. Takács and tried to comfort her with little attentions on the one hand, and with crude pleasantries on the other.

When Miette entered the Hadnagy Street living room that day she saw two strange women, whose greeting was noticeably frigid. For the entire duration of her visit she felt oppressed by the inquisitive, hostile stare of the younger one, who was undoubtedly the daughter of the other, a woman beginning to grow puffy, with the air of a rich bourgeoise, upon whom her mother-in-law lavished flattery and sweet words. The young woman, somewhat oily-skinned and obviously no longer in her first youth, whose face and entire manner, distasteful in themselves, betrayed besides a certain bitterness, was Aranka Vajnik. Needless to say, Miette had not the slightest suspicion that this girl cherished for her a boundless hatred.

She stayed at her mother-in-law's for half an hour; then, under some rather unconvincing pretext, rose and took her leave. It was in any case high time for her to go, because her conversation with Mme. Vajnik and her daughter—whose name she had not caught when they were introduced—would stop short after each exchange of amenities. Miette could have handled the situation admirably and with perfect ease, for her imagination seized quickly and with a sure instinct upon topics capable of interesting people whose intelligence was less keen than her own; but she felt much too tired and despondent to proffer her conversational gifts to these strangers, whose antagonism she felt instinctively behind their forced smiles. From the first moment an intuition, born of her rare sensitiveness, had warned her, despite her lack of any information on the subject, that this young woman had once been her rival. But she was not disturbed, and she made no effort to learn more of the circumstances. She got up and made ready to go.

"Goodbye, Mother dear. Father sent word that he would come to see you soon—but if he doesn't, don't wait for him; come to see us as soon as you can."

She gave her hand to Mme. Vajnik and her daughter with a cool, quiet smile. On the threshold she turned once more to say to her mother-in-law: "I understand the mails are extremely irregular just now. But if by any chance you get some news, please let me know at once; I am so terribly anxious."

It was nearly six o'clock when she found herself again in Hadnagy Street. It was a mild September evening, sweetened by the late flowering of the acacias in some nearby garden. She did not take her customary way home, but, in order to circle the hill, turned up the winding street. She walked quietly along the hillside, stopping now and then to watch the children at play. In an open square, two makeshift football teams were competing— all youngsters of ten to twelve, gathered about a ball made of rags that they had promoted to the dignity of a "football," and over which they were making a mighty clamor.

Miette opened her parasol, for the setting sun was scorching her neck in an apparent effort to expend its dying strength at one blow. To the left the street skirted a row of villas, and a few pedestrians crossed her path. An auto passed close to her, sounding its horn cautiously on its way up the hilly, winding road and leaving behind, as it disappeared, a glittering cloud of golden dust.

Miette stopped and looked toward the Vargas' villa, halfway up Mount Gellért. Suddenly she remembered the March afternoon she had spent there with Peter. Closing her eyes, she thought she could still feel the air suffused with fresh perfumes, and the bright young sunlight of that budding spring afternoon, so different from the setting September sun, wan and vitiated. Such sorrow overwhelmed her that she wanted to weep. She felt herself unutterably forsaken, absolutely alone in all the world. The visit she had paid that afternoon convinced her afresh that she could never find in her simple, childish mother-in-law either refuge or comfort. Lately she had been drifting farther and farther from Mme. Varga, too. She was slowly growing conscious of this woman's boundless vanity which, together with the emptiness of her soul, she masked, or at any rate tried to mask, beneath a façade of kindness and propriety. And among her other acquaintances there wasn't a single one she wanted to see, nor whose closer friendship she would have sought. Seeing herself thus abandoned, she was full of self-pity, and she would have been almost glad to attribute the sadness that so often overwhelmed her to this sense of solitude and desolation. Even in her inmost self, she wouldn't admit that her sorrow had a different, secret source that she persisted in ignoring—it was really her father's health that worried her. It seemed as if, in the course of the last few weeks, Father had abruptly and with startling rapidity grown old. His skin was drawn tight and thin, like parchment, over suddenly hollowed temples; his eyes revealed an inexplicable weariness; his beard seemed dull and was much longer, since for some time he had not had it trimmed. This long beard had completely changed the expression of his face; he seemed almost to have become a strange old man. At first Miette had tried to attribute this alteration in her father's appearance to the fact that he was grieving over the war and over the fate of the world; but before long she found this explanation too inclusive, too abstract, and when her eyes rested on his face now and then, the hazy, fearful thought took deeper and deeper root within her mind that behind this face, in the brain, in the heart, in the arteries, death was beginning to worm its silent, wary way. But whenever Miette arrived at that point she always summoned the strength to flee from the image of this certainty, and to banish this terror from her soul. Thus she succeeded in reassuring herself, in finding some pretext for regaining her confidence. But unconscious of it though she might be, the shadow of the fear remained secreted, like a pallid threat, in her heart.

The sun disappeared behind the hill and all the light was suddenly quenched. The air grew perceptibly cooler. Miette caught sight of a bench at the side of the road, sat down, and laid her parasol beside her. She looked straight ahead of her, seeing nothing of the shapes of trees and houses that seemed to melt into the soft, quiet dusk of twilight. She was thinking of Peter. She was trying to imagine where he might be just then. The appearance of the train that had carried him away, the aspect of this Russian country, of the little Russian stations that the train left behind; what could Peter be thinking and feeling at that moment? But in spite of her efforts, it all remained hazy and obscure. Since she had known Peter had been taken prisoner and sent to Russia, she had searched in the library for all the Russian novels she could find and had bought other books—travel books, books on geography and ethnography, everything concerning Russia. Her curiosity leaped, wildly impatient, to the conquest of that vast Russian world, but occasionally she would drop in discouragement some book she had already read and was looking through again, feeling vaguely that neither Tolstoi nor Chekov, nor Goncharov was the beacon that would illumine for her this strange, disturbing, infinite grayness that had engulfed Peter as the ocean seems to engulf a departing ship. An occasional sentence would capture her imagination, showing her for a fleeting second the vast snow-covered reaches of Siberia, but she would soon encounter names and words that would baffle her once more; thus when she read in some geographical work the names of Tunguska, Yakutsk, Yukaghir, Chukotski and Koryak, the valleys of the Ural and the Yenisei or the shores of Lake Baikal would elude her suddenly, disappearing in the hazy distance that hid from her the country of those fairy tales told her years ago by some old nurse in her grandmother's house during the long, dark autumn and winter evenings. She had listened to these tales, her child's heart oppressed by anguish, and in their shadow the very oil lamp seemed to burn with a dead light, and a curious smell of smoke, mingling with the wet dog's odor of the great St. Bernard drying himself by the fireplace, spread through the vast kitchen—odors that her vivid imagination brought back in all their pungency.

Just then a man in a gray suit approached the bench and, casting a glance at the parasol lying there, raised his hat.

"May I?" he said.

Miette withdrew her parasol in silence, and looked for a second into the face of the man who sat down at the other end of the bench. She had the impression that she had already seen that face twice today as she was climbing the hill. This man had stared at her, had turned back after having passed her rapidly, and had then crossed her path again, trying always to meet her eyes. She had thought nothing of it, but now that he had popped up next to her she began to seek some connection between the previous encounters and his present appearance. She turned her head and looked the other way. But the presence of this stranger had dissipated her thoughts and she was waiting, irritated and impatient, for the moment when she could get up and go. She did not want to rise immediately, thinking that her sudden departure might seem unnecessarily offensive and might even give this man the idea that she was running away from him. She wanted to show that she was above anything of that kind. These thoughts crossed her mind rapidly and meantime she remained seated.

After a moment the stranger began to speak. His voice betrayed his uncertainty and some misgivings.

"Excuse me, madame. I shouldn't like you to think me rude—I didn't greet you though I have the impression that we have already met—"

Miette turned her eyes calmly upon him. For a moment she surveyed with a cruel imperturbability the face of this man, enjoying the painful embarrassment apparent in his nervously dilating nostrils as he waited for her answer, and in the red spots on his cheeks. He was a man of about forty, with an insignificant, vacant countenance adorned by a thick mustache trimmed in the English fashion, which at the moment seemed to Miette disgusting. From his appearance and dress he seemed to be a city shopkeeper or a petty clerk. Having taken his measure in a keen, all-embracing glance, she answered with a quiet simplicity that the stranger apparently found very unpleasant: "No, you are mistaken—we have never met."

And in her voice and expression there was not only haughtiness and a serene strength, but a touch of wistful, pitying kindness as if she were asking forgiveness of this stranger who had put himself in a false position on her account. This tone completely disarmed the seeker after adventure. He rose, smiled awkwardly, and, lifting his hat in embarrassment, said, "I am sorry, then—I was mistaken," and departed hastily.

On other occasions, too, Miette noticed that in the course of her solitary walks, when she wanted to be alone with her thoughts, men would follow her or walk stubbornly beside her, their eyes fixed on her feet, her neck, her hair, her face, and she felt that these greedy glances were stripping her of her clothes. Often they spoke to her under one pretext or another, and sometimes she was obliged to answer sharply to compel their retreat. After each walk she would return home with the memory of these temptations that left, however, not the faintest trace behind. Yet these little adventures were constant reminders that the muffled forces of life and love were prowling about within her and that her body, which she knew to be beautiful, drew in its wake as she walked in their midst the desires of men, as a ship draws the trembling wave behind it.

There were evenings when, stretched on her bed, her hands crossed behind her neck, she could not summon sleep. It was then she felt she could not endure the thought that Peter was not near.

Over and over with feverish impatience she counted the days until Christmas, for she firmly believed Peter would then be back, and she was always picturing to herself in the greatest detail the nights they would spend together.

With a little moan in her tear-filled throat, she would stretch her splendid body beneath the blankets, racked with desire and longing.

III

After Peter's train had traveled for three days, Kiev rose out of the vast plain in the morning sunlight. An incredible array of domes, roofs, and factory chimneys lifted their gold and silver and soot-colored outlines in the distance.

Peter sat by the window. Startled out of sleep, he gazed without comprehension from the train window at the overpowering vision of the approaching city.

It was only gradually that he awoke to his surroundings, and when he raised his eyes to Ensign Kölber sitting opposite him, cautiously stretching his legs that were numbed by the long journey, he suddenly realized that in his sleep he must have jolted several times against Kölber's knee; it was then he had had the sensation, sharp and sweet at the same time, of touching Miette's knee! Now he was looking with indescribable disgust at Kölber's face, where the oily, dark-red stubble of a three-day beard glistened like a myriad tiny red needles. This Kölber was a bullet-headed, cat-faced boy, who could hardly be more than twenty-three; in his watery gray eyes lay an unchanging shadow of embarrassment, fear, and sadness.

At his right someone yawned like a panther, his chin dropping almost to his stomach in the process. This someone rubbed his eyes and asked Peter in a voice husky with sleep: "Where are we, friend?"

This was Stephan Bartha, who had left Bihar—where he had been the town-hall clerk in a small village—to go to war as a reserve lieutenant.

"At Kiev," answered Peter in a low voice.

Bartha, his eyebrows raised, stared in front of him, and his face with its hollow cheeks and drawn features revealed that he was deep in thought. His cheek bones were a brilliant red, as if he were tubercular.

Draughts of fresh air entered the compartment through the window of the passageway. The sun was high and was slowly beginning to warm the windowpane. Gradually the others awoke, for the wheels beneath them clattered incessantly as they passed over the switches. With Lajtai, Lukács, and Mezei there were six in the compartment.

Lajtai, who seemed the oldest of them, had a thick mustache trimmed short in the English fashion; he raised his nose—a little hollow like a saddle—high in the air and when as now he gazed out through the window, his face was stamped with an expression that was the climax of all bitterness.

Chief engineer of the Diósgyör Iron Works, and father of three children, he was something less than pleased with this journey to Kiev.

Lukács, whose smooth, repulsive face was pallid and leaden in the crude morning light, like that of a ruined gambler, was casually cleaning his other nails with the sharp nail of his little finger.

They were all second lieutenants, except Mezei, who was a first lieutenant. He sat in a corner near the door, seemingly plunged in painful thought, as if asking himself how it happened that he, an officer in the regular army, should be in the company of these creatures—these civilians dressed as officers who, he felt, were of another species—and whether it was really possible that not only he, but they, too, could be prisoners of war in good standing.

They spoke little, wondering whether new unforeseen surprises awaited them in this city, and apprehension oppressed the hearts of all. They felt that some mysterious, inscrutable uncertainty sat at the helm of their destiny.

Only Bartha spoke as he rubbed his bristly, itching chin with his palm, and raked his hair that was damp with sleep.

"Let's hope we shall find something decent to chew here."

Then he called to Kölber: "Have you a little cordial left comrade?"

"Ja, ja," answered Kölber in his Tyrolean accent (he could speak nothing but German) and held out his canteen.

When the train entered the station the prisoners' carriages were met by soldiers with fixed bayonets. The whole body of men, chafed by three consecutive days of traveling, jumped from the train like beasts released from their cages.

The Russian soldiers pushed them back with their bayonets. They shouted incomprehensible things to the prisoners in a rude, wild tongue, sounding as if they were trying to pick a quarrel. This reception had a painfully harrowing effect upon them all.

Peter had remained standing on the running board of the car, above the crowd. Always in his memory stood the vision of Miette in the little blue dress she had worn that day when they walked together for the last time on the platform of the Kelenföld station. Yet his attention was held by all he was seeing here on the Kiev platform, and these two opposing currents of thought mingled together in his brain.

A barefoot, flaxen-haired little girl, carrying a huge basket in front of her, cried incessantly, "Boulki, Boulki . . ."

She uttered the strange word in her tiny, melodious voice, as if in this swirling crowd she were calling desperately someone named Boulki.

But it was not difficult to guess that the word applied to the little snow-white, wheaten rolls that filled her basket.

In the midst of all these people who crowded the platform, a cripple was hopping about. You couldn't lose sight of him, for he wore a scarlet shirt and a scarf of a beautiful lemon yellow knotted about his throat. He must have been a good-natured fellow, for he let himself be shoved this way and that without a word of protest; sometimes he hopped to one side, balancing before him with the dexterity of a monkey the tray on which his wares were displayed, crying ceaselessly in his grating, parrot's voice: "Piroschnik! Piroschnik!"

He was selling cheap, dubious-looking pastries.

Europeans and Asiatics mingled in the crowd milling about the platform. There were dark-brown Tatars with their round caps and their *khalats*. Here and there stood groups of Russian peasants, wearing their greasy sheepskins even in this warm weather, with burlap trousers held by a rope at the waist, and shapeless shoes made of woven reeds. All their persons reeked with a heavy odor, suggestive of the stable. Beside them, the bearded Jews

of Kiev, sinister-looking with their long tresses and
caftans, resembled black marabous. The whole station
was swamped by the ceaselessly churning waves of
merchants and traders who had gathered from the vast
areas of the Russian steppes; there was even a little boy
standing in the crowd. He was dressed in a long black
coat that reached to his ankles, and clung with one hand
to his father's fox coat—the latter was evidently a horse-
dealer—casting frightened glances into the noisy turbulence of the mob.

When the news had spread that live, flesh-and-blood
prisoners were being brought direct from the firing lines,
a huge swarm of the curious surrounded them, eyeing
them from behind the Russian bayonets as through the
bars of a cage. The soldiers prodded right and left with
the butt ends of their weapons, shouting in their lusty
voices, and finally succeeded in leading the company of
prisoners to the space reserved for them at the front
of the station. There were a hundred and fifty in all,
officers and men, and none of them knew where or
when they had been separated from the rest of the
regiment.

They were met at the enclosure by Russian officers,
who promptly began to examine and search them and
their baggage.

A tall, powerfully built petty officer undertook to
examine the contents of Lieutenant Mezei's knapsack;
the latter, forestalling him, plunged his hands into the bag
first, drawing out his military field glasses, which he
smilingly offered the soldier.

"If you please, Sir, souvenir of Budapest."

The Russian cast a glance toward the officers to make
sure they weren't looking in his direction, but they were
talking at the moment to Lieutenant Rosicsky, who stood
stiffly at attention before them.

The Russian's bony, freckled face brightened, and with
a broad smile he slipped the gift into his pocket. After
that the search was only a pretense; some bags he didn't
even open, just feeling them self-importantly with his

large, bony fingers, while his face flushed with the
excitement of this new calling.

The inspection, however, lasted several hours, and those
who were searched by other officers did not fare so well,
for canteens, knapsacks, belts, and other things that might
be construed as part of their field equipment were taken
from them.

Peter was particularly pleased that he had succeeded
in saving the big military revolver, hidden at the bottom
of his bag. He did not know why, but he had a presentiment that he might still need it.

It was nearly noon when, the inspection ended, the
roll was called. No one was missing. There were fourteen
officers in all.

They were drawn up, four abreast, and one of the petty
officers who spoke a little halting German told them that
they were to remain in Kiev for the time being, and
to be lodged in the city barracks that happened to be
vacant.

When they left the square in front of the station a
huge throng, having learned in the interim that the
vengerski (Hungarian prisoners) had arrived, was waiting
for them. It was composed almost entirely of women and
children; a troop of giraffes or elephants could not have
created a greater sensation than this first detachment of
prisoners, who brought to the people of Kiev the mysterious
aspect of the enemy. Searching, frightened, curious eyes,
eyes laden with a thousand thoughts, stared at them and
clung to their clothes as they marched toward the city
between the bayonets of the soldiers.

The dense tide of the crowd surged about them, and a
muffled, confused murmur issued from its midst—but not
at all hostile or antagonistic, as they had at first believed.

Between the bayonets of the shouting Cossacks who
forced them back, the compassionate hands of women
offered food and packages to the prisoners.

A little old woman made her way to Peter and held out
a bunch of figs.

"Vosni radnjo! Vosni radnjo!" she said to him with

her trembling old lips, as if to say: "Here take it—it's for you, my dear child, take it, my child!"

And when she offered him the figs, her little tear-dimmed eyes glistened in her withered, wrinkled face and the tears she restrained distorted her lips, twisting her toothless mouth into a queer little grimace.

Peter held the sticky figs in his hand and did not know where to look. Pale and deeply moved, he gazed at the kind little old woman, who was shaking her head in tears, and whose eyes spoke her regret that she could not make herself understood to this foreign soldier. This old woman bore no resemblance to Peter's mother, and yet he had the feeling that in the midst of the human torrent eddying noisily about the streets of Kiev, his mother's heart had just risen before him.

Farther on, a young girl stopped him. A hat of sun-bleached straw shaded her face, tired and without beauty, that looked like a crushed fruit. With a timid, awkward smile she held out an orange to Peter.

"Bitteschön!" she said, her accent betraying the fact that she knew no more of German than the two words.

The hands of the others were also laden with all sorts of good things. Stefan Bartha was holding a cake and sausages as if weighing them.

He said to Peter, smiling but touched a little, nevertheless: "See, brother, what they shoot us with here!"

The farther they went into the town, the thicker grew the mob milling about them. Heads crowded the windows of the old Russian city. Women and young girls waved handkerchiefs, and in several places flowers were thrown to them. Their hearts, heavy with the terrible specters of war, suddenly lifted for a moment, and the storm that oppressed their spirits sank to a low rumbling.

The streets through which they marched presented a curious mixture of the architectures of two worlds. Beside palaces built in the European style rose bizarre Asiatic structures in wood, some small, some large, churches topped by heavy domes between slender or bulky towers and surmounted by the double cross; then fashionable streets right next to them, reeking of perfume, while squalid nooks stuffed with rubbish stood cheek by jowl with glittering Parisian shop windows. Smart officers in uniform elbowed humble, wretched *moujiks*. Tatars in their high furred caps and brilliant Kirghiz mingled with the scum of the populace, whose race and even whose sex it would have been difficult to determine. Motors flew by and proud, horse-drawn court carriages. Among these elegant carriages jogged ramshackle vehicles, hauled by lean steeds, rough-haired and shaggy, but sturdy beasts nevertheless.

At last they reached the barracks buildings where living quarters had been prepared for them. To judge by the preparations, they were going to stay in Kiev for a long time. Immediately upon their arrival they were given lunch—soup, meat—tough to be sure, but in generous quantities.

After lunch the officers were allowed to go through the town under the guard of soldiers' bayonets, to make purchases, to change money, or to telegraph.

Peter sent a short telegram to Miette, in which he said simply that they were at Kiev and that he was well. He sent an equally short wire to his mother. Telegrams were expensive, and Peter was careful of his money, half of which he had changed into rubles. He had about five hundred rubles and as much in Hungarian crowns. The other officers bought various small articles, but he spent nothing. While his comrades were in the shops he waited for them in the street, in company with a Russian soldier.

The street was bordered with shops of all kinds, and Peter amused himself by examining the articles in one of the windows.

Everything possible or imaginable was to be found there: pins, dried mushrooms, wooden combs, perambulators, furniture, saws, samovars, stags' antlers, telescopes, watches, carriage springs, feather dusters, opera glasses, wooden chairs, anvils, Caucasian daggers, sleigh bells, ax handles, carriage cushions, gilded bracelets, zithers, long, narrow bathtubs, door locks, and a huge heap of second-hand civilian clothing. The sight of this supremely absurd collection of bric-a-brac and the motley confusion of all these incongruous objects put Peter into good spirits.

Evening had come when they returned to barracks. After dinner then went to sit in the yard and chat a little. Slowly the darkness descended upon them. The men stretched themselves on the dry, dusty turf and began singing soldiers' songs, and the tunes affected them all with a deep, poignant emotion. The officers dropped their conversation; only the tips of their cigarettes burned like tiny brands in the brown, autumnal darkness. The Russian soldiers leaned against the wall and listened, too, to the foreign songs. Bartha, his legs dangling from the top step, accompanied the chorus in his deep, melodious voice.

Soon they turned in for the night. They were given no bedding, but stretched themselves out on wooden benches over which blankets, emitting a nauseating odor, had been thrown. One of the Russian officers, however, making his rounds, assured them that the officers would receive beds and bedding next day.

Peter shared a room with Franz Kölber, the Austrian ensign, who lay down promptly on his bench bed and to all appearances fell asleep at once.

But Peter did not lie down. Seated in the darkness on the edge of his bench, he began to peel the orange that the timid, ugly Russian girl had given him in the street that morning. As the juice trickled between his fingers and its pungent odor rose suddenly to his nostrils, winter evenings of other days, of his childhood years, returned to his mind. He felt his heart swell unaccountably. There, in the gloom, he sat and ate and was suddenly appalled at the thought that he was now in Kiev and would not be free for a long time, perhaps not for many months! Such a frenzy seized him that he began to fear he was losing his mind. In the midst of his anguished, confused thoughts he suddenly saw Michael Ádám standing before him. He saw his dark blue, faultlessly cut suit at the

Vargas' tea: then he saw him walking along the Danube esplanade with Miette—walking fast and passing without seeing him; and he saw Michael's face again as he raised his dark green velour hat among the snowflakes; again all those painful sensations that had beset him when he had been inadvertently switched into the midst of that senseless telephone conversation rose once more to assault his nerves.

He sat there in the blackness, on the edge of his bench, contemplating with revulsion these feelings that were taking possession of him. He had a foreboding that this specter of jealousy would never leave him in peace. He looked straight ahead with wide-open, staring eyes, as if this primitive, musty little room were filled with the creatures of a nightmare. Then closing his eyes and surrendering to his madness, he felt his spirit sucked into a whirlpool of pain.

Soon other thoughts entered his mind. He saw Miette before him in various attitudes, and bitter-sweet yearnings of love and desire made his whole body tremble.

He heard Miette's voice, so deceptively near that he might almost have believed she was really there. He saw her standing barefoot in front of the closet, arranging something in it, her nightgown falling to her ankles. Only one lamp near the bed was lighted, its glow softened by the shade, and that dim light faintly outlined, through the sheer gown, the beautiful young figure. He saw Miette's head lying next to his on the pillow, her hair spread all about in great billows of gold. He breathed the fragrant perfume of her neck and thrilled at the burning touch of her dry palm.

He lost himself in his thoughts, and because of the tension of his nerves, his faculties worked feverishly. From the beginning the idea of escape had been at the bottom of his mind; now it seized him irresistibly.

He decided to take only his revolver and his money. He would leave everything else, even his cloak and cap, lest someone should recognize him as a foreign soldier. His mind was still filled with the touching events of the

morning when the population of Kiev had proved its
sympathy as they passed through the city. "There are
people here, too," he said to himself, "who have human
feelings; perhaps they will even go so far as to help me."

He would slip into the yard, bareheaded and in his
shirt sleeves. When he got close to the edge of the barracks
wall he would jump over. Once on the other side, in the
street, escape would not be so difficult. He would hide
in some corner until morning and wait for the opening
of that shop where so many incongruous articles were
sold; there he would buy a second-hand civilian suit, a
hat, and boots. If he succeeded in all that, then his
money and, if necessary, his revolver, would help him
somehow or other to push onward. Since at the morning's
inspection he had seen the joyous grin that lighted up the
Russian officer's large face when he hid in his pocket the
field glasses presented him by Mezei—since then Peter
put all his hopes into the efficacy of his rubles.

Once more he reviewed all the details of his plan.

Outside the room was a long corridor through which
the outer passage could be reached. Sentries were posted
in the passage and in the yard, but they would certainly
be asleep. And if they weren't, it would surely be possible
to elude their vigilance on this pitch-black starless night.
If only he could get over the wall without attracting
attention, that would mean the success of his flight was
half assured.

He removed his vest warily, drew his revolver from his
knapsack, and tiptoed to the door.

Just then Kölber spoke to him in a tone that sounded
as if he had followed every one of Peter's movements
with eyes wide open in the darkness.

"Where are you going?"

His gentle, pitying voice gave Peter the feeling that
Kölber had been aware of the tremendous mental
struggle that seemed to him to have filled the whole
dark little room.

"I'll be back in a minute," he answered as calmly as
he could.

He was already in the corridor. He stood there motion-less for a moment, straining his ears toward the other end of the hall that was plunged in darkness; only at its farthest extremity a lamp burned dimly. His heart beat so violently that he felt its throbbing from his head to his very heels.

He entered the hallway, crossed it, and was on the point of slipping into the yard.

Just then something in the shadows beside him stirred, and a second later an electric torch, its light turned full in Peter's face, flashed in the hand of a soldier who was holding a gun and whose bayonet was ready for action.

"*Kuda vi idjitye?*" (Where are you going?) he yelled at him in Russian, aiming the electric light at him like a spear.

Peter mumbled something, trying meantime to explain by signs that he wished to satisfy a natural need.

The soldier, taking him by the shoulder, pushed him back with all his strength so that Peter lost his balance and fell against the doorframe.

"*Nazad!*" he roared; his eyes were popping from his head and his arm, extended in an imperious gesture, said clearly that the word meant: "Back!"

Then he pointed to a bucket in the corridor, half full of a fluid that was already diffusing a horrible odor.

Peter went back to the dark little room and tiptoed to his bed, where he collapsed just as he was, his face buried in the blankets.

IV

The first snow had already fallen. Every afternoon Miette settled herself by the living-room window with her embroidery. The snow was faintly luminous and the colors of her peasant shawl burned like cold flames about her shoulders.

One afternoon the doorbell rang, and she recognized her mother-in-law's voice before she entered the room.

"It's snowing terribly, my dear," cried Mme. Takács as the snow fell in veritable cakes from the shoulders of her plain black coat to the carpet.

"Good heavens! What a puddle I am making here!"

Her little pointed nose was ludicrously reddened by the cold, and small snowflakes clung to her blinking eyelashes.

"Have you heard the news?" she asked Miette, once she was settled in a large armchair that swallowed her almost completely. "Michael has been called to the war, and now Charlotte begs me to go and live with her in Brassó. What shall I do, my dear child?"

Peter's sister Charlotte was five years older than he and married to a lawyer named Pável. Charlotte, as a thin child with pinched nose, old beyond her years, had constantly found fault with Peter. She refused to take part in any childish pranks, always insisted that she was wiser, more intelligent, and more sensible than he. She grew to be a pretty girl, blond and attractive, desirable to men; but she was unable to hold any of them after they discovered the egotism masked by her studied sweetness. When she was twenty-four and verging on spinsterhood, she concentrated all her seductive powers upon Michael Pável, a law student. She succeeded in holding Pável. There was a certain wholesome brutality in his makeup. He wore his hair well brushed back and ate his breakfast in the morning wearing his mustache holder, so that all day long he looked as if he were ready to impale the whole world on the points of his upturned mustache. He was of Roumanian ancestry, and a foreign flavor still lingered in his rapid, nervous Hungarian.

Peter detested his brother-in-law. When he had been twenty and a second-year law student, he had found himself in serious money difficulties because of cards and other indiscretions. He decided to appeal to his sister. He knew that Pável, who had some personal means and had taken over his father's lucrative practice, was in excellent financial circumstances. He asked Charlotte if she and her husband would advance him a few hundred

crowns. It was Pável instead of Lotte who answered the
letter. Assuming a patronizing and extremely insolent
manner, he reproved Peter for his lightness of conduct
and prophesied that he would go to the dogs very quickly.
He concluded his letter with high-sounding, platitudinous
advice. But he did not send a penny.

For two long, bitter years, Peter groaned under the
burden of those small debts and finally emerged from the
experience cleansed, his will hardened. But Pável's letter
had left a deep scar. That was the principal reason why,
condemning himself at the same time, he was estranged
from his only sister.

Peter had told all this to Miette as the occasion arose;
so she had not been surprised when the Pávels took no
part in Peter's marriage save through a telegram filled
with flowery wishes. As time went on they maintained
their relationship for the sake of appearances, since there
had been no open breach between them; they sent several
cards to Brassó during their honeymoon, and Peter wrote
his sister a letter from the battlefield.

Mme. Takács was sitting in the large armchair in front
of Miette, her head a little to one side. Her eyebrows were
raised, her lips puckered, as if she were on the verge of
tears. She was little inclined to move to Brassó, but she
knew it was unavoidable. Szücs' turn had come to be
mobilized, so that Mme. Takács' cherished project of
uniting him with Aranka Vajnik had come to naught.

"Is your dear Father at home?" Mme. Takács asked
Miette affectionately, eyeing the door of Father's study
respectfully. They could hear an occasional reflective
cough or the creaking of the armchair beneath the weight
of the writer absorbed in his work.

"Do go in," said Miette.

Mme. Takács went to the door and opened it cautiously.

"May I come in?" she asked, a slight suspicion of
innocent coquetry in her voice.

Father pushed his glasses onto his forehead. He
pretended not to recognize her and inspected her several

times from head to foot, asking as he turned to Miette, "Who is this pretty young lady?"

"Don't make fun of me!" said Mme. Takács, flirting her handkerchief like a fan at Father. She sat down and gazed at the old man, wagging her head. Her eyes laughed and wept simultaneously.

It was her farewell visit. Two weeks later she was on the train bound for Brassó. She had sold most of her furniture and taken with her only such things as had tender and mournful associations. The little apartment in Hadnagy Street was rented by a Galician merchant who supplied onions to the army and had a whole flock of children.

Miette parted from her mother-in-law tenderly, her eyes filled with tears. She remained with her to the last moment and helped her pack, and when she left, Father and Miette both escorted her to the station. As Miette returned home that day she could not rid herself of a dull sense of depression. She felt that with her mother-in-law's departure, another strand of the life she shared with Peter had been broken, another fragment disappeared. This simple, neat, little old lady, with her fluttering eyes, her constantly moving head, and her sugary language, had really never meant very much in her life; but now that she was gone Miette had the feeling that her existence was the poorer by still another human being, and that she was more than ever alone.

Father, for whom Dr. Varga had prescribed some pills, seemed, thanks to the medicine, completely recovered; especially since, at Miette's plea, he had had his beard trimmed again and his face had regained its former expression. But Miette's searching, anxious eyes still found something in the old gentleman's features, in his gestures, and his dry little cough, that filled her with oppressive fear.

Miette went frequently to the Vargas' during these months and spent the greater part of her days there again, as when she had been a girl. There were occasional receptions in the doctor's apartment, where old faces and

new appeared. Occasionally she went to the theater, or
served on charity committees. She wrapped Christmas
packages, or knitted mittens for the soldiers fighting in
the Carpathians. These things forced her out of her state
of dull insensibility for an hour or two. Often she forgot
for whole days that fate had robbed her of life's loveliest
possession, and then she could be gay and high-spirited,
for the unused forces of youth accumulated within her
sought an outlet in her healthy nature.

Gradually, without even noticing it, she had abandoned
hope of seeing Peter at Christmas—that hope to which
she had clung tenaciously for months without exactly
knowing why. Day by day, war was spreading, gaining
so much ground as to submerge all plans and projects
for the immediate future.

The acutely painful longing with which, during the first
weeks, she had counted the days to Peter's return had
been gradually dulled and blunted in her heart, as time
deadens all suffering.

She had been reading a great deal. All the novels she
had gulped down, one after another, with the rapidity
and eagerness of a heart consumed by thirst in its solitude,
disposed her to revery. They opened for her those horizons
on human life which in the midst of our immense doubt
are at least a kind of vague explanation, attach at least a
negative meaning to the great mystery of the birth of
man and the goal of existence. Miette was not religious by
nature. It was due rather to the convent education she
had received that she went to church regularly and con-
scientiously, and that her evening prayers had become a
habit; but now in the very depths of her soul, weary as
she was and torn by the thorns of dark anguish, she was
turning toward God, in whose shadow she might find
rest.

Moved by fear and by some deep-rooted instinct, she
overwhelmed her father with a thousand loving attentions. She knitted a nightcap for him, she discovered by
adroit questioning what foods would tempt him, and
spent hours in consequence combing the city for a tin of

pickled Dutch herring, because Father had once expressed his liking for them. She spent whole afternoons in his room, reading him extracts from the novels that had particularly impressed her, after having told him the plot of the story. During these hours she told him stories as if he were a child.

These dreary winter afternoons, when twilight fell so early, brought back to her memory the vanished days of the previous year with Peter. In these rooms, lighted by the snow and the glow of the stove, she felt once more the sweet, searing thrills of bygone moments. She paused beside the stove, leaned her forehead against the warm enamel, and recalled their first kiss. So vividly did her imagination reconstruct those moments that not only did she see Peter, but she seemed to be actually touching him. An indescribable sweetness crept into her heart and she wandered through the rooms, driven by some inward restlessness, dropping to the couch now and then, as if all her strength had forsaken her. Her nervous tension was so great that it was only with the utmost difficulty that she refrained from giving vent in a piercing, heart-rending cry to the emotions surging within her—torturing uncertainty, longing, desperate loneliness, and ardent sensual desire. She carried these emotions about with her like a living, devouring fire, and it was only rarely that she could free herself of them or forget the suffering they caused her.

So far she had received three letters from Peter. They had all come from Kiev, where for the moment his fate held him fast. They described minutely the monotonous schedule of his life; they were full of hope and confidence, but Miette always read a certain constraint between the lines. She felt with instinctive penetration in reading these letters that Peter, in his desire and longing for her, was harrowed by intolerable physical and mental anguish but that he was careful to conceal those impulses in her direction, perhaps out of masculine vanity perhaps from a sense of shyness or tenderness. Behind these sometimes meaningless sentences, meant to encourage and console her, Miette always saw Peter's livid face, distorted by the agonies of captivity.

In one of the letters Peter wrote:

"I have been away from you four months now, my darling little Miette. Sometimes I feel I am aging a year every day. The day passes somehow, but when we go to bed and the light is out, there come horrible moments. I share a room with an Austrian ensign named Kölber, who left his fiancée at Villach. I have often heard him sobbing aloud at night, when he thinks I am sound asleep. My darling Miette, I can't tell you all that grips my heart at such times. It seems to me that I sit on my bed every night and do the same thing without realizing it. But God will help us, and I hope to be back before summer comes. Think always of me, as I do of you. Don't be discouraged if you don't hear from me, because the mails are not dependable. I have been letting my beard grow for three weeks; I'll send you a photograph soon. I look like a Russian Christ. You'll laugh yourself to death when you see it."

In none of his letters did Peter allude to his attempted escape.

Miette no longer hoped that he would return in the spring. She refused to cherish any hopes or to fix on a definite date in the near future, lest a new disappointment should hurl her into a new abyss of despair.

For some time Olga had been much in her thoughts, and one day she made up her mind to look for her; she learned from the Vargas the name of the sanatorium in which her mother had been placed and went there one morning. But she was told that the patient had been transferred some weeks before to an Austrian sanatorium, though just which one the doctor in charge didn't know; of Olga he could tell her nothing definite.

Spring came at last. Miette went now and then to the tennis courts, where the white balls were beginning to fly under the first mild rays of the young sun; but she found almost none of the old players. High-school students, still children, crowded the courts; it was rarely that a familiar face appeared, and when it did, it was that of someone already in uniform.

One evening there was a little party at the Vargas', and after dinner they sat down to cards.

The women were playing at a side table. Miette, taking no part in the game, went into the next room to rummage among the books in the hope of finding new reading matter. When she returned and sat down near the players she heard the end of a conversation begun in the course of the game. "But she was never ill, she always gave me the impression of being so full of the joy of life, so healthy and fresh!" Mme. Lénárt was saying in the tone in which one speaks of a person dead or very seriously ill, and as she spoke she shuffled the cards slowly and deliberately in her bony hands.

Mme. Varga was piling up little stacks of chips, and there was a trace of hostility in her voice as she said: "Gustave sounded her chest once about two years ago, and he said then he was afraid her lungs were affected. He told her she must be very careful of her health."

Miette didn't know whom they were talking about. From the men's table young Bogdány called: "I was at the hospital day before yesterday and the doctor who is treating her told me there was no hope for her."

Mme. Kramer laid her cards down on the table and, turning to Bogdány, said: "Will you be good enough to get the hospital on the telephone?"

The telephone stood on a small table. Bogdány went to it, lifted the receiver and asked for the number. Everyone at both tables had now laid down his cards and was watching Bogdány's face attentively. For several seconds there was a deep silence. Miette turned to Mme. Lénárt and asked in a low, timid voice: "Whom were you talking about?"

"Olga," she whispered, so as not to disturb the silence.

Miette had no time to collect her horrified thoughts, for with all her strained nerves she was watching Bogdány, who had been connected with the hospital.

He was speaking to one of his colleagues: "Will you be kind enough to tell me how Olga Syeremy is?"

Deep silence reigned once more, pierced only by the thin, ghostly, unintelligible sound of the faraway voice in the receiver.

"Thank you very much," said Bogdány as he hung up. His face was expressionless.

"Well?" someone asked, timidly breaking the silence that had fallen again.

Meantime Bogdány had gone back to his place, and it was from there that he replied: "She died at five o'clock this afternoon." He spoke impersonally, adjusting his glasses, then took up the cards that had been dealt him and arranged them carefully.

The silence of shocked emotion spread through the room and hung for an instant, while the news of this death pierced every heart like the icy blade of a dagger. But it made a different wound in each.

"The poor child!" stammered Mme. Lénárt in a voice that could hardly be heard.

Mme. Varga lowered her eyes and with slightly trembling fingers gave all her attention to making straight piles of the chips in front of her. The chill breath of death was perceptible for only a few seconds, no longer than it would take for a faint mist of breath to disappear from a clear windowpane. Mme. Varga laid her hand gently on Mme. Lénárt's arm, as if by this light, affectionate touch to awaken her from a bad dream. Her voice was soft and pitying, but it was possible to detect the sham emotion in her words, "It's your deal, my dear . . ."

The game was resumed, though they all spoke in subdued voices, as if there were a coffin in the room. Miette rose and went into an adjoining room. She was so weak that she had to lean against the table. Then she staggered into a third room that was in total darkness and threw herself into an armchair, while the tears gushed uncontrollably. She pressed her handkerchief hard against her mouth, for she didn't want those people out there to hear her and come to disturb her grief. She wanted to be alone with the memory of her poor little friend, and in her thoughts she begged forgiveness for not having told her that she had never turned away from her in her heart and had never stopped loving her after her lapse.

She was the only one to go to Olga's funeral. Some strangers stood beside the grave. It was one of those melancholy, ill-attended Pest funerals, but so drowned were her eyes in tears that she did not even see the few who were there.

V

It was early April, but the regions flooded by the Volga were still covered with snow and ice.

The commander-in-chief of the Russian army had ordered all the prisoners at Kiev to eastern Siberia. Peter's company had been sent to Tobolsk and reached the Volga bridge. Black sledges glided swiftly below them over the snow-covered surface of the great river.

At dawn they reached the station of Sviarsk on the farther bank. An escort of Cossacks was waiting for them at the station, their leader a bony-faced, red-haired *proportchik* (sergeant).

The ruddy *proportchik* did not wish to start out at once. He informed the commanding officer at Kazan that any attempt to cross the flooded regions along the Volga would still be very dangerous, but if they waited a few days longer the ice and snow would have completely disappeared, for the thaw was already setting in. He dared not take the responsibility for all the lives entrusted to him, nor for his own. Particularly, he felt a very keen responsibility for his own life.

About nine o'clock, however, orders came to set out without delay.

Despite the official prohibition of the sale of alcohol, a station employee at Sviarsk, a long, lean, fox-faced youth, gave them vodka on the sly in return for their good

money. The few mouthfuls had a bracing effect in this
damp, penetrating cold that bit through their trousers
into their legs and pierced their chests through and
through.

Meantime there were a number of interesting things to
be seen. Mounted Cossacks had been scouring the neighborhood in every direction and soon came into sight,
driving before them a crowd of grumbling Tatars who
swarmed about the station in their queerly shaped
sledges—narrow, with long, forked tails.

The prisoners climbed up and settled themselves as
best they could, with their orderlies and luggage, into the
hundred and fifty Tatar sledges arranged one behind the
other. The tails of these sledges, sweeping the snow like a
swallow's tail, were intended to prevent them from over-
turning in their headlong flight. Magnificent horses were
yoked to the sledges, powerful Tatar stallions, their huge
chests steaming in the icy cold.

The Tatar drivers, torn by the Cossacks from slumber,
had not even been given time to throw a little hay or oats
into the bottom of their sledges. Whips in hand, necks
sunk between their shoulders, they squatted in the beak-
shaped prows, resigned to their fate, awaiting the signal
for departure.

Among all these identical sledges there was one that
stood out from the rest; it was smarter than the others,
closed like a carriage, a festal sledge like a barouche. The
red-haired *proportchik* got into it and as the temperature
grew suddenly milder and a heavy rain began to fall, he
gave his orders from there.

It took more than an hour to organize the caravan and
to get all the sledges in motion.

Peter's orderly was a garment worker from Zemplen,
who understood Slovak. His father was a Slovak, but his
mother had come from the Székelys' country, which was
how he had come by the name of Moses.

This Moses Zemák was Peter's companion in fair
weather and foul. He had been made his orderly at Kiev,
where they had spent seven long, monotonous months

under a surveillance growing daily more rigid, in the
same barracks in which they had been lodged on their
arrival. They could see only one explanation for this
journey eastward—the Russian army had been obliged to
retreat and the prisoners must be driven back toward
Siberia.

Some of Peter's comrades rejoiced, for they thought this
great Russian retreat would bring peace in the spring.
This journey eastward filled Peter, on the other hand, with
dismay, for he could see only one thing—that by railroad,
by ship, by sledge, and by carriage, fate was drawing him
farther and farther onward.

As he sat there in his rumpled coat, humped over his
baggage in the sledge, looking beyond the infinite fields
of snow toward the Volga—shrouded by the leaden rain
in spectral gray as far as the eye could reach—his face,
after the winter months spent in Kiev, seemed much
older. His tormented mind, his brooding, had stamped
upon his face an expression of curious, profound, almost
animal sadness. During the few months of this captivity
he had aged several years; yet perhaps it only seemed so,
for he had let his beard grow and the heavy locks of his
long hair, which also had not been cut, fell to his ears.

Zamák, slow of movement, was still pottering about the
sledge, trying to put everything in order. With scrupulous
care he was tying to the sledge packages of food, which he
held as if they were the apple of his eye. He had a huge,
grotesque nose, shaped like a cucumber, and small deep-
set eyes whose quick glance leaped incessantly from one
object to another. There was so much natural humor, of
which he was well aware, in his uncouth manner, that he
deliberately exaggerated his awkwardness simply to
amuse the others. He had quickly grown popular with the
officers and men, and served as the target for all kinds of
jokes. Moses tolerated these pranks and pleasantries—
some of which were mild, but others painful—with an air
of superior wisdom and a wink of the eye. He would have
liked to convince himself at all costs that he was the
greatest coward on earth, whereas in reality, his was an

intrepid soul. As for Peter, whose profound grief he felt—
he did not know but only suspected its secret—he had
formed such an attachment for him that he would have
been ready at any moment to lay down his life for him.

When the traces were abruptly tightened and the whole
caravan darted forward on the smooth, immaculate snow,
more than one of the men, perched high on the narrow
sledges in the most ludicrous poses, tumbled down,
rolling like ninepins in the snow; whereupon their
luckier fellows burst into uproarious shouts. At the same
time, the little bells on the necks of the trotting horses
tinkled up and down the scale, and this procession, with
its men—some kicking in the snow, others laughing—
with the vast, circular plain surrounding them, made
Peter think of a gigantic circus, into whose arena hundreds
of clown musicians were making their entry to the
agreeable music of thousand-toned bells.

However, it was only at the beginning that the journey
proved exhilarating, either to the eye or mind. There was
no trace of road. They crossed untouched fields of snow
and in many places the sledges were plunged into ditches
and gullies. The mounted Cossacks who accompanied
them suffered most. Often it was only after heroic effort
that they were rescued, with the help of ropes, from bogs
beneath the snow, whence they and their horses emerged
covered with muddy water. The Tatar stallions were
better prepared for this pastime than the Cossack horses,
unaccustomed to the slippery river banks and the
dangerous crossings where the frozen floods of melting
snow were beginning to mutter.

Peter's Cossack was a stubby little lad who looked like
a good fellow. He trotted beside the sledge for hours in
silence, following all its movements with unremitting
vigilance and obvious good will.

At their first stop Peter offered his Cossack some lunch
and a cigar, and the soldier, cigar in mouth, strutted in
the midst of his comrades, spitting long, sharp jets of
saliva from the corner of his mouth into the snow,
exactly as if he had been born on the banks of the Tisza!

Moses struck up a great friendship with the Cossack. He spoke Slovak to him and somehow always managed to understand him. The Cossack told him that they should have reached their halting place for the night by midday, since it was scarcely eighteen miles away, but the thaw and the floods were forcing them into a wide detour and they would be lucky if they reached Ceitovo by midnight.

He had guessed correctly, for it was very close to midnight when they heard the barking of dogs from distant snow fields that gleamed pearly white as far as the eye could see beneath the pale rays of the moon. Far away on the horizon tiny orange lights glimmered faintly.

When the little group to which Peter and Zamák belonged reached Ceitovo at last, the others had long since aroused the village, and many had already eaten their supper and gone to bed.

Peter and a few other officers—among whom were Kölber, Bartha, and Lieutenant Neteneczky, who, small and fat and looking like a huge ball, was called simply "Netene"—were billeted in the house of a rich, hospitable Tatar.

The Tatar had two wives. Both were slovenly, with flat faces on which the paint was very apparent. They stained their front teeth, according to the Tatar custom, with some black substance, which rendered their smiles of welcome somewhat grisly.

"Children," Neteneczky whispered, "they are going to serve us with pitch for dinner here," and bowed to the Tatar women with as much courtesy as he would have shown to society women in the little city on the farther side of the Danube where he taught mathematics in the high school.

The host was a broad-shouldered man of about forty, with a powerful, bulky torso. They learned later that his name was Jak Michailov Ragusin.

The Tatar, after having greeted his guests, gave an order to one of his wives. She knelt before a chest of painted, variegated wood with copper nails and decorations. She opened it, and as the key turned in the lock, pleasant, melodious sounds, like those of a zither, issued from it. It was the famous musical chest of the Tatars—sensitive strings were so arranged that if a thief attempted to open it, the lock emitted sounds of alarm.

The women pulled queerly shaped cooking utensils from the chest, some of which were made of silver.

Meantime the guests disposed themselves as best they could about the large room. Peter's Cossack hastened to remove his boots, which were wet through and, together with the bandages that wrapped his feet, placed them carefully on the ledge of the stove, whence a thick vapor promptly arose.

But this had no effect upon the air of the room, which was already so heavy and dense that no new odor could possibly have added anything. Yet the boots and bandages did all they could in that direction as the steam issuing from them grew thicker and thicker.

There was a kind of small platform in the center of the room upon which the samovar rested, surrounded by moldy-looking metal cups. Carpets and animal skins were spread on the floor around the platform. But tables, chairs, or beds were nowhere to be seen. The room was heated not only by the stove and the family, but domestic animals contributed their share. Two calves and several sheep occupied one of the corners, hens and cocks slept on the other side. In the third corner of the immense room the Tatar's children slept among six white lambs.

The Tatar women gave their hosts steaming tea and hard-cooked eggs. The officers offered them sardines and other European food, which the amazed Tatars turned over and over in their dirty fingers without daring to eat.

The conversation was carried on by signs and gestures. It proceeded amicably, dealing with simple topics. After the meal they lay down on the straw-covered floor and, exhausted by the long, wearisome sledge ride, immediately fell into deep slumber.

Toward morning Peter's Cossack shook him awake.

"*Podjam, Gospodin Kapetán!*"

For some unknown reason he took Peter for a captain.

Perhaps because he was the only one of the officers who had let his beard grow.

Zamák had been standing outside the house for a long time, engaged in hurling frozen clods of earth at the ravens, who were perched by thousands on willow stumps around the house and had been making a hideous racket with their croaking since early dawn. Moses was trying to rout them so that they wouldn't disturb the poor sleeping officers; naturally, as each clod was thrown, the ravens flew off, whirling in black swarms and croaking louder than ever.

The officers, on awaking, felt their hands, their faces, and their necks, for there was no dearth of bugs and lively roaches in this Tatar house. Efforts to destroy bugs and other domestic parasites did not succeed in this country, for among the Tatars it was a sin to kill a cockroach; they looked upon it as a domestic animal, pleasant and sociable.

A fierce snowstorm was raging when they awoke. Having finished packing as best they could and bade farewell to their hosts, the caravan was once more ready for departure.

The haze was so dense as they started off that they had difficulty in distinguishing the sledge immediately preceding theirs.

At about ten they were obliged to halt at the Tatar village of Devlakitch, for the roads ahead of them were flooded. A thin coating of ice had formed, but it wasn't solid enough to carry them to the ford of the Sviaga River. Yet this village was so squalid and miserable that even the red-haired *proportchik* dared not stop. Therefore he gave the order to push on, whatever the consequences.

And the ice broke. One after another the sledges plunged beneath it. The feats of the Tatar stallions—their epic struggle with this treacherous, snare-pitted earth—actually bordered on the miraculous. They seemed to feel that these human lives had been entrusted to them. Neighing madly, champing the ice in fury, they forged onward, heads lowered, tense with the strain on all their muscles, over blocks of ice that were constantly breaking and turning beneath their feet. They slipped, they stumbled, but scaled and finally crossed them. The music of the jingling bells at their necks was lost in the crackling of the ice and in the shouts coming from every direction through the haze—hysterical, furious, despairing—some even filled with mortal agony.

At last after an hour of anguished struggle they reached the embankment and the ferryman's house without the loss of human life. The ferryman had two boats, but the towing ropes had been carried away a few days before by the flood. There remained only one way to attempt the crossing among the drifting ice cakes—with the help of what instruments they had, poles and spades. A huge throng crowded into the first boat; scarcely had they reached the center of the current when an iceberg, descending the stream, broke the rudder. The current carried those on board—Kölber and Netene among them—downstream, and till late at night the others remained in harrowing uncertainty of their fate. But they finally succeeded, no one knew how, in reaching shore.

The boat Peter boarded was steered by the ferryman himself. He was a heavily built Russian, with bushy hair and a mustache like a seal's. But the expression of his face was all kindness and softness. His large, shapeless, waterproof boots reached to his hips. He followed a different course from that of the other boat and at the instant of shock turned his moth-eaten craft to form an acute angle with the current. As they neared the shore they ran several times onto a sandbank, and each time he waded into the water in his big boots. The icy water reached not only his hips but his very armpits. Yet he moved about in it as another might move in a warm bath. He worked away with the help of harpoons and great hooked iron rods; submerged at times to the neck, he would cast encouraging little smiles at the men in the boat. He put infinite enthusiasm into his work.

Bartha, who was a landsman, clung with both hands to

the edge of the boat, shivering with cold, and shouting in Hungarian each time the boat pitched heavily: "Look out, brother; don't let us drown!" Whereupon they all shouted with laughter.

After a half hour of strenuous effort they were landed on the opposite shore, beneath the willows. Then there was another sledge ride, much like that of the day before, punctuated by tumbles into the snow, and early in the afternoon they reached the large Russian village of Serjebinsk. The weather had cleared, and the officers stopped for a moment in the square near the church to rest and bask a little in the sunlight.

As they sat against the wall on their piled-up baggage, waiting for the sledges to be changed, the wrought-iron gate of a pretty house on the other side of the square, with two dark poplar trees in front of it, opened suddenly and an attractive young woman with the air of a European approached them.

She addressed the officers in somewhat halting German: "May I invite you in for a little meal, gentlemen?"

She was slender, with the eyes of a gazelle, and a curious sadness lurked in her sweet, soft voice.

They all jumped up and introduced themselves with great ceremony to the strange young woman, who led them into her house; on the gate was fastened a brass plate bearing the curious inscription: "Zemsky Vrasch!" Once inside, they learned that they were in the house of the district doctor.

A few minutes later the table was set in the dining room and they were served delicious tea, preserves, cream, slices of tempting cold fowl, roast pork, sausages, desserts made of flour and honey, and all kinds of little cakes. The perfect cleanliness of the tablecloth, the luster of plates and glasses, the glittering silverware, all this was the work of their Russian hostess' lovely, delicate hands. She was no longer in her first youth, but there was infinite spiritual sweetness in her rather tired face, and a quiet beauty that was just beginning to fade.

The parqueted rooms were furnished in European style.

A piano could be seen in the living room, which opened onto the dining room.

Presently the doctor appeared. His name was Nicolas Ivanovitch Krylov. He was a tall, blue-eyed man, a little stooped. He cast mournful, absentminded glances here and there as his blond, silky locks kept falling over his forehead. He told them that in his youth he had lived for a long time in Germany, that he retained a very kindly feeling for the German people, and looked upon this war between the two countries as a terrible punishment at the hand of God. His wife had died recently, and it was his sister, Katerina Ivanovna Ilyina—whose husband, an artillery officer in the Russian army, had been taken prisoner in January—who kept house for him.

Then Katerina Ilyina spoke. "Sir," she said, turning her frank, sad face toward one of the officers, "I was informed a few weeks ago, through the Red Cross, that my husband had been sent to Hungary." Her voice trembling, she added apprehensively: "Do you happen to know how war prisoners are treated in Hungary?"

There was a moment of silence; then all the Hungarian officers spoke at once.

"Oh! In Hungary! Well, then he is all right! You may be quite sure of that, Madame."

They vied with each other in reassuring the beautiful Russian.

Katerina Ilyina pressed her handkerchief to her eyes. The doctor, also overcome by emotion, stared at his plate.

Lieutenant Vedres turned to the wife of the Russian officer and asked: "Do you know to what city your husband was taken, Madame?"

"Oh yes . . . Kemiermeso . . ." she replied in a tone of discouragement.

"Estregram . . ." said the doctor, realizing from the lieutenant's expression that he didn't recognize the city.

Suddenly Neteneczky burst forth joyously, "Kenyermezo! Yes, yes—near Esztergom."

"But that's very close to Budapest!"

"A few miles at most! And on the banks of the Danube; enchanting country!"

From all sides there were attempts to console her, and, her cheeks flushed, Katerina Ilyina let her eyes wander from one to the other of the officers, as she listened agitatedly to their description of the conditions of life down there.

Then, wringing her hands and twisting her fingers together, she cried piteously, "If only I could see my husband just once more . . ." And hardly had she finished the words when she burst into tears.

The officers comforted her with all the kindness of which they were capable; Peter alone, pale and silent, did not take his eyes from the table.

They sat around the laden table for another half hour, then the officers went out into the yard to assemble their baggage and load it into the fresh sledges that had just arrived.

Peter remained behind; he was still in the room when all the others had left, together with the doctor who had gone to escort the officers. He approached Katerina Ilyina who, choked with tears, was beginning to clear the table.

He stood in front of her and looked deep into her eyes; "Madame, I should like to speak to you . . ."

There was such a strange tone in his voice that the young woman, startled, laid the plate in her hand on the table and raised her eyes in astonishment to Peter's. Then she moved toward the living room and, opening the door, said agitatedly: "Come this way, please."

When they were facing each other in the living room, Peter asked: "What is your husband's name, Madame?"

"Alexander Petrovitch Ilyin. He is an engineer."

She riveted her eyes on Peter's face, as if trying to unravel the meaning of his question.

With an instinctive gesture Peter closed the door behind him, lest someone overheard what he was about to say. He was ghastly pale and supported himself against the table, closing his eyes as he spoke: "Madame—I am horribly unhappy; I cannot endure captivity—I'm afraid I shall go mad—I have lived only a few months with my wife, with whom I am desperately in love. Help me—so that I can escape and reach Hungary! If I succeed in getting back to my country, your husband's fate will be in my hands—I have influential connections, my father-in-law is an important official. I swear that I will do everything possible in your husband's interests."

Immediately, without giving the young woman time to answer, he continued in an access of excitement: "Believe me—nothing is impossible if only the will is strong enough—I think I can lag behind the caravan toward evening and come back here at night—you could prepare civilian clothes for me, and it might even be possible to secure some kind of papers. If I can only get to the frontier I should manage somehow to get home—perhaps across Roumania."

His forehead glistened with perspiration as he spoke, and he looked at Katerina Ilyina with a strange light in his eyes.

"Think of your husband, Madame," he added imploringly, and at the same time commandingly.

Peter's words stirred the engineer's wife to the depths of her heart, and she sank weakly into an armchair.

Peter remained standing before her, leaning against the piano.

Katerina Ivanovna was still unable to reply. She passed her soft hand over her forehead, feeling it, as if she wanted to force into a calmer channel the thoughts that were whirling madly behind it.

There was a long, profound silence—so long that Peter cast an anxious glance toward the door, fearing lest they be interrupted before she had answered him.

Katerina Ilyina finally raised her gentle light-brown eyes to Peter and said in a scarcely audible voice: "What you want to do is impossible! I would willingly risk anything to help you, but—believe me—I cannot send you to certain death. You don't know Russia and you don't know its police—oh, especially now, in wartime. You would be arrested at the very next town and—I'm not sure, of course, but probably shot down. It is tempting God, what you want to do—I'm not strong enough to help you—don't attempt it, I beg of you. How much longer can the war last? It can't go on for years like this —perhaps only a few months more. Listen to me, believe me—it will be better for you to wait for the end of the fighting . . ."

She fell silent and it was apparent from her expression that she was struggling once more with her thoughts. Then she continued as if she had reached her decision anew, on the basis of what she had just been thinking.

"No—no—it would be madness! Think! I have everything to gain—it is only your life that I'm risking— but my conscience will not permit me to advise this thing."

Peter was standing beside her, pale as death. He did not raise his eyes, but continued to stare fiercely at an invisible spot on the floor. "I pity you with all my heart," she said so low as to be scarcely audible, and pressed her handkerchief against her mouth.

Someone whom Peter could not see opened the door. He forced himself to smile, walked up to Katerina Ivanovna, and, bowing low, kissed her hand in silence.

He went out into the yard with the fixed smile still on his lips.

The sledges, to which fresh horses had been harnessed, were drawn up in front of the house, ready to depart. The officers were already perched high on top of their baggage.

It was about five in the afternoon. According to the instruction of the *proportchik*, they were to reach Ivanska, a Tatar village about ten miles to the East, before nightfall.

The sun had disappeared from the sky, and heavy gray clouds had gathered low over their heads. Enormous flocks of crows were croaking above the damp-smelling snow fields. Slowly the darkness fell, and the little bells of the Tatar horses filled the snowy, desolate plains with a strange music as the black sledges flew over them like a flock of migrating swallows.

A moment later the snow began to fall again in enormous flakes.

VI

It was already one in the morning and through the open window waves of warm, balmy May air entered the room. The hills of Buda were bathed in constantly clouding moonlight as light and shadow followed each other alternately across the sky. The hills seemed to hover and wave in the slow tide of these huge billows of light and shadow. A fierce wind howled through the trees, and high above the moon leapt through the clouds. This mute, mournful flight of the moon produced an almost frightening effect. Miette bent her white neck at an acute angle as she wrote. Every word, almost every stroke of the pen was accompanied by a quick, sensitive facial change. Tomi, stretched among the cushions, breathed noisily, almost like a human being, rising from time to time to stretch and look for a more comfortable spot.

Father had been in bed a long time; the house was so quiet that the slightest noise stirred fantastic echoes. One could hear the faint scratching of pen on paper in the silence of night.

". . . I received a letter from your mother yesterday. It is filled with tears and worries about you. What can I write to her, though? What consolation can she expect from me? I have lost almost all my energy and there is no one about who can comfort me. It is dreadful, being so alone. I don't really know which of us suffers most. I often find myself wishing that something would happen, some physical pain, or anything that would change the course of my thoughts that circle round and round in a mad whirl.

"I know I have no right to complain, I who live surrounded by the same people as before, in the same house, with the same familiar things. Father is with me, and my friends are here, too, while your own fate is horrible.

"And yet, Peter darling, believe me when I tell you that my fate is perhaps harder to bear than yours. I am a woman, weaker and softer perhaps than any other woman I know, while you men are differently constituted; sometimes I cry all night long. If you realize this struggle that is going on within me, please remember always that it is only because of you I am so miserable, and that God has imposed the same suffering on me as on you. And let your knowledge of my unhappiness be a consolation to you, in so far as my love can console you, for my suffering means that I love you, that I am waiting for you, that I want you; that without you my life, my room, my bed, everything is horribly sad and empty.

"You ask me how I live? I get up at about ten in the morning, then Mili brings me my breakfast in bed, because I am sometimes overcome by such exhaustion that I hardly have the strength to get up. The morning goes somehow or other, and I am as slow in performing my tasks as the days are slow in passing. I put both our rooms in order myself now, and often do the marketing, because Mili's legs always hurt. But I have plenty of time to do it before two, and sometimes it's three before we sit down to lunch. Now and then I stop to chat with the grocery woman at the corner—you know, the poor thing —her husband was killed. And then I go to buy cigars and spend another half hour there with Gisele. After lunch, I keep Father company for a while and toward evening go out with him for his walk. He's been looking ill again lately, and eats so little that it breaks my heart. I don't know what it can possibly be; I get no satisfaction from Varga, who keeps telling me it's nothing; but I'm so worried about him that I sometimes get up at night and go quietly on tiptoe to his room, and listen to his breathing in the darkness. Why aren't you with me then? It's horrible to rush through these dark rooms, that way, barefoot—in a nightgown. I don't know why, but some terrible suspicion, a kind of confused fear, drives me there. I am afraid, perhaps without cause. It is strange, but sometimes I am seized by forebodings of death, and now death is everywhere, all around us and close. I can't get used to the idea; I can't convince myself that Olga is dead!

"After dinner the Vargas often come in; we go to the cinema, too—you know the one, near the house; mostly Mili and I go alone because, you remember, Father can't endure the cinema. I have been twice to the theater altogether. I don't like to go, because I can't keep myself from crying. Elvira persuaded me to go to one of those convalescent homes and become a nurse like herself. I went twice, but I shan't go again, because these women with their starched white blouses and their antiseptic scent don't appeal to me. Elvira is so self-important that she gets on my nerves. She's in her element now, working from morning till night, and has already received some decoration from the Red Cross. I can't make myself look at these poor soldiers in their sickness and misery. Some of them are really ill, but some are humbugs, too. Young Madarás, for instance, has been loafing around the hospital for months, convalescing. And Elvira, with her gossiping tongue, brings me all the scandal, everything that they are saying about Mme. Galamb. Believe me when I tell you that people aren't worth bothering with. I prefer to be alone with my books.

"A few days ago I met Sigismund Pán in the street, in uniform. He has been mobilized into the infantry and was dressed as a private. God forgive me, but I was almost ill with laughter when I saw him! He told me that he had lost absolutely all respect for the monarchy, since soldiers like himself were allowed in the army. Paul Szücs came to the house on Thursday; he was in Budapest on a few days' leave. He has won the gold medal for bravery and he talks faster than ever. He swore by all his gods that the war would be over in two months, and he said it with such an air and in such a tone that you would have thought he was going to end it himself! He said to me,

'Little lady, you can spit in my face if Peter isn't back in six months!' Oh if it's only true! I can't believe in it anymore, but I was glad to see Szücs, to be torn for a moment from this awful lethargy in which I live. I like this Paul Szücs, and I told him to come soon again. I asked him if he wasn't thinking of marrying, but he said that he was an enemy of women and was through with them for the rest of his life. Late yesterday afternoon I was walking along the street with Father, and although it was getting dark, I am pretty sure I saw Szücs and Rose, the Vargas' maid, walking together. I pretended not to recognize them. They squeezed against the wall and Szücs put his hand in front of his face. But I think it was they, because when I met Rose on the stairs today, she turned red as a poppy.

"Of Johnny I know only that he is an ensign, and that he has been somewhere on the northern front for a long time. I got this news, too, from Szücs.

"My darling Peter, I am sending you in the next package six sets of underwear. I knitted the four pair of warm socks myself, but I bought the sweater ready made. Father sends you the tobacco, but he must have written you himself and I will enclose the letter with the package. We are not sending you more things, since you wrote that the packages are always opened and arrive with half of the contents missing. You didn't tell me in your last letter whether you received the little cushion I sent you. It is really awful that whole months go by before we receive answers, or our letters cross; there is no connection between them; it is as if, each from his own side, we were calling incomprehensible things to each other across this hideous distance!

"I received your last letter yesterday, the one you wrote on the way. Oh, how terrible that Volga River must be! I have already spoken to Father. He knows General Várkonyi, the commander of the Esztergom Camp, very well. I shall go there myself one day next week and do all I can for Alexander Petrovitch Ilyin.

"Take good care of yourself, my love! Don't be too

impatient. If we bear this trial submissively, you will see, God will help us and make up to us for all the suffering we have endured. I await your return as though you had left only yesterday; I still put your nightclothes near the pillow on your bed every evening. Not a single hour passes when I don't think of you. Father and I speak of you and keep you constantly in our thoughts.

"Now you know everything that has happened since I wrote my last letter to you. Oh, God, is it really possible that it will soon be a year since I last saw you? And the future is so uncertain!

"I am sending this letter to Tobolsk; I suppose you will have been there a long time when it reaches you.

"May God keep you, my dear one! Think of me, love me! Love your Miette, who is so sad . . ."

At this point she paused, for her eyes were filled with tears and she could not make out what she was writing. Her brimming eyes wandered from one object to the next on the desk with a poignant look of fear and supplication, as if she wanted to fly she knew not where, in search of help. Then she leaned her head on her arms and wept unrestrainedly.

Tomi crawled off the couch, went to her and, standing on his hind legs, begged for a place on her lap. But Miette pushed him away.

Gradually she grew calmer. With the little handkerchief that she held crushed in her hand as she wrote, she patted lightly and carefully the tears that had fallen on the polished wood of the table.

Then dipping her pen in the inkwell once more, she continued her letter:

". . . I shall never stop loving you. Hold me tight in your thoughts, as I hold you constantly in mine.

"It is past two in the morning; I can hear the moaning of the wind outside and the moon shines with a strange light. I am going to sleep now.

"I read a piece of poetry in the paper yesterday. I read it to Father, too, then I cut it out to send you, and now I can't lay my hands on it. It's disappeared, I don't know

where. The poem was called 'A Message to Tobolsk.'
Father had tears in his eyes when I finished reading it to
him. I read it over so often that I almost know it by
heart, so I am writing it down for you from memory.

I send you this by the mists,
Will it reach you, lieutenant prisoner?
O, distant Mongolia is infinite;
Thousands of leagues form your prison walls.
We live as of yore, we live,
The clock ticks, the lamp burns.
The sinister wind howls through the night of Tobolsk,
The white snowflakes fall in a dreadful harvest.
The valiant prow of my soul cleaves
The immense ocean, the Mongolian plain;
And beyond the mists, the abysses, the seas,
I clasp your hand, your desperate hand . . .

"May God protect you, my darling Peter! I send you
millions and millions of kisses. I think of you always, and
I am always yours, yours who loves you forever,

"Miette."

It was almost three before she was ready to get into
bed. She opened the window of her room and stood for a
long time looking out, watching the clouds careering
across the sky in the moonlight and listening to the
soughing of the wind.

A few days later, armed with a letter from Father, she
went to Esztergom to see General Várkonyi, the commander of the prison camp. She arrived in the afternoon,
and the general immediately accompanied her to the
quarters of the Russian officers to look for Alexander
Petrovitch Ilyin.

On the wide avenue of this city of war prisoners they
encountered a large group of Russians in their flat caps;
there were perhaps hundreds of them, but they looked so
much alike that it almost seemed as if a great number of
copies had been made of the same person. They carried
in their hands tin plates that clashed occasionally, and
they made Miette think of a flock of sheep, with little
bells at their necks.

"What is that?" Miette asked.

The general began to laugh.

"They are the Russian prisoners. We couldn't find enough cloaks for them, so we bought up the stocks of a bed-cover manufacturer. When they go walking they never fail to throw these cheap red blankets over their shoulders."

They reached the building reserved for the officers, whence issued a humming sound like a swarm of bees. There was singing inside, and through an open window came the sound of a balalaika.

The petty officer who was with them went in and reappeared a moment later with a Russian prisoner whose hair was rumpled and whose epaulettes were the only sign of his rank. He was a short, puny-looking man and staggered along beside the officer, as if he had just crawled out of a dark corner and was dazzled by the glare of light. When he heard that the general wanted to speak to him, his eyes betrayed mortal terror; perhaps he thought they were going to shoot him on the spot.

The officer led Alexander Petrovitch Ilyin to Miette and the general. Miette took a step toward him.

"Parlez-vous français?" she asked in a voice that gave evidence of a struggle with tears.

"Oui, Madame," Alexander Petrovitch answered, turning pale and casting an anxious glance toward the general.

"My husband is a war prisoner, too," said Miette softly, hesitating a little over the French words.

Petrovitch Ilyin, holding his breath, raised his eyes to hers.

"One day in Russia he was received into your brother-in-law's house and treated very kindly. He promised your wife that he would write to me and that I would try to make things easier for you."

The pallid man gazed at Miette and seemed not to have understood what he had just heard.

"Your brother-in-law is a physician at Tchelbinsk, isn't he?"

"Serjebinsk," he corrected her, throwing a nervous

glance behind him without any reason.

"I have already spoken to the general—you will have news in a few days."

Again Alexander Petrovitch cast a brief glance at the general, who evidently had a reputation for harshness and severity among the prisoners. The general did not look at him, but thoughtfully contemplated the ash on his cigar, deliberately detaching himself from any situation—like this one—not strictly in accordance with regulations.

"You are an engineer?"

"Yes, Madame . . ." He stepped back a pace, thinking that no one would notice; he was ashamed of his boots, which were worn to shreds.

Miette held out her hand.

"Goodbye, sir . . ."

Alexander Petrovitch looked at his own hands and, seeing that they were not clean, extended one reluctantly in an awkward and embarrassed gesture, so that Miette had to grasp his fingers as they hung hesitantly in the air.

She nodded and smiled, the general touched his hand to his cap, and Alexander Petrovitch Ilyin turned on his heel to go back to the barracks. But he took a direction exactly opposite that leading to the officers' quarters, and it wasn't until he had gone half way that he turned suddenly and went back the right way.

"The poor fellow is frightened," said the general as they walked back.

"Yes," said Miette, sighing. Her heart was filled to over-flowing with all kinds of sensations. She felt happy.

Next day she went in person to see one of the directors of the Ganz factories whom she had known for many years, and asked him to put the Russian engineer, Alexander Petrovitch Ilyin, to work.

VII

Brilliant sunshine by day and the silvery glow of moon-light by night accompanied the Russian steamer *Ermak* up the Irtysh River toward Tobolsk. The eastern shore rolled away flat and empty, while perpendicular cliffs alternated with undulating hills on the western shore.

The country they were traversing resembled that of the Volga, but there was no trace of snow anywhere, and the stifling closeness of the Siberian summer lay heavy over the marshy, yellow river. Occasionally the boat would pass a shabby wharf or a wretched, commonplace little village.

One afternoon a violent storm burst over this monotonous country, obliterating the outlines of both shores, while the waters of the Irtysh rolled muddier and yellower than ever.

After the storm the skies cleared toward the East and the sun peeped through the thick dark-gold clouds tumbling over each other. The whole landscape was flooded in a strange red-gold light that burst in slanting rays from beneath the clouds and lighted the tops of the willows with a celestial radiance. A large flock of wild ducks flew alongside the steamer through these slanting rays, their emerald-green necks glittering like brilliant turquoise necklaces in the golden light. They passed so low and close in their rapid flight that their heavy, shapeless bodies all but collided with the smokestacks.

Bartha and Vedres, who were sitting on the deck on their luggage, were amusing themselves by aiming at each duck as it flew by, imitating meanwhile the report of a gun. "Pan! Pan!" came the sound of an explosion, now from Vedres, now from Bartha.

After about ten minutes of these alternating "Pans!" Bartha asked Vedres, "Well how many have you brought down?"

"Twenty-one!" answered Lieutenant Vedres gravely and earnestly. He was an officer in the regular army, but there was nothing in him of the military man ossified by his calling. He belonged to that class of infantry officers who, before the war, remained first lieutenants until they grew bald, owing money to every headwaiter in the country, thoroughly disgusted with their profession, and always hopeful that a brilliant marriage would liberate them before long. But their reputations were such that the fathers of well-to-do families feared them like the plague. Vedres, a silent man with a dry humor, raised his arm to fire at a new flock that had just made its appearance and this time discharged a remarkable double volley into its midst.

Attracted by these noisy "Pan-pans!" Zamák, too, drew near and, blinking in the sunshine, measured the great wild ducks in their lazy flight with an expert eye.

"These birds are much larger than ours at home," he commented familiarly.

"Get away from here!" Bartha roared at him. "Don't interfere in gentlemen's affairs!"

Zamák sauntered away, not without a glance over his shoulder at the hunters as he exploded into laughter.

Peter was standing in the prow of the boat, watching the billowing yellow waves that broke against the keel. Sorrow, dark and leaden, weighed on his heart. The movement of the ship gave him the feeling that there wasn't a tree or a branch left behind on the shore that wasn't waving him a farewell; that under the somewhat shaky planks of the deck, the engines, making such a deafening clatter with their mad steel arms, apparently demolishing themselves, were through the very desperation of their efforts carrying him farther and deeper into the East.

Where, toward what fate, was it taking him over the waters of the strange river?—this Russian steamer reeking of tar . . . A year of captivity already! Flung from one spot to another in this terrible Russian desert! After the months of deadly boredom spent in the barracks of Kiev, they had wandered hopelessly through the flooded, snow-covered valley of the Volga, waiting for weeks and even months in wretched Tatar villages—Cheliabinsk, Kurgan, Petropavlovsk, Tetiuch, Sizram—savage, terrifying names of towns and villages that buried themselves like painful, lacerating thistles in the brain. Where and when would the *Ermak* land? On the shore in what dreadful year?

These aimless comings and goings, wrecking the mind and body, this uncertainty that destroyed the soul, had lasted now for a year. Their uniforms, their single pairs of shoes had long since fallen into shreds. It was with the greatest difficulty that Zamák's needle kept the rents and patches together. They looked like men whose clothes had been torn by wolves. Once, at the beginning of the summer, a Jewish merchant had whispered to them that Lublin had fallen and that the Germans were marching on Warsaw. For days and days this secret hope had pulsed within them like a wild heart throb—then the order had come depriving them of their swords and forbidding officers to wear the insignia of their rank. And now they were being driven eastward again; always farther, always deeper into hell!

If he could at least endure his fate like the others! The others, his comrades—they could laugh, they could play stupid, childish tricks on each other, but his thoughts congealed into heavy icicles that pierced and hung from his heart . . .

Perhaps this life wasn't reality—nothing but a strange, disturbing phantasmagoria . . . The Irtysh river—the *Ermak*—in front of them no one knew where, Tobolsk—could this be reality?

He looked down at the waves dashing against the boat's keel, and suddenly remembered the *Neptune*. He saw all about him the clear dome of the sky over Lake Balaton and the mirror of water gleaming beneath the sun's rays, so smooth that the silvery thistledown seemed to be skating over it. Yes, he saw Miette, her hair unbound, and, straining all his senses, he sought to recover the tiniest, subtlest memories of that Sunday afternoon, as if to find there the invisible, imperceptible point at which the thread of his former life had been broken.

"Miette—Miette—Miette," the wheels of the engine groaned as the *Ermak*, in its fearful struggle against the powerful current of the Irtysh, strove to pursue its course upstream.

Hundreds of conflicting thoughts crossed his mind, beginning with the moment when he had met Miette. Reckoning the time, he realized that it had been just two years ago to the day when he had been strolling through the streets of Buda one Sunday afternoon, asking himself whether or not he should go to the Vargas' tea. He had known nothing of Miette then, had been unaware of her very existence—and suddenly the memories of that afternoon swooped down upon him; so close did he feel those moments out of the past that he all but lived them again. Coming from a direction that he couldn't quite gauge, he heard over the hills of Buda the plaintive tones of a tárogato that seemed to be bidding a melancholy farewell to summer. Had only two years passed since then? The memory seemed to him to have emerged from some unreal, fantastic remoteness of his life.

Then the moment when he had analyzed the hand-writing—when following Paul Szücs, a white hand suddenly rested on the paper. It took the pen gently and the purple letters glided over the white paper with a thin sweet sound.

Miette Almády . . .

In his anguished heart he lived over again that moment when, turning his head, he had seen standing before him in the shaded light of the lamp a girl with dark gold hair smoothing her glove over her pretty hand. There she stood with lifted eyebrows and half-lowered lids, a faint, hardly perceptible blush mantling her cheeks.

Miette!

As he stood in the prow of the boat, his fixed gaze bent on the rushing waters, her image blended, by the strange power of hallucination, with the yellow, clay-colored waters. The weary *Ermak* panted up the Irtysh. Yes, Miette was standing there in the lamplight; her lips were curved in a gay, mocking smile as she looked down at him, with a little kindly contempt in her eyes for the whole science of graphology, and her head bent to one side in an attitude that was at once grave, meek, and virginal. Yes, that was the moment that had penetrated all his being. There was no escape from the sweet, agonizing pain of it. It emerged in sounds from the clatter of the *Ermak's* engines; it emerged in light from the Siberian dusk; it was a perfume in the breeze that fluttered along the western shore. Someone was playing a Mongolian zither between decks, and the vibrations of that melancholy music held it, too. It flowed in burning, restless streams from every direction like a persistent, distracting thought that will under no conditions release its hold on the weary, throbbing brain that is its prey.

"Miette, Miette, Miette," something in him sobbed, and his fingers clutched the rail so savagely that they all but buried themselves in the wood.

Suddenly these torturing thoughts abated their violence; and in their stead terrifying phantoms began whirling through his mind.

His thoughts of Miette were never for an instant free of Michael Ádám's figure, outlined somewhere against the background, now smudged and half-effaced, now lighted by the morbid glow of his tortured imagination. He could not explain this association of ideas, but his imagination, struggling in the darkness, continued to seize upon the well-groomed Ádám, in his faultlessly cut suit; and he would see the figure, to which he himself had given life, approaching Miette's bed. He knew that Ádám's father was a general, and that if Michael had been mobilized he must surely have obtained a safe berth in Pest.

He knew from one of Miette's letters of Olga's death, but the news had not troubled him—indeed, had hardly touched him. His own suffering made him an egoist, and for him Olga's death meant only that someone had vanished from Miette's horizon who in his eyes represented the rejection of virtue and feminine morality, represented freedom impatiently grasped at, and the outcry of famished love. On him Olga's death had had almost a tranquilizing effect.

The sun was very low on the horizon, its orb an amazing shade of violet. The left bank was growing more and more rugged and precipitous. The river, describing a gigantic, almost circular arc, received the dark waters of the Tobol, whose current forced its bed westward. The high banks were left behind and, before the sun had set, the city of Tobolsk appeared in the near distance on a flat peninsula whose landscape was at once magnificent, savage, terrible, and enchanting.

Describing a large curve, the boat made for the wharf just as another passenger steamer was leaving it.

A military detachment awaited them at the pier. They passed through the city in the heavy evening heat between the bayonets of Russian soldiers.

The dirty wooden houses of the lower city of Tobolsk, the principal Tatar section, extend along the bank of the Irtysh. Beyond the Tatar settlement, on the high upland, rises the city of Russian officialdom, dominated by the old fort that hides beneath its round watchtowers and within its bastioned dungeons hundreds of convicts and political prisoners.

The hill rises like a cliff above the Tatar city, and pedestrians mount a flight of wooden steps to reach the high city, where the domes of beautiful Russian churches glitter yellow, blue, and red-gold on sunny days.

The streets of the higher city, roads as well as sidewalks, are covered with excellent wooden planks of the thickness of a hand. Yet they are very much neglected, rarely cleaned and in many places rotted through. They are strewn, too, with decaying oranges, melon rinds, all sorts of refuse, and especially with the husks of sunflower seeds that everyone spits about everywhere.

At the moment only a few people, who looked like shopkeepers, were dragging themselves, minus collars or ties, along the street, apparently exhausted by the scorching heat. A well-dressed woman had stopped before a shop window and was interestedly examining the parasols and other fashionable articles on display, munching sunflower seeds all the while, cracking them with her teeth as a parrot does with its beak, and spitting out the husks in every direction.

The few people whom they met paid not the slightest attention to them. Only the children ran behind the marching prisoners. No one here felt the least interest in a new lot of captives, for the city had been filled with them for months, and when some woman did turn her head in their direction it was only to follow them with hostile eyes as if to say, "Ah, here are some new ones come to eat us out of house and home!" Prices were mounting daily in this overpopulated city.

It was at the river's edge that the prison city, built for ten thousand men, was situated. It was called *Pod-Chouvachi* (first hostelry), and surrounded by high palings and guarded by four towers, covered an immense area. The thousands of Hungarian soldiers taken captive at Przemyśl had been brought here.

Peter's group was the first taken to Pod-Chouvachi, but there was no more room in the officers' barracks. The privates stayed, but the officers and their orderlies were taken that evening to the lower city; to a one-story frame house on the river bank which had formerly been an inn for transient Tatar merchants.

This house, standing alone not far from the willow-bordered river bank, did not make a particularly favorable impression. Dung was piled over three feet high in the narrow yard, and the noxious vapors of the foul pools, left by the Irtysh as it receded, crept through the crumbling apertures.

"A plague on this vile hole!" muttered Bartha as they stopped before the door.

Within, the house looked still more forsaken. The rooms, empty of furniture, were strewn with dung, the walls were covered with an accumulation of century-old smoke and greasy soot.

Zamák held his nose between his fingers and never stopped chuckling as the scowling officers hurried through the rooms.

They spent the first night in the yard, where they spread their blankets on the ground.

Fortunately the nights are short in Tobolsk. The sun sets at an acute angle about ten at night, and rises shortly after midnight, at about one, not far from the point where it vanished. Moreover, those few hours of night are more like a twilit half-darkness, light enough for the reading of a newspaper if one strains the eyes a little.

They covered themselves from head to foot with their overcoats, for they were harassed by endless swarms of mosquitoes from the Irtysh. Many of these were no larger than a pinhead, but some were as big as small dragonflies.

They hardly waited for the sun to rise before jumping up.

Major Doroviev, commander of the prison camp, arrived early. He walked with a decided limp, though his wound dated from the Russo-Japanese war. He was evidently a humane person, and spoke to them in a friendly fashion, telling them that they were to stay temporarily at Tobolsk. They all knew by this time that "temporary" meant long months.

They got shovels, picks, and pitchforks, and began clearing up the yard first. The dung had to be removed and the pools filled with sand, so that the pure breezes of the Irtysh might cleanse them. The officers worked in their shirtsleeves, side-by-side with the orderlies.

When Peter felt the shovel in his hand he experienced a real thrill of joy and an eagerness for work such as he had known in childhood, when he built a little house at the bottom of the garden. The others, too, were stimulated by the hereditary building instinct, for they knew this was their own dwelling place that they were putting in order.

Lieutenants Vedres and Rosiczky went to town with a few orderlies. They returned at noon with a bulky package of nails, saws, and planes and a cart filled with planks and laths, mason's tools, whitewash, brushes, buckets, and mosquito netting. Soon the fresh, resinous odor of pine wood, the buzzing of saws, and the grating of planes filled the yard. The work sped under their hands.

The beds were made by nailing planks to legs and stuffing bags with straw to be placed on top. Each one nailed together a table and chairs, according to his own taste and ability. Joseph Baktri, Rosiczky's orderly, suddenly acquired great importance, for he had been a carpenter's apprentice at Kaposvár before the war. Now he directed the work, as a general directs the maneuvers of a battle, approaching one or another of the officers and taking the plane or saw out of his hands.

The atmosphere was filled with a new spirit of serenity, produced by the unalloyed happiness, dimly conscious of it though they were, of the builders of a country. Many of them, like true laborers, began to whistle as they worked, and when Joseph Baktri struck up a popular air, the others soon joined him.

Zamák was engaged in avoiding as far as possible any heavy labor. He would pick up a long plank from one spot and carry it for no particular reason somewhere else. He came and went among the workers with these long pieces of timber, like the phlegmatic clown in a circus ring among the attendants who are feverishly unrolling a carpet over the sawdust.

Neteneczky was sitting on a beam, drawing up plans for the furniture under construction. A few others, Szentesi, Szabó, Altmayer, and Lukács, mounted on stepladders, were cleaning the rooms and whitewashing the walls. The echoing rooms rang with whistling and singing that floated out into the street.

After a few hours Peter's hands burned as if he were holding hot coals; the saw and the plane had blistered both his palms.

Work continued uninterruptedly from early morning till late at night for a full week, till the old Tatar house was cleaned inside and out, from top to bottom. Stefan Bartha named their new home Misery Hotel, a name that sounded Russian somehow, and he went so far as to paint the name in large black letters on a pine board, which he proposed to fasten to the door. But Mezei didn't like the name and after much wavering decided to call it Hun-

garian Home. No one could oppose his choice, for he had
been in the service longest and the officers maintained a
certain kind of discipline among themselves.

Mezei sometimes made their lives more painful than
necessary because of a certain pettiness in his viewpoint
and conception of things, and because of his inelastic
army spirit; but otherwise he proved himself a first-rate
organizer, so that life was soon pursuing its even, orderly
tenor at Misery Hotel. For it was in vain that the sign,
Hungarian Home, framed in the national colors, hung
from the front of the house; everyone called it Misery
Hotel—with the exception of Mezei, of course, who
considered the use of that term a personal affront. Indeed,
the opinion that Bartha was a man of very inferior
mentality had rooted itself deeply in his mind, and he
reprimanded the orderlies severely when he caught them
saying Misery Hotel instead of Hungarian Home.

At first the officers took their meals in town, where for
eighty kopeks each they could get, in the Nomera Laskutnaya, a small third-class hotel in the lower city, a well-
cooked and inviting meal.

Although the Tsar had issued a strict ukase at the
beginning of the war forbidding all Russians to drink
alcohol, Igor Kroukof, the paunchy landlord of the
Laskutnaya, assumed an innocent air and pretended not
to have understood the Little Father's thundering edict.
Ice-cooled beer could be bought from him, and if one
flattered him a little and poked him in the ribs, an
excellent red Crimean wine could be had for a few rubles
—all, of course, under cover.

It was possible to obtain from patrons of the hotel
occasional news of what was going on at the front, but
even then it was difficult to form a clear picture of the
whole situation.

After two weeks of this regime the officers tired of it,
because there was always the annoying necessity of
forming into ranks at midday and marching through the
town under the escort of Russian soldiers.

They decided to do their own housekeeping. Their

greatest difficulty in carrying out this plan was the acquisition of cooking utensils and tableware, which threatened to swallow the balance of their money, so that the household had to contend with financial embarrassment from the start. Fortunately the Russian butcher and the Tatar tradesmen gave them plenty of credit; in fact, they almost insisted upon its acceptance. The Russian authorities had prescribed the exact daily ration of meat, flour, and other provisions to which each of the prisoners was entitled, but it was the duty of the *starshi* assigned to them to keep track of these things, and he wouldn't have dreamed of objecting to the appearance on the officers' table of better or more plentiful dishes, since he and his men were fed from the same kitchen.

Once Zamák was caught by a city police officer buying more meat at the butcher's than was allowed. This might have led to unhappy consequences, had not the clever fellow, with a charming smile, proffered the bullet-headed officer half a calf's haunch, which settled everything.

It was evident from the crowded life of the streets that Tobolsk was overpopulated. It was filled not only with exiles, Germans, and citizens of other countries, deportees and suspect Russians, but with Jewish and Tatar tradesmen as well—and with war prisoners into the bargain. They all looked upon each other as secret allies, and the streets, the marketplaces, the shops, the waiting rooms of physicians and dentists, the hospitals and the churches, all proved convenient spots for the exchange of news.

The number of Hungarian war prisoners at the Pod-Chouvachi camp had reached nine thousand. The officers were scattered throughout the city. Peter's group was on good terms with those of the Bear House, so called because in the Tatar house where they were lodged, a rich merchant had two bears shut up in solid iron cages. These bears were at least a source of diversion for them. When Zamák could be found nowhere else, he was sure to be standing in front of the bear cage, establishing friendly relations with its inmates.

Meanwhile Misery Hotel was growing into a fit and even pleasant human habitation. The dung heaps had been replaced by flower beds. The open space between was always swept clean as a floor, and, seated comfortably in the shade of a large poplar that grew there, Bartha, Vedres, Neteneczky, and Lajtai played cards every afternoon in their shirtsleeves till they were driven indoors by the mosquitoes. These card parties would often end in heated arguments and altercations, and, their faces purple, they would fling down the cards that Altmayer had drawn on cardboard in red and blue pencil. The kings looked like first lieutenants, the next higher cards like second lieutenants, and the lower ones like the most popular orderlies. Ulrich Rudenz (one of the cards) had Peter's face. But as no one, either among the lieutenants or the orderlies, had been willing to lend his features for that purpose, Zamák sacrificed himself and posed for the knave.

While the others played cards, Peter, whistling a little tune and completely absorbed in his work, carved chessmen from the gnarled poplar wood with a very sharp knife. As he cut into the wood with his knife, his fingers began to hurt, and he suddenly remembered that dreary autumn afternoon, when sitting at his desk in the Hadnagy Street house, he had carved on the little board the girls had given him the words, "I love you."

Rosiczky, who had bought a second-hand zither at a bazaar in the old city, sat on the doorstep of Misery Hotel all day, playing the Tatar instrument.

Peter shared a room with Kölber, a little room furnished with chairs, two wardrobes against the wall, coat stands, two night tables, and even two writing tables with drawers—all of smooth, white pine. Mosquito netting was stretched in front of the window.

There were seven rooms above; Bartha occupied one with Szabó, Lukács with Altmayer, Rosiczky with Lajtai, and Netene with Csaba. In the largest room Hirsch, Szentesi, and Vedres were lodged. A small room, apart from the others, was reserved for Mezei.

The fourteen orderlies lived in one large room downstairs and in another, the five armed men who composed the guard under the command of a *starshi*. The kitchen, the pantry, and a room that affected the air of a salon and had been combined into a living and dining room were also on the ground floor.

The guards were peaceful folk; they accepted small tips without the least scruple, and were as Netene declared nothing but a collection of caps, beards, and boots.

But there was one among them whom they scarcely dared look at. His name was Yurovski and he looked almost simian with his flattened nose and brutish features. When Yurovski was about, they spoke in low tones, though he couldn't understand a single word of Hungarian.

It was mid-September when Peter finally received the letter Miette had written in May.

He withdrew to his room and didn't go down for his meals, remaining all day under the spell of the letter. All the atmosphere of his former life was revived with extraordinary power and vividness. It was actually as if Father and Miette, his mother and Paul Szücs, Johnny and Mme. Varga, Rose, the Vargas' pretty maid, and deaf, round-shouldered Mili had gathered round him in the little room of Misery Hotel. Even Tomi was somewhere in a corner of the room, raising mournful earnest eyes from behind the little hanging tufts of his eyebrows.

Peter walked back and forth in the narrow little room, pausing at intervals before the night table, where stood two portraits framed in rough poplar wood. One was an old, faded daguerreotype, showing his mother as a very young woman. The other was Miette, only a little amateur snapshot that Sigismund Pán had taken. Miette was standing, hatless, the sun-drenched sand at her white-shod feet, Balaton behind her. Her eyes were squinting in the sunlight, and the wind was whipping her light blue dress around her legs.

He studied the photograph for a long time, then he

closed his eyes, but still continued to see her clearly before him.

Close by, beneath the willows, the tumbling and roaring of the vast yellow stream of the Irtysh, driven by mysterious forces, could be heard through the open window. And from some unknown, infinite distance in the north of Siberia, the wind blew toward him the smoke from the charred tundras that the flames were devouring.

PART THREE: GOLGONSZKY

I

Another summer had passed. The rays of the afternoon sun cast an unutterably melancholy light on the window-panes. One morning Miette, sitting in her negligee before the mirror of her dressing table, saw that her sad eyes were circled by dark hollows.

Lassitude, physical and moral, was gradually over-powering her. Sometimes she would sit down and begin a letter to Peter—but she hadn't the strength to finish it. feeling that she had nothing to say to him.

One morning she met Rose on the stairway. Suddenly she remembered their last meeting and said to her: "Tell me, Rose, what does this Paul Szücs want of you?"

"Of me?"—and she blushed crimson.

Miette wagged a gloved finger at her in a charming gesture that spoke volumes.

She often sent for Rose in the afternoons, and they would iron together in the kitchen. She liked the company of this white-skinned, graceful girl, whose wrists and ankles were so delicate that any highborn maiden might have envied them. There was something so bewitching about her loveliness, about the natural grace and charming jumble of her talk, that Miette could listen for hours without wearying of her pretty chatter.

Those were her best afternoons. First Miette loved to iron, and then Rose would talk of her native village, where her father was a carpenter. She knew all kinds of lively, pleasant little stories—what had happened to the schoolmaster or to the Jew's wife, the one who squinted. Rose told, too, of Patócs, a big fellow, strong as a bull and just as pugnacious; and of Szu Perke, the gypsy who

changed herself into a turkey every night; and then there
was old Baron Lidiczki—she wasn't sure that that was
his real name!—who bred everything, even "American
cats," in his castle and was such a great hunter that even
his reversible umbrella was loaded with six bullets.

Miette played big sister to Rose. She would amuse
herself by dressing her up or by making over for her an
old house dress. It gave her real pleasure to adorn this
slender-waisted girl, who had a perfect, natural instinct
for everything beautiful. Rose loved Miette so, she would
have been unhesitatingly ready to die for her. She rushed
to the Almádys' on the slightest pretext, and gradually
established herself there as a cat establishes itself in a
strange house.

One afternoon the doorbell rang, and presently Mili,
distraught, entered the room where Miette was sitting.

"Miss Miette—please—a foreign gentleman is here—
he doesn't understand Hungarian!"

When she was upset, Mili still called Miette "Miss."

Miette was making ready to go to the foyer, but
Alexander Petrovitch Ilyin was already standing in the
dining-room doorway.

He was so completely transformed that at first she
hardly recognized him. He carried white buckskin gloves
in his hand, wore patent-leather boots, and the gilded
epaulettes glittered on his new green-brown uniform. He
was freshly shaven and his sleek flaxen hair had been
carefully brushed back from his forehead.

Standing on the threshold, he extended both his hands
to Miette, and both joy and agitation were in his glance
as he said, "Vous souvenez-vous de moi, Madame?"

Miette, flushed and embarrassed, gave him her hand
smiling, but said nothing, for she had forgotten the
Russian officer's name. She invited him into the living
room and asked him to sit down.

He sat in an armchair opposite Miette. He told her that
he had been working for four weeks in the Ganz factories,
where he was treated with the consideration due his social
position, and that he could come and go about the city

as he pleased. He had received money from home, but had postponed his visit to her until his new uniform should be ready.

Firmly clutched in his fingers he was holding a little parcel wrapped in tissue paper.

Miette felt a little uncomfortable, for she was still trying to recall her guest's name, and she carefully avoided addressing him first. She showed him Peter's photograph. Alexander Petrovitch Ilyin looked at it for a long time, his face suddenly sobered and his lips moving slightly as if he were speaking to the picture. Then he placed it gently back on the table.

There was an occasional lull in the conversation, when Alexander Petrovitch would gaze thoughtfully at the floor.

Presently he rose and made ready to leave. He began to unwrap the little parcel with trembling hands, and the tissue paper rustled slightly as he crumpled it between his fingers.

The package contained a holy picture, a Russian icon that seemed very old, all yellowed and smoky in its frame of gilded wood that was worm-eaten here and there.

"Madame," he said, pale and a little solemn, as if he were speaking words he had learned by heart, "I come of a very old Russian family. For many generations my ancestors have prayed before this little icon, and God has always come to their aid. There is nothing of greater value that I can offer you just now. Please accept this from me, and you will see that God will sustain you, too."

He spoke the last words in a very low, almost choked voice.

Miette turned her head aside and began to weep, trying to conceal her tears. She was aware that Alexander Petrovitch was bowing low before her and kissing the tips of her fingers.

Father, who was working in his study as usual, rose from his desk and thrust his head through the half-open door to see who was with Miette. He was very much astonished to see a Russian officer cross the dining room on the balls of his feet, his lips trembling and his eyes filled with tears. He stood looking after him until the Russian had disappeared into the foyer, then went to his daughter. After learning what had happened, he stood for a long time at the window, his hands crossed behind his back, gazing pensively out into the street.

And September also passed. Often whole weeks would go by without news of Peter, then suddenly three cards would come in one mail. But they brought no news.

One Sunday morning in front of the church, Miette encountered Mme. Cserey, a distant relative, whom she had not seen since her marriage.

"I'm coming to see you tomorrow morning," Mathilde called to her, before disappearing in the crowd.

And next morning she actually appeared. She sat opposite Miette, her legs gracefully crossed. Her bearing, her manner, everything about her suggested the great lady; her ankles were as slender and delicate as those of a young girl. She had a little color in her face, and beneath the transparent skin a blue network of hairline veins was visible. Her body was built on slender, delicate lines; it was easy to imagine how beautiful she must have been. She was nearing fifty. Her husband had been police commissioner, but since they had inherited an enormous fortune, they had been at home in all the capitals of Europe. Their only daughter had died at the age of eight, and the tender, beautiful memory of the dead child colored all their life together.

She had Miette tell her all about her life, then explained that she and her husband had only recently returned to Hungary. The declaration of war had surprised them in Paris, but at the last moment they had succeeded in reaching Germany.

There were in her voice certain marked singing notes, a kind of musical tonality. She would occasionally give a word of slight French intonation, yet without any suggestion of affectation. As she pulled on her gloves— the color of faded chestnut leaves—in preparation for departure after an hour's conversation, she scrutinized Miette attentively. "How pale you are, my dear! I think you take things too much to heart. You mustn't look upon life too seriously, for you'll be punished later on. My heart aches when I think of you. You are young and beautiful. People remember you and speak of you. They remember you when you were still unmarried. I'm constantly asked, 'What's become of pretty Miette Almády?' People who have known you a long time imagine that you lead the life of a princess held captive by some spell at the bottom of a dungeon. Really, it's appalling to live like that. You must go out into the world. You know, if you hold your arm motionless in the same position for a long time it will grow stiff and insensitive, and if you hold it that way for a *very* long time, it will be paralyzed. It is the same way with our souls and our minds. Do you play bridge? No? That's too bad . . . There's a good bridge game at my house every Thursday. Then you must come on Saturday. There'll be a large crowd and I expect some very, very interesting people. You'll be an ornament to my drawing room. I don't know why, but women are not so pretty as they used to be. Don't you find it so?"

As Miette accompanied her to the door, Mme. Cserey, already on the landing, turned to say, "I'm counting on you absolutely. I'll send my carriage for you."

Mathilde's visit gave Miette's mind something new to feed upon and shook her out of her lethargy. She herself realized that she couldn't go on living this way, and she made her preparations very happily for the Cserey party. On Saturday afternoon she sent for the hairdresser, who arranged her hair in a new style, and when, her toilette finished, she stood in front of the mirror, she was satisfied with her appearance. She could still hear Mathilde's voice lapping about her in pleasant and slightly intoxicating music: "You are young and beautiful! People remember you and speak of you. What's become of pretty Miette Almády?"

She told Mili to come for her at midnight.

She was a little late and very nervous as she entered

the Csereys' large, colonnaded reception room, where twenty-five or thirty people were already gathered. The men were in dress coats or full uniform, the women in evening dress and covered with jewels. Diamonds glittered brilliantly here and there.

Miette felt that she had lost her social ease, and for the first few minutes, beneath her unaccustomed coiffure, her own voice sounded strange to her.

Mathilde took her by the hand and introduced her to some elderly women, who were apparently of the most exalted aristocracy. She exchanged a few irrelevant words with them and answered their questions in a voice that was rather muffled by shyness, aware that these empty phrases served only as a pretext to give them the opportunity of examining her from head to foot.

Dinner being announced, there was no more time for introductions. On Miette's left there was a middle-aged man who carried his head a little to one side and who would close his eyes every few seconds as he spoke in a low, well-modulated voice. Her right-hand neighbor was a very young man, the kind that at eighteen creates an impression of maturity, especially in evening clothes. He threw out his chest and sat his chair as if it were a saddle. He seemed to be holding reins in his lap instead of a napkin, and he looked straight ahead of him, speaking to no one. It was obvious that the starched bosom of his shirt was making him uncomfortable.

Miette cast a glance about her but could discover no face that she knew, though she had the impression that she must have seen some of them before. Her left-hand neighbor seemed especially familiar. She was glad that she would not have to make much conversational effort during dinner. She amused herself by studying the people sitting opposite her with that interest always aroused by faces one has never seen before: a woman of about fifty with blue-black hair, wearing huge emerald earrings ... a major in the gold-laced dolman of the cavalry, who spoke German, using only the most precise and elegant expressions ... a young girl whose perfect doll-like beauty was so insignificant that the eye passed unconsciously over her.

Throughout the meal Miette noticed that one of the guests, seated at the other side of the table some distance from her, looked long and often in her direction. Their eyes met several times. He regarded Miette with a certain emotion. He was a broad-shouldered, strongly built man, whose evening clothes fitted perfectly over his powerful shoulders, and whose rather commonplace, pleasant face reflected a wholesome, healthy spirit, making the sadness with which he gazed at Miette doubly apparent.

When they left the table Miette sat in the drawing room with her left-hand neighbor on a black, heavily carved Italian bench. The conversation turned to Italian art. Miette was not entirely uninformed on the subject, and she carefully gave in her replies some rein to her natural impulsiveness and originality. She soon realized that this unknown friend was listening to her, eyes half closed, head bent a little to the side, with sincere pleasure.

Miette felt her mind was clearer and more active after this talk, as if her brain and her intelligence had taken some beneficial gymnastic exercise.

They were speaking of Michelangelo, and he suddenly let fall the absentminded remark: "Henri de Regnier has written a little essay on him, which I prefer to any other."

He said it as if he were talking to himself.

Miette thought this man must be some important university professor.

"The opinion of beauty on the beautiful is always interesting," he said. "I have often watched young women of various countries in Italian museums. That is a wonderful moment—when those fugitive beauties come and go through the churches, greeting with their eyes their sisters, the Eternal Beauties."

As they were talking, Miette suddenly cast an almost involuntary glance toward the fireplace, as if she felt someone's eyes upon her.

A lieutenant of uhlans was standing near the fireplace. Tall, slender, and well groomed, he seemed to stare at her, yet she could not distinguish his face in the shadows.

A little disturbed, Miette resumed the conversation. Her new friend, who was looking straight before him with a dreamy, half-sleepy air, soon rose and took his leave of her.

Mathilde came to sit beside Miette.

"Well, how did it feel to be in the society of the great man?"

"Who is he?" asked Miette.

Mathilde reverently uttered the name of a writer whose novels Miette knew very well; he was a man universally known and respected, and Miette finally realized why his face had not seemed strange to her.

Mathilde led Miette to another corner of the huge salon to introduce her to a big young man with thick hair, who was standing in the center of a group, and who was a fashionable composer. He had a habit of crossing his arms on his chest in a rapid gesture at every possible opportunity. His face was extraordinarily dark and covered with tiny pock marks. His brilliant, jet-black eyes, whose pupils it was impossible to distinguish, cast swift, darting glances in every direction. These eyes were filled with distrust of people and things, so that, before lighting a cigarette, he would first make sure by a rapid glance that the object he was holding was really a cigarette, and he would do the same thing with the match.

The man who had been gazing at her so incessantly during dinner was now standing behind her, as if he were waiting for something. Involuntarily, she turned her head in his direction.

"Madame," said the stranger, "I have a message to give you—"

So odd was his tone as he spoke, that the words promptly took on an enigmatic character in Miette's mind.

"From whom?" she asked with eager, frightened curiosity.

In a low voice the man answered, "From Olga."

Miette's breath failed her.

"Who are you?"

"I am Elmer Koretz."

Miette asked no more.

After a moment of silence, Koretz began to speak again. He didn't raise his eyes to Miette. He could scarcely control his emotion.

"She said to me before she died, 'If you should ever meet Miette, tell her that I loved her very much . . . I was terribly sad not to be able to say goodbye to her.'"

He stopped. Miette closed her eyes for a long moment, then asked softly: "Poor darling, did she know she was going to die?"

"Yes, she knew."

Miette hid the pallor of her face in her hands and whispered: "Tell me about her."

"Olga loved you very much. She always talked of you. She often said to me, 'You see, I am only a poor, frail creature, full of faults and weaknesses. Miette is altogether different.' She always spoke of you as of an extraordinary personality. She made the delivery of this message to you a special obligation."

She gazed at Koretz dreamily, as if now she wanted to learn all she could of this man, who had taken her poor, unhappy little friend away. She said, with something like hostility in her voice, "How did you treat her? Did you love her?"

Koretz bent his head slightly. Then he answered: "Yes! She was a plaything in my life—but one of those playthings for which one commits murder, if necessary, or sends a bullet into the brain. She was twenty years younger than I, and I treated her like a child—"

"How did she die?" murmured Miette.

"That's a long story; I will tell it to you. Except for you, there is no one to whom I can speak of her . . . In the last months she often had violent attacks of fever, and I tried in vain to persuade her to consult a specialist. I wanted to send her to Davos, but I couldn't go with her, and she wouldn't take a step without me. She was capable of deceiving me about her temperature and

would even deny that she had any fever! Finally I took
her myself to a famous specialist. The doctor examined
her and said: 'Go home again like a good girl, little black
devil; there's nothing the matter with you!' Of course, I
had arranged in advance with the doctor to send me the
correct diagnosis, but not to the house, to my office. Next
day I received the doctor's letter. I hadn't hoped for
good news, but what I received was crushing; it was
virtually a sentence of death. I scarcely dared go home,
I was so afraid she would see something in my face. After
lunch she sat on my lap, fooling around like a baby; she
was in high spirits. She was patting my cheeks and eyes
gently with her little hand when, quick as a flash, she
suddenly pulled my wallet out of my coat pocket. It was
something she often did, because, without the slightest
reason, she would sometimes be almost sick with jealousy.
She would run away with my wallet and ransack all its
compartments, looking for love letters and demanding
explanations of the most insignificant memorandum. We
would run all around the room, chasing each other, and
sometimes she would jump over the furniture with her
plunder. I generally enjoyed this game, because she was
sweet enough to eat when she played it; but that day I
suddenly remembered that the specialist's letter was in
my wallet. I seized her hand as she fled, but she wrenched
herself away, and my terrified gesture contrived to make
her really suspicious. I was determined to get the wallet
back at all costs; but she upset the table and managed to
get away from me. I shouted furiously, and when she had
got too far away from me to reach, she turned, panting
with rage, and shouted back, "Ha, ha! . . . I've caught
you this time!"

"She ran into the bathroom and locked the door. I grew
frantic, and pushed against it with all my strength. I am
no weakling, but the door was stronger than I. By the
time I had broken the lock she had found the letter and
read it to the end. I was absolutely beside myself; I tore
the letter from her hands. and fell all but fainting into a
chair, as I realized how horribly cruel that abrupt

revelation must have been for her. A moment later I saw that she was sitting on the floor at my feet and crying. She raised her eyes to me as if she wanted to ask forgiveness. 'It doesn't matter—don't be angry,' she said, her voice all drenched in tears. 'I thought it was a letter from a woman . . .' "

He remained silent for a moment.

"What happened after that—they were the most agonizing days of my life. Four weeks later she was dead."

He stopped. Deep creases lined his forehead, and the expression of his face was savage. He seemed to be struggling against the pain that was racking him.

Miette pressed her handkerchief to her mouth. She turned away a little, leaning against the back of the chair, so that the lamplight should not shine on her face.

They sat thus in silence for a long time. Koretz rested his hand on the table, carefully tracing with a finger the design of the inlaid wood.

At last, her voice somewhat lighter and clearer, as if she had partly controlled her emotion and forced back her tears, Miette asked, "Is her mother still alive?"

"Yes; she is in a sanatorium near Vienna."

Then they relapsed again into silence, both full of their memories of Olga, seeing her alive before them under the most varied circumstances.

To change the course of their thoughts, Koretz asked Miette, "How long has your husband been a prisoner?"

"Over a year now."

"Do you live with your family?"

"With my father."

They began to talk on a note of friendly interest, telling each other the circumstances of their lives—a thing made possible by their common memories of Olga.

Miette noticed that little groups would occasionally pass in front of them or stop not far away with stealthy glances in their direction, and she felt that they were talking about her. All evening she had been aware that she was making a distinct impression upon people.

Turning deliberately toward the fireplace, she was astonished to see that the uhlan was still standing there in the semi-darkness, his arm on the mantel, his eyes fixed on her. He seemed to have been standing in the same place for a long time.

Miette felt a little thrill go through her at this discovery, for his conduct was almost equivalent to a declaration. Under the compulsion of that strange gaze, glowing upon her out of the shadow so as to give almost the effect of touching her, she adjusted her gown with an involuntary movement at the shoulder as if to cover it, though the dress was not cut very low and only a bit of the rosy shoulder could be seen, its perfect line soon lost in the folds of soft reed-green silk. The small area of naked flesh shone with the tender, exquisitely shaded velvetiness of a peach, and her lovely thick hair, arranged so distinctively that evening, gleamed in the lamplight whenever she moved her head, warm copper tones glinting in its rich russet masses.

She glanced at her little diamond-studded wrist watch, cried in surprise, "It's past midnight," and got up to go.

Koretz rose too, and offered to see her home.

"Oh, thank you . . ." said Miette, a touch of protest in her voice.

She was standing, her body turned a little to the side, and without exactly seeing him, she felt—it was more like a divination—that the uhlan was approaching her.

Koretz bowed low before Miette.

"Goodbye," she said warmly, and gave him her hand in a gracious gesture.

When she turned, the uhlan was standing before her. She raised her eyes and looked at him, an incomprehensible tremor at her heart.

He stood before her, his hands thrust deep into the slanting pockets of his dolman. He had one of those faces that captivate the imagination at first glance. A dark skin, and in his bronzed, clean-shaven face, steel-blue eyes, whose calm gaze seemed to rise from the depths of his being. This strange, intense scrutiny actually seemed to touch each object toward which its hard light was directed. There are eyes that plunge like daggers into the soul, but there was nothing sharp or acid in this man's eyes. They pierced whatever they looked at through and through to the very bones, but they allowed themselves to be pierced as freely in return. Infinite candor was reflected in the depths of those eyes, and a multitude of undisguised thoughts. This candor held something almost terrifying, demanding as it did the same complete and absolute candor from those whose souls his clear glance probed.

It was a strange face, unlike any other. The short, unruly hair extended beside the ears in fine, downy little flaps, gray-blue, like the delicate feathers beneath the wings of certain wild birds.

He was tall, slender, and distinguished-looking, and spoke with complete assurance to Miette.

"I have been waiting a long time to exchange a few words with you."

She looked up at him in surprise.

"Do we know each other?" she asked, a little disconcerted as she resumed the seat she had just left and arranged the silken cushions about her. She could not have described the agreeable sensation of buoyancy that pervaded her, nor the slight giddiness for which she couldn't account.

The uhlan sat down in the armchair.

"In any case, I know you . . ."

He enveloped Miette in a surreptitious glance—from her narrow, pointed, gold slippers to her hair that was like a huge, rust-darkened red lily.

"Since when?"

"I used to see you often on the tennis courts some years ago . . . Then we met a long time ago at a tea. You weren't married then. And the day before yesterday I saw you in Buda, near the Danube. You were walking along the lower bank with a little terrier on a leash, and you were very much engrossed in your thoughts."

"Really?" asked Miette, for she didn't remember ever having seen his face.

"Yes," said the officer, "but it hasn't been difficult for me to remember you all these years."

A faint flush spread over Miette's cheeks which, together with her embarrassment, heightened her beauty. The uhlan contemplated her for a long moment in admiring silence.

"You were talking just now of a girl who died recently?"

"Yes, I was grieving for a former friend of mine."

"I know. Her name was Olga."

"You knew her, then?"

"Only slightly. But I know her story well. She was a gallant child. And it was because of her gallantry that life compensated her to some extent for her death in the flower of her youth. She lived, loved, and reveled royally in life's pleasures. I have heard that she traveled extensively. She tasted of life in Paris, marveled at the Bosporus, walked on the green turf of England and along the slopes of the Swiss Alps . . . What more could anyone want? And she was given money lavishly to squander—and she squandered it."

Miette remained silent for a moment; then asked thoughtfully, as if she were assembling the impressions she had formed of Koretz: "This Koretz loved her intensely, didn't he? Do you know him?"

"Yes, I know him and find him very agreeable. He enjoys an excellent reputation as a businessman. He is feared, because he is hard and ruthless, but he would have made any sacrifice for that girl, not like some men."

"Are you a regular army officer?"

"I? God forbid! No, I am in the diplomatic service."

"I am sorry, but may I ask your name?"

"Oh—forgive me—you are right—I should have begun with that. My name is Ivan Golgonszky."

Miette had a dim impression that she had heard that name before.

"In what city is your husband a prisoner?" Golgonszky asked.

"In Tobolsk."

"I once spent some time in Tobolsk. I vaguely remember the governor's palace, the fort, and the Tatar section—" Then he added thoughtfully: "I have a number of friends in Russia."

"How is that?" asked Miette in surprise.

"I was an attaché in Moscow for two years."

Miette, interested, leaned toward him. "Tell me a little about the Russian people—about Russia. I know nothing about the country except the little I have gleaned from reading novels, and that little seems to be very confused."

Golgonszky drew out a cigarette case, snapped open with a deft movement the lid of the exquisite little gold box, and offered Miette a cigarette.

She lit it and, taking the glass of champagne that a servant had meantime placed at her side, moistened her lips. Again she arranged the silken cushions about her and, sitting in the lamplight, drew in the smoke of her cigarette and listened attentively to Golgonszky. Yet she only half understood what he was telling her of the life in Moscow, of the club, of hunting in Russia, for all her attention was concentrated on the face of the speaker, and on the play of his hands which he thrust deep into the slanting pockets of his dolman, only to draw them out again the next moment. She found more strength and distinction in these hands than she had ever seen in the hands of any other person.

Listening to Golgonszky's recital gave her an excellent excuse for watching him at the same time. She noticed his strong, dazzlingly white teeth, and followed the movements of his thin, well-shaped lips that were richly red and over which, as he talked, played the subtle gradations of some secret amusement or irony; try as she might, she could not help thinking of Peter's teeth, which were yellower and more irregular.

Golgonszky felt that Miette was watching him and he, too, was watching her. He went on with his story but more and more absentmindedly, interrupting himself now and then as if he would have liked to make an end of it.

They both knew that each was studying the other with hidden thoughts.

Golgonszky terminated his narrative abruptly, and fixed Miette with a frank gaze.

The young woman's cheeks grew faintly pink, and she glanced at her watch. It was one o'clock in the morning. Time had passed disconcertingly fast.

Miette rose, and Golgonszky followed suit. They looked about the salon, occupied now by only a few guests.

Mathilde came up to Miette.

"There is no need to hurry, for I sent your maid away a long time ago; she came for you at midnight." Then, turning to Golgonszky: "Ivan, you will see my niece home."

Golgonszky bowed.

Miette noted two distinct exaggerations in the words Mathilde had just uttered—first, in elevating Mili to the rank of personal maid, and second, in blandly dubbing Miette her niece, though they were only distantly related. And the young woman felt a slight pang of remorse, as if her own conscience had been burdened with these untruths.

Golgonszky turned to someone who had addressed him, and for the first time Miette noticed on his hip the chamberlain's insignia, the knot and gilded cord flat against the seam of the dolman. She could not have said why this discovery should fill her with emotion.

They bade their hosts good night and she preceded Golgonszky down the stairs. At the door below a chauffeur wearing a flat cap and tan leather boots laced to the knee opened the door of a powerful limousine for them. The interior of the car was lined in dove gray and fitted with a smoking set, electric lights, clothes brushes, perfume bottles, a speaking tube, and other paraphernalia of luxury and comfort, like a first-class hotel.

The huge car sped noiselessly through the silent streets of the center of town. Miette felt more distinctly that faint, agreeable dizziness that was confusing her head and heart. At each turning their arms brushed against each other, and they surrendered themselves to the light, pleasant movement of the car as, in changing direction, it swung them now to one side, now to the other.

"*Au revoir!*" Miette murmured as they separated in front of her house, involuntarily giving the word an enigmatic inflection.

But she regretted it immediately, for Golgonszky bowed and took leave of her with cool, courteous reserve, as if he were suddenly withdrawing all the interest he had ever shown in her.

As she climbed the stairs she pondered the matter, wondering if this sudden coolness had been calculated, or if it were simply Golgonszky's usual manner. She decided upon the latter explanation, without being able to convince herself completely.

Before starting to undress she studied herself for a long time, revolving with lifted arms before the mirror, looking more graceful than ever in the cool reed-green of her gown. At last she went to bed and, cuddled shivering beneath the blankets, began to think. She felt she had lived more intensely that evening than in the whole preceding year. Life seemed to her richer and wider, as if invisible walls had crumbled all about her, and beyond those walls she saw herself in a new and interesting light. She thought of that writer, the famous man with the tired eyes, who spoke so low and who had given her his exclusive attention—which was an honor in the eyes of the other guests. She suddenly remembered that some people had stopped a few paces away from her, whispering to each other their opinions of the young woman whom the great man had singled out, and she thought she could hear their smothered words of admiration. She thought of Koretz, whose mind she had occupied for months without knowing anything about it. Greatly moved, she conjured up her memories of Olga and, suddenly reverting to Koretz' story, she seemed to see the expression on Olga's face as, beyond the overturned table, she fled triumphant with the letter she had succeeded in carrying off.

She saw herself walking with her little dog on the bank

of the Danube all unaware while above, leaning on the parapet of the esplanade, Golgonszky watched her . . . . She wondered what impression the sight of her made on the young man, and she tried to recall the most minute details of that walk, what her movements had been, how she had held her hands and head. She tried to remember what she had been wearing that day—shoes, dress, gloves. Then she saw Golgonszky as he had appeared to her that evening, emerging out of the shadow, approaching her after he had left the mantelpiece against which he had leaned for so long. Her thoughts returned continually to Golgonszky, and again she felt that faint, agreeable, elusive giddiness. She recalled his strange face, his clean, dazzling teeth, his voice, his eyes, the chamberlain's cord, the touch of his hand, and her memories of this man, like tiny darts of pain, began to gnaw and feed upon her heart.

Dawn was beginning to slip through the double curtains before Miette finally grew drowsy. Its rosy light entered through the open window and, half asleep, she heard high up on the hills a blackbird's sleepy, uncertain notes announce the morning.

II

The railroad running from the Tyumen River to the city, connecting Tobolsk directly with Moscow and St. Petersburg, was completed.

Tobolsk, capital of the province as well as an episcopal residence, communicates with other parts of Asia by way of the yellowish waters of the Irtysh, which rises on the Chinese frontier. This river, thanks to its tributaries, the Tobol and the Ishim, opens the road to the West, and the smaller steamers that navigate the Antarctic can reach the port of Tobolsk by way of the Irtysh.

The area of the province of Tobolsk is almost four times that of old Hungary. But this immense territory is peopled by scarcely two million inhabitants. Through the marshy steppes of the North wander Tatars and nomad folk who, on their big-headed, tangle-haired horses, accompanied by their huge white dogs, hunt wolves to the very outskirts of the primeval forest, and on the eastern border go so far as to drive the Siberian tigers from their lairs.

These are the Ostyaks, short of stature, their necks buried in their shoulders; occasionally they go down to Tobolsk in their reindeer- or dog-drawn sledges, but they are principally engaged in the bartering of pelts. Their business transacted, they return speedily to their own country, as if they dreaded all contact with civilization. They know the marshy tundras that stretch to infinity as well as they know their own hands, but they will guide the Russians who live along the river banks through these marshes only when it serves their own purposes. There is no army in the world capable of wresting this empire from them.

North of Tobolsk, the primeval woods and marshes grow wilder and wilder; toward the South, however, pine and birch forests alternate along the pleasant banks of the Irtysh with beautiful fields of wheat and rye during the three months of the warm season.

The officers were allowed to go to the city two or three times a week, provided they were accompanied by an escort. Officially these outings were called "shopping tours." But there was no pleasure in traversing the lively city streets under the escort of an armed guard, for it often happened that they would meet convicts from the fort walking, like themselves, under the guard of a few Russian soldiers with fixed bayonets.

The young men solved the problem in this way: As soon as they reached the town they led their escort to the nearest pastry shop, telling him to order what he liked. But when they returned the first time after a half hour's promenade, the Russian was still devouring cream tarts. He had gobbled up half of the shop's supply, and the officers had to pay some twelve rubles to have him released.

A few days later, having grown more wary, they settled Nicolai Ivanovitch Pirilov, who accompanied them, on a bench in the street, and Vedres bought him some mints that cost only ten kopeks. Nicolai, whose mouth was covered with so luxuriant a beard and mustache that he couldn't even articulate distinctly, was quite satisfied and, left to himself, began sucking the sweets peacefully. He ate them to the very last, though his tongue was on fire. This Nicolai was a good-natured fellow, but they wouldn't have tried that trick on the Gorilla—the name they had privately given to Yurovski.

When they went to town, the officers would walk up and down in front of the shop windows, giving their special attention to the women. Those of the better class were dressed in the French fashion and took special pride in their elegant footwear. There were many pretty feet to be admired, but as the weather turned wintry, the women hid their delicate little shoes in high, heavy snow boots. There were few really pretty women. The round, well-fed faces with their high color were generally disfigured by small, snub noses.

It was not unusual, however, to meet real beauties among the Kirghiz and the Cherkess women in the lower city, near the bazaar of the Tatar quarter. The middle-aged women wore simple gray dresses, but the young ones were clad in light colors, lilac, sky-blue, and violet. They bound bright kerchiefs, peony red and lemon yellow, about their heads, from beneath which their almond-shaped eyes lifted shy, dark, velvety glances. Their glossy, raven-black hair gleamed as if it had been drenched in oil, and a few of them were dressed as if they had come straight from Muscovy.

The younger girls adorned themselves with ribbons, coral necklaces, glass pearls, and silk scarves; their breasts were bound by corselets, their waists by velvet girdles, and their fur caps were embroidered with multi-colored pearls and coins. Ribbons of gold-stitched velvet encircled their foreheads, and strands of horsehair and multi-colored ribbons were braided into their hair, with gold and bronze coins fastened to the ends of the long ribbons. Their tiered skirts glowed with brilliant color.

Bag-shaped white veils covered their faces, for they were Mohammedans, but they were obliged to keep their veils lowered only before men of their own religion; they would raise them willingly, even significantly, with a gesture that held both grace and coquetry, before Europeans.

Peter, watching these women in their brilliant peacock finery, felt nothing more than curiosity. His spirit was paralyzed by such utter apathy that the numbness spread to his very bones and nerves. In every woman he had encountered since his captivity, he saw only an imperfect creation, discovering flaws, defects, or some kind of lack even in the most beautiful, while the figure of Miette, body and soul, hovered unattainably high in his imagination. He thought continually of Miette and of Miette only—her slender, graceful ankles, the warmth of her body, the perfume of her breasts, and the sweet, burning savor of her moist lips.

Often, when he was alone in his room, he would sit for whole hours at the table, his face buried in his hands and his eyes closed; all the countless memories of his life with Miette, sad and happy, would pass before him. He saw her smiling, yawning, or looking straight ahead with knitted brows. This endless retrospection closed his spirit to any outside influence in his present life. When he happened to pass perfumed, desirable women in the streets of Tobolsk, he felt no throb of sensual desire.

The others, of course, ran at every opportunity after any woman who was in the least attractive. Since Zamák had made new clothes for the officers and the Russian commander had granted them permission to resume the insignia of their rank, they mingled with much greater assurance among the women of Tobolsk.

In addition to the natives, many Jewish merchants and interned German families were living in the city.

Everyone knew that Bartha was courting a plump, black-eyed Jewish widow who, to be sure, was no longer very young, but whose beauty had not yet entirely faded. During their excursions in the city, Bartha invariably disappeared under some pretext into a winding little street of the Starishlo quarter of the old settlers, and Szentesi, having slipped along behind him one day, reported that Bartha had stopped before the window of a little yellow villa and stood there, one hand resting gracefully on his hip, while a woman's curly head had leaned out of the window and listened smilingly to the cavalier's gallantries. It was all the more extraordinary since Bartha, except for military commands, understood not a word of German. Yet they seemed to understand one another, no one knew how.

Vedres always walked with a tall, beautifully formed German girl. Neteneczky, on the other hand, disappeared regularly among the Kirghiz women.

Only a few weeks had elapsed, and each of them was already involved in his own secret amorous intrigue. They never discussed these things with each other, never teased each other about them, nor made the slightest allusion to them, letting each man go his own way, as if these affairs with women were natural functions which it was unseemly to mention.

In most cases these transient intrigues, as time went on, embittered the hearts of the captives and cast a shadow over them. When they returned at night from one of these expeditions, to seat themselves around the same table in the community dining room, their thoughtful faces often held the reflection of the souls of these women who had entered their lives at Tobolsk.

Peter and Kölber alone continued to struggle with the memories of their former lives. Kölber wrote in his diary every night, and the details of that diary took the place of letters to his fiancée.

At first Peter had tried to keep a diary, too, but he hadn't the heart to go on with it. He never even wrote to Miette, except when the heavy, confused thoughts that tortured him had accumulated to a point where he was forced to relieve his heart at all costs in a long letter and to hurl far from him the burden of his overwhelming grief.

To see him sitting on a tree stump in the yard of Misery Hotel, his arms propped wearily on his knees, mouthing his empty cigarette holder—a mammoth's bone he had bought at a bazaar—it would have been easy to believe that the mind of this young officer—who had grown a full beard since his captivity—had been turned.

The men were soon forced to give up sitting in groups around the yard, for winter made its entrance abruptly, accompanied by keen, biting winds. All day clouds raced in pursuit of each other and, once the sun had set, the cloud-heavy sky glowed purple and crimson to the East and Northeast, as if the northern lights had managed to penetrate to that part of the country. The trees lost almost all their leaves, wild tempests raged at night, and soon the last ship had left port.

It rained incessantly for days; the sky was a depressing gray, and the change in temperature affected the spirits of the officers, who were dejected and irritable. Card-playing amused them no longer, no letters had arrived for a fortnight, and life was growing more and more unendurable. Mezei and Neteneczky quarreled over some wholly insignificant trifle and didn't speak to each other for two days.

Those rainy days were followed by a few short, sunny ones, but then a thick fog enveloped the country, a fog containing so little moisture that even metal objects remained dry in it. The tundras to the North were burning, and the smoke of those gigantic fires drifted down as far as Tobolsk. Through the fog the sun wandered like a lavender-silk balloon that had escaped from its moorings.

And one morning the snow appeared.

From that day, the thermometer continued to drop. Toward the end of November they awoke to find it twenty below zero. The mosquito netting was removed from the windows, and double panes had to be put in; but the panes were always frozen, and every morning the Siberian winter drew its mysterious message in strange characters on their surface—marvelous flowers of silvery ice.

But the city grew more and more lively. The uneven streets which had been almost impassable in summer were suddenly transformed into sledge roads, transparently white, that glittered like a polished mirror. The snowy roads of the northern marshes became passable, too, so that the sledges of the Cheremiss and the Ostyaks were soon thronging the streets of the lower city.

In the upper city the people flocked to the Grand Boulevard. They were all clad now in polar garments; the women in brown snowshoes slid along the polished sidewalks, and the greatest variety of furs was to be seen. Bear and sable mingled with Siberian fox. Wolf and hare-skins were used in enormous quantities, and occasionally a black-and-yellow-striped tiger would appear in regal dignity embracing the broad hips of a rich Tatar woman.

The Siberian horses, harnessed to sledges from which hundreds of little bells dangled, celebrated those sunny winter days with loud neighings as they waited in front of the shops and nibbled for very joy at the fresh snow.

Life in Tobolsk took on a new, fresh glow during those cold, clear winter days.

It snowed for whole days without a moment's respite. The last number of the *Russkoye Vyedsmoste* told of violent snowstorms raging in the northern tundras.

The inmates of the Bear House decided to arrange a great Christmas entertainment, and were working day and night to get their program ready. They visited Misery Hotel to gather what talent they could, but since they were unable to persuade Bartha to sing Hungarian songs at the projected party, they succeeded in obtaining only three performers from that house.

Lajtai promised to give a lecture on blast furnaces— a promise that was received with joyous enthusiasm— and the lecture, a bold innovation in the history of cabaret performances, was placed second on the program, after the intermission. The hussar ensign, Gustave Mathi from the Pod-Chouvachi camp who, dressed as a woman, was going to recite indecent verses in a soprano voice, would follow him on the program.

"Why don't you call on Rosiczky?" said Bartha to Lieutenant Remete, who was chairman of the evening.

"What can he do?"

"He's learned to play the zither and he does it so beautifully now that he'll soon be able to go begging for us all!"

Rosiczky actually did play the Tatar zither like an accomplished artist, and he promised to play some Volga Christmas songs.

Altmayer, who had studied painting, volunteered to draw caricatures, and showed samples of his talent. To tell the truth, his caricatures bore no resemblance to anyone, but they were very amusing, nevertheless, so Altmayer was included in the program.

"Do you think the show will be a success, old man?" Bartha asked Remete who was sitting on one chair, with his feet on another and his hands clasped across his knees, negotiating his important business from that position.

With an eloquent gesture, Temete answered, "You still don't know what the principal number is to be—we shall have readings from the dictionary."

The "dictionary" was a ribald manuscript defining certain terms current at the Pod-Chouvachi camp in the usual barracks humor.

Among the men of the camp, Remete had discovered one who had been a prestidigitator in a Park cabaret at Budapest; he was enrolled under the name of Jean Kolompár, but there had been a time when he went by the fine, artistic name of Souh-Ahram. By his own account, he could swallow any number of china plates and pull them intact from his trousers a moment later; he ate candles as if they were sausages, and then took them —lighted, of course—out of his pocket. Besides, he could change water into ink, and give magnificent imitations of the nightingale's song and the pig's grunt. At any rate, he undertook to do all these things. His offer was accepted, but Remete promised him a thrashing if his act should prove unsuccessful or bring disgrace upon the performance. Nevertheless Souh-Ahram declared himself ready to play his part; so there was fair hope that the evening would be a success.

A few days later, Zamák, who pried about everywhere with his long nose and ferreted out everything in advance, brought the cheering news that a Swedish transport was due the following Thursday with all sorts of gifts for the prisoners.

Even more than over the expected gifts, the officers rejoiced at being able at last to send to their families detailed letters that would not run the risk of mutilation or rejection by the censor.

After dinner that evening, once Kölber was in bed and asleep—or at least pretending to sleep—Peter began writing to Miette.

On the pinewood table, his writing materials were arranged in the same rigidly meticulous order as formerly on his desk at the bank in Pest. Even here he preserved these little habits of his earlier life. The paper cutter and the blotting pad must be on the left; the ruler, writing paper, and sealing wax on the right. He had made each of these things himself. The paper knife had been cut from a large fish bone, and the top of the blotting pad had been made out of a tin preserve box.

The room lay in silence, and the dense smoke of his cigarette drifted about the dusty electric bulb.

It was nearly midnight, but through the thin partition could be heard the sounds of Rosiczky's zither, for he was practicing assiduously for the coming Christmas party.

Peter bent over the sheet of paper and began:

"My little Miette, my dear and only treasure:

"I don't know whether you have received my last letter, the one I wrote you on October 10th. I'm afraid not, which is why I am telling you again that I have not received the package or the money that you said you were sending. Please don't ever send me anything more, since it's no use. Even letters arrive very irregularly, and as for packages or money, we never by any chance receive them at all.

"Just now, we are supposed to be getting 50 rubles a month, plus 6 for light and heat; but that, too, comes very irregularly. For instance, today, December 1st, we have just received our October pay! I had planned to buy an old fur coat for the winter. Finally I found a good wolf-skin—somewhat moth-eaten, it is true, but it will do me for this winter. The Tatar wanted 200 rubles for it, but when he learned I was a Hungarian he let me have it for 30—because I hadn't another kopek. The funny thing is that the Tatar's last name is Venguer, which means "Hungarian," and he insists that his grandfather was a Hungarian. Of course he doesn't know a word of our language. One of the oldest streets in the lower city is called Venguerski Ulica—why I don't know. They say that when Napoleon entered Russia at the beginning of the last century, a troop of Hungarian war prisoners came as far as this town and settled here.

"Our days go by, gray and monotonous. But occasionally something happens to rouse us out of this ghastly torpor. Last week there was a German airplane raid over Tobolsk, and you can imagine our feelings. I saw it with my own eyes, though to tell the truth they didn't look any larger than matchboxes. It was a very strange sensation that the sight awoke in us; I can't describe to you all the thoughts that went through my head; the others felt the same way, naturally, and it was many days before we could shake off the effects of that occurrence.

"Last Sunday an Austrian countess, a Red Cross worker, came here, but I heard of it only through my comrades, for the countess wasn't brought here. She was shown only the Czech prisoners, who are very comfortably housed.

"Just now our greatest need is firewood. We are sending a delegation to the staff captain tomorrow to ask for an increase in our daily wood ration, for we are sometimes very cold. For some unknown reason an order has just been issued forbidding us to go to town, and special permission must be obtained even to consult a doctor. That doesn't disturb us particularly, however, for we are now settled and acclimated here, just as a fox eventually settles in and grows accustomed to his cage. Besides, this kind of restriction rarely lasts more than a week or two at most.

"I play chess constantly; you'll see—when I get back you will parade by my side as the wife of a chess champion!"

At that point he paused, wondering whether this levity would appeal to Miette. He looked down at the lines he had just written, which confronted him with an alien air. Where would Miette be now and what would she be doing? Among what people had chance thrown her and would she be interested in what he had written there?—the wood ration—the German airplane—Venguerski Ulica—the old coat—

Perhaps when this letter reached her she would be returning from some reception or tea, filled with new desires and new emotions. And he seemed to see the weary gesture of her hand as she laid the letter aside. Oh, how beautiful Miette was in evening dress! And how smart she must be in the clothes she must have had made since he left!

And he—what had become of him? He looked at his neglected hand lying on the table, and made up his mind that, beginning next day, he would look after his finger-nails.

Then he went on with his letter.

"For the rest, I am applying myself to the study of Russian and already speak it very well.

"I don't dare think how things are going at home. The local newspaper—the Telegram—is constantly filled with Russian victories, and we read in every number that they continue to advance. They are always trying to frighten us by saying that the war prisoners are going to be removed from Tobolsk! Ah, if only it were to go to Nijni-Novgorod! But we are afraid we shall have to go farther east. Yesterday, for instance, they cut off the electric current, saying: 'Who will pay the electricity bill if you are sent away suddenly?' It was only after a long argument that they consented to turn the lights on again.

"Christmas is near. We are getting up a party and entertainment for ourselves, but there is still another pleasant surprise that we are preparing for the holiday and which we are anticipating more eagerly than we did the Christ child in our younger years. It is this. Bartha has discovered an old billiard table in the Tatar bazaar of the lower city, and he's been haggling for it for weeks. We pooled all our money and even cut down on food, so we could get the billiard table before Christmas. If we can only get it, we'll be living in clover . . ."

Here he paused again and for a long time contemplated what he had written. Would Miette smile as she read the lines? His imagination pictured the smile playing about her lips, that smile that always lighted Miette's face when she read a letter.

Then he went on:

". . . Another thing I should like to buy for myself is a pair of sealskin boots—they are comparatively inexpensive here.

"Yesterday we had a fine walk through the upper city all around the fort. To tell the truth, we reached the top only after much trouble, because climbing those snowy, slippery hills is not without its difficulties. The fort is interesting. On the side that overlooks the city there are no openings for ventilation; it's nothing but a great, thick, blind wall that gives you a horrible sensation when you think there are human beings doomed to remain forever behind that wall—not only murderers and civil prisoners, but political prisoners, too, penned up all together in the same dungeon! It helps me to bear my fate with an easier heart, for at least I enjoy the open air and the hope of seeing you again.

"We have received, through the mediation of two volunteers, a very distressing letter from our men who were taken to another part of the city and of whose fate we know very little. They beg us in this letter to send them some old clothes, for the poor fellows are actually freezing! Alas, what can we send them, when we have nothing ourselves! Our only hope now is that the Swedish transport may be bringing us some winter clothes . . ."

Peter arose and opened the window for a moment, for the cigarette smoke was filling the little room to suffocation; but first he covered the sleeping Kölber with his wolfskin, and then waited with chattering teeth for the cold air to dispel the smoke. The snowstorm had abated but the cold had grown all the more biting.

"It sometimes seems to me that I shall never see you again and that those months during which you were mine were nothing more than a heavenly dream in my life.

"Do you still love me? Do you still remember me? That is the one thought that still binds me to life—that you are thinking of me and waiting for me. If I should ever learn that you had forgotten me and given your heart to another, I believe I should go mad with grief.

"May God keep you, my darling Miette. Give my affectionate greetings to Father, and you—I kiss you a million times in spirit. Your wretched Peter, who loves you tenderly and passionately."

When he had finished his letter, he leaned his head on his arm, listening for a long time to the wild clamor and turbulence of the thoughts and feelings that possessed his heart.

It must have been two in the morning. Rosiczky was still awake. Through the thin partition crept the dreamy notes of the Tatar zither, evoking from the songs of the Volga all the melancholy of the Russian Christmastide.

III

Miette didn't see Golgonszky for some time after the Cserey party. One morning about a month after that memorable dinner, Mathilde took her to the riding school, where she met a number of acquaintances. It wasn't easy to recognize these people at first, for they were all in riding clothes.

They seated themselves in reed armchairs in the large gallery overlooking the arena and watched the riders. The thick layer of sawdust deadened the rhythmic noise of the horses' hooves, though the wooden veneer of the wall echoed with a hollow sound whenever a hoof happened to strike it.

Miette watched all this attentively, with the feeling that she was sitting in a gigantic cask; between the staves human voices rang out, echoing curiously, together with the cracking of whips, the clinking of the curb bits, the panting, plaintive snorts of horses impatient to be off. She had never visited the riding academy before, and her eyes feasted in delight on the magnificent spectacle of an ebony black horse in motion. The animal seemed to be made of a single piece of solid, shining black rubber. He pranced as he trotted, and the play of his muscles rippled in broad waves over his gleaming chest.

Miette was aware, amid the neighing, wildly snorting horses, amid the noise of the saddles and the sound of the bits, of the strong smell of ammonia, the warm steam that rose to her nostrils from the horses' bodies, and the acrid odor of sawdust, and felt as if she had been borne back to the years of her childhood. She remembered her grand-mother's house, the court at the back and the stables below, where sharp, warm odors mingled in the darkness with the fragrant smell of fodder. And she saw old Father Gregory sitting barefoot in front of the stable on a faded old horse blanket, rubbing bacon fat into his moldy boots. He concentrated all his attention and zeal on this task, and the boots sparkled in the sunlight between his clumsy, chapped old hands.

In the pleasant, drowsy atmosphere of the riding school, she was losing herself more and more deeply in her child-hood memories, when suddenly she caught sight of Ivan Golgonszky. He was sitting not far from her with a group composed of two women and an elderly gentleman. They, too, were watching the riders. He wore civilian clothes, topped by a greenish-brown hunting hat, in whose wide band two slender woodcock feathers were fixed. His hat pushed back a little, one leg crossed over the other, he lay comfortably back in his armchair in an attitude at once careless and graceful.

Miette's heart gave a sudden, wild lurch at the sight of him. She turned away quickly, but she could no longer concentrate on the arena, despite the amusing spectacle it presented just then. A rider had just fallen with a loud thud from his white horse into the sawdust, scattering yellow clouds of dust about him, to the accompaniment of lusty cheers from all sides. The gentleman leaped to his feet and acknowledged the plaudits, throwing kisses right and left, like a mountebank. Then he shook the sawdust out of his ears, as a dog shakes water.

Meantime Miette felt her knees trembling with weakness. She cast a glance in the direction of Golgonszky's group, which had risen and seemed to be on the point of departure. They passed close by. Golgonszky bowed to Mathilde and was about to resume his hat when he caught sight of Miette. He stopped short, then turned a little and raised his hat once more to Miette. His look and his gesture betrayed surprise and hesitation, as if he wanted to come back to her.

Miette acknowledged his greeting with a frigid nod.

The party with whom Golgonszky was leaving consisted of a thin, stooped old man and his wife and daughter. The old man gazed arrogantly at the world out of hard, pale, baggy eyes; the girl greeted Mathilde with a curt nod. They were very obviously people of the highest nobility.

Miette saw Golgonszky turn his head for a moment before going out. She was annoyed with herself for having chosen that very moment to look back so that he caught her glance.

"Wouldn't you like to ride, too?" Mathilde asked her.

"Oh, no!" Miette answered, but her eyes grew thoughtful.

She already saw herself dressed in riding habit, and decided that the slim jacket, the wide, extravagantly flowing skirt, the soft high boots, and the stiff felt hat on her head would be most becoming to her. But she suddenly realized that it would cost a great deal, a very great deal of money, and Father had been advising her lately to practice economy.

Walking home, she kept thinking constantly of the tall, bony girl she had seen with Golgonszky. She hadn't been able to see her face distinctly, but she told herself that it didn't much matter whether she was pretty or ugly, for she certainly was very rich and very nobly born.

Could she be Golgonszky's choice?

She felt an unreasonable dislike for this girl, and was filled with strange dread at the thought that Golgonszky might marry. But having reached that point, she roused herself in horror from her reverie, as from deep slumber, and cast glances of dismay about the street.

"I must get rid of such thoughts," she said to herself, hurrying on.

She stopped for a moment before the window of an expensive grocery shop, then went in and bought a box of preserved fruits, of which Father was very fond.

A postcard and a letter were waiting for her at home. That was unusual, for she seldom received mail. The letter was from Peter. She put it aside to read last and glanced rapidly at the card. It came from the front, from Paul Szücs.

"We are riddling the Russians with bayonet thrusts; we continue to advance, we are pushing them before us like wheelbarrows" (wrote Szücs).

Miette took up Peter's letter with a dim hope. Perhaps this letter would restore equilibrium to her troubled soul.

This was the letter that Peter had written one November night while Rosiczky's Tatar zither accompanied his thoughts.

And it reached her only now, with Christmas close at hand.

"Do you still love me? Do you still remember me?

That is the one thought that still binds me to life—that you are thinking of me and waiting for me . . ."

She read the end of the letter twice, but the words left no impression on her mind.

Father came to look for her, for he knew Peter had written and he was filled with curiosity and impatience.

"What does he write?"

Miette handed him the letter, her soul empty.

Father withdrew into his room with the letter. He put on his spectacles and plunged contentedly into it. For some time now he had been wearing in the house a black silk skull cap that Miette had made for him. At first he had rebelled against it—such headgear was appropriate only to old gentlemen; but he soon accepted it and ended by wearing it with pleasure.

After luncheon Miette lay idly on the couch, her heart uneasy. Sometimes when she entered the room and saw Peter's photograph on the dresser, she felt that it was watching her with living eyes. This time, too, the portrait stared at her, but with a look that made her lower her own eyes.

She thought of the sensations that the morning's encounter had released in her. She examined herself as if she had been a complete stranger whose perceptions and moods were controlled by forces outside herself.

She saw clearly that little by little she was being transformed into two different personalities, and that these two Miettes whom she carried within her were developing contours more and more distinct.

One was the Miette who had gone to the station with Peter and bidden him goodbye. That trembling, weeping young woman of twenty-one was still down there in the shadows among the tracks, straining her ears amid a confusion of thoughts—listening to the diminishing clatter of the receding train.

The other Miette was the one who had come home from the station; whom the current of time had borne on its waves and whose soul had been transformed by its motion. This Miette was a year and a half older than the other, and her thoughts were straying afar; time and circumstances together had brought her to a strange pass.

These two Miettes had nothing in common. They met, occasionally—the older and the younger—and surveyed each other in amazement.

She always managed to set her mind at rest by reasoning of this kind, when remorse for her secret thoughts of Golgonszky began to gnaw at her.

Why shouldn't this new Miette be free to think and to live? In any case would she not die the instant that Peter returned? She would disappear like a shadow, and in her place the old Miette would be down at the station again, awaiting the incoming train.

Having reached that conclusion, she would plunge anew into her reveries of Golgonszky, abandoning herself to the faint, sweet giddiness of her thoughts.

And thus her days passed . . .

Since the encounter at the riding school, she was conscious of seeking pretexts every day—sometimes twice a day—for going to town; she would take long walks in the secret hope of meeting Golgonszky and would often lead Tomi interminably back and forth along that section of the Danube esplanade where Golgonszky had once seen her, though walking was no pleasure in this cold, snowy weather.

Before that, she had been in the habit of taking Mili's oilcloth bag in the mornings and going hatless as far as the corner grocery to do the marketing. Now she wouldn't have done it for all the wealth in the world, lest she should meet Golgonszky in the course of that brief excursion. Thus she was never any longer alone; always and everywhere Golgonszky walked beside her, invisible. He directed her thoughts, her actions, her steps. His hand opened her wardrobe and chose the dresses she wore on her walks, for in her thoughts she always consulted his taste—which, since she had no knowledge of it, she could only imagine.

These long walks developed into increasingly eager and increasingly desperate pursuits. In the heart of the city

and in the outskirts she sought a chance encounter—and
finally stumbled upon it weeks later, in the most unexpected place.

One afternoon at about five she was leaving the Vargas'
apartment. She was wearing her simplest house dress
with a heavy shawl thrown over her shoulders.

As she turned on the landing Golgonszky suddenly
stood before her. He wore a long brown officer's coat, and
stared in amazement at Miette, while an expression of
glad surprise flashed across his face.

"Do you live in this house?"

Miette could hardly conceal her emotion. She felt her
heart throb painfully, and her legs grow so weak that they
scarcely supported her. She answered in a voice that was
only a breath: "Yes—and where are you going?"

"I am looking for a doctor—I must speak to him about
my orderly."

"Dr. Varga?"

"Yes."

"Do you know him?"

Golgonszky began to laugh.

"I shouldn't dare say so—but I remember very well
attending a tea at his house several years ago—"

"Yes?" asked Miette, lingering on the word, for she
had suddenly realized why Golgonszky's name had
seemed familiar to her from the beginning. She remembered now that Olga had once mentioned him.

This discovery occupied her thoughts to such an extent
that she scarcely heard Golgonszky's question. A faint
blush spread over her face.

"What did you ask me?"

"Where do you live?"

"There—in that corner."

"Alone?"

"With my father."

There were a few seconds of silence during which
Golgonszky gazed with rapt admiration at Miette's face.

She turned her eyes away and fixed them for no reason
on the middle of the court, grasping the landing rail with

both hands and thrusting the toe of one slipper through the iron baluster curve, as if she were about to climb it. There was uneasiness and a childish grace in that action. Then she turned her head and looked again at Golgonszky, blushing still more deeply. Her sensitive face, which invariably reflected the subtlest play of her thoughts, was now a mirror of confusion and torment, for she felt that her soul lay clear upon her face, betraying her. Those few seconds created an atmosphere of discomfort; she felt herself struggling in a net that held her prisoner.

Golgonszky understood and tried to force Miette's eyes to meet his own, whose effect on her was so strange.

"How beautiful you are!" he murmured.

Miette stared at him in alarm. She wanted to say something, to reply lightly and disdainfully to those words that affected her so potently and seemed to pierce her inmost being. She wanted to turn them off, so as to strip them of their significance and so shake off their influence; but she found herself incapable of uttering a single word. Shivering, she drew the shawl about her shoulders and felt her whole body tremble.

There was another moment of silence that opened up dizzying abysses before them; then Golgonszky resumed: "I mustn't keep you any longer—you might take cold!"

"Oh no!" said Miette, realizing at once that she shouldn't have said it and giving him her hand abruptly to counteract the effect of her words.

She looked down carefully at the hand she had given Golgonszky, as if it had retained the impression of the contact with his.

Then she ran to the door of her own apartment. Before entering, she looked back and caught a momentary glimpse beyond the landing of the brown officer's coat.

She went to her room, sat in an armchair, and cast an apprehensive, hunted glance about the room. She knew that extraordinary things were happening, that her emotions were overwhelming her, engulfing her as in a dark, fathomless welter of waters. What she felt now was almost a sense of suffocation.

She felt in this man something unexpected, something unaccountable, that she had never felt in anyone before, and that affected her and disturbed her by its very novelty. That face, with its preternatural blend of ugliness and beauty, that was comparable in no single detail to any other face, had on her the overwhelming, startling effect of a fearsome hallucination.

What was to become of her? She felt that the power of that face, and of the soul behind it, was gaining greater and greater mastery over her. She knew that she was rushing toward the abyss, she saw herself on its steep slope, and thought in terror of the danger that threatened her. An urgent, inexplicable longing took possession of her to obey this man's orders, and she had the feeling that her soul was being seized, lifted, borne away—by what ineffable power she knew not—on the path of his whims and commands. She felt herself permeated by a gentle, soothing desire to lean her head against Golgonszky's breast, that she might be near him and enjoy the peaceful delight of the contact; a desire, too, to offer him what up to then she had not known she possessed, what she had not known existed—that deepest, most secret sense of intimacy—new in essence—that had been born in her beneath the power of Golgonszky's eyes.

She was powerless to raise barriers within herself against this feeling—she couldn't keep herself from constant thoughts of him.

The days passed, uniform and uneventful, but her emotions continued to drag her thoughts after them, like a long, heavy chain.

With closed eyes she repeated over and over again those few muffled, restrained words that Golgonszky had uttered so simply and yet with an effect of such agitation: "How beautiful you are!"

For days she went nowhere, as if the disquieting influence of their last encounter had appeased her for a time, and as if Golgonszky's glance had broken something within her that dissipated her strength yet filled her with burning delight.

At first she couldn't even sleep; she would lie for an hour or two, exhausted and unconscious, haunted by the sweet turbulence of a troubled dream; and as soon as she opened her eyes she would resume the thread of her thoughts where she had dropped them when she finally drowsed.

She knew occasional moments of clarity and lucidity, when she would feel herself again and be convinced that it was only her loneliness and state of desolation that were playing this cruel game with her. On such occasions she studied herself with the eyes of a physician, building up vague, confused theories designed to prove that during the long, dreadful months of unassuaged longing, her body had doubtless stored up the seething juices of feminine desire that were now fermenting and spreading their malignant poisons through her blood; and that all this going on inside of her was the momentary disorder of an abandoned body and had nothing to do with her soul.

Yet her soul was saturated in this new, mysterious kind of poison that was rioting through her veins, ravaging and devouring her.

On Christmas afternoon she received an enormous box of roses. She opened the envelope nervously and read with a sense of disappointment the name of Alexander Petrovitch Ilyin on the visiting card.

Even at the New Year, Golgonszky gave no sign of his existence.

A few weeks later she resumed her long walks, and waited impatiently for a visit from Mathilde, hoping that through Mme. Cserey she might meet him again. The news that the Csereys had left for Vienna and would not be back for a few months was a crushing blow.

Yet she had neither the strength nor the courage to make any kind of sign to Golgonszky, fearing lest a meeting should prove fruitless and even destroy the feeling that already existed, beautiful in its very abomination.

At the beginning of February she received a letter from Peter's sister in Brassó, saying that she and her husband would be in Pest before long and would call on her.

They arrived on a dreary, snowy afternoon, and Miette did everything in her power to display some measure of friendliness toward these people whom she had never seen in her life and with whom she had nothing in common.

Even Father emerged from his study and gazed at the callers out of his tired blue eyes with the kindliness born of his family feeling. It was obvious that his attitude was one of special benevolence and indulgence and that for Peter's sake he forgave them their shortcomings.

As she poured tea, Miette couldn't make up her mind whether it was the man or the woman who made the more disagreeable impression upon her.

Michael Pável, all animation, with his brusque, choppy manner of talking, his overwhelming vitality, his shock of hair combed straight back, and his pronged mustache, made her think of some absurd object that, rubbed with a woolen cloth, emits the crackle of electricity. She found him insufferable, with his bad Hungarian pronunciation tinged with a Slavic accent and his forced humor that was intended to prove what an entertaining person he was. Equally distressing was the familiarity with which this repulsive man had entered the room, promptly addressed her with the intimate second-person "thou" and even taken her into his arms, patting her on the back.

Charlotte, whose nose had grown thinner with the years, was abundantly provided with that provincial complacency that makes women of her type so un-attractive.

As they talked she took inventory not only of Miette but of the room and the furniture, without, however, expressing her approval or any opinion whatsoever. It was apparent from her survey that she was searching for whatever pieces of furniture Peter might have brought with him—part of the paternal legacy, perhaps—with the idea at the back of her mind that they might revert to her.

She kept Miette coldly at a distance as if she knew what the young woman must have been doing during these two years of separation from Peter—and her attitude betrayed a certain bitterness because she had no evidence against her.

Nevertheless, she let slip a few remarks on the subject of conjugal fidelity, and her voice took on a slightly acid, didactic tone as if she had something with which to reproach Miette.

Pável nodded approval of everything his wife said.

This attitude was so offensive to Miette, who felt herself a hundred cubits above them, that she racked her brain for some suave word whose expertly directed dart would wound these two people to the core; a word to which the thread of the conversation would lead imperceptibly and whose edge would be keen as a razor blade's. But she decided upon reflection that the struggle was unworthy of her, and agreed instead with everything they said, contriving to overwhelm her guests with affability and exaggerated compliments.

Charlotte was trying to parade her husband as a man of extraordinary spiritual depth and great mentality. "Michael said this—Michael said that—Michael knew in advance"—such were the words constantly on her lips.

Little by little the impression grew that if Michael had been consulted beforehand there never would have been a war.

Meantime, with a rapid movement of his stubby-nailed hand, Michael was twisting the ends of his mustache, whose hairs, glued together by some cosmetic, had collected all the dust of the street.

"Tell us about Mother," said Miette, interrupting Charlotte.

"Mother? Poor thing, she's always the same. Till the last minute it was understood that she was to come with us, but when the time came to leave, she shrank from the long journey. I wasn't at all surprised. Traveling is a horror nowadays—all these terrible military trains. When is all this going to end? Thank God, Michael has an advantageous post for the present."

"Won't you stay for dinner?"

"Oh, thank you so much, my dear, but we are already engaged—Michael's friends, you know . . ."

And her eyes told what distinguished and powerful circles were opened to them by Michael's connections.

Miette was glad to be so easily rid of them. She didn't ask them to come next day, nor inquire how long they expected to be in Budapest. She pretended to take it for granted that they were leaving next day.

When they had gone she had the feeling that this woman had robbed her of something; robbed her of the clear, sweet image she had kept of Peter, for there was some fleeting resemblance between Charlotte and Peter, particularly about the eyes and mouth—the kind of resemblance between brother and sister that lies in the secret lines of the face and that only a stranger's eye can detect.

She was aware of an unpleasant, distressing sensation— as if, after a long interval, she had seen a poor edition of Peter.

The days and weeks that followed brought not the slightest variation into her life. She spent long, dreary afternoons alone with her thoughts and her fancies that clung to Golgonszky and to a world apart. But after a while the tumult of her thoughts seemed to subside, exhausted.

She had been neglecting Rose recently, but now she began sending for her often, even having her come down after dinner when the Vargas had gone out to some party.

Miette would already be in bed, propped up among the pillows, and, sometimes shouting with laughter, she would listen to the tales Rose brought her of what was going on in the house. She told her of the scenes between the caretaker and his wife, who boxed each other's ears, an occurrence she had seen with her own eyes; and she knew all sorts of queer tales about the parties given by Mlle. Prandella, who lived on the third floor and entertained her guests with her accomplished violin playing. Rose seasoned this gossip with her own often very original comments.

One evening she was sitting beside Miette's bed with the air of one who has a new and interesting tale to tell.

"Does Madame know Mr. Sinka? He lives here, on the fourth floor, in a small apartment on the court. One room and a kitchen—he's a bachelor, have you never seen him?—a little, thin, grizzled man—he works, I don't know where, and looks as shabby and poor as Job. The other day, the cook said to me, 'Look, Mr. Sinka is taking something to Mme. Kádár again!'—that's the laundress who lives next door to him. The next day I watched— Mr. Sinka goes out in the morning on his way to the office, carrying a package wrapped in a brown bag. He knocks, Mme. Kádár sticks her head out at the door, they nod and smile good morning to each other. Mr. Sinka gives her the package, says goodbye and goes. When he comes in at night, he knocks again at Mme. Kádár's door and she hands him the package—the same package, mind you, wrapped in the same brown rag. That goes on every day. Guess what is in that package: a brick, Madame! Mrs. Kádár puts Mr. Sinka's brick in the oven in the morning and it keeps warm there till night; the hot brick is to warm Mr. Sinka's bed. Oh, this terrible coal shortage!"

Such stories brought by Rose to Miette's bedside at night cast a light on the life stirring between the walls of that house.

One evening Miette asked her, a mischievous gleam in her half-closed eyes: "Tell me—is Paul Szücs still courting you?"

"Me? What is Madame thinking of . . . !"

Quickly she picked up her scarf, jumped up, and ran laughing from the room.

Miette's eyes followed her good-humoredly.

She thought of the girl's dancing step, her slender figure, her delicate contours, and it seemed to her that Rose, with her dewy freshness, her gay laughter, and her charming prattle, shed about her the sweet fragrance of a wildflower.

A few days later Koretz recalled himself to her in a

most unexpected fashion. He sent her a bag of fine flour with a letter.

"Don't be surprised at this unusual gift," he wrote. "Nowadays it is equivalent to a box of sweets or some flowers."

Flour rationing had been in effect for some time then.

Miette telephoned Koretz to express her gratitude for his gift and ended by inviting him to tea. She asked Father to come in that afternoon, and the two men chatted together with apparent pleasure, exchanging sensible opinions on the present situation, economic conditions, and the outcome of the war. Miette listened as if they were talking in a foreign tongue, for she never looked at a newspaper and shunned in distaste all news of the war.

Koretz' manner to Miette seemed a little nervous and uncertain. Occasionally he let his brown eyes rest upon her, and in his warm glance lay the unmistakable light of desire and admiration.

Miette tried to escape the insistence of those eyes and, save for a glance of frank trustfulness, gave him no response. She felt that a serious sentiment for her— burning in the depth of this mature man's being—was concealed beneath his extremely reserved and respectful manner, and that a single look from her would be enough to fan this budding passion to a leaping flame. And just because she knew it, she was all the more cautious, for she knew, too, that Koretz would never mean anything more to her than a safe and pleasant friend, and she wanted to keep him so.

After that visit they were in constant touch with each other. Koretz often telephoned to Miette to inquire whether she was in need of anything.

He was useful to her as a guardian might have been, for during that period housekeeping entailed innumerable difficulties, and the restrictions on food as well as on all other necessities made life almost unendurable.

Spring was slowly approaching.

One day in April the physician, who was also a director

in charge of a Buda sanitarium, died. That death brought a change into Miette's life, for Dr. Varga was appointed to the vacant position, which carried with it the privilege of an apartment in the sanitarium; a few weeks later the Vargas moved.

From her window Miette watched the movers carry the heavy furniture out of the house on their backs, the straps taut over their shoulders.

She had not felt of late that she had many things in common with the doctor and his wife, yet her heart was rent by unutterable pain just then. She felt that the furnishings of her former life were being carried away and that her very past was being moved farther and farther into the distance, that her girlhood memories were lost in the now empty Varga apartment, and that the horrible circle of abandonment and solitude surrounding her was spreading in ever-widening rings to some point beyond the walls of her room.

One morning she went to the fortress on the hilltop to ask for the money due her as Peter's wife, for she felt the need of even that trivial sum.

She was sitting on a bench at the upper station, waiting for the funicular, when suddenly she saw Golgonszky.

He didn't see her. He was standing a few steps away from her, reading a newspaper. This time he was in civilian clothes, and apparently was also waiting for the funicular.

Miette had the feeling that her heart was hammering through her whole body, from the tips of her feet to the crown of her head; she felt, too, that she had turned pale as death and that all her strength was forsaking her.

Golgonszky was nearer the entrance door, where several people were already waiting, and so she ran the risk of losing sight of him. For a second she considered passing in front of him, which she might have done very naturally, pretending not to see him. But she kept her seat, for she had a presentiment that an inscrutable destiny, directed by mysterious forces, was approaching her in the person of this man. It would be futile, she told herself, to try to avoid this destiny or go forward to meet it; she would leave everything in the hands of chance.

Golgonszky folded the newspaper, looked absent-mindedly about him, and caught sight of Miette.

He hastened immediately toward her.

"How long it is since I've seen you!" he said softly, after having bowed and shaken hands with her.

"I never go anywhere," said Miette, choosing her words with care, lest she betray her deep agitation.

They began talking and didn't notice that the funicular had come and gone down again.

"Where are you going now?" Golgonszky asked.

"Home."

"Wouldn't you like to walk a little?"

Miette looked at her watch, as if her decision depended on the hour.

"Yes—I should."

They set out and before long had reached the Fishers' Bastion, which was almost deserted.

"How do you live? What do you do? How do you spend your days?" asked Golgonszky. And, without waiting for her answer, he added: "I pity you so profoundly—all of you."

"Why?"

"Humanity is suffering the cruelest torments imaginable these days. Take yourself—"

"Oh, I'm resigned to my fate," said Miette lightly.

But Golgonszky refused to be interrupted and went on heatedly: "God created you to live, to sparkle, to shine, for your own pleasure and the pleasure of those about you —as long as you remain so glowingly young and beautiful. There is something in you that captures the imagination. You are so beautiful that everyone is dismayed when you enter a room where there are strangers. You frighten and mortify the women, and you inflict pain upon the men, that particular kind of nostalgia that every man experiences when he sees a remarkable woman who is not his and who he knows never can be his. You are more than merely beautiful! You radiate the charm of the unattain-

able, and that makes you perilously desirable. It bewitched me, too. It distracted me, unsettled me, filled
me with a strange, disquieting sensation. I remember the
first time I saw you. You were sitting in a corner in the
shadow of a lamp. I was leaning against the mantel. I
watched you, my heart troubled as if I sensed the
approach of an intangible apparition that held the clue
to all those riddles of life that occupy our thoughts and
provoke our speculations; those riddles that we identify
with the purest desires of body and soul, and the loftiest
esthetic taste. Look here, I'm a cynic. I maintain over
and above everything else the rights of self. I feel myself
possessed of mighty forces, burning will power, insane
recklessness, to conquer what I need, what I feel will
appease the terrible, consuming thirst tormenting me in
the depths of my being, tormenting every man in the
same way. When I saw you the first time I looked at you
as men look at any pretty woman. Then I examined you
more and more attentively and I said to myself, 'Yes,
there she is, that is the woman I have so often imagined,'
and with the ravenous hunger of a flesh-eater I felt that
here was royal prey whose delicious blood I might
absorb into my veins. What you felt, what you thought of
me, how I affected you—that wasn't important. The only
important thing was this terrible compulsion blazing,
spreading within me. Should I have been successful? I
don't know. I believe I should. But, you see, I avoided
the conflict, beautiful as it would have been even in
defeat—with its thousand thrills, its imagined triumphs,
its throbbing sensitiveness to the loved one's proximity,
its fevers and agonies of inflamed desire—for therein we
reach the highest level of life. The most beautiful thing in
the world is the pursuit! To hunt, like game, a woman's
weakening will! I gave up this struggle because I felt it
would have been an infamy. You have a husband, and
to trample upon someone who cannot defend himself, who
is absent—that is a piece of cowardice that is more than
my conscience could tolerate. If you were a free woman,
or if your husband were here and I could take you from

him with my teeth and my nails, by violence with a
revolver, or with money—that would be another thing.
But this way—the man who is absent possesses a strength
I cannot fight. Isn't that true?"

"Yes, it is true," Miette whispered, appalled by those
words that filled her at the same time with unutterable
rapture.

Golgonszky removed his hat, allowing the gentle breeze
to fan his forehead. They stopped by the stone parapet
and gazed—but with eyes turned inward—far over the
city that lay stretched at their feet, with its domes, its
towers and gray-roofed houses enveloped in a fine mist,
and its clamor that reached their ears, softened by
distance.

"You see," said Golgonszky, "you are as much a
prisoner as your husband. You, too, have desires and
needs to which perhaps you cannot even give a name. It
must be so, for life speaks in a loud voice, in a powerful,
penetrating voice as if issuing from the throat of a young
bear, and that voice cries and pierces the walls of the
rooms in which you lock yourself. And I often have the
impression that I hear that cry . . ."

Miette didn't answer. With the tip of her gloved finger
she traced mysterious letters on the stone parapet. She
had neither the strength to protest nor the courage to
raise her eyes. She felt that Golgonszky was reading her
soul with his words.

"I don't know," he continued, "which of you two is
enduring the harder captivity. He is locked up in a
barracks and guarded by bayonets. Those are external,
alien powers; but you must build a barracks around
yourself, by your own strength, and you must forge your
own bayonets and direct them against yourself. Up there,
life is dull, everything is stupefied by torpor, the days are
lost in sullen indifference, in nothingness—but you, you
live here in this magnificent, intoxicating city, where the
very stones sing, where feverish life escapes through the
walls, and where everything you see about you stimulates
you, draws you, excites you."

Miette drew a deep breath—like a sigh that escaped from her heart. She was struggling with herself, unwilling to betray her emotion.

It began drizzling, and they took the road leading downward.

"I am going back to the front," said Golgonszky, "and I shan't see you for a long time. It may even be that I shall never see you again . . ." then he added, "for any one of a number of reasons; death on the battlefield is always a possibility, though that hardly enters into my calculations; I believe that the real reason is in myself— you may have noticed that I have been avoiding you."

After that they walked side by side for a long time in silence. A thousand thoughts whirled through Miette's mind, but when she wanted to express them she couldn't grasp a single one—it was as if they eluded her nimbly at just the crucial moment.

She wanted so much to say something and, in the giddiness of her joy, she sought desperately for a word that would pierce Golgonszky's heart and dwell there like some ponderable object. But nothing came to her mind, and she didn't regret her silence overmuch, for she felt that its spirit was winged, and that Golgonszky understood her speechless language.

They reached the trolley station without further words.

A moment later the grating car issued from beneath the viaduct.

Miette held out her hand to Golgonszky.

"Perhaps we shall see each other again," she said in a low, peculiarly warm voice, and allowed her hand to rest for a moment in his.

He stood there, motionless, till the car had started, and Miette turned her head to look at him.

When she got home she caught up Tomi, who was waiting in the lobby, with a quick gesture, held him high in the air, touched her nose for a second to the dog's cold muzzle and threw kisses at him. Then she pressed him fiercely against her heart and dropped him to the floor again—her customary way with Tomi.

Her soul was in a frantic state of turmoil. She paced the apartment, whistled—a thing she seldom did—and ran her fingers, in passing, over the furniture and window-panes, as if to draw arpeggios from these inanimate objects.

Then she clasped her hands behind her neck and continued to walk about in that position, almost losing her balance each time she turned.

"He will come back!" she whispered to herself. Then she sat at the piano and opened an old music book. She couldn't play, she had no talent for music, but she placed her beautiful hands carefully on the keys and played some childhood scales out of the yellowing old book.

For days and days she went nowhere. Sometimes she would stand for whole half hours at a time in the corner near the stove that was her favorite spot, her eyes fixed on some invisible point. Or else she idled, dreaming, on the couch. Her eyes closed, she would repeat to herself over and over again the words she had heard on the Fishers' Bastion, and she saw Golgonszky's bared forehead under the light breeze as he stood by the fretted stones of the parapet, looking into the distance beyond the clouds, and she saw that a lock of his hair—strange blue-gray hair, fine and silky as bird's down—had been blown against his temple by the breeze.

So, among dreams, a few weeks slipped by. Time seemed to have taken wings.

One afternoon Mathilde came to see her.

"Summer will soon be here," she said. "What a pity that we can't go to the seashore! Oh, why this horrible war? We'll have to go through Germany again—"

"Take me with you," said Miette, without raising her eyes, as she poured coffee from an antique silver pot.

Mathilde's face lighted joyously. "Would you go with us?"

"I was only joking—I couldn't go in any case," and she tried to change the subject.

But Mathilde refused to abandon the idea.

"After all, why couldn't you come with us? It would

give us infinite pleasure, and a little trip would do you good, too."

"Oh, it's not so simple—and I have no clothes—"

"Clothes? Let me see your wardrobe . . ."

With an expert hand Mathilde began making a selection from among the coats, traveling costumes, and hats. Though everything dated from peacetime, it was of the finest quality, for Miette patronized only the best shops.

Mathilde would listen to no further objections.

"I am going to talk to your father," she said, and with her light step passed quickly into Father's room.

They left three weeks later.

Miette reveled in this new kind of comfort, the comfort of traveling when another attends to all the details, and especially when that other considers no expense. Traveling is an art and Cserey was a past master at it.

They spent several days in Vienna and from there went to Salzburg.

Soon after they left for Berlin, where war's privations were already apparent in the streets; but money still made it possible to discover hidden corners of luxury. Miette was often distressed to see small fortunes slipping through the Cserey's hands—but this seemed to be the usual thing with them. They vied with each other— husband and wife—in making Miette's trip as comfortable and interesting as possible—unforgettable, in fact. They lavished upon her marks of their care and tenderness— it seemed to give them extraordinary pleasure to do so.

Then they left for Swinemünde by the sea.

It was now summer, and the torrid days had arrived.

He who sees the sea for the first time finds himself face to face with God—and Miette had never seen the sea.

She stood on the beach, listening to the majestic roar of the incoming tide. Under the influence of this music of the Infinite, her thoughts of Peter grew confused.

Frequently during the day she would go alone to bathe and, surrendering herself to the gentle play of the waves, would luxuriate in feeling her body grow lighter in the water.

During the bathing hour she discovered the charm of a new kind of solitude; she would sit for hours on a jutting rock, breathing in the enchanting breath of the sea. She would look far out, moving not even her head, while innumerable thoughts, sweet and bitter at once, passed through her head and the spray of the sea fell and dried on her face.

She thought of Golgonszky, and heard his voice in the wind and the roar of the waves.

One day as they walked on the beach toward evening, Golgonszky suddenly appeared before them, as though he had sprung from the earth.

He wore a light summer suit and his face was bronzed by the sun. He seemed a little nervous, and avoided Miette's eyes, as if unwilling to see the effect his unexpected appearance had upon her.

He told them he had business in Berlin and had come to the seaside for only a few days.

It was some time before they had a chance for a word together, but a little later, when all the questions with which people pelt one another on such occasions had been exhausted, the Csereys stopped in front of a newsstand.

Miette and Golgonszky walked on a little way.

"I am not here by accident," said Golgonszky, speaking rapidly and low, and glancing behind him to estimate how much time would be given them for this private conversation.

His voice was filled with passion and with pain.

"I looked for you in Pest, and learned there that you were here. I could no longer bear not seeing you—and here I am! You have kindled in my soul an emotion that drives out every other thought—I am no longer master of myself—every vestige of what is called character, control, reason, has fled—I have not come here of my own will— I have reached the end of my will—I have been dragged here by force."

He stopped abruptly, for he was undergoing an agonizing struggle. He took off his hat and bared his burning forehead to the wind. With narrowed eyes he gazed into the distance, as if he expected an answer from the roar of the sea.

Meantime the Csereys had rejoined them.

"Ivan, I hope you're going to dine with us," said Mathilde, giving Miette the newest postcards—for her affectionate care embraced even such trivialities.

They dined on the terrace.

They had been invited to the villa of a German deputy after dinner, but Miette refused the invitation, for she felt that she couldn't endure being among strangers until midnight.

Never before had she wanted so much to be alone, and after dinner she went directly to her room.

She stretched herself on the couch and closed her eyes, listening to the distant murmur of the sea, pierced now and then by the melancholy hoot of a ship's siren. She lay completely absorbed in her thoughts, one down-flung hand just touching the carpet.

It was still light, but the folds of the draperies were being softly blotted out by the dusk. Cool breezes from the sea fluttered through the open window into the room.

She must have been lying there a long time when suddenly, hearing footsteps at her door, she leapt up.

Pressing her right hand to her forehead, she stared at the door. She was sure it was Golgonszky.

Her heart was throbbing violently.

Golgonszky appeared in the open doorway, then took a few steps toward her, and thus they stood, facing each other.

During those few seconds of silence, dizzying sensations whirled about them, as if they stood at the brink of an abyss.

Miette felt she was lost.

A tremor of fear shook her, and she retreated to the table. She felt that she was about to burst into tears, and, desperately twisting her hands, she looked straight at Golgonszky, her face transformed in alarm. Gasping and broken came her words: "I beg you—Golgonszky—I implore you—leave me. You see that I am weak—you cannot do this to me—I beg you—in God's name—go away . . ."

The last words were spoken almost sobbingly.

Golgonszky gazed at her for a moment without stirring. His face was very pale.

He bowed in silence and left the room.

Miette collapsed by the window and rested her forehead in her hands.

The room grew dark about her.

The next morning she received a letter from Budapest, in which Elvira told her—with an exaggerated caution that served only to alarm her the more—that for the last few days Father had not felt at all well.

She left for home immediately.

IV

The officers in the Misery Hotel were grouped in front of the photographer, a German Jew, to have their pictures taken on the occasion of the second anniversary of their captivity.

Following Mezei's instructions, they had grouped themselves on the steps of the house, so that above their heads could be seen the placard bearing the official name, Hungarian Home, which they had decorated for the occasion with fresh foliage and small Hungarian flags.

They were fourteen in all, and for two days Zamák had been ironing the officers' clothes so that the trousers should be well creased for the picture.

They had given the place in the center of the group to Mezei, for he was the oldest among them in point of service, and their nominal chief. Neteneczky, who was by nature over-courteous, had even brought him a chair.

Mezei, as the most important personage in the group, had folded his arms over his chest and flung back his shoulders.

Behind him, to the right and left, stood Bartha and Vedres. Vedres was standing practically at attention; he had assumed—God knows why—the somber expression of a prophet of ill omen, and had been waiting patiently since long before the scheduled time, his eyes fixed on an invisible spot.

Bartha leaned familiarly on the back of the chair and, one hand before his mouth, never stopped laughing, for he couldn't take his eyes from the photographer's trousers, which looked as if they had been unearthed from the darkest corner of the Tatar bazaar. There was a long rent in the back, and the piece with which it had been ineptly patched dangled half loose. The legs were ridiculously tight and ended in accordion pleats above the shoes with their turned-up tips.

The photographer, who answered to the name of Gützow, hopped about on his long legs in front of the camera like a dizzy crane. As he arranged the group of men, he would catch now at his glasses, now at his trousers, both of which were always on the point of falling. He was a jolly fellow, and called incessantly as he hopped: "Nur ein' Moment, meiner Herrschaften!"

When he had finally succeeded in arranging them to his liking, he seized his long chin in his hand and, head cocked, surveyed the group critically.

To the right of Mezei stood Lieutenants Lukács, Szentesi, and Hirsch. Lukács had assumed an affectedly sweet expression, a constant habit of his that irritated his comrades. Behind his smile and his suavity was an enigmatic quality, an inscrutable purpose that, even here in captivity, he revealed to no one. Vedres was of the opinion that here was a man who, if he should ever find himself in a hole, would sell them all for two kreutzer. Lukács seemed to feel the general atmosphere of unfriendliness, and went always armed in a kind of unfathomable Oriental servility and obsequiousness; as for his profession, they knew only that he was the director of a club in Budapest, devoted chiefly to gambling.

Szentesi, who even at the most critical moments never parted from his razor and his mustache holder, now waited, with freshly shaven cheeks and waxed mustache, for the click of the camera, his honest sheep's face turned toward the apparatus. They all loved Szentesi—who was called "Little Stump" because of his short, squat figure —for they knew that if the need arose he would give his last shirt for his comrades. He was a good, simple, brave-hearted fellow, recognizable a hundred feet away as the typical tradesman. He had a prosperous business at Györ, which his father had deeded him during his life-time. By his own admission, he had been the worst student in the whole province, though he had managed to get his bachelor's degree at the age of twenty-one, after his father had for years been sending half the shop's contents to his professors. Those had been the worst days of his life, and their memory made it possible for him to endure his Siberian captivity with a lighter heart. After his exam-inations he had served a year as volunteer and married soon after. When war broke out he already had four children, the eldest being twins.

Hirsch was an insurance agent in Pest. He was without doubt by far the skinniest, longest-necked young Jew in existence, but concealed beneath his unattractive exterior a wealth of kindness and humor. He walked with so decided a stoop that he looked like a fishhook waiting to be baited. He couldn't rid himself of the attitude im-planted in him by his former profession, and even now he was contemplating Gützow as he hopped about the camera, and wondering for what amount, and on what scale, he might be induced, circumstances permitting, to insure his life.

To the left stood Altmayer, Csaba, and Szabó. Alt-mayer was the son of a Viennese cardboard manufacturer, but during his childhood had discovered in himself a talent for painting, which had disinclined him for his father's respectable trade. He had spent several years in Munich where, instead of painting, he had learned a complete repertory of drinking songs, which were a great asset here. Altmayer had organized a quartet made up of Bartha, Rosiczky, Szabó, and himself, to sing these songs.

Fate had flung Szabó among them from somewhere in

Transylvania, where he was studying to be a lawyer. Csaba, on the other hand, was an agricultural engineer, and assistant manager of a lordly estate beyond the Danube, which was why he would pause occasionally before the displays of the grain merchants and run the wheat of Tobolsk expertly between his fingers.

"Good Lord, what couldn't one grow in this soil!" he was wont to say.

He and Szabó—who even before the war had abandoned all hope of passing his bar examinations, and who flung himself rapturously into any adventurous scheme—discussed this project night and day; once the war was over, they would turn everything they had at home into cash and come back to Tobolsk as farmers. All they would need do would be to apply modern market-gardening methods to a few acres of land. The plan seemed not unfeasible, for land could be rented so cheaply in the neighborhood of Tobolsk that, according to Hungarian standards, it seemed more like a gift than a lease.

Szabó, whose imagination had wings, could already see himself, rich and round-bellied, in the midst of a huge, improved leasehold.

Csaba had begun experimenting with market gardening in a fenced-off corner of the yard. He remembered that on their arrival they had carried a huge heap of manure from the yard of Misery Hotel to the banks of the Irtysh; now all he had to do was to plant large quantities of Russian cabbages and tomatoes there. Thanks to his own system of fertilizing and watering the ground, his very first attempts produced results that were admired even in the Tobolsk public market.

There burned in this young Hungarian, with his warm brown eyes, a passion for teaching and demonstrating. He wasn't satisfied till he had succeeded in gathering all the young men about him, and he explained to them with such enthusiasm and so radiant a countenance the various methods of using scientific fertilizers that in a very short time he had transformed most of his comrades, as if by magic, into earnest and resolute farmers.

Lukács and Kölber alone remained unaffected.

Lukács made notes all day and drew mysterious figures on sheets of paper, having invented, according to his own account, a new card game that was to take the world by storm. Kölber rarely spoke to anyone; one had to drag each word from him, and he lived for his diary alone, whose manuscript could now hardly be crowded into the drawer of his narrow little writing table.

But the others developed an increasingly keen taste for gardening. Each had his own plot of ground and the rows of vegetables soon stretched down to the Irtysh. Csaba maintained that the following year they would be making money out of it.

One evening Bartha had brought home with him a large white dog that he had lured with a piece of sausage from the vicinity of the governor's palace. He looked like a Hungarian sheepdog, though his body was longer and he was tall as a wolf. Judging by his collar, he must have come from a well-to-do home.

They baptized him "Comrade" and declared him common property.

At first Comrade didn't feel at all comfortable among these strangers, and growled especially at the approach of Neteneczky, who always addressed him tenderly and spoke to him as to a child in swaddling clothes. But it wasn't long before he felt by various signs the affection and fraternal comradeship that was being tendered him, and since, moreover, the food seemed to be to his taste, he made friends with them all, and opened his heart to each of them. Misery Hotel was promptly transformed for him into a veritable canine Eldorado, for from morning to night they all showered him with attentions, so that he began to feel his own importance.

He had elected Zamák as his bed-companion, and every evening, sitting at the threshold of his room, the latter would relate to Comrade the history of his family as far back as his grandmother. He invented a special dog language and Comrade would listen patiently and with apparent interest to these interminable tales.

The photograph group would not have been complete without Comrade, and after much debate they placed him in the foreground at Mezei's feet.

After Neteneczky, Lajtai, Rosiczky, Kölber, and Peter had taken their places in the group, Gützow signed to them to be silent and not to move. Peter was standing to the right of the group, looking with his bearded face like a youthful portrait of Lajos Kossuth.

Behind the camera, the orderlies were watching with an absorbed and lively interest.

Before Gützow pressed the bulb, Bartha shouted to the orderlies: "I see that you'd like to be in the picture too. . . . All right, come along, and sit on the ground in front of us!"

Smiling broadly, the orderlies obeyed; Zamák had to be seated by force, for he insisted on being photographed standing and kept getting in front of Altmayer so as to hide him completely.

At last the group was ready. Everyone stood motionless and the expressions assumed for the pose froze on each countenance. Gützow tucked up his left sleeve, and with the gesture of a prestidigitator reverently grasped the shutter of the camera, crying: "Eins, zwei; eins, zwei; eins, zwei—hopp!"

Whereupon he closed the instrument and bowed low.

Zamák shouted, "Hurrah!" and they all took up the cry.

Gützow approached the officers and asked pleasantly: "Hat es ihner weh getan?" and he chuckled, baring his black, broken teeth, proffering this stale photographer's witticism to each in turn, as he would have proffered a sweet.

"Yes," answered Hirsch, in a sepulchral voice and with some temper.

"Wieso?"

But Hirsch replied only by an evasive movement of the hand. He glanced at Szentesi, who nodded agreement with a bitter smile.

Gützow didn't realize that for these men this was a day of anguished mourning, rounding out as it did the second year of their captivity. The year that was taking flight before them paused for a second, hovering above the dark cloth with which Gützow had covered his camera, and stared at them from that point of vantage, plunging its eyes like a ghost in their hearts.

Each of them was asking himself: How much longer will this horrible persecution last that will drive us all mad in the end? When will this hellish torment into which body and soul must slowly, imperceptibly sink to decay— when will it terminate?

The hope of peace hovered always about them like a carrier pigeon settling himself for an occasional brief rest on the dilapidated shingles of the roof of Misery Hotel. When they returned from town at night, each had some piece of news to impart to the others, gleaned from interned Germans, from Jewish merchants, or from some acquaintance among the citizenry. They discussed these items of news in the community room downstairs, often until midnight. Sleepy though they were, they would prop themselves on their elbows about the big, round table and argue spiritedly over the meaning of some enigmatic piece of information.

They were quite aware that discipline in the Russian army was practically nonexistent. Not a single Russian artisan or tradesman or peasant with whom they talked made a secret of it. They all longed impatiently for peace. Russian villages to the North were already sheltering hundreds and hundreds of deserting soldiers, whom the villagers hid in their own houses. The story began to circulate that the Little Father himself wanted peace at all costs and was in secret communication with Emperor Wilhelm. That piece of news was brought by Zamák, who imparted it with so weighty an air that one might have believed he had been talking a half hour earlier with the Tsar himself.

At all events, it is certain that the process of dissolution in Russia, like the stifling smoke of the flaming northern tundras, reached as far as the yard of Misery Hotel and kept the young men there in a constant state of perturbation. Two parties were formed. One was made up of invincible optimists, while the members of the other contented themselves with incredulous flourishes of the hand.

Peter belonged to neither of these parties. Occasionally, on the strength of some piece of news, he would abandon himself to the exuberance of joyful emotion, only to sink once more into the same dark lethargy.

Vedres, who was among the optimists, wagered a hundred rubles with Csaba that revolution would break out in Russia by Christmas, and that spring would see them back in Hungary. Csaba, who was planning an extensive market-gardening development for the spring, would hear of no such thing. Meantime, neither of them could produce the stakes to cover their hundred-ruble wager, but they took it very seriously nevertheless.

Meanwhile events pursued their course, like those terrible silent landslides in the bowels of the earth, giving no indication as to just where, when, and in what direction the surface will be split asunder, though everyone feels beneath his feet the movement of mysterious forces and awaits with anguished heart the moment when God's hand will precipitate whole continents into the abyss.

It was an open secret that corruption was demoralizing the whole country over incredible areas. They learned from a Russian dentist that a shocking famine at the front was making devastating inroads among the soldiers, while carloads of foodstuffs were rotting in the huge warehouses of Vladivostok.

Traffic on the Russian railroads grew daily worse; the whole system was in confusion like an immense fish net that had got hopelessly tangled. The powerful railroad syndicate, the largest and best-organized combination in Russia, had fallen into the hands of the Cadet party; this fact alone seemed to seal the fate of the Romanoff dynasty, since in those days whoever controlled the means of communication—railroads, ships, mails, and telegraph

—was the all-powerful master, capable of making the vast body of that mighty empire dance to his tune.

The popular opinion was that General Broussilov's offensive, breaking through the enemy's front, had rekindled for the last time the hope of victory in Russia. Yet the results of that notable triumph petered out into little more than the acquisition of hundreds of thousands of prisoners, Germans, Austrians, Hungarians, and Turks, with whom the Russian commander-in-chief filled the cities to bursting, and whose maintenance resulted in a general increase in the cost of living. Fresh consignments of prisoners arrived almost daily at Tobolsk, and one day an order was issued forbidding the occupants of Misery Hotel, as well as all other war prisoners, to go to town before ten o'clock in the morning; at that hour the city's civilian population had already bought out the marketplace, so that very often the orderlies returned with nothing but beef bones, liver, tripe, and rotten cabbages. Fortunately, fish were abundant in the Irtysh; the orderlies wove large nets that covered the dams like huge spiderwebs. The head of the fishing department was Gyurka Suhajda, Mezei's orderly, who before the war had earned his living as a fisherman in the Tisza, and had long since made a net for himself. Necessity had now given this industry an unexpected impetus, and under the supervision of Csaba, Szentesi, and Saabó, all the orderlies fished in the Irtysh from morning to night.

The latest news could always be gathered in the neighborhood of the bazaar. It reached that point like the palpable swell of a distant earthquake, when the streets of Petrograd, of Moscow, of Kiev, of Kazan and other large cities, began to shake. The famished crowd, clamoring wildly for peace and for bread, broke into daily riots. The police had lost their old formidable power, and even in the case of mutinous garrisons, the insurgents were handled with circumspection and mildness.

Vedres would return from town smiling broadly.

"Your hundred rubles are doomed, my dear Emeric," he would say to Csaba.

But the latter would reply only with a skeptical gesture.

While in the street, in the villages, in the garrisons, and at the front, the well-organized Socialists were mining the ground for revolution, they were at the same time hurling their demands for peace—in the Duma, in the ministries, in the government halls—at the Russian bear who, standing on his four ponderous paws, was beginning to sway perilously and to growl savagely, his eyes filling with blood.

Up to now the *moujiks* had waged war fanatically; for in peacetime the threat of Siberia, of the Sakhalin Islands, or of Knon, and now the machine guns at their backs, had accustomed them to blind obedience. These devout people, passive, bending their backs to everyone, hastening to kiss the hand of every priest they met in the street, burning perpetual vigil lights before the holy icons in their poor, clean little rooms, and in practically every railroad waiting room and restaurant, however deserted. These people—who made the sign of the Cross in terror at the very sound of the Little Father's name and trembled with fear when their eyes happened to fall on the Tsar's mournful, bearded picture—were gradually losing confidence, first in themselves, then in their immediate superiors, their leaders, and finally they began to suspect the priests themselves. Their gently morbid souls sought comfort in the doctrine of some new people. They were growing indifferent—this unhappy people—to the preachings and would have been willing to die at the stake to save their wandering, uneasy souls.

This uncertainty, the lack of a common ideal and a controlling will, these were the reasons why the burning flood that ran hidden beneath the earth had not yet been able to open a way for itself and burst to the surface, though the whole country was already seething with a passionate longing for revolution.

The war party was striving to assemble all its strength. They continued to raise the Greek Cross high, proclaiming everywhere that if the Little Father won the war, this Cross would adorn the tower of Saint Sofia in Constantinople. The Tsar would be the Pope and pastor of the Eastern Church, and he would unite all the Slavic nations in a single flock. And then would begin that other struggle—that truly magnificent struggle against the Catholic Church—so that at last the Word might be fulfilled: "One stable, one Shepherd!" But it was the Little Father himself who had least faith in that proclamation. A few hysterical staff officers and hot-headed Pan-Slavic politicians were alone responsible for the proclamation and cried at the top of their lungs that the war must go on.

So uncertainty continued to hold sway. The *Telegram* announced that Great Britain was to send a million soldiers to the front for the winter campaign, and Russia two million.

This news injected fresh life into the discussions of the inmates of Misery Hotel.

Csaba said in his turn to Vedres: "Your hundred rubles are doomed, my dear Joseph!"

So it went day after day. Things moved so swiftly, events followed so rapidly upon one another's heels, that they often made the same taunt to each other on the same day.

After a few weeks everything settled down again, and deep gray horizons of appalling monotony unrolled as far as the eye could see.

One afternoon an ugly incident occurred in the yard of Misery Hotel.

Bartha and Csaba came to blows. How and why it would have been difficult to fathom, for up to then no dispute had ever arisen between the two men. But their minds were now filled with wild and bitter emotions, and it may have been due to blind chance that the quarrel should have blazed up between just these two.

Bartha was sitting outside in front of the house, under the birch trees, writing a letter. Not far away, Csaba, seated on a tree stump, was engaged in sharpening a rusty hoe. The file drew a grating, ear-shattering sound from the hoe.

"Get the devil out of here with that squeaking!" cried Bartha nervously.

Csaba only raised his head and continued more energetically than before.

"Get out of here!" Bartha roared, beside himself.

"That's a little emphatic," said Csaba ominously.

Bartha flung his pen down on the table, shouting: "You dirty blackguard!"

Csaba put the hoe aside and strode up to Bartha. "What did you say?"

For a moment they confronted each other, motionless, their eyes glittering. Csaba made a gesture as if to strike, but Bartha, no longer able to control himself, forestalled him and struck with all his might, while Csaba dodged quickly, taking the blow on his neck.

The next second Bartha recoiled, staggering, for Csaba's bony fist had caught him under the eye. The table was overturned, the inkstand rolled onto the ground, and the ink with which Bartha had been about to write to his mother was spilled in the dust.

A wild fight ensued, the two men hurling themselves savagely upon each other.

Vedres was first to interpose between the two raging men.

"Children! Look here! Children!" he cried, his voice woeful and despairing.

It wasn't easy to separate them. Even after their arms were pinned firmly to their sides, they continued to glare, pale and panting, into each other's eyes. Down Bartha's unshaven, chalk-white cheek the blood flowed from a long, gaping wound under the eye down to his mouth, and dripped on the dirty collar of his shirt.

Bartha was taken to his room, where Mezei held a long conversation with him in undertones.

Csaba went into the community room and sat in the darkest corner.

"What was it all about?" Rosiczky asked.

But Csaba didn't answer. He stared straight ahead of him, frowning.

They made up the same evening. Bartha came down to the community room, walked up to Csaba, held out his hand and said: "Servus, Emeric!"

Csaba jumped up. He wanted to smile but couldn't, and they clasped hands in silence.

But they remained gloomy and depressed for days and days after that, and no one heard the sound of their voices. For five days, until his wound healed, Bartha did not leave his room.

For some time Peter had been attending morning mass every Sunday in a little church in the upper city. He was not naturally devout, but the spiritual torment and suspense that sometimes left him mortally exhausted seemed eased there in the church. High up, to the organ's accompaniment, the chant of the cherubim floated out, sung by a three-part choir, and the ritual of the Russian mass and the piety of the people kneeling at the altar steps below somehow comforted his heart.

He was a little early on that particular Sunday, and the services had not yet begun. There were only a few people in the church, chiefly old ladies; among them he noticed a young girl kneeling on the flagstones at the back.

He couldn't explain to himself why his glance strayed continually to this girl who, with her simple attire, her high black boots, and her pretty hat trimmed only with some artificial red eglantine berries, had attracted his attention from his first glimpse of her.

He couldn't see her face distinctly, but even in this kneeling position there was a natural grace in the carriage of her head and in the movements of her joined hands that arrested Peter's attention.

Above the organ's accompaniment, the Kheruvimskaya began mounting softly. The fresh voices of young girls, women's contraltos, and warm tenors rang out behind them. The angels' chorus, in four parts, filled every corner of the church.

Peter watched the kneeling girl steadily.

When the service was over he remained standing in the church doorway, waiting for the crowd to emerge.

The girl was one of the last. Peter recognized the red berries on her hat from a distance.

As she passed him she raised her eyes to his for a moment. Her face was pale, and in that white face two great black eyes glowed. She looked at Peter, as a woman might steal a glance at a stranger in the street. But her eyes were full of feeling and their glance plunged for an instant into Peter's soul.

His gaze followed her. She walked with a beautiful swaying grace, descended the steps of the church, and turned toward the main street, but stopped for a moment in front of Licharov's pharmacy to inspect the bottles of perfume in the window.

For a second Peter considered following and speaking to her. Then he turned away and took the road home, as one who has nothing to seek in the lives of others.

Once at home, however, the girl's hat, with its red berries, occupied his thoughts throughout the whole of luncheon.

V

Around ten at night Francis Almády had barely laid his head on the pillow and stretched his arms over the blanket when he was overwhelmed by a curious, unaccountable sense of weakness, so acute that he felt an immediate presentiment of death.

This terrified him. He knew he was doomed, but he had counted on two or three more years of respite. But now this consciousness of imminent death—this he found horrible, inconceivable!

A moment before he had felt quite well. And now, suddenly, the mysterious force called life seemed to be escaping from his body, which had grown empty and cold, especially below the waist, and his two hands lay exhausted and helpless on the blanket as if the departing soul had already withdrawn from his limbs and lingered only in the lungs, the heart, and the brain.

A cold perspiration beaded his forehead and he stared with a grim, inward gaze at an invisible spot on the ceiling.

Death had come. Curious how very clearly his brain grasped that fact! And what a strange contrast between his suddenly sharpened intellect and his pathetically impotent body.

If only Miette were here! But half an hour ago when she had left for the theater with neighbors, he had felt unusually well and strong. How had this happened and why should it have come upon him so suddenly? It was weeks since he had suffered any pain; and it was two months since he had last felt really ill, when Miette had been obliged to hurry home from Germany.

A soft October rain was falling outside.

If only Miette were with him now! Why had he let her go?

The windows ought to be opened. There seemed to be no air in the room. His lungs hurt him as if he were inhaling fire.

If he could only have a glass of water! Perhaps this unbearable burning sensation would stop . . .

He tried to call Mili, but no sound came, despite his most strenuous efforts. Gradually, he grew calmer.

After his exertion he felt a gentle—yes, even a pleasant —sense of fatigue and relaxation. The departing soul, having been set free, wandered back into the life that was past.

Suddenly he remembered himself as a little boy, and the bygone years appeared to him as from a dim distance.

He saw his mother again, with her old-fashioned high topknot, standing in front of the kitchen door, and he heard her voice distinctly. In the brilliant midday sunlight he saw the rows of pot-bellied jars of cucumbers standing on the narrow ledge built for them around the house; he saw how they basked and ripened in the sun, and how their parchment lids puckered and blistered.

He saw his father, with his ruddy beard; he saw him

walking along the wooden sidewalk of the little town, carrying his stick over his shoulder like a rifle.

He saw the large schoolyard with its mulberry trees and the moving shadows of their foliage on the white-washed walls. He had the sensation of actually being there among the many little barefoot peasant children—in the schoolroom smelling of the damp wool of heavy overcoats, where the oil lamp hung by a piece of twisted wire that seemed to turn a luminous red in the thick afternoon sunlight.

It all returned distinctly to his mind.

Suddenly he was in the college classroom, and he saw a chalk-drawn circle on the cracked old blackboard; he heard the squeaking of the chalk; he saw some formula indicated by root signs: $A+B$, $c+d$—but the rest grew confused in his memory . . .

His mind, exhausted by the effort, rushed on, grasping at everything within its reach. But he could do no more than skim the surface of his memories here and there, then leap forward in huge, incredible bounds, like the reflection of a broken bit of glass manipulated in the sunlight.

Now all that faded into nothingness and he saw himself, a young law student, with his clothes and his small budding beard worn in the fashion of the Eighties. He heard about him the familiar noises of old Pest—the horns of horse cars, and the long blast of the Mohács steamboat's siren below the Chain Bridge.

Then he was seated at his regular table in the restaurant that had formerly been the Szikszay; it was an evening flooded by summer warmth; he sat on the terrace beneath an awning, on the noisy pavement in the glaring gaslight, and drank sparkling soda water. He never drank anything else.

From there his memory leapt to the whitewashed walls and huge files of the Hall of Archives where he had spent long years of monotonous labor. The penetrating smell of yellowing old papers filled the air. How many years, all exactly alike, had he buried between those walls! How many sunny days of life and youth had sped by outside while he rummaged among those old documents that reeked of death.

His memory turned eagerly to the doe-eyed girl who was to become his wife. How lovely she had been, how beautiful that slight forward bend of the neck! Her whole being exhaled the charm of youth, the fragrance of virginity. Had there ever been anything lovelier than she, with her silken, auburn knot of hair, and the lobes of her ears that looked as if they had been molded of some fragile sugary substance, her voice with its cool musical notes, her clear eyes, her candid smile . . .

Well, she was dead, too—and amid what torture, poor child, as she gave her own spirit in the bringing of another into life . . .

Since then there had been nothing worthwhile in his own life, save for those Saturday nights that still held some beauty, when he reached her parents' home and sat in the lamplight on the porch of the old manor house, among the scents of the shadowy garden, while the evening breeze plucked the soft dreamy chords of an aeolian harp in the window.

Little Miette sat on his lap, and while he talked to her grandfather her tiny hands played curiously with the charms hanging from his watch chain. One day, holding up a carved carnelian, she had asked, raising her grave eyes to his: "Is it candy?"

As he thought of Miette, a sudden warm flood of pity swept through his heart. What would become of her now if she were left alone? But perhaps, after all, the war would end? The war! What was happening to the world? It was like a specter, chimerical, awful . . . Airplanes zoomed through the air—fantastic! He remembered when he had first heard that zooming over the roofs, that strange, muffled roar that filled the deep court of the house! How many things had been achieved during his lifetime! The telephone!—who would have believed it? The cinema. It wasn't wise to think of these things—it sent an icy shiver down the spine. And Peter—what was he doing now?

Was life worth living? Was this all of life?

How short it seemed! No more than the flash of an eye . . .

And now death was coming, the mysterious end—oh, dear God, what nameless horror!

Everything would go on as before. Wagons would roll by tomorrow and their clatter would ascend to the windows. The same voices, the same noises in the street —motor horns, bicycle bells, all would remain unchanged. Would the dog know that his master was dead? He ought to pray—but he could no longer collect his thoughts. Too bad he couldn't have finished his last volume of the *Decisions of the Supreme Court* . . .

He experienced infinite comfort in thinking of his work. He would not vanish altogether without leaving a trace of himself in the world. Those two squat little volumes would remain in the libraries, and his name would be in the biographical dictionaries. And suddenly he thought he saw a little black-framed notice in the *Budapest Journal*, headed by the name "Francis Almády."

If only Miette would come back!

Money, pension, debts—what would happen to all that? Would they ever find their way through the memoranda lying topsy-turvy in his desk drawer? He should have made a will and left precise instructions . . .

Dear Lord, wasn't that a noise in the hallway?—If it should be Miette after all! The thought made his heart beat so violently as almost to revive him.

Yes, he heard the door being closed cautiously.

Miette had been astonished when she came in to see a thin ray of light beneath her father's door.

She opened the swing door gently and, filled with apprehension, thrust her head through the opening. "Father dear, aren't you asleep yet?"

He stared at her, a strange fire gleaming in his eyes.

Miette, frightened, approached the bed.

The old man stretched his arm toward her, but it fell back, helpless, on the blanket.

"I feel ill," he said feebly, his eyes imploring, his lips

twisted as if he were about to weep. There was ineffable humiliation in his look, as if he were asking forgiveness.

"What is it you want?" asked Miette, her voice transformed as she grasped his hand.

He wanted to speak, but he was no longer able. His eyes remained fixed on Miette's, and he uttered a long, piteous moan. Miette leaned over the bed, slipped her arm beneath her father's head, and pressed her face against his white beard.

"Father darling, what is it?"

Her voice sounded like that of a ten-year-old child.

Trembling, she watched her father for a few seconds, then rushed to the door and sent a long cry for help toward the hall: "Mili, Mili!"

Meanwhile, Francis Almády had lifted himself with extraordinary ease and was sitting up in bed. Miette went to him and put her arm about his shoulders.

"I am getting up," said the sick man, a firm, somber resolve in his voice and on his face; but hardly had he uttered the words when he fell back into Miette's arms.

His eyes filled with strange shadows. He was still seeking Miette's eyes, as if he wanted gently to make her understand something—something terrible.

Miette felt that the last moment had come. She wanted to cry out, but only trembled from head to foot. Yet she met her father's eyes and, at the cost of so great an effort that she thought she would faint, looked into them, a gallant, tearful smile in her eyes and on her lips.

She raised her head for a second to turn it toward the door when Mili appeared, her face convulsed by fright, but taking the situation in at a glance, the old servant promptly disappeared to hurry for a doctor.

Francis Almády lay motionless on his pillows. The electric bulb of the night lamp on his bed table threw a clear light across the bed from beneath its silk mushroom-shaped shade. The white beard, the firm skull gleamed in the clear light; the skull seemed almost lifeless now; a heavy silence surrounded him, a silence that held terror.

Every time he expelled a breath, the white hairs of his beard quivered.

The expression of fear and helplessness apparent a moment earlier on that face had disappeared, and now the eyes were straying, and seemed to be gazing into distant spaces beyond the walls. There was gentleness, gladness, the radiance of a soul at peace in that transformed gaze.

Miette, terrified by the unearthly expression of his eyes, dared not look at them.

She pressed her face against her father's hand, and knelt beside the bed.

"My darling little Father!" she murmured, and began to cry softly.

Thus a half hour—an hour perhaps—elapsed.

At the end of that indefinite interval a stranger came into the room and placed a leather case on the table; then he tossed his hat and overcoat, damp from the rain, on a chair. The collar of his coat was turned up and he wore only a night shirt beneath it. His eyes were red and indifferent. His bushy eyebrows were ruffled as if he had tangled them deliberately.

He approached Miette, took her arm, and helped her up.

"Come, dear lady, please—"

Miette stood beside the table in the half darkness, outside the circle of light cast by the lamp. Holding her breath in dread, she watched what the doctor was doing to her father. She felt an unaccountable respect for this strange, gruff physician, the respect that each of us feels under similar circumstances, as if the physician had at his command some supernatural, mysterious power and could struggle against death. Her burning eyes followed his every movement, but she saw nothing. The doctor had turned his back, hiding the bed completely. When he bent over, the turned-up collar of his coat formed an acute angle, curiously sharp. His shadow stirred gently on the wall, and occasionally something would ring against the night table—the sound of a light metallic object placed on a glass top.

All this took a long time and the atmosphere of the room was heavy and tense.

At last the doctor straightened up and took a full, deep breath.

"What is it?" Miette inquired breathlessly as the doctor turned gently toward her, the stethoscope still in his hand.

He didn't answer at once, but as he returned the instruments to his case he shrugged his shoulders slightly and, as if he were speaking to himself, said as kindly as possible: "We must all die!"

Francis Almády was dead. The doctor's fingers lowered the eyelids over the staring eyes.

Miette drew near the bed, her arms outstretched. She fell to her knees on the spot where she had been kneeling a moment before, and stayed there, motionless.

Hours thus passed while, face hidden in her hands and in the coverlet, she spoke voiceless yet impassioned words to her father. There were several people in the room; now and then she would feel someone take her by the arm, whisper pitying words into her ear, implore her to rise.

But she didn't stir.

Elvira and Dr. Varga had arrived, too. It was they who toward morning raised her by force. The long kneeling had made her knees stiff; she could scarcely stand. So they helped her to her room and led her to the bed. It wasn't necessary to turn on the electric light: the gray dawn of the rainy autumn morning was flooding the room.

Miette did not go to bed. She simply lay down, fully clothed, on the bedcover and sent everyone away. She lay on her back, feeling the pain caused by her long vigil weighing like a foreign object on her knees.

From the next room could be heard occasional whispers and the floor creaking faintly beneath cautious footsteps.

Mili's restrained sobs could be heard, too—an old woman's sobs, gentle and monotonous.

PART FOUR: ZINAIDA

I

For four months now, the boundless snowfields of the Siberian winter had swallowed the letters of war prisoners. The convulsively cramped fingers of war had shattered the Russian mail service. Little by little Tobolsk seemed to have been torn away from the terrestrial globe and now, completely separated, was flying with its snow-covered streets in an entirely new direction through space, solitary and soundless, like a cold, white, silent star.

Peter was sitting outside on the doorstep, wrapped in his wolfskin coat. It was about eleven in the morning, and a brilliant, blinding sun glittered on the crisp, dry snow.

It was just past the New Year, January 1917. Throwing back his head, Peter leaned it against the post and closed his eyes, exposing his face to the ardent rays of the sun. He sat thus for a long time, unmoving, fearful lest those wintry sunbeams, so tenuous that they seemed to draw their warmth from his own eyes, should take fright and vanish.

Vedres, in a short coat, his hands crossed behind his back, was describing monotonous circles on a narrow little skating rink he had contrived in a corner of the yard. The snow, surrounding the rink in an even border, was like the large white frame of a huge mirror. Vedres' tall, slender figure was sharply reflected in the clear blue-white depths of the ice as, one leg raised high, he skimmed about in loops and spirals. Formerly, when Vedres had skated on the ice at Szeged, his brilliance had dazzled all onlookers; but now Comrade was his only admirer. The dog sat in the snow, wagging his tail, his head and eyes eagerly following Vedres' glidings, apparently convinced that His Excellency the lieutenant was revolving about for Comrade's sole amusement and obviously doing his best to play the appreciative spectator.

Vedres' skates were of his own making and of very primitive construction. He had fastened short, hard wooden laths to the soles of his shoes, after having affixed to the lower edges of the laths stiff, thick pieces of wire.

Deep silence, intensified by the heavy layers of snow, reigned over the yard. Only the regular scraping of the skates on the hard ice was audible, a tiny sound like that of a woman's needle slipping over the taut silk in a light embroidery frame.

The other inmates of Misery Hotel were fishing in the Irtysh. Kölber alone was upstairs in his room. The men were breaking the ice in the river with axes, and behind his closed eyes Peter was aware of those blows of the axe coming from far away, like the strange tinkling of glass heard in a dream.

Peter was thinking of Zinaida. Zinaida Ignatovna Larina—that was the name of the girl he had seen for the first time one Sunday morning four months ago in the upper city, in the Church of the Virgin Mother, the Kashanski Sobor.

This yellow-painted Russian church, with its blue cupola and white pillars, rose on the public square like a multi-colored cactus. The upper part of the main door was decorated by a fresco in the Italian style, representing the Resurrection.

Peter remembered how the girl had been kneeling on the tiles at the back of the church, and how, when the mass ended, he had recognized her in the crowd from a distance by the red eglantine berries on her hat.

The following Sunday he had seen her there again, and once on a weekday, when he had gone to church very early, the girl had been kneeling in the same place. There was no one else in the church but a ragged old man on his knees, apparently sobbing, his arm resting against a column and his head on his arm.

Peter stood against the wall, listening to the deep, mysterious silence that filled the dark church. The silence seemed full of all kinds of whispering voices. The angelic choir of the Kheruvimskaya still rang, as on that first Sunday, from the mute, empty organ loft, though now it seemed fainter and farther away, as if from a star. And it faded away as the beadle opened the door of the sacristy at the other end of the church and, stepping on tiptoe from slab to slab, crossed the slumbering church.

This time, too, Peter waited near the porch for the girl, who cast upon him the same indifferent glance as at their first encounter.

He saw no more of her face than he had seen before, since her great, dark, wide-open eyes riveted his attention for the few seconds of their meeting—eyes that held a little apprehension, humility, and a gentle melancholy—inscrutable eyes with a quality that robbed Peter of the courage to address her, despite the fact that in the church he had resolved to accost her as she left. He had thought up a few Russian sentences that he believed would prevent her from thinking him a nuisance or a common flirt.

All he actually wanted was to talk to her. He had often felt, during this third year of captivity, an irresistible desire for contact with a new, unknown personality. Life had stopped at Misery Hotel and seemed to weigh upon them like stagnant water. All the memories of their youth, all their adventures with women, all the anecdotes and the most trivial details of their lives had been recounted to one another incalculable times. At night they sat together in their community room with empty souls. Those diverting experiences of Bartha's with Professor Rák no longer amused anyone—Professor Rák who, after eight years of unremitting enmity, had, at the baccalaureate banquet, drained with Bartha the cup that sealed their reconciliation and ended the evening as dead drunk as Bartha himself. At first they had laughed till they cried over it, and once Szentesi had awakened the sleeping Bartha to ask him: "Tell me, just what *did* happen when Professor Rák drank the ink at the May festival?"

Now they yawned so that their jaws were threatened with dislocation when Vedres told his stories of barracks life before the war—the one about Colonel Stoll, who was so vain that he had his cloak padded like a woman's waist. And even Szentesi's adolescent memories, his intrigues with the shapely servant girls of Györ, whom he had been fortunate enough to succeed in seducing with a few ounces of English sourballs, and to whom Szentesi's father—while the former was still a student—had had to pay considerable sums of money—even those memories were like withered, shriveled spiderwebs hanging dustily from the walls. And the tale of Neteneczky's passion for Miss Influenza—so called because of her hypochondria and her mother's fear that everything, even a fly, menaced her safety—had lost its savor. After three years of a perspiring courtship in the style of 1830, Netene had failed, despite all his bombast, to attain the rich dowry! And they all turned a deaf ear now when Lukács told of his fabulous card parties at Monte Carlo and his romance with a Sicilian princess.

Those stories, told in greater and greater detail, spun out till their breath failed them, were at last exhausted.

Each evening they sat down to the table with wearier spirits, and the silence and emptiness about them grew daily more appalling. Recently all their attention had been given to the problem of acquiring firewood and provisions, and their thoughts revolved only about their most primitive and atavistic instincts.

"What would she have answered if I had spoken to her?" Peter wondered as, at the church door, his eyes followed the girl whose gait had something of the buoyancy of a butterfly. The features of her pale, beautiful, slightly strained face, like a frostbitten fruit, bore witness to the Russian in her and to that appealing melancholy that is so characteristically Russian. To judge by her simple but tasteful clothing, she might have been the daughter of a physician or of a minor government official.

Next morning Peter went to church again. Zinaida Ignatovna was there, kneeling on the flagstones. Peter stood leaning against the wall behind her, contemplating her slender neck for a long time. He had an impression that the girl felt he was there behind her; but this supposition was groundless, for Zinaida Ignatovna, her head bowed, was deep in fervent prayer, though after a moment she turned her head slowly and fixed her eyes on the spot where Peter was standing. It was all over in a second, yet that simple movement of the head made Peter's heart leap. It seemed to mean that, in the depths of her soul, she was occupied with the same thoughts as he.

"When she leaves the church, I shall speak to her," he said to himself, trying to bolster up his courage.

He stood outside in front of the church door, blinking in the sunlight, watching some eels that had fallen from a fisherman's wheelbarrow. The sun's rays, lemon yellow this winter morning, beat blindingly on the Cyrillic characters of the gilded shop signs opposite and on the window of Licharov's pharmacy. How long Zinaida Ignatovna lingered in the church! It was amazing! The few people who came every morning, all of whom Peter knew by sight, had gone a long time ago. Thinking that the girl might have left by another exit, he glanced inside; she was still kneeling there, as if putting Peter's patience to the test.

At length he heard her light footstep and waited for the glance for which he had always hoped when she had passed him on previous occasions. But Zinaida Ignatovna passed him that day with lowered eyes.

This unexpected treatment upset him so completely that he dared not address her on this occasion either. Her averted glance meant that she was well aware that this captive officer, with his dark brown beard and sorrowful eyes, who, even in his poor cloak, looked clean and trim, came to church only on her account.

Did she wish to ignore his advances, or was she only naturally shy and reserved?

These thoughts flashed through his mind as his gaze followed the girl's descent of the broad, high steps leading to the church.

The next moment he regretted his cowardice and followed her. Zinaida Ignatovna had reached the bottom of the steps and was already in the street. Peter was hoping that he might still overtake her in the silent, deserted church square before she had disappeared into the hubbub of the main street.

He was very excited and took two or three steps at a time in his anxiety to catch up with her; but reaching the last step he slipped on its frozen surface and fell full length to the ground, sliding and rolling on the icy pavement, trodden smooth by the crowd, to the very feet of the girl.

Zinaida Ignatovna turned in dismay and made an involuntary gesture, as if she wanted to help him up.

But Peter was up in a flash. He had turned very red and felt deeply ashamed, his first thought being of the absurd and humiliating position in which he had placed himself.

He was completely abashed and stood blushing before the girl, brushing the snow from his elbow.

"Oh—I beg your pardon," he said, and grew more than ever confused, realizing that his apology made no sense.

A sympathetic smile hovered about the girl's lips, for it was a ridiculous situation. Then she turned and walked away, without looking back.

Peter took the opposite direction. Large chunks of snow adhered to the back of his coat. Several passersby turned to smile at the sight.

Having reached a side street, he tried to get rid of the snow by making ludicrous passes at his back.

He had a bitter taste in his mouth and he could have wept. As soon as he got home he threw himself on the bed and lay there motionless for hours.

This stupid affair had utterly disheartened him. He couldn't bring himself to smile at it, for his spirit had developed a raw sensitiveness, and he was too enfeebled to remain unaffected by such things.

For four whole weeks he didn't go to town.

Eventually, however, one Sunday before Christmas, he went back to the church. He stood against the wall on the opposite side of the building, paying no attention to the girl, who was kneeling in her customary place.

But when the service was over he waited, against his will, in the church vestibule. He had intended to go straight home, nor did he know what strange power held him at the door of Kashanski Sobor, through which rolled the majestic surge of the organ. And those deep-toned waves seemed to be sweeping the throng of worshippers through the narrow door, for the attendance that day had been unusually large. Like some prismatic mass, the people spread over the white snow of the square in front of the church.

Finally, among the gaily colored shawls of the Russian peasants, Peter caught sight of Zinaida Ignatovna's berry-trimmed hat.

The girl cast him a long glance as she passed him, as if she were asking for an accounting of the four weeks during which he had been invisible.

That glance had a sudden electrifying effect on Peter. He walked up to her and asked, simply and quietly: "May I walk home with you?"

"No, thank you," she said gently. She trembled and her face turned very pale. She continued on her way but presently turned her head uneasily, as if she regretted what she had just said.

Now Peter's mind was in complete confusion. He waited until she was about twenty feet ahead of him, then followed her. He lost sight of her for a few seconds in the midst of the crowd on the main street, but soon her hat emerged from among the fur bonnets of the other women.

In front of the governor's palace the girl turned into long Petrovka Street.

Peter followed her.

Zinaida Ignatovna stopped in front of a small one-story house. Before crossing the threshold, she looked back once more, then disappeared into the house with obvious reluctance.

Peter stood still in the deserted street, then slowly began pacing the sidewalk, whose wooden boards were covered with a thick coating of snow and ice.

A host of disturbing thoughts swarmed through his mind, and he was bent on discovering all he could about this girl.

He stopped, as if he were waiting for someone, in front of the adjoining house, evidently a locksmith's, for a large tin key hung above the door.

After a few moments a kindly looking old woman appeared at the door. She wore the multi-colored national Sunday costume of the women of Little Russia and was apparently about to pay some call.

Peter asked her: "Who lives in the house next door?"

The old woman felt flattered that he should have spoken to her and answered affably, her voice soft and weak, like that of an invalid: "The daughter of Ignatov Sergey Larina, Miss Zinatchka."

She pronounced the diminutive Zinatchka so gently, she put so much tenderness into the word, that Peter's heart filled with warmth at the picture thus conjured up of the unknown girl.

He asked no more questions. He wanted only to know her name, and having taken note of the house number above the door, he returned to the main street.

He entered a florist's shop, selected a small bouquet of roses and had them sent to Zinatchka, without a card.

From that day he stopped going to church.

The atmosphere of the Christmas holidays blotted from his mind every memory and every thought of the girl, who had meant to him nothing beyond a slight heart throb, and a thirst—a vague nostalgia for life, for love, and for womanhood.

It was now five months since he had received any word from home. Miette's last letter had been dated in July; since then he had received no news. He had frequent visions of Father, as if he were standing in plain view. He didn't know Father was dead.

But his thoughts of Miette and his memories of the old

life were utterly exhausted, and when he tried to think of her, he felt that he was staring for long hours into maddening darkness.

He avoided such thoughts. Especially did he flee them when, from the depths of his being, rose the question, "Has Miette remained faithful?" Then he saw Michael Ádám's distinguished figure, an ironic smile on his thin, attractive lips beneath the clipped little blond mustache.

He went to town one afternoon after New Year's Day. He wanted to buy a pair of sealskin boots, for which he had been saving money. He had had the necessary sum in readiness for several days.

In front of the watchmaker's shop a young woman was approaching him, her cap pulled down over her ears, her sable coat clasping her throat tight and even covering the lower part of her face. He soon recognized her as Zinatchka.

She must have recognized him first, for even from a distance her glance betrayed mingled surprise and pleasure.

She stopped in front of Peter and looked into his eyes for a second with a glance that held a little mischief, but more timidity and confusion. Peter stopped, too.

Zinatchka spoke first.

"Was it you who sent me those flowers not long ago?"

The question took Peter by surprise and he couldn't answer at once. He could only scrutinize the girl's face, which seemed to him composed of two different profiles— lending it a peculiar interest.

The mouth was pretty; the corners of the lips curled delicately upward, and behind the fresh mouth gleamed small, sharp white teeth, one of which had grown out of alignment. In the pale face, great, dark, wide-open eyes were now fixed questioningly upon Peter.

He stood before the girl, after her unexpected greeting, as if he were standing before a superior officer.

"I wanted to know you," he answered, meeting Zinatchka's eyes calmly.

With a little sadness in her voice she asked him, "What do you want of me?"

"Nothing. I am married and I love my wife. You would have been the first person I have ever known here."

Zinatchka walked on slowly, but with a gesture of invitation to Peter to walk beside her.

"How long have you been a prisoner?"

"Two and a half years."

"Good heavens!" she whispered.

They were both silent for a moment.

Peter gazed at her round chin and at the fur beneath it, moist with her breath.

Zinatchka looked back at him and asked gently: "Do you want to walk home with me now?"

"Yes, but I shall have to notify the guard. I told him I would return in ten minutes and I'm afraid he may be looking for me. Let us go back to the bakery shop."

They started out. Courteously Peter gave the girl the inner side of the street.

"Do you live with your parents?"

"I have no parents."

"With relatives?"

"No. I live with an old man who was my father's servant. My mother died four years ago."

"And your father?"

"My father? He has been dead for twenty years. I was still a very small child when he was exiled to Tobolsk."

"What was his profession?"

"He was an officer, a Cossack captain. Poor man! He was accused of maintaining secret relations with the political prisoners at the fortress of St. Peter and St. Paul. Of course it wasn't true, but in those days they sent anyone to Siberia whose enemies made a charge of that kind against him!"

"And how did you come to Tobolsk?"

"My mother brought me with her. I was four years old. We were allowed to visit the fort on Sundays. My father died during that first year."

"And your mother?"

"Four years ago. I have lived all alone since."

"Have you no friends?"

"Yes, but I prefer to be alone."

They had reached the bakery, where the *starshi* was conversing with his brother-in-law, a hump-backed baker. Peter went in, gave the *starshi* a ruble and told him he would return in half an hour.

Then they walked through Petrovka Street, lined mostly with one-story dwellings, toward Zinatchka's house.

At the door the girl held out her hand.

"If it would give you pleasure, come to see me some time."

"When?"

"Do you want to come tomorrow?"

"Tomorrow I can't. I am allowed to come to town only twice a week. Thursday, perhaps—"

"Thursday, then—at five."

They shook hands and Zinatchka disappeared into the house.

That had been on Monday, and today, this very afternoon, she was expecting Peter.

As he sat there in the yard, his closed eyes still turned to the sunlight, his heart grew heavy, and he considered not going, escaping this visit under some pretext.

What did he want of this girl? Now that he had made her acquaintance and knew who she was, she no longer interested him. All those thoughts induced by the kneeling girl, by her easy grace and sorrow-drowned eyes—they had simply been suggested by the yearning of his desolate soul.

His mind was filled with bitterness and boredom at the thought of that afternoon's call. He went, but with the idea of getting a disagreeable duty over with.

Zinatchka was waiting for him, the samovar steaming. Her little one-story house had only two rooms. The two small windows of one overlooked the street, and the room was permeated with a peculiar odor as of balm mint and the smell of newly varnished wood. The narrow little room was pleasant and gave an impression of extreme cleanliness.

Along the wall were ranged several lyre-backed chairs, which the father of the late Cossack captain had bought during a campaign in Poland. The rest of the room's furnishings consisted of an upright piano, a glass case, and a triangular table. There were a few Russian books and a guitar on the table that stood against the wall, the books being the works of Pushkin, Goncharov, and Dostoevsky. On the wall above the piano there was a large dark picture representing St. Nicholas, the miracle maker. Beneath the icon burned a small, perpetual vigil light, whose flame illuminated the tiny porcelain egg suspended by a red ribbon on the saint's breast.

On the opposite wall hung a small velvet slipper that served as a pincushion, a monogram of braided hair under glass in a black frame, a sword, some Turkish weapons, and a Cossack ship model.

Between the two windows there was an enlarged photograph whose frame of carved wood was surmounted by a wreath of cornflowers that had withered to silver gray. The picture showed a big Cossack officer and a young woman. He wore a tall, black bearskin cap and heavy epaulettes. His face and expression suggested those pictures of men with regular features and curled mustaches painted outside the doors of provincial barber shops to testify to their owner's skill in the tonsorial art. This was Sergey Ignatov, Cossack captain.

His wife was beside him. Apparently the eyes of the captain's wife had been obliterated in the process of enlargement, and the artist, perhaps some vagrant Caucasian photographer, had with a few over-zealous pencil strokes attempted to remedy the defect, with the result that two fish eyes, hard and terrifying, stared straight into space.

The other room was visible through the open door. It contained a small bed covered by a linen spread and, beside the bed, an iron-banded chest with an arched top.

Zinatchka invited her guest to sit down and poured tea for him. A cherry-red woolen scarf was wound about her neck and she wore a simple brown cloth dress that one could easily see she had made herself.

It was obvious from the atmosphere that the room was not ordinarily heated. Blasts of warmth issued from the small, dark blue porcelain stove where a lively fire crackled. The lamp was already lit, for night had begun to fall. A colored paper shade, painted with battling Chinese dragons, covered the electric bulb that hung above the little gilt-legged table.

Zinatchka offered Peter a cigarette, first rolling the cigarette paper into a funnel, into which she poured the Russian tobacco, powdered like poppy seed.

It was difficult to start the conversation. Peter was wishing the whole thing over, and the girl was obviously nervous. She kept passing her hand over her neck.

Her glossy black hair was cut short, like that of Russian students. It was combed flat and smoothed back behind her ears, giving a virginal expression to her pure, fresh face.

Peter watched her eyes, which were now sparkling, now profound, and the next second grew dreamy and mysterious to the point of melancholy.

"How were you taken prisoner?" asked the girl, with the obvious intention of coaxing the conversation along.

Peter told her of the events of that night of August 1914.

Zinatchka drew the scarf about her shoulders, leaned forward slightly, and listened, wide-eyed. Her melting eyes reflected a thousand thoughts.

"When did you marry?" she asked later, holding her cigarette between her fingers in a curious, awkward fashion. She pouted her lips and puffed out her cheeks as she exhaled the smoke, and it was apparent that she was smoking today only in honor of her guest and the special occasion.

"A few months before the declaration of war."

"You loved each other?"

"Very much."

"How did you meet her?"

Peter suddenly grew loquacious. He told her everything; it was as if now he wanted to recall aloud those crucial moments that he had already rehearsed so many thousands and thousands of times in silence.

Above the table the steam of the tea and the blue smoke of their cigarettes drifted in the lamplight. Peter stared at the smoke and again saw the two girls sitting near the piano at the Vargas' first tea; he saw Miette standing at the door of the Almády apartment as he took leave of her, and Father sitting in the dining room of the lighted apartment, reading his newspaper at the table that had been laid for dinner; he saw Miette and Michael Ádám as they passed him on the Danube esplanade, and the most minute details, every facial expression, every gesture, words and voices, returned as poignantly to his memory as if they had been miraculously revived. He was talking of his past life to this Russian girl, to this stranger, as if in some country beyond death he were telling these things to a bodiless soul.

And everything seemed so unreal!—the queerly shaped furniture of the little room, easily recognizable as the remnants of a more pretentious household; the idea that he was now on the other side of the globe in Asia, at Tobolsk, and that the large attentive eyes of Ignatov Sergey's daughter, reflecting tenderness and secret intimate thoughts, were fixed upon him in absorbed interest.

Meantime the *starshi*, who had placed his loaded gun in a corner, was chatting in the kitchen with Dmitri, the Cossack captain's old servant, after having guzzled tea till there wasn't a drop left in the iron pot.

Dmitri was past sixty, and with Zinatchka's help performed all the household tasks. His long gray hair fell to his ears, and beneath his absurd little shoe-button nose grew a forest of mustache and beard; he wore clothes of some coarse material, and Russian boots, and through his belt was thrust a metal comb, which he never used.

After an hour Peter took his leave.

"Will you come again?" asked the girl.

They agreed on another meeting.

Peter felt an impulse of deep, unalloyed gratitude toward the girl and kissed her hand as he bade her goodbye, though the glance she gave him made him promptly regret the gesture.

When he got back the others had finished dinner. After his own meal he didn't go down to the community room where they were in the habit of congregating at night, but went directly to bed.

With deep sighs that seemed to pierce him through and through, he abandoned himself to his thoughts. That afternoon had roused all his dormant, weary memories. Closed wounds, covered by scars, had reopened within him, and were bleeding and throbbing like ghastly living organisms.

He thought of Miette and felt himself wrung by infinite pity, as for a forlorn and friendless child.

He saw her stepping out of her morning bath, enveloped in steam, and the warm, moist air of the bathroom was filled with a wonderfully soft and fragrant perfume.

But suddenly Michael Ádám's figure appeared to him again, and the merciless, searing torment of jealousy began to tear at his flesh, as if to strip it to the bone.

II

That winter, for lack of coal, the streets of Budapest remained plunged in darkness, and even in the most fashionable restaurants along the Danube esplanade the smartest patrons ate cornbread. But despite all that, the city was drunk with joy, for there were more German soldiers in France than French or English; from the Russian battlefields to the North, there flowed into the country enormous quantities of booty taken from the enemy—guns and cannon; Russian prisoners arrived by hundreds of thousands, and to the South, Hungarian privates had just missed taking prisoner the king of Italy!

Two months after her father's death, Miette had received a letter from Ivan Golgonszky.

"Everyone tells me (he wrote) that you do not allow even your friends to see you. I cannot express the pity I feel for you. I'm afraid that the thoughts with which you so jealously surround yourself can only oppress your spirit. It is with this fear in mind that I am writing you. I hesitated a long time before I could make up my mind to write to you in this vein, but now I have a double motive for approaching you in the most blameless fraternal spirit.

"I cannot endure the knowledge that you are abandoning yourself helplessly to unending grief, going over and over the same painful, merciless thoughts.

"I should like to help you, but I do not know how to go about it. I, a strong soul, witness your plight with impotent rage. Why do you allow yourself to be thus overwhelmed? I want nothing from you; I want only to comfort you. Make one sign in my direction, the faintest, most imperceptible sign, and you will make me happy."

Miette hadn't answered the letter.

She didn't want to rouse herself from the curious dream life that had been hers since her father's death.

She was astonished that people should interpret her situation so differently. The Vargas and the Csereys had urged her for weeks to come and live with them, to stay with them until Peter should return.

They all believed she had abandoned herself to grief and that she cried day and night. They couldn't realize that she actually felt contented in this even, monotonous existence and that the silence and solitude surrounding her had grown to hold for her life's deepest, purest meaning.

She guarded this silence and solitude about her, even though people to whom she had denied herself said she was half mad.

She knew that she had offended the Csereys, that Mathilde was really angry with her; Mathilde had been passionately eager to have Miette live with them. It wasn't the same with the Vargas. Elvira wasn't angry, because she had invited Miette only out of a sense of duty, and in order to show herself in a generous light; she was secretly grateful to Miette for having declined her offer.

In her mourning clothes that made her look paler than ever, Miette came and went about the apartment, feeling mortally weary, as if her general sense of lassitude had begun to affect her heart. She would sit for hours in her father's room, where she had left everything untouched; she imagined him there before her, and recalled one by one all her memories of him—how his chair had creaked when he was at work; his short little, somehow mechanical, cough; the movement of his hand when he stroked his beard toward his neck, from top to bottom; the queer, whistling sound of his empty pipe stem when he drew on it before filling it; the pleasant little noise of pencils being sharpened; the dry rattling of crumpled papers; the questioning glance of his blue eyes, suddenly raised; in a word, the thousand tiny remnants of sound and color with which, for her, her father's room was filled.

She gathered up these memories with infinite care; she kept them together so that, thanks to them, the dead man might still live beside her. She knew that some day or other they would leave her. Some were already fleeing, but she darted in pursuit and recovered them.

So the winter months passed.

She had still received no reply from Peter to the telegram notifying him of her father's death; no one knew whether he had received it or the letter she had sent shortly after. Everywhere the Russian mails had stopped.

This silence, this speechlessness surrounding Peter's life made her own solitude all the deeper.

Try as she might, she couldn't realize that there had been long years of her life when she had frequented tennis courts, society, when everything connected with life and movement had interested her. How was it possible, since her present life was more beautiful, better, purer than anything in the world—these long afternoons, these still, monotonous days that lulled the soul to rest on a peak of unearthly silence.

In March a fresh blow fell. The bank, to whose Claims Department Peter had belonged and which, up to then, had been sending her his salary regularly on the first of each month, abruptly suspended payments.

It was true that the value of the money had been reduced by two-thirds, but it was none the less the economic foundation of the establishment and easily sufficed to pay her own and Mili's living expenses.

The bank, which was not one of the small group of first-rate credit houses, had suddenly become the center of a tremendous scandal involving supplies furnished to the army, and hardly had the scandal blown over when the bank failed.

Miette had paid no special attention to the affair; but in April, when her quarterly rental was due, she was forced to take a pencil and to face some appalling facts. The money she had inherited from her mother—which her father had kept in a savings bank—had been invested by him a few months before his death in war loans. The interest represented a certain revenue, but the value of the money depreciated from month to month.

It was the first signal of alarm to arouse Miette, forcing her to turn from her life of abstraction and reverie to face reality. But she neither took fright nor lost hope. She who had suffered the fierce onslaughts of anguish and convulsions of weeping that had shaken her to the soul remained completely untouched by her financial reverses, profoundly as they would have affected her under other circumstances.

From the first moment she was determined not to accept help from the Csereys or the Vargas. Her pride protested against the thought of living on anyone's charity. She felt that such a situation would disturb her spiritual balance.

As for Peter's relatives, Michael Pável and his wife, she didn't even give them a thought.

She decided to go to work. Her mind turned to Koretz.

It was about a year since she had seen him, but she still thought of him trustfully and even with a feeling of warm friendliness.

One May morning she went to his office. A number of people were already waiting in the anteroom. Her appearance in her black dress and long mourning veil created a sensation among the impatient group of petitioners.

The secretary informed her that she would have to wait at least an hour. But scarcely had he taken in her card when he returned and ushered her inside.

Koretz, surprised, hurried forward to meet her.

Miette sat in the clients' armchair beside the desk.

"I have come to you with a rather unusual request," she said, somewhat embarrassed. Koretz' eyes were all attention and devotion. "I want to work. My situation has become difficult since my father died. You know perhaps that the bank where my husband was employed is being liquidated. What am I to do now? I have no relatives. Only the Csereys and others still more distant. Besides, I have a horror of accepting help from anyone. I'd like to work. My handwriting is good, I speak German and French fairly well; I learned stenography at school, and I believe I could readily pick it up again."

She blushed and grew a little confused as she murmured, "I don't know if that's enough for a secretarial position," and her black-gloved hand played in embarrassment with the handle of her umbrella.

Koretz looked at her, visibly moved, and his voice betrayed his emotion when he said, after a moment's silence, "What you ask of me I should do for any woman in your situation—"

Miette gazed at the tip of her umbrella, intent on keeping herself in hand, lest she be unable to restrain her tears.

After a moment he asked, "Don't you think that such unwonted labor would be too heavy a burden for you?"

"Oh, no!" she answered eagerly. "I love work, and I think it would be good for me to have something to do."

Koretz offered her a cigarette, with a gesture of apology for not having thought of it sooner.

Miette declined it, smiling faintly, but indicating by her manner that she considered their present interview a purely business matter.

"Give me two or three days to think it over," said Koretz. "Truly, I was prepared for anything save that you should come to me with a request of this kind."

Miette rose and held out her hand to him.

Koretz accompanied her to the door. Her hand on the knob, Miette paused for a second. "Tell me, what salary do such positions pay?"

There was such candor, such innocence in her expression that Koretz gave her a long, smiling glance.

"I can't fix it for you exactly just yet—" he said mysteriously.

Next day she received from Koretz a note, to which a check was attached. "Dear Lady (he wrote): I have given much thought to your request, and I have arrived at the conclusion that the position I could offer you would bring you into contact with old employees, atrophied by routine. Such contacts would not be very pleasant. On the other hand you will understand how impossible it would be for me to explain to these crotchety, nervous men—to each of them singly and on each occasion—that their attitude toward you must be all I would have it. As for employing you in my private office, that is something which for various reasons I cannot take upon myself.

"Please accept the enclosed sum and return it to me how and when you like. And if you are in need of anything else, whatever it may be, I beg of you to apply to me. I shall feel only too happy, too deeply moved, if I can be of service to you."

Miette looked at the check. The sum was so enormous that it almost frightened her. Holding the letter in one hand and the check in the other, she raised her eyes, frowning as if she were trying to fathom all of Koretz' secret thoughts.

"One thing is certain," she decided after a moment's reflection, "and that is that the gentleman has misunderstood the purpose of my application, or at any rate he is not altogether convinced that there wasn't an ulterior motive behind my visit—an offer in disguise. Why not? In these days of misfortune and ruin such a man—like any purchaser certain to pay a good price—is used to receiving offers of even the most jealously guarded family treasures. Why should a woman's honor be the only exception? He must have thought that the test would lie in his sending me this insanely huge sum. He had nothing in mind, but he managed things so that if I myself were harboring the thought, the way would be open to me. Which proves him intelligent, good-hearted, magnanimous . . . . His is a simple, clear, wholesome mind that doesn't manufacture useless complications. He is like all traders, all merchants who do business in the grand style—his heart and his safe are always open—I buy, I sell—he buys only first-class goods, and what he gives in exchange is certainly worth its weight in gold, for he is honest. He's right; perhaps in his place I should have done the same thing."

She looked at the check again.

"Well—so that's what I'm worth!" she thought, holding the paper between her fingers.

She sat immediately at her desk to write her reply before the impression made on her by the letter could wear off.

"Dear Friend (she began, using the word 'friend' deliberately, for now she felt a kind of superiority and assurance): Regarding the secretarial position—I have been thinking it over for the last two days, and I believe you are absolutely right. That kind of work is not for me.

"Meantime, I have managed to cope with the temporary difficulties of my present situation, and I am returning to you, with my very warmest thanks, your proffered help. I shall always think of you with gratitude and sincere friendliness."

She took the letter to the post office herself.

Next day Koretz' office boy appeared again, carrying a long narrow box. He said there was no answer and didn't wait.

There were two roses in the box, and on the enclosed card only the words: "Yours devotedly and respectfully, Koretz."

Miette saw in those two roses the expression of a simple, open-minded man's humble retreat. She felt the delicate significance of his having sent her only two roses and not a bouquet. She thought without resentment of this kindly man, of his brown eyes, of his sincere glance. She was pleased with the outcome of this struggle between them that had been carried on quietly, in the depths of their beings, with unuttered words. If they wished, they could deny to themselves the thoughts invisibly woven through their correspondence, thus doing away with the fear of embarrassment should they meet again.

Miette picked up her pencil once more and resumed her calculations. She found her situation less desperate than she had believed in her first access of alarm. She would sell her remaining securities one by one, and by living very modestly she could manage for another year.

She decided to go away. She felt herself irresistibly driven to that step, for now she was no longer at peace. The events of the past week had drawn her out of her dreamy state and dispelled the strange, sepulchral silence in which she had been wrapped since her father's death. All that had happened in the last few days—the letter from the bank, her trip to Koretz' office, the anteroom, the secretary, and the moment when she had said to Koretz, "I know German, a little French, and perhaps stenography . . ."; then the exchange of letters, and finally the check whose light touch she could still feel at her fingertips—these things had pierced her existence like crude rays of light, like the burning rays of actual, objective life, dissipating the heavy fumes of grief from the rooms of her apartment.

And yet with all her soul she longed again for silence and solitude.

She remembered that when they were planning their honeymoon Peter and she had sent for a whole army of pamphlets from foreign watering places. Those pamphlets were still somewhere in the bottom drawer of a cupboard. She sat down on the carpet and spread about her the brilliant pictures of those variegated landscapes. After much hesitation she decided upon St. Hilben, a little place hidden somewhere in the mountains near Salzburg. With its purple rocks, its peaceful-looking lake in a low valley, its quiet waters with their air of having existed from time immemorial, with the dark green of its firs, and its little cottages that looked as if they had been built of match sticks, St. Hilben seemed to promise everything she so passionately craved.

She left toward mid-June, not quite three years after that August evening when she had taken Peter to the station.

God alone, and a gentle subdued desire for death, were with her as she boarded the train.

III

One afternoon Zamák arrived at Misery Hotel with the sensational news that he had just seen, with his own eyes, the all-powerful Tsar of the Russias. He had saluted him and the Emperor had returned his salute.

Bartha and Vedres had him seized by the other orderlies, and twenty-five strokes were administered for his impudence in having dared assert that he had seen the Tsar and, what was worse, that they had saluted each other. This time the twenty-five strokes were dealt gently, symbolically, as it were, but he was warned that if he ever allowed himself to concoct such a tale again it would be a serious matter.

Yet, for once, Zamák had told the truth!

In the main street, next to the Laskutnaya Hotel, there was a house that looked like a villa, with a large balcony on the street side where a man in civilian clothes had been sitting all day, reading the newspapers.

In the street below, the mob gathered in speechless awe. Devout peasants made the sign of the Cross and shook their heads. They stayed there until the guards installed on the ground floor rushed out and dispersed the gapers with the butt ends of their guns.

The gentleman in civilian clothes was actually Nicholas Romanoff, Tsar of all the Russias, whose name in Russia, a few months before, had meant more than God's, for it appeared sixty times on the calendar in red letters, while God's appeared only thirty. A few months ago he had commanded a hundred and eighty million men and ruled over a sixth of the earth's surface. Twenty years before, such vast multitudes had assembled at the time of his coronation that the distribution of sweets and drinks among the people on Hodinka Field had cost the lives of fifteen hundred peasants, thrown to the ground and crushed in that pandemonium. Now, on the balcony of this Tobolsk villa, he was called simply Colonel Romanoff.

When the Duma, after a turbulent nocturnal session, had dethroned the Tsar, and Prince Lvov had been compelled to turn over the Duma, drunk with the new wine of its young freedom, to Kerensky, the most clamorous of the Socialist leaders, a locked railway carriage had already left Switzerland secretly for Moscow. In this carriage, his elbows on his knees, sat a bald-headed man, deep in meditation, answering to the name of Vladimir Ulyanoff. He had the angular face of a satyr and flat Tatar eyes, in whose depths burned the flame of a fearful oath he had taken against all humanity when his brother had been hanged for attempting the life of the Tsar and he himself had been put in irons and exiled for six years to Siberia.

This man called himself Lenin.

The Tsar stood on the balcony of the villa, his hands deep in his pockets; he wondered when he would mount his throne again; he had no suspicion that that mysteriously locked car had crossed the Russian border and was approaching Moscow. It was drawing nearer, nearer and nearer.

The Tsar had reached Tobolsk by way of Tiumen on August 20th. The two ships landed at night, but when the Tsar learned that they were to be lodged in the Tatar city, he refused to disembark. Kerensky had accompanied them to the station on their departure and had promised that they should occupy the bishop's house. But later the Emperor submitted to his fate.

The guard, brought from St. Petersburg, occupied the ground floor of the villa; the second story was turned over to the Tsar, his family, and his suite. Save for a few foreign-born servants, only Prince Dolgoroukhoff had accompanied the royal entourage into exile.

The Emperor used the corner bedroom with the balcony. From the adjacent room the notes of a piano and the singing of women sometimes floated down to the silent streets of Tobolsk. In this room the Tsarina Alexandra lived with Mme. Virubova, a small, ugly, deformed woman with a thorough knowledge of spiritualistic practices. The Empress always called her Anya, and played and sang duets with her every day.

A picture of St. Michael hung on the wall of the Tsarina's room and beneath the dark icon a tiny flame burned day and night. And there was also a mysterious black wooden chest, bound in silver, where a bloody shirt was kept locked like a sacred relic. This shirt had belonged to a Siberian horse dealer, a hypocritical tramp of the Asiatic race of the Chamans. His name was Rasputin. Prince Yusupoff had killed him the preceding winter, and the officers of the guard had thrown his corpse, like the carcass of a dead cur, through the ice of the Neva.

But the Empress Alexandra kept that soiled and blood-stained shirt to the day of her death.

The lovely Tatiana, the crippled heiress to the throne, and the rest of the children were crowded into the other rooms.

The street on which the house stood led to the Pod-Chouvachi camp, and when the Tsar stood on the

balcony the war prisoners, officers and privates, marching
between their escorts, always offered him the regimental
salute as if they were on parade. This ceremony was a
welcome diversion for the men. Necks turned toward the
balcony, they executed the command "Eyes Left!" and
their heavy boots clattered on the wooden pavements of
Tobolsk. Standing on the balcony, the Tsar thanked the
prisoners with a gesture. Six months before, the interminable columns of the Imperial Guard, in their heavy
bearskin caps, on their beautiful black or snow-white
horses, their gilded tips glittering in the rays of the
winter sun, had marched in dreamlike pomp and splendor
past Tsarskoye-Selo. But it was possible that that parade
gave the Emperor less pleasure than this salute from the
tattered regiment of war prisoners.

Peter often stopped in this street and watched the
bearded man standing motionless on the balcony for
hours, his hands behind his back, staring at some invisible
spot on the ground.

He stood there as on the bridge of some spectral,
broken-masted ship that, borne on the eerie wings of a
howling tempest, pursued its mad course toward fearful
abysses.

Peter watched the Tsar and thought of his own fate.
The balcony of the Tobolsk villa never failed to capture
his imagination; and as he stood on the street, leaning
against the wall, his eyes raised to the Emperor, he
suddenly recalled the Almády apartment. He saw the coat
rack of light wood with its carved antlers in the anteroom;
the wide apple-green carpet in the hall; and in the dining
room the aged leather armchair that creaked like a
saddle when sat on. He saw in the living room the large
inviting couch where Miette, breathing almost imperceptibly, napped after lunch, her shoulders gently relaxed,
her body wrapped to its toes in her long silk shawl;
the life-size portrait of Miette's mother in its gilded frame
above the piano. He could hear the familiar little sound
made by his knife, his gold pencil, and his watch chain as
he laid them, before retiring, on the marble top of his

night table; the antique black clock between the windows, its pendulum swaying back and forth with a soft tick-tick. He could visualize Miette's bright braids of burnished hair that seemed heavy as gold lying spread over the pillows; the wicker chair in the bathroom, with the soft pink bathrobe, whose pattern had faded, and the crumpled silk nightgown thrown over its back; two little red mules abandoned in front of the tub; the bathroom redolent of that pleasant odor emitted by delicate soaps and various cut-glass bottles; the water that gushed hissing from the taps, then, in a shushing spray, the cold, invigorating shower over his back and neck—all that lay between those walls, in those rooms where his body and soul had been at peace; all that constituted his lost life, engulfed, flown—so far away that his spirit was drowned in its memory.

Perhaps the Tsar, standing motionless on the balcony, experienced similar sensations as he let his fancy roam among the well-known voices, the familiar colors, the provocative perfumes of Tsarskoye-Selo. Perhaps he dreamed of the soft contact of the armchair that had adapted itself to the line of his back, and of the objects that felt comfortable to his hands and fingers, as he touched them gently, to the very grating of his door latch that might have come to seem like a human voice . . .

The wind sent a scrap of paper scurrying through the street, drawing the rapt and staring glance of Nicholas Romanoff after it. Slowly his eyes passed along the street, but their vacant gaze held no spark of interest.

Then they fell upon Peter and paused there. Peter stiffened under that scrutiny and saluted as at the touch of some peremptory hand. The Tsar bowed his head, and made a slight gesture of the hand. That was his way of thanking anyone who saluted him from the street. Lately he had been tormented by evil forebodings and the thought often came to him at night that he, too, would be slain like so many of the Romanoff emperors before him. He saw his future assassin in every person whom he glimpsed from his balcony, and it made him almost happy to be able to respond with a friendly gesture to anyone's salute.

Peter remained where he was for a moment, then turned abruptly toward home, as if ashamed of his childish gaping.

After a few days the Tsar on the balcony had become as familiar a sight to the people of Tobolsk as the cross on the dome of Otche Nache Church, and when they passed the villa they no longer even raised their eyes.

But this man disturbed, tormented, fascinated Peter with the power of an apparition seen in a dream. He would sometimes stand breathless for half an hour, watching the Tsar's hand resting on the iron rail of the balcony, and the thought would cross his mind that this was the hand that might have stopped the war; and he would be back at the bank, assistant head of the Claims Department; Miette might already be the mother of two children, a little boy and a little girl, every fold, every ribbon, every knot of whose dainty clothing would testify to Miette's taste and skill. The little boy would be called Peter and the little girl Mari. He saw both children on Father's lap, and he saw them in the little bedroom of Hadnagy Street, where his mother would give them eggnogs to drink—just as he had imagined it all once before, as he was being rocked on the deck of the *Neptune*.

He stared at the Tsar's hand as if it were a particle of God, a visible, palpable, formidable limb of the pain-wracked body of human destiny.

It had been a year in July since he had received his last letter from home. Since then he had had no news either of Miette or of his mother. Sometimes, as he walked along the street or worked at home or sat at his meals, he would shudder suddenly at the thought, like a knife thrust through his heart, that Miette might be dead.

Yet that thought was more bearable than the other— that Miette had been unfaithful, had betrayed him. If Miette were dead, it would be easy for him to face death here. For in any case that must be his fate, sooner or later. At Pod-Chouvachi camp the prisoners already had their own cemetery, and it was a miracle that during these three years none of the occupants of Misery Hotel had been borne to the grave. The poor food, the lack of heat, and the depression that preyed on their spirits—weren't these things draining them of all their vitality!

Yes, if Miette were to die, death here, in Siberia, would be his salvation. But to perish after three years of devouring hopes, expectations, and desperate speculations—to succumb here in captivity, knowing that Miette was sitting beside another man in the discreetly lighted corner of some smart restaurant, her pretty hand playing absent-mindedly with the petals of a flower on the snowy tablecloth, while the other's burningly thirsty eyes caressed her shoulders, and new sensations surged in her heart like the rainbow bubbles in their champagne glasses—that was such an excruciating thought that there was nothing left to do but die, foaming at the mouth in rage and agony, with groans torn from the heart's living flesh, with the fearful screams of a man overwhelmed by an avalanche of pain.

Oh, if he could stop thinking of it! Sometimes, all his nerves taut, he would strive to catch a glimpse of that other's mysterious face and the only face he ever saw was Michael Ádám's.

"If I ever get back—I'll kill him!" he often said to himself, and thousands of times he planned the most minute details of that murder. Several times, in the solitude of his room, he actually rehearsed the whole scene aloud to the very end, with animated gestures. He saw himself, revolver raised in his hand, turning burning eyes on his adversary; he saw Michael Ádám's brilliant, ironic smile beneath his little clipped blond mustache shrivel suddenly in a hideous grimace at the fear of death.

As he rehearsed this scene, he sometimes took fright at his own voice, and he would stop abruptly, his body suddenly grown rigid. At such times he was like a somnambulist, to whom someone has called a warning. He would throw himself hastily on the bed, hiding his face as if he were ashamed to confront himself with what he had been doing, and his heart would freeze at the thought that all this was a symptom of mental disorder, that he could no longer hope to escape insanity.

Nearly every day some officer, gone mad in the third year of his captivity, was taken from Pod-Chouvachi to the hospital. And here, too, among themselves, there were some who behaved so strangely that the others whispered together behind their backs. Kölber's manner seemed particularly suspicious; for months he had been unwilling to speak to anyone.

Perhaps Peter too sometimes did things—of which he was unaware in his weariness and confusion of soul—that made the others whisper together behind his back and say, "Poor St. Peter!"

Bartha had nicknamed him St. Peter because of his beard, which was already half a foot long. The name had clung to him, and now his comrades never called him anything else. Even the orderlies, behind his back, called him Lieutenant St. Peter.

He had a feeling that he would have gone mad long ago but for his continued visits to Zinatchka. He could bare to this girl the most intimate secrets of his heart and she listened so sympathetically, her eyes so absorbed, that he always felt his soul revive beneath their deep, innocent gaze.

He had known Zinatchka now for ten months. Every week, and recently twice a week, he had gone to call on her. They were bound together by a pure friendship that even in their subconscious minds held no trace of love. At least, so Peter believed.

He always told Zinatchka exactly what had passed in his mind during the few days of their separation. He bared all his thoughts to her, nor did he suppress even those that reveal a man's soul in all its nakedness. He told her of his desire for Miette and the torments of his jealousy; he gave her a scrupulous accounting of those moods in which he felt the sweet, mysterious attraction of suicide, and of those unreal moments when his mind grew uncertain of the very actuality of existence.

He talked to her of these things as a sick man talks to his physician. He shuddered at the idea that he was going mad and he carried his soul to Zinatchka, submitting it to her tender care.

She always listened attentively. Her eyes were full of sympathy and affection, and she made him repeat numerous details. Then she would find an explanation for everything. She was possessed of so much tenderness, so much intelligence and serenity, that Peter always left her with a mind less weary.

When he had nothing more to tell, Zinatchka talked, recalling the memories of her childhood. She knew amusing anecdotes about old Dmitri, who had scarcely more intelligence than a dog but who, on the other hand, surpassed even that animal in fidelity. Even now Dmitri wouldn't venture to turn the electric current on or off, and one day, when Zinatchka tried to explain to him what the telephone was for, he put his hand before his mouth to hide the fact that he was smiling at Miss Zinatchka who took him for such a fool and tried to make him believe such tales. Of all mechanical triumphs, it was the bicycle that impressed him most, and when Zinatchka sent him to town to market and he remained away for hours, you might be sure he had found a bicycle leaning somewhere against a wall, and that he couldn't tear himself away from it. He would crouch beside it, pry breathlessly into its mechanism, and was convinced that if the bicycle wanted to, it could speak.

Dmitri's soul was filled with the fear of God and with superstition. He believed in the power of burnt salt; he believed that if the candles kept burning on Holy Thursday there would be no illness to fear for the coming year; that the mushrooms wouldn't grow, once a cat had looked at them; that every Jew carried a bleeding brand on his breast. He never ate melon, because a split melon reminded him of his grandfather's cleft skull, his grandfather having been murdered with a butcher's cleaver by a Tatar bandit. As a child he had seen that skull split in two, but the Tatar had shown him mercy—probably that he might assure himself of his own compassion and good-heartedness, if he should feel remorseful later on.

Zinatchka, at the invitation of a friend, went to spend six weeks of the summer at Omsk, and Peter felt her absence keenly. But they exchanged letters, and these letters were filled with indications of their mutual affection.

The news of successive political events struck Misery Hotel like so many flashes of lightning. As a result of the news of the Revolution, the mental state of its inmates grew constantly more pessimistic, for they knew that this upheaval could bring them no good.

Two thousand Hungarian and Austrian officers at Pod-Chouvachi camp had been sent farther east to the shore of the Amur River, for the military powers feared that the war prisoners might liberate the Tsar. The inmates of Bear House had been taken away several days before. At Misery Hotel everyone went in fear of being placed aboard ship one fine day and sent east. Their situation had grown much worse recently; for four months now they had not received the fifty monthly rubles that had assured them at the beginning of a carefree existence, even though the ruble had dropped to half its value. Still, the possibility of their having to leave Tobolsk seemed to all of them a calamity.

Csaba's kitchen gardens now stretched to the bank of the Irtysh. That year the cabbages, turnips, onions, and tomatoes had been so abundant that they had been able to send some of them to the Tobolsk market, and since the new order had gone into effect, this was their sole, scanty source of income. When the men at Pod-Chouvachi lacked provisions, volunteers would come to ask for a few bags of onions or cabbages.

One evening Mezei entered Peter's room.

"Peter, my boy, there's a volunteer downstairs. Will you see him in my place? I must finish my report."

Peter went down to the community room. A kerosene lamp was burning on the table, for electricity had not been installed here. It was still light outside, but this ground-floor room had no proper window.

The volunteer was standing near the door, and when Peter entered he clicked his heels and saluted.

"Lieutenant, I respectfully report that we need three sacks of cabbages for our volunteers."

Peter walked absentmindedly to the table to fill out a receipt, for Mezei wouldn't allow a step to be taken unrecorded. The vegetable department had its own books, and everything was set down therein, to the last tomato.

Peter filled out the receipt and handed it to the volunteer, who stood at the other end of the table to sign it. As he bent his head over the table the full light of the lamp struck his face.

Spellbound, Peter scrutinized it, feeling as if he had just been dealt a terrific blow over the heart.

The volunteer was Michael Ádám!

He stood beside the table in his war prisoner's tattered uniform, trousers torn at the knee, elbows patched, broken shoes held together somehow by strings.

Peter jumped up and seized Ádám by the shoulders. He held him in a grip of steel, that he might the better see his face. He stared at him as at a terrifying vision. With eyes bursting from their sockets, he continued to gaze at him, apparently incapable of believing his own eyes.

"What's your name?" he asked in a voice that was hardly more than a whisper and sounded like the voice of a madman.

For his part the volunteer eyed him in consternation, not knowing what to think.

"I am Dr. Michael Ádám—" he answered, his voice a little apprehensive, but resentful, too, and cool.

Peter released him and leaned against the table, looking as if he were on the point of swooning.

"How long have you been a prisoner?" he asked, without looking at him.

"Three years. I was at Tomsk for two and a half years, and was sent here six months ago."

He fastened his eyes on Peter who, pale as death, rested one arm on the table where his wild eyes were fixed.

After a moment Ádám asked timidly, "May I ask the reason for this question?" Anxiously he scanned the face of this unknown lieutenant, ravaged by fierce emotion.

Peter raised his eyes to him but was incapable of uttering a word. The corners of his mouth drooped and the unuttered words trembled on his lips. At last he cried abruptly, his voice choked by sobs, "You knew my wife!"

Hardly had he spoken when he dropped to the table, laid his head on his arm and began sobbing aloud.

With an involuntary movement Ádám pushed aside the smoking lamp, lest Peter's elbow upset it.

Then he moved a step away from the table. He stood there as if at attention. He was stirred to the depths of his heart by this scene, and ransacked his brain, wondering who this lieutenant's wife might be whom he was supposed to know.

Suddenly Peter regained his composure, raised his eyes to Ádám and whispered, "You don't know who I am?"

Ádám gave Peter a moment's scrutiny. "I have seen you here at camp several times, Lieutenant. I know you by sight, but I don't know your name."

Peter sent him another long glance as if to give him time to think. Then he said in a low voice, "I am Peter Takács. My wife—"

Ádám lifted his hand suddenly, as if to forestall Peter, and cried sharply, "Miette!"

It was the first time in three years that Peter had heard that name pronounced by another's lips. It stabbed him to the heart. It was as if the name had come alive, as if a corpse, on being called, had leapt to its feet.

Once more his head dropped to the table, once more his sobs shook him with savage violence.

Ádám drew a chair to the table, sat down and laid his hand on Peter's convulsively heaving shoulder, in an attempt to check this paroxysm of grief.

"Don't cry!" he said gently. But his own eyes were fixed intently on a corner of the table that someone, in a moment of boredom, had rounded off with a jackknife.

Gradually Peter grew calm. He raised his head but

turned his face aside, ashamed that he had been unable to control his tears. It was the first time that this had happened to him since his captivity. He rubbed and pressed his cheeks as if he had just awakened from the stupor of a deep, heavy sleep. He wrinkled his brows, then relaxed them again, but kept his eyes shut. His beard was full of tears that stung his face and were beginning to tickle. He started to take out his handkerchief but changed his mind and carefully pressed the tears from his face with his finger.

He coughed gently several times to clear his throat, as if to make sure his voice wouldn't fail him when he began to talk.

Propped on his elbows, he leaned across the table and looked long at Ádám. In a low voice that was eased of its pain, he said, "It isn't so hard for you. You're a bachelor—"

Beneath Ádám's clipped blond mustache his pleasant, ironic smile appeared.

"I had been married three weeks when the war broke out—"

Peter eyed him in astonishment.

"You're married?"

"Of course. I married Eva Toronyi. Didn't you know her?"

The name stirred something in Peter's memory. Yes, Johnny had said to him the first time he had been in Miette's house, while she and Olga were in the bathroom, "Michael? Michael is courting Eva Toronyi."

There was a long silence, which Peter was the first to break.

"Stay and dine with me. I have a bottle of Crimean wine; we can drink and talk."

"I can't stay; I must give notice in advance. Tomorrow perhaps—"

Peter went with him to the door. They embraced on parting.

After dinner he began pacing the yard—at the lower end, beside the wall, where no one ever went. It was a summer's evening at the end of August, already past nine, but the violent orb of the sun was only now beginning to disappear behind the poplar woods along the banks of the Irtysh. A sickening cloud of smoke spread through the heavy, stifling air, for up in the North—perhaps a thousand miles away—the tundras had been aflame again for days and the dry marshes of the Lena were being devoured by tremendous fires.

Bartha and Vedres were amusing themselves by making Comrade jump over their sticks. The dog welcomed this diversion with joyful barks, clearing the sticks that were held shoulder high.

Mezei, Csaba, Szentesi, and Lukács were sitting under a tree at their card game.

Rosiczky had settled himself on the doorstep and was playing his zither.

Half an hour later, the yard was silent. They had all gone to bed. Peter still paced back and forth at the lower end of the yard Little by little utter darkness fell about him, and the large, feverishly glittering summer stars of the Siberian night covered the heavens.

It must have been midnight when he went to his room. Only then did he realize how profoundly those hours of monotonous pacing had exhausted him.

Kölber was asleep, or pretending to be. His sleep was always a kind of strange waking; his breathing was scarcely perceptible, and he seemed merely to be lying there with closed eyes.

Peter felt no desire to sleep. To busy himself with something, he put his linen to soak, then sat at the table and began playing solitaire to compose his thoughts that were setting his temples afire. But he couldn't keep his attention even on the cards and soon went to bed.

He stared with wide-open eyes into the darkness. For the first time in three years he was happy. He thought of Miette with a tenderness replete with humility and begged her forgiveness for having associated her in his imagination —that had been floundering in a vacuum—with poor Michael Ádám; he felt now as if a malignant, purulent

abscess had been cut from his heart. The knowledge that
the jealousy that had tortured him for three years had
been directed against hollow phantoms suddenly
enveloped Miette's figure in an aura of purity and grace.

A new sense of life was dawning for him. Why should
he allow himself to be consumed by these hideous
anxieties and chained to his love for Miette as to a
pillory, where the agonies of jealousy were wolves that
tore him asunder? Had he not reached the threshold of
insanity, and only because his morbid imagination had
driven him there?

Now he was free of this horrible nightmare. Every pore
of his body and soul began to burn with a wild and eager
thirst for life. Now he was suddenly sorry for himself and
felt that after three years of agony he had a right to
anything.

It would be a crime for Miette to betray him—an
atrocious, unpardonable, vile crime. Yes, it was well that
Miette had remained chaste—

But in his case, it was different. In the depths of his
being the despairing instinct of self-preservation stirred,
and he must save himself from madness. He saw no
unfairness just then in this method of reasoning.

He thought of Zinatchka, and he recalled the little
room with its pleasant odor of balm mint. He saw the
girl's glossy black hair, her wide, silent gaze, and he
imagined the soft lines of her shoulders hidden beneath
the cherry-red cotton shawl as she sat shivering a little
in her armchair.

He was seized by so violent an impulse that he sat up in
bed and for a long time strained his ears in the darkness ...
a strange impulse that drew his confused thoughts toward
the daughter of the late Cossack captain, Ignatov Sergey.

IV

Every afternoon, in the park of the watering place of St.
Hilben, a private orchestra entertained the few visitors

who happened to have strayed there. They played old Viennese waltzes so sorrowfully that the melting notes of the cornets seemed to be weeping for the beautiful days of the past.

Along the park's sandy path, overrun by weeds here and there, an old officer walked, leaning on his stick. The graveled sand crunched beneath his shoes, and one of his trouser legs, which hid a wooden stump, creaked, the two sounds mingling in a curious blend. This veteran, wearing a threadbare uniform of the Imperial Tyrolean Infantry, looked so ancient that it seemed likely he had lost his leg during the old Bosnian campaigns.

In the late afternoon, when the yellow, slanting sun rays touched the tops of the tall lindens, the environs of the hotel, deserted all day, took on a little animation. There were only a few people left sauntering about the park, chiefly officers sent by the military administration to spend their convalescent leave at St. Hilben.

The mountain air pervaded this old garden with the cool, indefinable fragrance of distant, snowy summits. But sometimes toward noon, or in the early afternoon, the heat that gathered in the valley grew so unbearable that the very birds fell silent among the foliage. The green-gold light of the sun pierced the dark pine forests on the mountain slopes, while on the distant heights surrounding the valley glittered the pale mauve of eternal snows.

Below the park the cold waters—a beautiful indigo blue in color—of the little Hilben River leaped among large flat stones, and, still lower, a ramshackle watermill was visible.

The natural beauties of this wild, majestic landscape, worthy of an artist's brush, were blended in some indefinable manner with the tedious atmosphere of the bathing establishment and the everlasting smell of cooking.

Miette was entering upon the second week of her stay. She was sitting on a bench under the old linden tree in the late afternoon sunlight, listening to the music of the orchestra's wind instruments, invisible behind the bushes.

Her arm rested on the back of the bench. She sat in a

rather weary attitude, and her dusty shoes gave evidence that she had just come from a long walk in the mountains. Every day after luncheon she was in the habit of climbing to the church on the mountain top, whence there was a magnificent view of the valley and the emerald lake between its walls of rugged rock. When she reached the edge of the village she never failed to sit on the sun-warmed wall of the stone bridge, to watch the wheel-wright at work. The old white-bearded man worked outdoors in his shirtsleeves and wooden shoes; his work bench was placed in the shadow of an apple tree, and the yellow elm shavings flew gaily about beneath the blade of his plane. Roughhewn wheels, milky white as fresh butter, were flung pell-mell about the green grass.

She had formed the habit of sitting for long intervals near this workshop, because something about the wheel-wright's powerful bald head reminded her of her father.

From the stone bridge she had come directly here to the park and now, in the sorrowful mood induced by the music, she abandoned herself to her thoughts.

Why was she here, in this wild, alien spot, where she had no thought or feeling in common with a living soul, nor anything to say to anyone? She was a little sorry already that she had decided to leave home. This strange, monotonous landscape weighed on her soul with inexpressible sadness.

She felt that her life had strayed into a labyrinth, and in whatever direction her thoughts turned, she found nothing anywhere but chilling uncertainty. No letter had come from Peter for eight months. Was he still alive? Perhaps he had been dead for months. Once she had heard of a similar case; who could tell?—perhaps years would pass before she could get any definite news of his fate. Hundreds of millions of men were being tossed about in that maelstrom of war and revolution out there, and it would be as difficult to discover traces of the life or the grave of an anonymous war prisoner beyond those immeasurable distances as to find a pebble hurled into the stormy sea.

It was just three years since she had taken Peter to the station. She sounded her heart to find out what she still felt for him. But she found her heart desperately empty.

What would she feel now if she should receive news of Peter's death?

Or rather, what would she feel if, tomorrow or the day after, he should appear suddenly at her bedroom door? How would they resume their broken life?

To these questions she could give herself only vague replies.

She felt it would be good to die—to make an end somehow, to fall asleep among these gloriously colored mountains, to sink down softly on this bench and never to wake again—while behind the bushes the brasses breathed forth with a strange melancholy the dreamy waltzes of old operettas.

What more could she expect of life?

In a few months she would be twenty-five. And this morning she had noticed again as she combed her hair that her white horn comb was filled with long hairs. Yes—that had been going on for months, and each morning these fugitives, these golden hairs, were more numerous, and with each of them a spark of her life and her youth was extinguished. When she braided her hair in the morning and fingered the long, heavy plait, she could feel how much thinner it had grown. And in that attenuated braid she seemed to be touching the dread, intangible, frail body of fleeting time.

As she thought of her hair, such sorrow filled her heart that she could have wept in self-pity.

She remembered, before her departure, having met in the corridor of the house the caretaker's eldest daughter, who had been living with relatives in the country for three years. She scarcely recognized the tiny, barefoot eleven-year-old child of former days in this fourteen-year-old girl, as tall as herself and with the air of a young woman. It was then for the first time that the thought smote her heart—good God! is this how time passes? In this child's transformation she recognized with terror the significance of those three years that had drawn her life, too, in their wake, onward toward death.

In the morning, after dressing, she settled herself with some embroidery on the veranda, and saw the young woman from Linz, whose acquaintance she had made, walking along the main path of the park. They exchanged a few words every day, and greeted each other with a smile and a nod of the head. Her husband was somewhere on the Italian front.

This young woman wore a light summer dress that the faint breeze molded to her body, revealing the obvious signs of pregnancy. Miette was seized by a curious sensation each time she caught sight of this woman. She thought of what her own lot might have been if Peter had given her a child; and as, with long sweeps of her arm, she moved her needle, followed by its flying strand of pale green silk, across the taut silk in the frame, she saw herself leaning over the lace-trimmed cradle, and she saw the child, trying to catch the empty air in his tiny fists, wrinkling his little nose, and she heard the shrill cries of budding life rise from his small throat toward the ceiling.

Pictures of this kind often crossed her mind, and then a warm, mysterious tide would surge through her heart. If she had a child, her empty heart would be suddenly filled with light and warmth.

But was it really empty?

Since she had left Budapest, left behind the rooms she knew so intimately—the creaking and slamming of the doors, her father's study table with its green cover on which the rays of the morning sun gleamed, the square glass paperweight where rainbows were reflected, the tinkling of the bell in the anteroom, Tomi's barking, and Mili, stooped, one shoulder thrust forward, coming and going through the rooms, the colors and lines of the curtains, and the faint, mellow, agreeable odor exuded by very old furniture in well-cared-for rooms—all that was so far away from her now! And as the days passed here, her imagination was being liberated and refreshed. There was nothing here to hold her bound.

During her long strolls over the woodland paths a thought often brushed her heart like a cool wind brushing the face, murmuring to her that there was something else in life besides mourning and spiritual anguish. There are so many things to check and arrest the attention of a solitary pedestrian—the rustling of a tree, sunlight striking the clouds, the flight of a bird. And this very moment—what is that life, so different, so far away, of which the brasses sing to her as she sits on the bench?

How many hearts must still be throbbing, how many flames of love and youth still burning in the world!

Was all that quenched in her?

She thought of Golgonszky.

The strange, deep gaze of his eyes had more than once recurred to her memory. And each time she had succeeded by a sudden, agile twist of her mind in escaping their gaze. In a kind of panicky flight she had hastened to turn her thoughts elsewhere, as if some dread power—the secret of sensuality and of sin—was hidden in those dark eyes whose glance pierced her very soul.

Now she felt it was in vain that she strove to escape those memories. She recalled the evening at the Csereys and the moment when Golgonszky, his hands deep in the pockets of his dolman, had approached her from the fireplace; she recalled the unusual face that from the first moment had captured her imagination. And she felt once more that inexplicable throbbing of the heart that she had felt then. Those memories raced one after the other through her mind, and everything came back to her—the moment when they had sat together in the motor, when she had seen him at the riding academy, when she had met him in the hallway and his brown coat had disappeared around the turn of the stairs, when they had walked along the Fishers' Bastion and he had declared his love, the hotel bedroom near Berlin, and now the last episode—his letter.

Why, really, hadn't she answered that letter?

Actually she had been racking her brain for weeks,

trying to think what to write, but everything that occurred to her seemed either too intimate or too cold.

". . . send me the slightest, the faintest sign . . ."

She was trying to face that idea now.

If she wrote him, he would doubtless come at once. And what would happen if Golgonszky should spend a few days with her here?

He would come of his own accord, and not at her summons. Would it be her fault if she should meet someone here whom she had known for a long time?

They would take afternoon walks in the mountains. Toward evening they would listen together to this sweet, sad music. The atmosphere about them would be filled with the enchantment of this strange, insubstantial love. The fluttering wings of a thousand new thoughts and sensations would encircle her heart, and she would feel anew that sweet, inexpressible agitation that she always felt in Golgonszky's presence.

Perhaps she would even yield him her lips, once. Here, under the trees, toward night, in the warm darkness, fragrant with foliage. And whom would she be wronging if she did?

What divine, glorious compensation that kiss would be for the three lost years of her life! She thought of her hair that was falling out, and the agony of this transient existence wrung her heart.

She closed her eyes and that imaginary kiss thrilled her to the very core.

But what would happen if she should be overcome? If she hadn't strength enough to resist her passion, and she became Golgonszky's mistress?

She felt so sickened by the thought that a shudder of horror passed through her at the fleeting picture of herself lying shamelessly naked in Golgonszky's bed.

Nothing was farther from her mind just then. She felt that after such a fall there would be nothing left for her but suicide; the searing torment of conscience, the self-disgust, and the pangs of remorse would destroy her peace of soul and crush her.

What had given her the strength so far to resist these fearful ordeals, save the sense of her own purity? She carried it always with her, as a bankrupt carries his jewel case. This exists, this is left, and so long as we have it we can always begin a new life. When we go to bed at night, the treasure rests in some corner at the bottom of the closet, and the mysterious power that it radiates is the surest balm for the fugitive's tortured spirit.

Engrossed in her thoughts, she hadn't noticed that the music had long been silent, and that darkness had fallen about her.

From the restaurant terrace the clatter of dishes could be heard, and here in the warm darkness the fireflies were beginning to dart about. They fluttered around, then hid their phantom glow among the foliage—like incandescent wires, some short, some long, that had detached themselves from heaven knew where and were now displaying the mute, green lines of their flame in the darkness.

Miette returned to the terrace for dinner.

She had been sitting there hardly half an hour when it began to rain; the rain pattered on the dry leaves like flames crackling among the trees.

A fresh wind arose, and the awning over the terrace seemed eager to fly away into the dark, wet night as though driven by some irresistible longing, and its rusty iron supports suddenly broke out in a plaintive moaning.

Such a wave of sadness overwhelmed Miette that she almost burst into sobs. The dull grief of solitude and desolation weighed heavily on her spirits.

When she went up to her room she was gripped by a strange terror of the long corridor—with its ornaments of chamois and ibex horns—which for some reason was never lighted.

She didn't go to bed immediately but, wrapped in a light shawl, sat huddled in an armchair, her knees up, engrossed in one single thought. So long did she remain in that position, so perfectly motionless did she sit, that an observer might have supposed she had long since fallen asleep.

For five days it poured incessantly, the unremitting downpour characteristic of the Salzkammergut mountains that obliterates all life. She could go neither to the waterfall, to the mill, nor to the church, which were her friends; she could no longer sit for hours near the wheelwright's workshop; all day she was shut up in her room, and what strength remained to her spirit crumbled away in captivity. At night she would imagine strange, invisible creatures crouched in the corners of her room, and suddenly she would be seized by the fear of insanity.

She couldn't fall asleep and would sit up in bed till dawn, her hair disheveled, sobbing spasmodically in the darkness, unable to make herself stop.

In vain did the dawn begin to break; the leaden sky, gloomy and overcast, the monotonous dripping of the rain, bore her farther and farther toward complete despair, in which the thought of death was uppermost. There were days when, locked in her room, she would continue her distracted pacing from window to door for whole hours before going to bed, sometimes falling to her knees and praying aloud.

She wrote to Golgonszky:

"Dear Golgonszky:

"Since I received your letter I have never been in the proper mental state to answer it.

"Thank you for your friendship, for your sympathy, and for having thought of me.

"I am at St. Hilben just now, whither I have fled for rest.

"I am alone. Alone with my thoughts and my memories.

"Cordially,

"Miette."

When she put this note into the envelope she knew that it was the faint call for help for which Golgonszky had been waiting.

She knew that as soon as he received the letter he would immediately hasten to her.

But when and where would it reach him? Was he still alive even? And if he were alive, would he really come?

As a matter of fact, almost a whole year had elapsed since he had seen her. And who knew what he felt for her now?

Should she mail this letter? She would still have time to think it over in the morning when her mind would be clear.

Revolving these vague thoughts, she fell asleep—but next morning her first concern was to go to the post office to mail the letter.

She began to look up timetables. Several times she went to the station and pictured Golgonszky's arrival. He would come in the evening, for that was the best train for visitors; she herself had come by that train. In the evening at seven o'clock, when the sun was disappearing behind the tops of the linden trees, but the concert was still going on in the park.

Because of the meager traffic, only one hired carriage was stationed at the St. Hilben depot for the use of visitors. She took a long look at it, thinking, "He will take that carriage when he comes."

Where should she wait for him? Perhaps she would be walking along the main path of the park and would wave him a welcome as the carriage passed her. But she didn't like that plan. For a moment she thought of going to the station, as if by accident. Then she felt that would be overdoing it. Finally she decided she would wait for him in front of the hotel, in one of those wicker armchairs burnt by the sun, reading a novel or busy with some piece of embroidery.

The very first evening, at the hour when the train was due, she was sitting in one of those armchairs. She listened to the long whistle of the incoming train, the panting of the locomotive, and reveled in those emotions that were enriching her heart with new delight.

She saw the yellow cab emerge from among the trees at the entrance to the park. She heard the crunching of the pebbly road beneath the wheels, and the groaning of the springs. Her heart leaped when she saw there was someone in the carriage, though she knew it wasn't

Golgonszky, for the letter couldn't even have reached him yet.

Before going to bed, she walked up and down her room for a long time, now throwing herself on the couch of the bed, only to resume her restless pacing the next moment.

All her time she spent in the fever of excitement induced by suspense and hope, and her heart was tormented by waves of sensual restlessness.

In the morning she would remain seated for a long time in front of the mirror, studying her face. At the corners of her eyes she discovered lines of weariness and grief, wherein were written all the secret, lonely thoughts of the past years of her life. Examining those marks of fatigue in her face, the terrifying sense of her fleeting life pierced her heart once more, like the feeling that grips one who reads his doom in some illness or some accident of fate.

Golgonszky arrived on the fourth day.

Everything happened as Miette had imagined it. She was sitting in front of the hotel when, at a few minutes after seven, the yellow carriage emerged from the bushes, carrying Golgonszky.

He hurried straight to her.

She didn't ask him why he had come, and he said nothing, explained nothing, as if everything were to be taken for granted.

After the first few words of welcome, Golgonszky went to his room and changed his clothes. Miette waited for him in the park below, and they walked in the direction of the mill.

Not by so much as a word did they touch upon what was oppressing their hearts, what was overwhelming them with doubt and unutterable torment. They walked slowly under the tall lindens, from whose crests the sun had disappeared. They spoke of irrelevant things, in unnaturally low voices that betrayed the one thought pervading their minds—that they were walking side by side, in an atmosphere of complete isolation, as if in all the earth no one existed but themselves.

Miette was glad that Golgonszky didn't mention her letter, that she might pretend unawareness, that she needn't talk about it—it was better so. The unuttered words weighed on her soul and she was anxious that nothing should be said between them—that Golgonszky should simply stay with her for a few days; and then she would let him go like a fading dream.

The dusky twilight was gathering about them as they returned to the main path of the park and ascended the terrace to dinner.

They did not linger at the table but went down into the garden and sat on a bench, not far from the electric-lighted door of the hotel.

They contemplated the starry sky and Miette had a feeling that the divine light of one of those stars was piercing her very heart.

Something clutched at her throat, she wanted to cry; her nerves were tingling with unappeased desire.

They were both silent. Miette knew that after this silence Golgonszky could no longer put off speaking to her of the one thing that dominated his mind; she was waiting for those words, she wanted that moment to be over; and as the silence lengthened, she longed to drop her head on Golgonszky's shoulder.

But he was still silent. He sat in the darkness, his head on his hand as if he were mortally weary of this fearful, unremitting struggle against himself, as if the maimed, dispirited words could find no way out of his mind. This muteness was more eloquent than any words. Miette could no longer endure the silence. She rose uneasily.

In a low voice, as if something had suddenly smitten her to the heart, she said—"Excuse me—I must leave you—I am a little tired—"

She was about to hold out her hand, but saw that Golgonszky was preparing to go in, too.

When they reached the dark passage at the head of the stairs he seized her hand in his.

"I am desperately in love with you—"

The passage was in utter darkness—feebly illuminated

only at the lower end by the reflection of the stars through the window pane. Against the wall beside the window were outlined the dark shapes of ibex antlers.

Miette yielded her mouth helplessly to Golgonszky's kisses.

The sound of footsteps was audible on the stairway and they separated abruptly. Miette did not look back but disappeared into her room.

Golgonszky stood in the darkness for a second longer, then he, too, entered his own room.

He stood leaning against the frame of the open window, as if he were plunged deep in thought or were waiting for something indefinite—what, he didn't quite know himself.

Outside the wind stirred gently in the foliage. The lamp below shed a faint light over the garden, and from the greenhouses, hidden somewhere in the darkness, floated the perfume of white violets.

He stood there motionless for a long time.

Suddenly, somewhere near Miette's room, he thought he heard a door being opened softly.

A second later Miette entered the room and remained standing near the door. In the semi-darkness she seemed to be clothed only in a pale negligee, and her hair was loose. She paused beside the door, leaning against it so as not to fall, for her legs could scarcely hold her. She closed her eyes and pressed both her hands to her breast.

Golgonszky went to her and took her into his arms.

She was trembling from head to foot, prostrated as if laid low by a lightning stroke of terror, of the consciousness of sin and of sensual ecstasy.

V

The willows along the banks of the Irtysh were beginning to yellow, and occasional cool gusts of wind rippled the surface of the water as if the distant Arctic Ocean had turned its face for a few brief seconds toward Tobolsk.

It was their third winter of Siberian captivity.

Returning from town one morning, Peter entered his room and stopped in astonishment on the threshold.

Kölber was sitting on his officer's kit in the middle of the room, his back to the door, his arms folded. A stuffed knapsack lay on the floor beside him, and all his belongings were packed. His cap on his head, his overcoat wrapped about him, he sat there like a passenger on the deck of a steamer.

"What are you doing there?" Peter asked in surprise.

Kölber turned his head slowly.

"I'm waiting for my passport."

Peter opened amazed eyes, not quite understanding what Kölber had said.

"Your passport?"

"Yes!"

"What passport?"

"Don't you know! I'm leaving this afternoon—I'm going home!"

For the flash of a second Peter's mind was a jumble of joyous thoughts, but suddenly he was seized by a fearful suspicion.

"Who told you that?"

A mysterious smile crossed Kölber's face.

Peter ran out and rushed down to the community room, looking for someone with whom he might share his shocking suspicion.

They were all gathered in the community room, mute horror written on their faces, and Peter saw at once that they were discussing Kölber.

"He said goodbye to us all a half hour ago," Mezei said.

Peter sat down on a chair, incapable at first of a word.

"What are you going to do with him now?" he asked after a moment.

Mezei began walking up and down.

"What can we do? I'll send him to the commandant this afternoon."

The next moment Kölber entered the room. He sat on a chair, a little apart from the others, crossed his arms and spoke to no one. He seemed to be suppressing an occasional smile, and changing shadows passed across his eyes. It was apparent from his absentminded expression that he was carrying on a conversation with himself.

From the moment of his appearance, a blank silence had settled upon the room, as if a dead man had appeared in their midst.

Bartha tried to whistle, while Vedres yawned loudly and patted his mouth with his palm. But there was a stabbing pain at their hearts, and they ventured only stealthy glances at Kölber.

At length Vedres turned to him and, to break the suffocating silence, called affectionately: "Wie geht es dir, Franci?"

Kölber shuddered as if startled suddenly out of sleep. Turning to Vedres, he answered simply and courteously: "Ich? Danke schön."

A little later he went to the window, looked into the yard and began singing:

"Kinder! Die kein geld mehr haben
Bleiben dann zu Haus!"

The notes floated out into the yard and seemed to linger there. An orderly, washing his plate at the well, stopped and looked toward the window with the expression of one who has heard a heartrending cry.

During lunch, Kölber suddenly grew nervous. His hands began to shake, his forehead was bathed in sweat, and he cast agonized glances about him.

Mezei, sitting beside him, stroked his head silently. After lunch, Vedres offered to take him to the commandant at headquarters, and Kölber agreed docilely to everything.

They were already on the threshold of the outside door when Kölber stopped, beckoning to Peter: "Don't despair," he whispered in his ear, "I'll take care of you too . . ."

He put his finger to his lips mysteriously, to indicate that, while he waited, he must say nothing to anyone.

Peter went up to his room, stretched himself on the

bed, and, propped on his elbow, gave himself up to his thoughts. He cast an occasional glance toward Kölber's empty bed, enfolded in a kind of terrible silence.

He saw Kölber before him, turned toward the wall, sleeping, or pretending to sleep. On the striped pillow, stuffed with dry grass, he saw the pale blond head, and the neck red as a turkey's crop.

He couldn't stay in this room. He went down to walk in the garden, but there, too, he was the prey of such restlessness that he soon gave up his monotonous pacing along the birch hedge where he was in the habit of walking.

He decided to go to town to see Zinatchka.

She wasn't expecting him that day, and she saw at once by his face that something unwonted had happened.

"What's wrong?"

"Nothing," he answered evasively.

"Has someone died?"

"No. Kölber's been taken to the hospital. I'm so desperately sorry for the poor wretch!"

He closed his eyes and added, "Will you give me a little tea?"

They had long since been using the intimate form of address. But it was not the intimacy of love or even of close comradeship; between them it represented a kind of abstract, exalted relationship, with a profound, almost sorrowful significance—like the ceremony of some strange religion uniting all men through the word.

When Zinatchka went out, Peter looked wearily about the little room. The icon above the upright piano, and beneath it the little crimson flame of the vigil light in its blue glass; between the windows, the enlarged photographs of the Cossack captain Ignatov Sergey and his wife; the curiously shaped triangular table where Zinatchka had just put down her work, a garment she was basting; the little porcelain stove that looked like a stubby, irascible little man; the sharp odor that filled the room, and the poor, shabby carpet—it all seemed to him ugly now, atrocious.

He buried his face in his hands to shut out these objects to which so many memories already clung.

Everything that surrounded him here seemed unreal just now—as if the shabbily upholstered chair arm where his inert hand rested was the palpable part of a nightmare. Was it really his hand—traces of oily grime still visible about the nails—looking like the hand of a laborer?

That morning he had been helping someone take apart the rod of the well and oil the upper pulley that had been creaking for days like a man being strangled. And these shoes on his feet! Why was he here? What did this word Tobolsk mean? Heavens, how the glass in that frame had cracked! Where could Johnny and Szücs be now? What a strange pain he felt in his chest!—almost as if something had burst in his lungs. How old was his mother now?—fifty-five? He would ask Mezei not to make Lukács his roommate. Or should he say nothing? What difference did it really make? Oh God, how horrible everything was!

Zinatchka came back. She brought tea in the steaming samovar that filled the room with a warm pungent odor. She said nothing, but her eyes, full of pity and apprehension, kept stealing to Peter's face, as if she were afraid of something sudden happening any moment. She had never seen Peter's face so somber.

There was a long interval of silence.

It was a deep, agonizing silence, broken only by the clink of cup against saucer as Zinatchka pushed the tea over to Peter. But Peter didn't touch it. His eyebrows raised, he stared at some invisible spot as at a specter.

Humbly, timidly, Zinatchka laid her hand on his.

"You're nervous today," she said gently, putting all her heart into those few lightly breathed words.

Peter closed his eyes, as though utterly exhausted by the struggle with his own thoughts. Suddenly he shivered and seized Zinatchka's hand.

"Say something! Say something—it doesn't matter what—but talk!" he cried in the voice of a very sick man whose throat is parched by the torment of burning thirst, and who pleads for a drink.

"What's the matter?"

Peter put his hand to his forehead. He was livid.

"I'm afraid—I'm terribly afraid I'm going mad too."

For a moment Zinatchka's strength forsook her. She trembled all over and wanted to cry out. Her knees slackened, refusing her their support; her heart seemed to have stopped. But it was only a momentary weakness; quickly she pulled herself together and said in a scarcely audible voice; "You're silly! What are you talking about?"

She sat down for a moment on the couch.

"Do you want me to sing something for you?"

Without waiting for his answer, she went to the triangular table and picked up the guitar. She threw one of the sofa pillows on the floor and sat down at Peter's feet.

The guitar strings had a dusty twang, and at first the notes were cold and lifeless; but gradually they grew warmer, a subtle glow passing into them from the girl's fingers.

Peter looked down at her, absentmindedly watching the play of those slender feminine fingers over the strings.

Zinatchka began to sing. She could convey a thousand emotions, a thousand sighs, a thousand presentiments in her thin, slightly husky voice.

She sang a popular old Russian song, native to the shores of Lake Baikal:

"Two lads went on the ice—on the ice—on the ice!
To get a fish for dinner—for dinner—for dinner!
Mashunka, do you hear what the wind is wailing?
Mashunka, do you hear what the winter calls to you?"

The words and the notes of the guitar fell about him— soft, silent flakes of snow.

When she had finished the song she let the guitar slip noiselessly to her knees, as if its spirit had fled.

She bowed her head on Peter's knees, and for a long time sat there motionless.

Almost unconsciously, Peter touched the girl's head, and at the feel of the soft hair under his fingertips he felt a sweet emotion surge through his heart.

"Can I be in love with her, too?" he wondered.

The fading memory of Miette stirred a dull pain in him now, like the memory of a dead love.

Nicolai Ivanovitch Kirilov, the guard who had accompanied Peter that day, had been talking with old Dmitri in the kitchen all this time, until his head had finally dropped to his chest and he had fallen asleep. Dmitri, his eyes half closed, sat on the bench by the fireplace, his hands on his knees, playing "mill." He would break off occasionally, only to begin again. When he found it necessary to drive away some impertinent fly that had settled on his silly little ball of a nose, he would simply move his fingers in an awkward gesture before his face.

That afternoon Peter stayed with Zinatchka for a long time.

Early in September, Pod-Chouvachi resembled an ant hill that had just been overturned. The commander-in-chief of the Russian army had ordered the disruption of the whole camp, for fear its ten thousand prisoners might revolt and liberate the Tsar.

Camp was accordingly broken, and began moving eastward, toward Chabarovsk.

The camp doors that faced the Irtysh were opened and the vicinity of Pod-Chouvachi took on the appearance of a huge junk market. Everyone was trying to get rid of his superfluous belongings at a good price.

The inmates of the Bear House and all the officers billeted in the town were taken away at the same time.

Within a few days the population of Tobolsk was reduced by ten thousand. The city market was eased of a fearful burden, as if some gigantic foreign body had been severed from it.

The Tsar stood on the balcony and waited in vain for the parade of the ragged troops of war prisoners, to which he had grown so accustomed.

The inhabitants of Misery Hotel were to remain in Tobolsk pending further orders.

A few days later an unexpected event threw them into a state of feverish excitement. Mezei, having gone to headquarters one day, brought back the news that, after a year and a half, the mail had just arrived. Joy, despair, apprehension were mirrored on the faces of the men. It was almost with a shudder of foreboding that they realized the fearful darkness of the past eighteen months would soon be dispelled for them—like a dark room, locked for years, whose door has just been broken down and its interior illuminated by the light of a lantern. How many dead will lie in the darkness, and who will those dead be?

Less than an hour later, the captain himself, accompanied by two subordinate officers, brought the mail. The silence of death descended upon them as he distributed letters and telegrams in the community room. As each man received his mail he walked, pale-faced, from the room and disappeared either into his own room or into the garden, so that no one might see his face as he read his letters.

The captain gave Peter five letters and a telegram. He looked at the addresses, and felt himself eased of a horrible weight when he saw, one after the other, Miette's handwriting and those of his mother and sister Charlotte on the envelopes.

Once in his room, he opened the telegram first. He unfolded it from the top and looked at the date first; it was almost a year since it had been sent.

Then, steeling himself abruptly, he read the text.

It said:

"God is merciless to me. Father died tonight without having suffered long.

"Miette."

He reread the words in the desperate hope that perhaps he hadn't understood them the first time; or that by a kind of miracle the letters might change under his eyes. And again he read it, three times, four times, while an icy chill stole through his breast, as if hoarfrost were settling on his throat and heart. This sensation of cold spread to his arms, and the fingers in which he held the telegram grew icy.

He couldn't take it in that Father had been dead almost a year. He remembered that only yesterday, sitting here on the edge of his bed, he had thought of Father. Now he saw the bald head on which the yellow lamplight played—his blue heavily pouched eyes, his little stiff white mustache and the soft grey beard about which there was always a faint, scarcely perceptible perfume.

For him Father had still been alive yesterday. And he shuddered to think that each time he had thought of Father during the past year, it was a dead man about whom his thoughts had revolved.

He didn't open the other letters till later. In the first, Miette gave him the details of Father's death; in the second—dated two months later—she wrote that the bank in which Peter had been employed had failed, and her third letter, consisting of only a few lines, was a cry of despair hurled into the void. In this third letter she complained of having had no news of Peter for ten months and of not knowing whether he were alive or dead.

His mother and sister wrote of trivial matters. They told him they were well and awaiting his return impatiently.

Peter didn't stir from his room till late in the evening. For whole hours he lay stretched on his bed, without stirring; then he jumped up suddenly and started walking restlessly back and forth as if struck by an overpowering idea.

After dinner he called Zamák.

"Sit down there, on the chair!"

Zamák sat down. His shrewd lively eyes sparkled, for he understood that this was going to be something important. He held his ragged cap politely on his lap and his eyes followed each of Peter's movements attentively.

"I'm going to escape," said Peter at last after a lengthy silence.

He paused in front of Zamák.

"Do you want to come with me?"

"Yes, Lieutenant!"

Peter sat down on the bed and meditated.

"We've got to find a way."

Zamák leaned forward, his eyes alert. One could almost hear their thoughts revolving in the air.

After another lengthy silence, Zamák spoke first.

"May I, Lieutenant—I've had something in mind for a long time—"

Peter fixed him with a questioning glance.

Zamák drew his chair closer, cast a glance about him to make sure that no one could hear, and lowered his voice to whisper, "We must dress as monks—it would be easy to escape that way."

Peter stared at him, apparently uncomprehending. Zamák, with a gesture habitual to him when he had something important to say, balled his fists, leaving the little finger free to tap the edge of the table.

"Lieutenant, please listen to me. Beggar monks are not arrested by the patrols, and when they get to a village the peasants make the sign of the Cross after them and even give them food—and they travel without paying on the railroads."

Peter did not answer at once. Their unmoving eyes were fixed on each other. Zamák made a gesture as if to say, "Well, isn't it true?"

Peter recalled the mendicant monks whom he had often seen in the streets of Tobolsk and particularly in front of the shops of furriers. Those monks, poor hirsute devils, their garments wretched and filthy as if they had been made of earth, generally walked barefoot, a small wooden crucifix clasped in the left hand, and in the right a narrow tray covered with black velvet. One never heard the sound of their voices, but they approached each passerby, raising the crucifix high in the left hand, while with the right they proffered the little black velvet-covered tray in a gesture that could not be misunderstood. Those who were inclined to give alms placed on the velvet board a few kopeks destined for God.

After a long silence Peter began speaking.

"You know, I don't believe that's such a good idea—the Reds are killing the priests nowadays."

"Yes, but no one harms the poor beggar monks."

"Where would we get the clothes?"

Zamák waved reassuringly.

"I'll take care of that, Lieutenant. They're made of cheap camel's hair, and that coffee-colored stuff can be found anywhere in the Tatar section."

"And will you be able to sew them?"

"Overnight. Has the Lieutenant a little money?"

Peter gave Zamák the rubles he had laid aside, and Zamák tiptoed out of the room.

When Peter was alone, he paused in the middle of the room, clasped his hands and, staring at the intertwined fingers, cried, "Lord God!"

All night long he dwelt on the details of his escape. He was the prey of such agitation that he couldn't close his eyes for a single second. The very idea that in a few months he might be home brought him to the verge of sobs. During three years of his captivity an immense store of repressed energy had accumulated within him and was now being released.

Home! He felt that, knife in hand, he could carve a path for himself across the bodies of men. He might be arrested? He might be shot? So be it!

The thought of this precarious adventure was like a sweet narcotic to his heart

Next morning he went to Mezei's room.

"I want to speak to you about something very important," he said, after he had taken a chair facing Mezei.

Mezei looked him straight in the eyes and after a moment's silence said, "You want to escape."

Peter nodded.

Mezei was not surprised. He could see in Peter's face

the impressive calm produced by a steadfast resolve. He didn't even try to dissuade him.

"It's your affair!" he said thoughtfully and a little sadly. A moment later he added, "Do you want me to collect a little money for you among your comrades?"

It was the custom in the prison camps, when one of them wanted to attempt his escape, for the others to make a collection for him. And the daily reports were falsified as long as possible so as to give the fugitives a slight advantage over their pursuers. But on the other hand, there was never any discussion of the ways and means of escape. That was each man's own secret. They never gave each other any advice because they felt advice of this kind would entail such responsibility that the soul of the adviser might be harrowed by remorse for the rest of his life.

Peter shook his head. "Thanks! I need nothing just now."

When he left Mezei's room, Lajtai and Szabó were already at the door. They both wanted to speak to Mezei, too. They exchanged only one brief glance, but it was enough to make them realize that they all had the same intention. The Siberian post, mute and inanimate for eighteen months, had sent its long shriek ringing through their souls and shaken them out of their lethargy. Who knew what they had contained—those letters that the captain had distributed among them so casually yesterday? Neteneczky had been pacing the yard all afternoon, his head pressed against his clasped hands. No one had heard Rosiczky's zither that evening, and Szentesi and Hirsch had spent the whole night writing letters.

Early in the morning Zamák went to the Tatar quarter. He sauntered along the streets until finally, in some waste lots at the end of town, he discovered two mendicant monks. They were sitting at the edge of the ditch that bordered the road, eating black bread and onions. Zamák settled himself beside them without honoring them at first by so much as a glance. He pulled a blade of grass from the ground and began rolling it between his fingers.

"It's beginning to get cool," he said, after a while.

"Yes, already," answered the older of the monks, looking up at the clouds in the autumn sky.

The younger didn't even look at Zamák. He said nothing but, grave-faced, continued to eat industriously.

"Where do you come from?"

"From Omsk."

"Where are you going from here?"

"We are going back—to Omsk."

They remained silent after a moment. The younger cast a sidelong glance at Zamák, and began speaking too.

"You are a Hungarian soldier?"

"I? Yes. Can you tell by the way I speak?"

The monk nodded, and went on eating. Silence fell once more. Then Zamák resumed: "Tell me—when you meet patrols, do they ever question you?"

Before answering, the elder carefully returned the dried bread to his wallet.

"Us? What for?"

"Because of your papers. Have you papers?"

"Of course we have! We visit the villages in accordance with the Pastoral Epistle—from Omsk to Tobolsk, from Tobolsk to Omsk."

That did not please Zamák.

"Have you ever been asked for your papers?"

"Not I—"

Meantime Zamák had been stealthily examining the cut of their gowns. Carefully he scrutinized the chaplets about their necks, the small crucifixes, and, with an absent air, picked up the little black velvet-covered board that lay in the grass. When he had learned all that was necessary, he took leave of the monks with a few affable words.

He went to the shops to buy the necessary things. The large package containing the material for the robes he didn't carry home till later in the evening, lest someone should see him. He locked himself into Peter's room, and they worked all night. Peter helped him to sew, continually pricking his fingers at this unaccustomed labor till the blood came.

Toward morning he fell asleep, exhausted, and didn't wake till noon. The excitement of the venture had penetrated to his very bones and he felt himself wrapped already in a kind of gentle, buoyant atmosphere of death.

That afternoon he went to see Zinatchka. When they were alone in the room he seized her hand suddenly and looked deep into her eyes.

"Tomorrow at dawn—I'm going away—" he said quickly, to get it over with as soon as possible.

"Where?"

"To my country. I want to get away. I've received a letter from home. My wife's father is dead. There are other troubles, too. I can't stay here any longer."

He spoke rapidly, as if these were unimportant things, to be taken for granted. Yet he couldn't look Zinatchka in the eyes, and he felt the girl's hand grow clammy and cold between his own.

She withdrew her hand, walked slowly to a chair and sat down, pallid as a corpse.

Peter went to her and laid his hand slowly on her shoulder. For a long time he could say nothing. Then he began in a whisper, "Zinatchka—you have always been good to me—I shall never forget you!"

His eyes suddenly filled with tears. He seized the girl's cold, limp hand, kissed it, and held it pressed against his cheek.

Then there was another long silence. Peter wished he were already out of this room, but he dared not get up to move toward the door, feeling that this movement would break the girl's heart. His own heart, too, was heavy with grief.

Zinatchka turned to Peter with a gesture as if she would have spoken. But no sound came from her throat and, apparently at the end of her strength, she dropped her hand on the red velvet covering of the walnut couch.

Then, gathering all her courage, she tried to smile. In a

very low voice, she said, "How strange—from now on—
we shall never see each other again!"

Peter didn't answer. He looked around the room to
bid farewell to the enlarged photographs—on whose glass
the sunlight of that October afternoon shone sadly—of
the Cossack captain, Ignatov Sergey, and his wife. His
eyes lingered for a moment on the linen curtain at the
window, on which a Siberian landscape was embroidered
—post horses being relayed in front of a wooden *irba* on a
snow-covered mountain slope. His eyes took leave of the
little triangular table, where Zinatchka's work box stood
open and some sewing lay that she had begun. Farther
along the wall, the vigil light still burned in the little blue
glass under the dark icon of St. Nicholas, but its flame
faded in the beautiful golden sunlight that fell athwart
the room, just grazing the glass.

Zinatchka touched his shoulder, as if to rouse him from
a dream.

"Go, now—" she said gently, tenderly, and it was
apparent that she wanted to put an end to his suffering,
too.

They kissed silently on the threshold. Peter left the
house hastily, but once on the street, he paused for a
moment and turned to listen. There wasn't a soul in
sight. The silence of the autumn afternoon lay empty and
lifeless about him. He fancied Zinatchka's strangled sobs.
But that was more of his imagination. He hurried as
quickly as possible to Misery Hotel.

During dinner he said nothing to the men, but later,
when they were getting ready to go to bed, he went to
each one's room to bid them farewell.

They exchanged few words, embraced and kissed him,
or said goodbye with a silent handclasp.

At dawn, though the day had hardly proclaimed itself
and everything around them was still in complete
darkness, Peter and Zamák crept with pounding hearts
through the outer door of Misery Hotel, their somber
coffee-colored robes blending with the darkness.

They reached the bank of the Irtysh, where they

followed the willows upstream. Little by little the day broke. They turned for a last look at Misery Hotel, the faint outlines of whose dark, shingled roof began to emerge in the dawning day.

"If we reach Chuksheska tonight, we can take the train there," Zamák whispered.

Low in the sky the crescent moon shone with an apple-green light.

They hastened onward.

VI

Miette had been Golgonszky's mistress now for almost three months. What she had most dreaded—the gnawing reproaches of her conscience and the haunting impulse to suicide induced by them—had come to pass amid throes of such searing agony as she could never have imagined.

Since their return from St. Hilben they had met almost every day. Golgonszky never came to her apartment, yielding in this to Miette's wish, for she felt that it eased somehow the burden of her sin.

But she could hardly wait for the twilit hours of those autumn afternoons when, collar turned up and face almost completely hidden, she might hasten along the tree-lined avenue at the other end of Buda toward Golgonszky's apartment.

As soon as she entered Golgonszky's room and the door closed behind her, she would fling herself into his arms with joy and delight, as if some mortal danger had been threatening her and this was the moment of her deliverance.

What had the timid impulses of her girl's heart, of her marriage, and her love for Peter been by comparison? Often that thought recurred to her when Golgonszky sat crouched at her feet, his face buried in her dress, racked by the agony of his inability either to express or to show what he felt for her. And she, too, was drowned in desire from head to heels, strangled by something within her that wanted to shout, to weep, to laugh, to free her in one long shriek of this unappeasable strain.

What were those nights in Florence by comparison, the rocking of the *Neptune* that first summer, and the moments of her brief conjugal life when she had given herself to Peter—moments that had so soon become a habit?

It was generally about five when she arrived for these trysts that sometimes extended far into the night. She had bought a pair of little red mules and an apricot negligee which she left with a little toilet case in Golgonszky's closet. These prolonged tête-á-têtes, behind carefully closed doors, stimulated their passion for each other to unimaginable heights. Only now, through Golgonszky, did Miette come to realize the power of her beauty and the irresistible charm of her body. She felt that she held this man's fate in her hand, and could do with him as she wished. But his influence over her was as great, and she knew that she had given her life and her destiny into Golgonszky's keeping.

The idea that this love might some day come to an end, that for one reason or another Golgonszky might disappear from her life—she knew that it would be the end of her.

Sometimes the pangs of jealousy began to torment her, and since she could find no cause for them in the present, she would turn to the future or her painfully sensitive imagination would attack Golgonszky's past.

"Whom did you love before me?" she asked in the course of a night of burning passion, as she sat on Golgonszky's lap while the tip of the mule on her naked foot brushed the carpet.

"No one," said Golgonszky.

"Who was that general's wife?"

"Which one?"

"The one Olga told me about—that little blond woman—she saw you everywhere together. Was she ever your mistress?"

"No!"

"Did you ever kiss each other?"

"Yes."

Miette dug her ten fingernails into Golgonszky's face and glared at him, her teeth clenched, her eyes blazing.

Laughing, Golgonszky released his face from the grip of those tender passionate claws.

"The general's wife? Do you know who the general's wife is? My sister! She is five years older than I, and my father's child by his first marriage. Didn't you know that?"

Miette felt a little abashed. Then she seized Golgonszky's lips between her pink fingers, as if she meant to hold him prisoner thus while she questioned him.

"Who is that very ugly girl with whom I saw you at the riding academy?"

Golgonszky freed his mouth of the living padlock.

"Whom do you mean? Jeanne——?"

And he mentioned the name of a well-known and very exalted family.

"Did you love her?"

"I? Never. But she's still in love with me. She keeps sending me letters."

"Let me see them!"

He looked at her for a moment, then said calmly but severely, "I will not let you see them!"

Miette knew that she had been wrong to ask. She flung her arms around Golgonszky's neck, as if she were flinging herself on his mercy, closed her eyes, and pressed her burning face savagely against his cheek.

One afternoon, having reached Golgonszky's apartment on the exact hour, the valet opened the door for her and told her that his master had not yet returned but would be in at any moment. Then he disappeared, his manner conveying no shade of offensiveness or familiarity, only kindness, meekness, and devotion. He was the only living being whom Miette knew there; he brought them tea and served them whenever Miette stayed to dinner. She never saw anyone else, though there were more servants at the other end of the apartment.

Miette sat down and looked about the room. She liked its simple, austere furnishings, unostentatious yet distinctive and inviting. She always felt pleasantly giddy among this furniture, her heart faintly oppressed.

But now the waiting and the solitude induced a sense of uneasiness, and she couldn't sit still but began pacing the thick carpet.

The snow was piled several inches high on the window-sill outside, and the stillness about her was so weird that the room and its appointments, these witnesses of so many hours of their tempestuous passion, affected her like an awesome hallucination.

What had happened to her? Into what fearsome adventure had she been dragged? What drug of passion, what diabolic incense had stretched her, stupefied by its deadly fumes, on this couch with its heavy silk cover reaching to the floor!

She was beginning to feel almost frightened and gazed about her in that state of tremulous dismay that seizes upon the spirit in eerie moments of too complete solitude or too profound silence, bestowing life and personality on inanimate objects.

Little by little the silence and the solitude began to shake her to the very depths of her soul.

What would become of her? Where would this wild, guilty love lead her?

She looked at her watch; it was already a quarter past five, and the minutes dragged more and more slowly.

At last the outside hall door opened. A second later she thrilled to the sound of Golgonszky's voice through the closed door. Immediately the sense of oppression vanished, and she drew near the door, waiting with taut nerves for the moment when she could fling her arms about his neck.

He came in and when, after a long embrace, he disengaged himself from her arms, his face showed traces of fatigue and ill humor.

"I must go away tomorrow!" he said gloomily.

"Where?"

"I've been negotiating all this time, but I can't hang onto my present post any longer. I've been transferred to the staff as aide to General Scharer."

"And how long will you be away?"

"I don't know—I can't hope for a furlough just yet—there's been too much criticism already of my lengthy absence."

A thousand thoughts flashed through Miette's mind. What would happen to her if she were left alone now? If Golgonszky should never return? Perhaps he might have avoided going and had only agreed in order to put an end to this affair that was carrying them both farther and farther down the slopes of sin! He had once said himself that it was infamy to rob one who couldn't defend himself. Perhaps he had been stung to remorse by some accident, by some unexpected impression, by the torments of his own soul—and perhaps this remorse had conquered his passion for her.

The eternal suspicion of the female suddenly blazed within her.

But, scanning Golgonszky's face with bated breath, she soon rejected her idea, for that face reflected such grief that nothing could have been concealed behind it.

A long silence fell between them while despair plunged its steel blade into Miette's heart. With the eyes of one condemned to death, she asked, "Must we part now?"

As gently as possible he answered her, "It's only a question of a few months."

In a voice that was scarcely more than a breath, Miette said, "And if Peter—returns?"

Peter's name fell heavily between them, for Miette had never yet uttered it in Golgonszky's presence.

But he answered promptly as if he had been waiting for this perilous question and had prepared his reply beforehand, "That cannot happen so quickly; if the war stops soon, lengthy negotiations will be started."

Golgonszky felt that the shadow of the absent man had appeared between them. He rose nervously to stride up and down the carpet.

All the time that they had been lovers they had never spoken of him, but now his name was in the room, impalpable, oppressive.

To Golgonszky, it meant a face never glimpsed, hidden in the disturbing shadows of mystery, a face to which his imagination strove vainly to give form. Had he ever seen his photograph, even? As for Miette, she still fancied she could hear from an infinite distance his last words down there at the station when, leaning from the running board of the officers' carriage, he had seized the outstretched fingers of her hand and said: "Be careful—you might stumble—"

Golgonszky paced the carpet with measured steps, from window to closet. He seemed to be waiting till Peter's name—still hovering like an eerie mist in the air—should be dissipated.

Then he paused, leaning against the closet, "I'll be back before spring—I'll write every day—"

Miette went to stand close to him and, with a movement of inimitable sorrow and grace, laid her head against his breast, as if she would seek there a place where she might rest forever.

They stayed together until two in the morning.

"Goodbye, my dear—" Miette murmured as they parted outside in the snowy darkness, before she entered the cab.

She didn't go to bed when she got home, but sat at her desk and began to write. She didn't weigh her words; she was simply pouring out her emotions on the white paper; this wasn't a letter, sentences linked together, but the burning fragments of unendurable pain, of impassioned longing that never attained expression but were quenched, sputtering, like glowing coals flung into water. It was one of those letters that ease a stricken heart.

She couldn't sleep at all, and very early next morning she sent the letter to Golgonszky, so that he would receive it before he left.

After he had gone and when she had grown accustomed to the thought that her lover was no longer beside her, no longer in the same city but among strange, distant scenes, where her fancy was unable to follow him, she felt that the joy of life had vanished from all the world. Especially

toward the close of day was she overwhelmed by a sense
of apathy. The hour of their trysts seemed to her appal‹
lingly empty. There was nothing left to enkindle her, to
bind her to life.

During the first weeks she sat at her desk till late into
the night, trying to relieve her heart in passionate letters;
but now that the long love trysts were at an end (though
their glowing memory lingered in her heart) she had more
and more time to reflect upon what had happened to her,
and frequently she forced herself to stand before the
tribunal of her conscience.

Still no news of Peter. She had received no answer
to her last four letters, and it was more than a year
now since, despairing of any reply, she had given up
writing.

Peter's fate lay hidden behind the heavy clouds of the
Russian Revolution, and Miette tried to deceive herself into
thinking that everything would have been different if
Peter's cries of love and desire had succeeded in reaching
her.

Often she wondered if what she had done was a sin,
and whom she had sinned against. She could always find
arguments to persuade herself that she had not sinned
against Peter, considering these years of her life as somehow outside of time, without beginning or end—a dream
she had dreamed, unrelated to actual life. And when
Peter came back, her feeling for him would be renewed
where it had been broken off four years ago.

What was life then? And of what use was a woman's
body, a woman's youth? To what end had God destined
this heavy, silken hair, this tender white breast, the soft
curves of these hips, the classic beauty of the whole body
—if not for love?

She thought of Olga—Olga who, flinging convention
and prejudice to the wind, had rushed toward death in
view of all the world—in the divine, reckless, endearing
nakedness of love. Who would dare—by what right, by
what law—to demand an accounting of this dead girl's
rights?

Where could she turn for a pattern and a guide, when everything and everybody contradicted themselves?

Woman's body was made to be offered to man. Only the time and the manner of its offering had any significance.

A few weeks after Golgonszky's departure, she began to feel the need of contact with the outside world.

First she went to call on the Csereys, who had spent most of the previous year in Vienna—which made it unnecessary for her to give any explanations to justify her protracted absence.

She scrutinized Mathilde's face with a secretly fluttering heart, wondering whether Mme. Cserey didn't suspect something of what had happened between her and Golgonszky; but she discovered nothing—Mathilde knew only that Miette and Golgonszky were acquainted, but that was enough to fill Miette with apprehension.

"And our friends?" asked Mathilde in the course of the conversation. "Really, I don't know what's become of any of them—"

She mentioned many unfamiliar names, thinking that Miette knew these people; then she remarked casually, "I haven't seen Ivan either for a long time. I heard he had gone back to the front. Golgonszky, I mean. Do you remember him?"

"Oh yes," said Miette, and promptly changed the subject.

She was sure now that Mathilde suspected nothing.

Yet Mathilde was a woman whose unfailing instinct could discover—with a bloodhound's scent—all the amorous secrets of her circle. Everyone trembled beneath her smiling, malicious, and slightly ironic glance. But then, how could she have known anything! They had been so discreet that they had never even let themselves be seen together in the street.

Miette had been selling her securities, one by one, and there was hardly enough money left that month for the household expenses, modestly as she and Mili lived.

Now, sitting opposite Mathilde, who had always shown

her such unfailing kindness, and feeling through her chatter the carefree well-being produced by riches, she was on the verge of confiding the difficulties of her financial situation. She was convinced—and rightly—that Mathilde would be only too happy to help her and that such help would be proffered in the most sisterly spirit. Weren't they kin and hadn't Mathilde always found real joy in giving Miette pleasure?

But as she formed the sentence on her lips, she felt that with the first words she would burst into tears. Listening with feigned interest and an absent smile to Mathilde's vivid, sprightly conversation, she was turning over in her mind the idea that she might sell her piano. Abruptly, as if reading her thoughts, Mathilde touched her hand gently and asked, "Miette dear, how do you live? Don't you need anything?"

Suddenly Miette felt herself braced, and smiled as she answered very convincingly, "No—really, I don't need anything!"

A few days later she went to visit the Vargas. Elvira had been to see here a few times in the interval, but she hadn't seen Dr. Varga for over a year. She found him aged. His beard was turning gray, and he seemed dispirited and tired. She promised to visit them oftener in the future.

Little by little other contacts were renewed. Sigismund Pán, who had been discharged from the service, came to call on her one day, and it was through him she learned that Johnny had been badly wounded the year before. A shell had struck him in the face but, according to Pán's information, he had left the hospital.

Paul Szücs had boxed the ears of a Czech colonel in a Prague café. He had lost his rank, been stripped of his decorations, and condemned to five years' imprisonment. This last piece of news was brought by Rose, who through some secret agency mysteriously kept in touch with Szücs.

Rose went to the Vargas' now only as a guest. She had inherited some money from her family and was studying millinery, and all her ambition was centered upon establishing a shop of her own. She was already negotiating for a little place in a side street near the Park. She came to see Miette frequently and asked her advice about everything. She would bring touching little gifts—crocheted doilies, lace trimming for a dress—once she brought a ham that had been sent from home, and the last thing had been a hat she had made herself, all her love and adoration for Miette worked into it. She always presented these gifts at the last moment, blushing to the ears, and generally with the words: "I have brought Madame something—would she be so good as to accept it?"

Little by little, signs of spring began to appear.

One afternoon Miette entered a pastry shop. She sat near the window, and ordered a cup of chocolate. An afternoon newspaper lay open on a chair. Huge headlines shrieked the latest dispatches from headquarters. Miette gave one glance at the paper, and abruptly turned her eyes away. She had a horror of newspapers and of everything reminding her that a war was going on. It was April, and springtime.

A black velvet hat shaded her face. One couldn't tell whether her eyes were blue or dark green. Under her hat, the soft silky curls of her red-gold hair were visible at the temples.

There were only a few people in the shop. Miette leaned her elbows on the table and rested her chin on her clasped hands. She raised her delicately arched brows a little, bent her head to one side, and stared steadily into space. She was bored, waiting for her chocolate. Her eyes wandered idly among the customers without really seeing them.

Suddenly, she shuddered violently, opening her eyes wide in horror. Convulsively they clung to one spot, and her breath stopped in her throat.

A young lieutenant was sitting at a table near the wall, alone, apart from the others. His arms crossed on his chest, his head bent slightly, he stared before him into space.

His appearance was weird and horrifying. Half of his

face was completely gone. There, at the arch formed by the temple and cheekbones, a huge, fantastic cavity was dug. This hollow began high up on the forehead and continued along the cheek to the mutilated, broken chin. A thin, pink skin suggesting the color of raw flesh was stretched across this cavity, and the parchment-like skin shone as it it had been waxed and rubbed with a chamois cloth. Every vestige of a human countenance had disappeared. The eye socket was open and the orb of the eye, surrounded by a ring of moist, revoltingly bloodshot flesh, was bare of brows or lashes.

The other side was the quiet, melancholy face of an attractive young man: a large brown eye, with long, almost childish lashes, a delicately arched nose, a firm, narrow, beautiful mouth, and a virile chin.

Miette gazed at him transfixed, unable to avert her eyes. She had recognized him instantly; it was Johnny, the cadet. Yet when the two sides of his face were presented simultaneously, she no longer dared be certain it was he. All her memories of the young man surged suddenly into her mind. She saw him at the moment of their departure on their honeymoon journey. He, too, had been at the station to see them off, and had saluted silently when the train began to move. He had been pale, and the look in his eyes had remained with her. Johnny had never told her so, but she felt, she knew, that he had been desperately in love with her, as only young people of twenty can love.

Johnny paid his bill, rose and moved toward the door. The two waitresses leaned toward each other, following him with rounded eyes and grimacing as if they had swallowed something frightful. Everyone looked at him with the same shocked expression.

Johnny walked toward the door without a backward glance. As he passed Miette's table, she called in a voice hardly louder than a breath, "Johnny!"

The lieutenant turned in surprise toward the direction of the voice. He went up to Miette. "Greetings!"

She gave him her hand, and he bent automatically in

an instinctive movement to kiss it, but changed his mind halfway, as if it had suddenly occurred to him that this lovely hand ought not be touched by his scarred and mutilated mouth.

So he stood awkwardly, holding Miette's hand in his.

She flushed with emotion, straining every nerve to conceal the shadow of fright in her face and eyes.

"Well—how are you, Johnny? How long it is since I've seen you!"

"All right," he answered in confusion "—there's nothing new."

"Wait a moment till I pay my check. Where are you going?"

They went out together. They happened to be in such a position that it was the disfigured side of Johnny's face that was turned toward Miette. But he signed to her to precede him and quickly placed himself on the other side.

"But tell me—how are you, Johnny?" said Miette, putting all the tenderness of which she was capable into her voice.

He answered with a few vague words.

"Can you still crow, Johnny?" she asked affectionately, warm laughter in her voice; but before he had time to answer she realized by a glance at his face that the question had been a mistake. The wound had destroyed part of his tongue and palate, and there was something strange and hollow in the sound of his voice.

Without waiting for an answer, she began to talk hurriedly.

She told him all that had happened to her in the five years since they had last seen each other. She spoke of Peter and told him of Father's death. She told him how terrible those days had been for her, and how she had believed she would never recover, but how she had returned little by little from desolation to life.

They came to a little cross street, and when Johnny turned into it, Miette, walking and talking by his side, followed him. They had taken a few steps when she interrupted herself and stopped. "Why do you take this street? It's much shorter by way of Kossuth-Lajos Street—"

"It's all the same, really—" Johnny answered casually.

Miette didn't insist, for she realized that it wasn't through abstraction that Johnny had chosen this little street. He wanted to spare her the ordeal of walking beside him along the main street because, even when they were still far off, people stared at that face, so horribly disfigured as to seem the work of a fiend, and once they had passed, turned round to look after him. Miette was so touched by this thoughtfulness that, feeling the tears rise in her throat, she had to stop speaking for a few minutes. When this wave of emotion had receded, she resumed quietly, "And then, afterward—you know—"

Walking thus, with Miette doing most of the talking, they reached her house. Johnny wanted to say goodbye to her at the door, but she seized his hand.

"No, Johnny, I shan't let you go. You're going to come up with me and talk to me a little. I'm so happy to see you—"

Upstairs, in the apartment, she called to him from her room, "Find the cigarettes; they're in the shell box."

Miette had changed her dress. When she emerged from the bathroom, her neck and hands were fragrant with fresh toilet water. She stretched herself on the couch, crumpled a large silk cushion under her elbow, and said to Johnny, "Now, come and sit by me and tell me exactly what's happened to you since we last met." She stretched her beautiful arm toward the box, saying, "Give me a cigarette."

"It was in autumn that I was wounded," he began. "I can't tell you much about that because I lost consciousness, and when I came round again I had been in bed and bandaged for a long time. I had no idea what was under the dressing. Then I was brought to Budapest. Here, at the hospital, I became engaged."

"Engaged?" said Miette, opening her eyes wide.

"Yes, but unofficially, just between ourselves. A little

society girl who had come to the hospital as a nurse. The daughter of a high official in the postal service."

"And when will the wedding be?"

"The engagement was broken—" Johnny answered.

They fell silent. Miette didn't want to ask why, and Johnny didn't tell her. He was sitting on the edge of the couch, leaning forward a little, his elbows on his knees, weaving his fingers together and making the joints crack, as if there was nothing very interesting in all this. Yet, as he sat there, staring at the floor, the grief in which his soul was submerged was plainly written on his face.

Now, too, he sat so that the unmarred side of his face was turned toward Miette.

With bated breath Miette scanned that face. After a long silence she whispered, as if her heart had stopped beating, "Did she jilt you?"

His hand shook a little as he knocked the ash from his cigarette.

"Yes. When the dressing was removed from my face. She never came back to the hospital after that day."

Leaning on her arm, Miette recoiled with a little shudder.

Johnny didn't look at her. Slowly he blew the smoke from his mouth, trying to make rings with it, as if nothing else interested him.

Miette dropped her head slowly to the cushion and closed her eyes.

There was another long silence, then Johnny began, "Listen, Miette—I'd like to tell you something—but don't be angry at my telling you a thing like this. I've not told anyone else—"

She didn't answer; she only opened her eyes.

"A fortnight ago," he went on, in the voice he might have used to tell a funny story, "I was in Buda with a few comrades. We had dined at a small restaurant and drunk a little wine. At about two o'clock I started home, alone. It was raining; I was wearing my officer's raincoat, and I had pulled the hood down over my cap. I was walking along the boulevard, close to the wall, to protect

myself from the rain. Suddenly a woman caught hold of
me—a street girl. She had grabbed me on the right side—
as you are seated now. She pressed herself close against me
and said—"

Here he broke off and raised his eyes to Miette.

"You won't be angry if I tell you this?"

"Go on!" Miette murmured.

"Well, to be brief—she took me home with her. We
turned into a side street, and she rang the bell of a
house over whose door a lamp was burning. And as we
stood there, suddenly this woman saw my face. Her
fingers stiffened against my chest, she uttered a fearful
shriek and pushed me away from her—" Johnny took a
deep puff at the cigarette.

"And she fled into the house," he added in a scarcely
audible voice.

Once more a long silence fell between them.

Then he rose and said, "Well, goodbye, Miette—"

Miette was lying full length among the cushions, her
eyes closed. Johnny took her exquisite hand that seemed
lifeless now.

"Goodbye!" he repeated in a whisper.

"Don't go yet!" said Miette, keeping a hold on his
hand.

He sat down again. Miette's hand lay in his. They
remained in silence thus for a long time. Suddenly
Miette's hand stirred and softly brushed Johnny's neck.
She drew his head down to the couch, so that his forehead
rested on her arm and his face lay against her breast.

And again they were silent, for a long time—a long,
long time, each feeling the wild throbbing of the other's
heart. One of Miette's hands lay on Johnny's neck and
held him there.

"How life has shattered us!" whispered Miette.

The young man made a movement as if to go; but
Miette drew him toward her once more. With a sudden
gesture, she drew him very close and Johnny's stricken
face was buried in Miette's fragrant negligee.

The room now lay in almost complete darkness.

Miette clasped Johnny in her arms and gave herself gently, like an offering, to the young man.

VII

In the Russian village of Kirienko, at the western frontier of the province of Tobolsk, snow had covered the house of Vassily Gregorovitch Urumov as if in an effort to bury it forever. At the lower end of the yard was the stable, for Vassily was a carrier and kept two camels. He was a God-fearing man who lived peacefully with his old wife and every evening prostrated himself for hours, drawling out prayers and chants before the icons.

A little light was allowed to penetrate into the stable through a small aperture scarcely larger than the palm of a hand, covered by a jagged fragment of broken glass and held in place by mud instead of putty. Outside the day was waning. The noisy breathing of the camels could be heard now and then in the darkness.

From a heap of straw thrown into a corner came the murmur of muffled voices.

"And what did your sister Julia do then?"

"She left the village and went into service at Kassa," said Zamák to Peter.

"Was she a pretty girl?"

"Yes! Only her nose may have been a little too long. Like mine, for that matter!"

Zamák had a provincial way of pronouncing certain words and particularly affected the locution, "for that matter," using it in season and out.

They were silent for a few moments, then Zamák continued.

"Do you hear, Lieutenant, how the wind is howling outside?"

Every night they talked together in the corner of the narrow little stable, whose air reeked of the damp, sweetish fumes exuded by the big, warm bodies of the camels. But at least the pitiless cold couldn't assail them here; the Siberian winter, with its frozen face and teeth keen as a sharp knife's edge, couldn't gnaw at them here. During those long evenings Zamák told Peter all kinds of involved stories, told him in detail all the incidents that occurred to him of his childhood years.

It was almost three weeks now that they had been living in Vassily Urumov's house. After having stolen from the yard of Misery Hotel three months ago, they had hoped to be able to take a train at the next village and cross Siberia without difficulty. They hadn't dared go to the station at Tobolsk, lest they should be recognized. But this precaution had been useless, for they soon realized that there were detectives and police agents posted at the most important stations, asking every traveler for his identification papers. Revolutionary Russia had no great love for mendicant monks.

Therefore, as soon as they neared an important center, they would leave the train before it reached the depot, preferring to travel afoot for days in order to avoid the city.

They had lost much time, and winter had overtaken them. Sometimes the main road vanished beneath their feet and the whole countryside was nothing but an endless prairie over whose immaculate whiteness a lonely Kirghiz sledge, carrying a physician or some hard-pressed traveler, would draw its tracks that vanished into the horizon.

It was very bad weather for pedestrians. There were times when they couldn't do more than ten versts a day. They were often caught in violent snowstorms that seemed destined to go on forever, blasting, stunning, blinding them.

Here and there a few black posts would rise in the snow. That was a hamlet. Sometimes they would be obliged to wait for weeks in one of these little villages before they could go on. Whenever they could, they would take the train. But it sometimes happened that they were driven off. Trains crammed with soldiers rolled through the snowy desolation from east to west, while from west to east thousands of prisoners were being conveyed to the depths of the country, away from the vicinity of the crumbling front. There was no room in these military trains for civilian passengers, and Peter and Zamák were sometimes forced to remain for whole weeks in some filthy little Russian village.

It was in this way that they had come to the house of Vassily Urumov.

"I'll help you cut your wood, brother," offered Zamák, as they entered the house to ask for shelter.

"You know—we'll be satisfied with the stable. At least it's warm there."

Vassily Urumov even gave the "monks" food. Weren't they quiet men, pleasant in the sight of the Lord, especially the one with the long beard, in whom the sorrow of Christ seemed to dwell?

"At least they'll pray for us, Tanya Ivanovna," he said to his wife.

In the course of the day, Tanya Ivanovna herself brought them steaming cabbage soup and corn bread.

She was a bony, round-shouldered old woman, not very different from the other peasant women of Little Russia. Her face seemed carved like a wooden icon, with empty, kind, stupid eyes, and her chest was hollow as a trough.

"You can sleep in the house," she said to the monks.

But they preferred to stay in the stable. It was better, anyway, than sleeping in the same room with the two old people.

They tried to make themselves useful in Vassily Urumov's house. They cut wood, carried water, fed the camels. They stayed till the beginning of February, when they succeeded in boarding a train that jogged along with them toward the West.

What a journey it was! It seemed impossible to get into the compartments. They weren't compartments, really, but hideous black holes into which the cold—silently, perfidiously—thrust its icy knives. Sometimes they were hurled against a soggy mass of invisible people. They felt like worms that might at any moment be crushed. Whole mountains of luggage were thrown about topsy-turvy. Zamák was perched somewhere on top, under the roof of the car, while Peter made a little place for himself among the mass of boxes, legs, and shoulders. Somewhere a candle was lit. Heads, bags, boxes, Red soldiers, and street women in tatters emerged abruptly from the darkness. The soldiers shouted at the tops of their lungs; the civilians were silent, as if their tongues had been torn out. A Red soldier placed his boots against Peter's shoulders, to keep from sliding off the pile of luggage, and held that position for hours.

But all this was of no importance. After the horrible monotony and the desperate years of waiting in Tobolsk that had brought them to the verge of insanity, these were beautiful days—yes, freezing, painful, frightful, but beautiful, nevertheless—days of action, days of progress toward the country of their birth!

The train took them some hundred miles; then they had to wait again for weeks. Once, when Zamák had already swung himself aboard a train, he hastily jumped off again.

"Where are you running to?"

"Don't go in there, Lieutenant!"

"Why not?"

"There are two real monks in the carriage!"

Still, by the end of February they had reached Khabarov. They slipped into a Jewish wine shop near the station, where they proposed to await the departure of the evening train. The other half of the café was fitted out as a grocery and reeked of rancid cheese and motor oil. They were given smoked herring and moldy bread for their meal, but at least the shop was warm. A rusty, red-hot little iron stove crackled away, intensifying all the unpleasant odors of the shop. They had sat on a bench against the wall all afternoon. The greasy table before them was covered with crumbs and the skeletons of the herring they had eaten. Zamák's head fell now and again to his shoulder and he began to drowse. Soon Peter fell asleep, too.

They were awakened suddenly by a dull roar from the street. The unintelligible sound drew nearer and nearer, and gradually shouts of joy could be distinguished above the clamor. Next moment the turbulent crowd was passing the shop. Peter and Zamák, startled out of a deep sleep, gazed at each other in bewilderment.

The little old Jewish shopkeeper—whose hands and beard smelled of cloves and who wore a dirty red cap of knitted cotton on his head—was standing at the door of his shop. When he had heard what it was all about, he flung his arms toward heaven and signaled hysterically to Peter and Zamák.

"Friede! Friede!" he shouted, beside himself with joy.

Peter and Zamák rushed out into the street. A delirium had taken possession of everyone. No one could utter an intelligible or coherent sentence; people were weeping and throwing themselves into each other's arms.

When the crowd had reached the lamp post at the corner, someone climbed up on a bench and began reading aloud, through the clamor that was renewed at intervals, the special edition of a Russian newspaper he had brought with him from the train.

"February 19th (he read aloud, articulating each syllable clearly and distinctly). The Advisory Council of the Russian People has sent a telegram to Berlin. This telegram protests against the advance of German troops, the termination of hostilities having been proclaimed by the Soviet Republic. The commander-in-chief of the Russian army has already begun the disarmament of troops on all fronts."

The news spread like a train of gunpowder through the crowd. The reader commanded silence by a gesture and continued:

"The People's Council, its hand having been forced, has agreed to sign the Peace . . ."

At the sound of that word such a thunderous clamor arose that the reader dropped the hand holding the newspaper. He gazed for a moment over the heads of the roaring crowd, where hats and arms waved frantically in the air. He was very pale as he looked at them; their cries were deeply moving. Then once more, with a gesture of his hand, he pleaded for silence and continued:

". . . according to the conditions proposed by the Four Powers at Brest-Litovsk. The Germans have taken Rovno, Luzk, and Duvno. The Austrian and Hungarian troops are advancing unopposed toward Kiev."

The last words pronounced by the reader were inaudible as the crowd broke into a fresh uproar. Peter elbowed his way to the reader. "What have the Germans taken?"

The reader looked at the newspaper again.

"Rovno, Luzk, and Duvno."

"And where are the Hungarians?"

"Before Kiev!" he said, getting down from the bench.

People flung themselves on him from all sides, besieging him with questions.

Peter seized Zamák by the shoulders.

"Do you hear, Zamák. The Hungarians are before Kiev!"

There was the quiver of a sob in his voice.

They hurried directly to the station.

"Lieutenant—please," said Zamák, overtaking Peter with difficulty. "Is Kiev far from here?"

Peter answered with a gesture of discouragement.

"Let's get to Yekaterinoslav first!"

"How far are we from there?"

"More than five hundred miles!"

"And from there to Kiev?"

"At least three hundred more."

Zamák whistled between his teeth and slackened his pace, keeping slightly in the rear, as if he thought it was hardly worth hurrying in that case. He had imagined they would get to Kiev next morning.

Their journey to Yekaterinoslav involved more difficulties than they had foreseen. The trains piled up on one another, and in all the villages the examination of identification papers grew more and more rigid. Everywhere the stations were filled with fugitive prisoners.

Nevertheless, at the end of four weeks they reached Yekaterinoslav. There they learned that a train was leaving for Kiev at ten o'clock that night. They had an hour and a half to wait. They sat on the floor in the fourth-class waiting room, since there was no more room on the benches. A huge crowd of excited people milled about them. Many were sitting on their luggage, their eyes closed, their heads drooping, as if the thought of the trip had made them sleepy. Men and women were huddled together. There were Red soldiers in rags, talking in an unfamiliar dialect. One of them had an ulcer on his nose.

Suddenly a heavy hand fell on Zamák's shoulder and a tall *proportchik*, his face seamed with pock marks, signed to them both to get up and follow him.

He led them into the corridor where the crowd was less dense and, glaring at them, said, "Show me your papers!"

Zamák turned livid with terror, and Peter felt all his strength forsake him. The ferocious-eyed *proportchik* held out his hand for the papers.

Peter looked him straight in the eyes and said calmly, "We are fugitive Hungarian war prisoners."

The *proportchik* showed not the slightest surprise at this unexpected announcement. With a movement of his head he indicated the door.

"March! I'm going to take you to headquarters!"

Peter didn't stir. With all his soul in his eyes he looked at the *proportchik* and said, "What do you want of us? We want to go home, to our families!"

He raised and opened both his hands, and showed his empty palms.

"Look—we have no weapons—we have been prisoners in Tobolsk for four years. Let us go! Peace has been signed!"

The *proportchik* leaned forward and shouted furiously into Peter's face, "Brest-Litovsk, eh?" snapping his fingers contemptuously. To him this peace evidently meant less than nothing.

"You are an officer?"

"Yes."

"And the other?"

"Private."

The sergeant measured them with his glance.

"You are going home to get ready to attack us again!"

Peter wanted to answer, but the *proportchik* motioned him to silence.

"Never mind! Let's go to headquarters anyway! March!"

But still Peter didn't stir. Zamák, who had meantime been eyeing the big revolver hanging at the Russian's belt, murmured, "Let's go, Lieutenant!"

They started off. The *proportchik* followed them three paces to the rear, indicating the direction they were to take. The military headquarters was situated near the tracks, some three hundred feet from the station.

At one point a Red soldier joined the *proportchik* and they began talking together. But he soon left.

Zamák took advantage of the opportunity to whisper to Peter, "Lieutenant—listen—as soon as we pass that first lamp post, let's both run."

"To the right?" Peter whispered, without turning his head toward Zamák.

"No—to the left!"

To the left, beyond the tracks, an empty field lay in the dim light of the moon.

Hardly had they taken ten steps after having passed the lamp post when Zamák turned, quick as a flash, and with all the strength he could muster, dealt the *proportchik* a blow in the eye. Whereupon he and Peter began running at top speed, to escape as quickly as possible the circle of light cast by the lamp post.

At the impact of Zamák's blow the *proportchik* had bellowed like a frenzied beast, then, seizing his revolver, had fired several times in the direction of the fugitives. Eight or ten soldiers who had been leaning against a wall nearby jumped up. The sergeant yelled something to them, pointing in the direction of the field, whereupon they too began shooting, one after another, at the fleeing men.

Suddenly Peter felt as if his leg were being pulled violently from behind. A second later he fell. Then he heard the heavy tramping of feet about him and felt terrific blows on his face and such kicks in his sides as he thought would crush his lungs and heart. Then he fainted.

When he regained consciousness his hands were bound, and he was seated on a bench in an office at military headquarters. A Russian soldier sat beside him, his cocked gun between his legs.

He felt burning, throbbing pains all over his body. He could scarcely open one of his eyes, it was so swollen. In the lower part of his right leg the pain was excruciating. Clotted blood was turning black on one of his hands.

"That's the leg that was hit!" he thought, and he tried to move it gently.

He looked around but saw no trace of Zamák.

Zamák was stretched out on a bench in the next room. It was a strange sight, this sprawling, long-nosed monk, his arms hanging, his face waxen, his eyes closed, a little crucifix clutched convulsively in his left hand.

Zamák was dead.

VIII

It was the middle of May. Returning around noon, Miette found a telegram on her table. It was only three words: "I am back." No signature. But Miette immediately knew that the telegram came from Golgonszky. The three words were suggestive, compelling, pleading, and imperious. They meant that Golgonszky would expect her at the customary hour, five o'clock.

Around two, she took a bath, dressed in her lavender silk shirt, slightly perfumed with Golgonszky's favorite lily of the valley, arranged her new spring hat, turquoise blue with cherry flowers, for a long time before her mirror, with almost painfully beating heart. When she reached the avenue, warm sunlight shone on the fresh, spreading foliage of the trees. This clear daylight troubled her and made her a little uneasy, and before entering the house she cast a glance about her to see if there was anyone near by from whose scrutiny she need shrink.

But the street was deserted. Only a woman sat propped on her elbows at a window of the house opposite, and Miette had the feeling this woman was watching her. She regretted now having stopped to look around, because this strange woman must certainly have noticed that, too. And if she had noticed it, she would have every reason in the world to seek mysterious explanations for the presence of this very smart young woman, dressed in a pearl-gray spring costume, who, walking with nervous haste, appeared suddenly around the bend of the avenue, and turned her head in a movement of instinctive caution to look about her before entering one of those little houses that looked like a private residence in this deserted street.

She was probably a neighbor of long standing, who knew that Ivan Golgonszky lived in that house. She would have to be quite stupid if she failed to make the plausible connection between these two facts.

But Miette didn't bother about all that now.

She ran through the hallway and glided swiftly and stealthily, impalpable almost as a breeze in its airy flight, into Golgonszky's room.

Tears, laughter, a passionate little cry, and a multitude of thronging emotions were crowded into her voice, as she held out both arms to Golgonszky.

"You are here!"

Overwhelmed by joy, Golgonszky took her silently into his arms.

"You're going to stay for a while, anyway?" she asked, disengaging herself after the first smothering kiss.

"Yes! I don't believe I shall have to go away again."

He surveyed Miette with eyes of rapture and wondering delight. He had never yet seen her so beautiful. He gazed at the snowy gloves that he helped her remove, at the rich tawny hair that, once the hat had been impatiently pulled off, seemed aglow with new lights; at the slender, exquisite lines of her figure, at her narrow feet, and small pointed shoes—those restless, eager dancers—and above, at the opening of her dress where the fresh triangle of skin, scarcely larger than the palm of a hand, was visible; and his eyes returned again and again to the place where the slope of the warm, velvety skin, revealing the tender outlines of the rounded bosom, suggested a rosy, bewitching nakedness.

Her face was so flushed with the joy of seeing him again, such gay, teasing little flames glowed in the depths of her eyes, her voice melted in such cadences of tenderness and ardor, that Golgonszky was seized by a fierce desire to prostrate himself before her and smother her in kisses.

But all this was reflected only in his eyes.

He retreated a step and looked at her.

"How beautiful you are!" he murmured ardently.

"Oh—!" Miette cried, quickly averting her face that was rosy with confusion.

She was so constituted that a compliment always upset and disconcerted her, though she herself knew by now that she was beautiful.

Miette had never been so happy as during those days following Golgonszky's return.

Once it happened that she lost track of the time and, forgetting that the sun rose earlier in summer, she stayed with Golgonszky so long that the day was beginning to break when she reached home. She spoke for a moment to the caretaker who opened the door for her, and inquired after his family so that her calm voice might disarm suspicion.

But she plunged even more deeply and madly into her passion, as if she felt a presentiment that her happiness would soon reach its end. It happened frequently now that she spent the night in Golgonszky's apartment, not reaching home till noon, and on those occasions she always told Mili beforehand that she would sleep at the Csereys'.

And indeed, prompted by some obscure fear, she did arrange to sleep at Mathilde's occasionally, in order to establish an alibi for herself, thinking that the dates of these nights could not fail to grow confused and obliterated as they faded into the past.

And more and more often she awoke in Golgonszky's bed.

On these beautiful summer evenings they were drawn irresistibly to the gentle slopes of the hills, and Miette grew daily more venturesome. Formerly she would never have dared show herself in the street with Golgonszky, yet now they took long walks every evening outside the city limits.

In the course of those long walks she gave him an exact and detailed accounting of her days during his absence. She told him of her first visits after so long an interval to the Csereys and to Elvira; she described to him her sensations as with a pounding heart she scanned Mathilde's face, fearing lest she suspect something. But she carefully concealed from him the fact that she had had to sell her piano; she still denied him permission to enter her apartment, even kept him from casting a single glance therein.

She told him of Paul Szücs' adventure, as she had learned it from Rose, giving him a minute description of Paul's exterior from the tips of his shoes to the crown of his hat, always a few sizes too small for him. She imitated his volubility and his habit of swallowing half of his words when he said "L'il la'y," for example, and the infinite number of "old fellows" introduced into his conversation—all so faithfully that finally Paul Szücs with his pimpled face and his shoulders stretching his coat to the bursting point rose in flesh and bone before Golgonszky.

Miette told him of the misfortune that had befallen Szücs for having boxed the ears of a Czech colonel.

"You must have so many friends and connections among the generals—try to help him."

Golgonszky, in whose estimation Szücs had risen high because of this reckless blow, promised to do everything in his power.

Miette spoke of Johnny, too, and described her meeting

with him. That is, she described it as far as she could. Her story had almost reached the brink of the abyss, but her voice betrayed no tremor, for the thought of Johnny never gave her the feeling that she had committed a sin. And she knew that she would never see him again.

One evening she was walking down the hill on Golgonszky's arm, completely oblivious of the fact that she might be seen. Suddenly she was aware of the approach of a group of three persons—an elderly couple with a rather plump young woman who must have been their daughter.

As they passed, the girl looked full into Miette's face. Miette seemed vaguely to recall having seen that face somewhere before, a very long time ago. Intuitively she felt that this was the same person who had been leaning on the windowsill, and had seen her entering Golgonszky's house after having cast a cautious glance about her. Yes, that woman at the window had seen her on other occasions, too, and it seemed to Miette as if she had been spying on her always.

Yet she searched her memory in vain; she was unable to recall who this person with the suspicious, spiteful eyes might be.

She didn't want to think about it, yet she couldn't rid herself of a sense of oppression.

"Do you know who lives in the house opposite yours?" she asked Golgonszky.

"In which house?"

"The two-story one—just opposite."

"Ah, yes—the Vajniks, or Vojniks—I'm not sure of the name."

Miette, to whom the name meant nothing, felt reassured.

But this incident prompted her to greater caution and when, a little later, the question arose as to whether the summer should be spent at a Hungarian or a German watering place, Miette decided it would be better to stay at home.

Entering the apartment one afternoon, she saw that the valet who admitted her was strangely distraught.

"The master is ill."

"What's the matter with him?"

"We don't know yet. He has a high fever."

Miette, sick at heart, ran to the bedroom.

Golgonszky lay in bed, his forehead burning, the skin of his face glistening and strained with fever. He turned troubled eyes like dark chasms to Miette.

Tenderly she took his hand that was hot as a glowing coal.

"What's wrong?"

Every word was an agony to Golgonszky, and the few that he managed to utter were gasping and labored.

"I don't know—inflammation of the lungs, I believe!"

Miette leaned over to kiss his fever-cracked lips, but he pushed her away.

"Be careful—I believe the epidemic—you must go at once—because—"

He couldn't go on; the raging fever seemed to have clouded his mind. He turned away and raised his eyes toward the ceiling, as if seeking there the elusive words.

"Has the doctor been here?"

"He is coming—" said Golgonszky with a tremendous effort, and his apprehensive eyes seemed to indicate the door.

Just then Miette heard Dr. Varga's voice in the ante-room. She had barely time to escape into the next room. As she fled, she upset the chair by the bed.

The bottle of mineral water and the glass, together with the tray that held them, fell clattering to the floor.

Dr. Varga entered the room. He might have believed that the chair had overturned of itself, had he not caught sight of a hand on the knob of the door that led to the bathroom. Detached, apparently, from its body, the hand groped blindly for the key on the outside of the door, then, like a pink, terror-stricken little animal, fled in distraction with its prey through the narrow, dark slit.

A woman's hat and a pair of white doeskin gloves were thrown on an armchair. Those long gloves still retained the shape and outline of the warm, feminine arms from which they had been torn hastily and flung on the chair.

But the doctor paid no attention to any of these things. He approached the patient.

In the bathroom, Miette thought she had escaped in time. But a thousand thoughts whirled through her mind, like so many searing arrows. She pressed her face against the door and, all her nerves in a state of fearful tension, listened to what was going on in the next room.

"He's going to die—" she thought, and the idea clutched at her fiercely.

"He's going to die—now, in the doctor's arms—he's going to die, as my father died—"

And here she was, taking refuge behind this door; with her own terrified hand she had turned the key, had separated herself from the dying man! He was going to die, and she wouldn't see in his eyes, so soon to be quenched, the last gleam of his soul, his last goodbye; she wouldn't know what that glance had said, or wished to say. The dead man would leave her with she knew not what enigma, what silence to drive her mad. She felt that if she were beside him now her eyes could detain the soul ready for flight. Well, why not? Who forbade her to kneel at the dying man's bedside?

A sudden determination was born within her, and a startling thought took possession of her mind. She seized the key and turned it.

Then, like a sleepwalker, she entered the room.

Dr. Varga, who was listening with a stethoscope to the heartbeats of the sick man, turned his head just then.

When he caught sight of Miette, the hand that held the medical instrument remained suspended in midair. He stared at her in amazement as at a vision.

Golgonszky turned his clouded, uncomprehending gaze on Miette in bewilderment.

Miette, very pale, stood before them.

There was a moment of silence. Then a thousand clamorous thoughts pursued one another through the silence.

At last the doctor drew a deep breath and, turning half to Golgonszky, half to Miette, said in a voice he strove to make natural, "The outcome of this disease depends entirely on the heart—and there's nothing wrong with the heart."

He smiled and carefully replaced the stethoscope in the upper pocket of his waistcoat.

"My fever is down already," Golgonszky whispered, simply for the sake of saying something. And he turned his eyes this way and that as if in pain. He seemed to be making an agonizing effort to understand why Miette was standing by his bed—and he didn't know whether she was reality or a dream of delirium.

"I shall come back at about ten," said Varga. On the point of moving toward the door, he seemed to hesitate. Should he speak to Miette or act as if he hadn't seen her?

She turned toward him and spoke. There was a singular, astounding serenity in her voice as she said, "I should like to talk to you."

Varga bowed and picked up his bag.

Miette put on her hat and gloves.

They left the room together.

When they reached the house door, Varga suddenly passed his arm through Miette's.

"Before you say anything, listen to me. Why are you trembling so? I can feel your arm shake. You're thinking now that I shall go home, pause on the threshold, clap my hands together, and say to Elvira, 'Just imagine what's happened!' Now listen to me! I'm a physician. I carry secrets within me that no one knows but myself."

He stopped for a moment, slackened his pace, and tightened his hold on Miette's arm, as if he wanted to draw her into the channel of his own thoughts. "If I were a preacher, I should say to everyone, with this epidemic raging: Nothing matters any more; hurry to save whatever may still be saved. Morality? Social prejudice? All that never enters my mind. Only the physician in me thinks."

He stopped and mopped his forehead with his handkerchief.

Miette closed her eyes, whispering, "I love him desperately."

The doctor spoke thoughtfully as they walked on, "Then it's serious. That means that you still have a bitter struggle ahead of you." He gripped Miette's arm again.

"Never mind!" he said at last. "I'm not afraid for you. I only pity you—you will have so much to bear."

They had reached the end of the avenue. He turned, faced her, and took both her hands in his. Looking into her anguished face, his voice was filled with unutterable pity and tenderness as he whispered, "My dear little Miette—"

Her lips trembled and she dared not look into his eyes, but contemplated his beard, where it seemed to her so many white hairs had woven their way since she had last seen him.

She raised her arms and clasped them about his neck. Pressing her face against his shoulder and trembling from head to foot, she began to weep.

"There! There!" said Varga, deeply moved, as he held her in his arms and tried to soothe her; then, in a different tone, more lightly: "This Spanish influenza is extremely contagious, and I really ought to tell you to keep away from the patient. But what would be the use? Everything depends on the individual constitution and perhaps even more on chance. You might be as likely to catch it locked up in your room. In any case, I know an infallible preventive—you mustn't be afraid of it! So, if you like, go back to him and nurse him. And don't worry—everything will be all right."

Smiling, he shook her two hands and disappeared around the corner.

Miette hurried back to the sick man.

"What have you done?" Golgonszky asked as she entered the room, his expression revealing the thoughts preying on his mind.

"It was better that way!" Miette murmured and,

seating herself on the edge of the bed, pressed his burning hand against her cheek.

She stayed with him till late into the night, till she was sure that he had fallen asleep and that the fever had somewhat abated.

And in the same way she spent all her time during the following days, withdrawing only when Dr. Varga paid his visit. She didn't want to show herself to him again, feeling that it would somehow be taking advantage of his kindness.

It didn't take very long for Golgonszky's vigorous constitution to prevail over the disease; but even when the danger was past he was unable to leave his room; there were still some adhesions in one of his lungs.

But he could get up now and walk through the thickly carpeted rooms in his long silk dressing gown that made him look like a maharajah. The exhilaration of escape from death filled his heart, and each day he waited more impatiently for the moment when Miette, a vision of grace and beauty, would appear on the threshold of his room.

Since his illness, they had spent more and more time together, and now Miette set out for Golgonszky's house immediately after luncheon every day.

Summer was long since over, and the sunny October days had arrived, but he still suffered occasional attacks of fever.

One night after Miette had gone, Golgonszky, beset by premonitions of evil, opened the windows and, muffled in his warm overcoat, listened to the silence of the dark, damp autumn night.

Suddenly, coming from he knew not where, he heard far away in the darkness the sound of firing.

They were the first shots of the Revolution.

Not until next morning did Miette learn that revolution had broken out. She ran down the street and, as though drawn by some invisible power, plunged deeper and deeper into the crowd.

It was eleven o'clock. There she was, in Rakoczi Street, caught in the raging tempest of those first hours. She saw the heavy trucks, crammed with soldiers, racing by at top speed, and she listened in anguish to the terrifying sound of guns being fired toward the sky. She was heedless of the fact that she was being jostled this way and that and squeezed tight among alarming-looking people. In front of her stood a toothless man in riding breeches, shouting over and over the same incomprehensible words. Over this man's shoulder and towering above the myriad heads she saw the silver helmets of the mounted police appear, welcomed by shouts of joy from the crowd who showered them and their horses with a white rain of chrysanthemums.

Everywhere shrieks that rent the heavens, the ceaseless firing of guns, and the pungent smell of powder filled the air!

She no longer knew where she was and, borne onward by the human current, suddenly found herself in the Uloi-ut, where the gates of the military prison of the Maria Theresa Barracks had just been torn from their hinges. Some prodigious force had twisted those heavy iron bars like so many bits of wire.

Through the vaulted porch she looked into the medieval court, where the liberated prisoners were being carried in triumph on the shoulders of the mob. She saw women of the laboring classes, their hair falling down under their hats or shawls, holding cocked infantry guns which they apparently had difficulty in dragging about. It was a meaningless gesture—their possession of these guns—yet there was something diabolic in the idea.

People were running about in all directions, and the air was hot with the fire of some suffocating spirit of vengeance. She felt vaguely that this was the end of something, that the suffering hitherto repressed was breaking forth in clamorous cries and with destructive might; that all this was as the gesture of a finger pointing to annihilation, and suddenly it seemed to her that she saw Peter's face appear, aged and transformed, in the features of some of these soldiers who were running past her, and that what was happening was directed against herself, that it was her punishment, her arraignment, the judgment of God upon her.

Exhausted by fatigue, covered with mud, and tortured by a thousand doubts, she hastened to Golgonszky's house.

She found him deep in thought.

"What's going to happen?" she asked, trembling.

He tried to explain the situation to her, arriving finally at the inevitable conclusion that most of the war prisoners would be home within the next few weeks, though the fate of those in the depths of Russia was still altogether uncertain.

Miette listened with a stricken heart.

Of all that had happened that day and of all that Golgonszky had explained to her, she grasped only one thing clearly—the war was over, and she must accustom herself to the idea of Peter's imminent return.

She felt that the question she was about to put would rend them both; but her heart was oppressed by such uneasiness, such intolerable suspense, that she could no longer remain silent.

She said, as if to herself, "What will happen if Peter comes back?"

She buried her face in her hands, as if she were trying to hide from something shameful.

Golgonszky paced the room, his hands behind him.

"There are several possible solutions," he said, lingering over the words and choosing his expressions guardedly.

"We don't know what's happened to him. Suppose the same thing has happened to him as to you? Who knows?"

He cast a surreptitious glance at Miette's face, as if to observe the effect of this idea upon her. But Miette was staring ahead, her eyes fixed and expressionless.

"If that's the case, everything would adjust itself."

Twice more he paced the length of the room before continuing.

"If it isn't—well, the situation will have to be faced—one decision or the other made—"

He interrupted his pacing to seat himself beside Miette and take her apparently lifeless hands tenderly into his.

"Listen—let's not torture ourselves with this just now —to make any decision at the moment would be useless— we must have some definite information first. And don't think that it's a question only of months. That's possible, of course, but I have an impression that it may be years yet—one or two anyway. Take it for granted that nothing will change for the time being."

Events confirmed Golgonszky's judgment, and their life returned to its accustomed channels.

Since her conversation with Dr. Varga, Miette found it easier to answer the questions that still agitated her soul, that still froze her blood. She often pondered what the doctor had said to her, but his words had not brought her complete deliverance. There were times when her own spirit protested most passionately against her present mode of life. One day, rummaging at the bottom of her closet, she found an old straw hat of Peter's, yellowed and battered; she remembered the summer evening when they had dined at a little inn in the woods and someone had inadvertently sat on Peter's hat. She remembered how happy she had been then—how blissfully happy under the great Indian chestnut trees. And she suddenly felt Peter's spirit so close to hers that, overwhelmed by the power of her memories, she went to her desk and wrote him a letter.

She wrote only a few words.

"My Darling Peter, what has become of you? The years go by and still no news of you. This suspense kills me, crushes me. Where are you? Are you still alive? To whom am I writing this letter? Perhaps it will fall like the others into a void. I implore you, give me a sign of life!"

She had written similar letters, each time with the feeling that her heart was being torn in two. But then months would follow when she couldn't and wouldn't think of Peter.

Meantime she had received only a postcard, already a year and a half old; and that was as if she had received nothing at all. Neither his mother nor the Pávels had heard anything from him. Miette's correspondence with her mother-in-law had grown more and more desultory.

One morning Rose came to see her.

"Oh, madame," she said, blushing and confused, "I've come to ask you about something of the greatest importance to me."

She had changed very much since Miette had last seen her, and in her pretty, black, fur-trimmed coat she looked like a smart young woman with a certain position in life.

"It's about Mr. Szücs . . ." said Rose diffidently.

"Is he free, then?"

"Oh, yes! Even before the Revolution! He was locked up with another young Hungarian, but they broke through the wall. He walked from Prague—across the mountains. If you'd seen him—how ragged he was and famished! I hid him for three weeks, but then the Revolution broke out. What ought I do now? Shall I marry him?"

"Has he asked you?" Miette cried in astonishment.

"Yes! I don't suppose—of course I wear hats now, too —but still, I said to him, 'Look here, what are you talking about? You—a gentleman, a society man'—I supposed all this grand talk of equality had turned his head. But he told me he had never been a gentleman. His father was a blacksmith, yes, and mine was a carpenter—and then, too, we are both Calvinists . . ."

"Do you love him?"

"Heaven knows—he's a good fellow—I don't say—"

"And he—does he love you?"

Rose smoothed a fold in her skirt and murmured, "He seems to—"

Miette felt the tears well up in her heart; she felt that she would gladly give her own life, her whole entangled existence, for Rose.

She spoke low and gently, "Marry him. You will have children and you will be happy!"

There was a note of unutterable sadness in her words.

When Rose left, Miette wouldn't let her kiss her hand.

Two months later, as she was walking through the woods alone, she met them.

They were coming toward her, arm in arm, like a young married couple. Szücs, taken by surprise, had the look of a man caught in a guilty act.

Miette hurried toward him, holding out both her hands.

"Szücs!" she cried, in a voice of mingled joy and sorrow, as if she were greeting a dead memory of her past life.

Szücs, robbed by emotion of the power of speech, took her hand.

Miette turned to Rose, threw one arm around her neck, and kissed her.

Szücs turned red as a lobster at the sight; his eyes opened wide and filled with tears.

IX

Even the Russian calendar now bore the date of 1919.

It was a sultry July evening. In the yard of Misery Hotel Mezei, Vedres, and Neteneczky were sitting in their shirtsleeves under the big birch tree, playing a quiet game of cards, as they had been doing almost every evening for the last four years. Since Lajtai had escaped the preceding autumn, they had played a three-handed game.

At the other end of the yard Altmayer, whistling a tune and reeking hideously of turpentine, was working at an easel. He was painting, from a little photograph, a life-size portrait of the dead wife of a Tobolsk wood dealer. He painted these pictures for so ridiculous a fee that he received occasional orders, and thus managed to keep himself in pocket money. The portraits were pretty and pleasant to look at, their one defect being that they bore only a very distant resemblance to the dead persons.

Szentesi and Csaba were in the vegetable garden, checking the current crop. Hirsch was working upstairs in his room, drawing economic charts, for Misery Hotel had by this time become the recognized source for the Tobolsk vegetable market and, thanks to the garden profits, they could at least feed themselves decently.

Their only desire now was to stay in Tobolsk till the

frontiers should be definitely opened and they could go home without interference. Here at least they had something to eat, they could gather wood for the winter, and protect themselves more easily against epidemics.

From all sides they received information indicating that the other prison camps had become the darkest breeding places of human misery. Since the outbreak of the Revolution, tea, sugar, and hot water, which had sustained them during the reign of the Tsar, had been stricken from prison rations. In the eastern camps especially, enclosed by barbed wire, typhus, malaria, cholera, and scurvy raged, wreaking fearful havoc among the prisoners. The bran balls, cabbage soup, moldy oatmeal, and salt fish of the Tsar's regime were happy memories, growing dimmer with each day; for since the beginning of the Revolution, they had been given camel's flesh, yak, cats, dogs, and decayed fish to eat, disgusting foods that emitted a hideous odor. The tedium of winter, the spiritual disintegration of these masses of incarcerated men, the inhumanity of the camp commandants and guards, the famine, the cold, the lethargy, the nostalgia and despair—all these things reduced the prisoners either to a state of complete apathy or to the mad delirium of souls driven beyond the limits of endurance. It was simply a question of the strength or weakness of the spirit bequeathed by God to each. Thousands and thousands, broken beneath the burden of starvation, had gone over to the Red army. It is true there were some among them in whom the appetite for murder and the thirst for blood were innate. For them, such days had dawned as they would never have dared dream of, for now they could steep their hands in blood as a child dabbles and bathes his fingers in the waters of the brook. Since the Soldiers' Councils had been formed at Moscow, and hundreds of thousands of *moujiks* swept back from the front to the rear, the castles and farms of landowners were being pillaged everywhere, and he who lusted to kill had only to take his choice among the middle-class citizenry of any of the lands of Little Russia.

The half-dark, water-soaked, wooden houses, the prisoners' barracks and buildings with their roofs battered and broken by the winds of Siberia, absorbed little by little the promise of the World Revolution. According to the Siberian maxim, "The People's Council of the Soviets owe their power to Hungarian bayonets, to Jewish tongues, and to Russian stupidity."

From the depths of the prison camps the Hungarian soldiers poured like the victims of some frenzied delirium. Under the Red flag they entered the Russian conflict, understanding only vaguely the aims of the Revolution. When they seized their weapons, it was a wild, death-defying gesture of utter despair. Where and for what they were fighting was to them a matter of indifference. There were Hungarian troops who fought one month on the side of the Reds and the next month on the side of the Whites, and it happened not infrequently that there were Hungarians on both sides, fighting each other. That was better at any rate than working at the construction of the Murmansk railroad in the province of Archangelsk, in whose marshlands the prisoners died to the last man, constantly being replaced by fresh draftees. They had to work at a temperature of forty degrees below zero. A Hungarian hussar named Bucko, who had escaped from there, stopped in at Misery Hotel on his return to Tobolsk, having made the acquaintance of its inmates in former days. He told them how even men whose legs had been frozen were forced to work, though they were hardly more than walking skeletons.

It was Bucko, too, who told them that Yurovski, the gorilla man who had disappeared from Misery Hotel during the first days of the Revolution, had with the help of his friend, Niculitch, assassinated the entire imperial family in the cellar of the mining engineer Ipatiev's villa at Ekaterinburg. The bodies had been dismembered, soaked in benzine, and burned in the forest. But of course it was impossible to verify these incredible rumors.

Occasionally, when they were in town, they would come upon a fugitive prisoner from whom they would invariably

hear some tale of horror. The bands of prisoners assigned
to wood cutting in the forest were beaten like Negro
slaves. Those who complained were shot down. In the
neighborhood of Nijni-Novgorod, soldiers drunk with
vodka had set fire to barracks containing three hundred
Hungarian prisoners, after having barricaded the exits so
that they couldn't escape. Some hideous, bloodcurdling
form of insanity had taken possession of this gentle
Russian folk, known in other days as the Candle of God!
The disabled war prisoners at Omsk were dying of hunger,
their cheeks sunken in, their teeth dropping from their
mouths, because they were left without food. With the
butt ends of their guns and nagaikas the guards repulsed
the few old peasant women who, moved to pity, would
have given them bread. The screams, the groans, the
wails of dying men swelled to so brutish an uproar that
even those who had preserved their sanity whole fell
before long into a state of hysterical frenzy. When one
died, his nearest neighbor carried off his clothes. A
lieutenant who had stopped in at Misery Hotel during the
first days had told them that three-fourths of the camp of
Novo-Nikolayevsk had perished in the course of the preceding winter. There was a time when twenty thousand
unburied corpses lay in heaps on the ground through the
freezing winter months; and when the spring thaws set in,
the whole city had been mobilized to dig trenches in an
effort to avert the plague. Since the establishment of
Communism, the private industrial enterprises of war
prisoners had been stopped everywhere—enterprises that
had been yielding them handsome profits. And during the
great famine, the prisoners were compelled to sell their
clothes in order to obtain food. Thousands and thousands
had to drag themselves painfully through the winter,
coatless, in tattered summer clothes and slippers made of
rags.

Only such men were freed as promised to help destroy
the middle classes. Officers were not allowed to return
home lest, once there, they should begin a new war.

Under these circumstances, the inhabitants of Misery

Hotel led a blissful existence. It was their good fortune to have been forgotten. Among the tens of thousands of prisoners, seven officers and a few orderlies no longer counted. The lame captain, Doroviev, who kept their roll call up to date at headquarters, had for two years been stocking his own larder and that of his brother-in-law from their vegetable garden. They owed it to this fact that they were still there. This Doroviev, with his bull neck, red cheeks, and flaxen hair, was a good-hearted, kindly hound along the bank of the Irtysh; he would go in and hold long conversations with the men. He laughed heartily at Neteneczky's jokes, and since Altmayer had painted his wife's portrait free of charge, a feeling of warm friendliness had existed.

Yes, life was still bearable at Misery Hotel. In the spring, cool winds blew from the Siberian fields along the Irtysh; in the vegetable garden the tender blue-green heads of kohlrabi, the inverted, frilled crinolines of the cabbage expanded with amazing rapidity; the tomatoes reddened within a few weeks and grew heavy on their stems; the delicate onion shoots thrust their spears through the earth, and the whole garden was decked in fresh bridal hues. The sky, too, was brightening; from dawn till dusk the wind drove before it fleecy herds of brilliantly colored little clouds; blue and gold light bathed the heavens in a luminous flood and, like some celestial folk migration, enormous flocks of wild ducks, their necks glittering, sped with the wind, together with brown wild geese and white swans and dawn-colored herons.

And now summer had come again.

It must have been about ten in the evening, but the yard was still light. Mezei had announced the last round of cards, for the silver clouds of mosquitoes were beginning to rise from the Irtysh.

Comrade was stretched on the threshold, half asleep, fanning himself with his tail. Suddenly he raised his head, began to bark, and rushed toward the gate.

A moment later Peter entered the yard. He walked with

a stick and seemed ten years older. The men had difficulty in recognizing him, but as soon as they did they jumped up and flung their arms around him, and in a few seconds all seven were clinging to him, besieging him with questions, fingering his clothes as if they couldn't believe their own eyes.

An armed guard had brought Peter down from the fortress and turned him over with some papers to the *starshi*.

Since the mosquitoes made it impossible for them to remain in the yard, they all went into the community room and seated themselves about Peter to listen to his story. Some of them sat on the table. The orderlies came in, too, and stood against the wall. They all began asking questions at once. Mezei motioned to the importunate ones to be silent and touched Peter's arm.

"Please begin from the day you left here!"

Then Peter spoke. His voice was a little husky, and his eyes held the weariness of a sick man doomed to death. He told them in detail the story of their flight from the moment when he and Zamák, disguised as mendicant monks, had slipped through the door of Misery Hotel in the dark dawn of that September morning. Now and then there would be a long pause as he seemed to be collecting his memories.

"I was taken to the hospital that same evening, after the *proportchik* had arrested us at Khabarov, to have my wound dressed."

"What became of Zamák?" someone asked.

Peter shrugged his shoulders.

"I don't know! I suppose he found his way home. I never saw him again."

"How long did you stay at the hospital?"

"At the hospital? Till early in October. My wound got worse and they were on the point of amputating my leg."

"Is it all right now?"

Peter extended his wounded leg and looked at it as at some foreign object.

"The bullet was removed, but there's still something wrong."

"Where did you go after the hospital?"

"They took me to Omsk, where they kept me till Christmas. One day I was so sick of the suspense that I asked the prison sergeant what they were going to do with me. 'Be patient, brother,' he said, 'maybe they're going to shoot you—how do I know?' You can imagine how comfortable I felt. But in January they brought me back to Tobolsk, and I was court-martialed and sentenced to four months in the fortress—and this very night I was freed."

The other men stared at him.

"You've been here in Tobolsk for four months?" Mezei asked in amazement.

Peter nodded. "Yes," he said softly.

"And why didn't you give us a single sign of life?"

"It was impossible. I wasn't allowed to get in touch with anyone. Everything was taken from me at Omsk, and I hadn't a single kopek left to bribe the *starshi* with."

Then he looked around and asked almost timidly, "Have no letters come for me?"

Mezei shook his head slowly.

"None of us has received any. There has been no mail for more than a year and a half—not since you left!"

Next moment Peter was scrutinizing, one after another, the faces of his comrades. He found Csaba stouter and Hirsch bereft of his few remaining hairs. The others had scarcely changed.

"And you all—how are things with you?"

"So-so!"

But they were aware of Peter's perplexity at finding their circle incomplete.

"Where are the others?"

"Lajtai and Szabó escaped. A few days after you."

"And Rosiczky?"

Mezei didn't answer at once.

"He's gone over to the Reds. He's become an agitator. I'm sorry for him, he was a good fellow. But he went mad.

That scoundrel Lukács dragged him along with him. He wanted to incite the rest of us to revolt too!"

Peter's eyes were still hunting for someone.

"And Stefan Bartha?"

For a moment no one answered. Finally Szentesi said in a low voice: "He is ill."

"What's the matter?" Peter asked, his brows drawn in consternation.

"The lungs—"

"Oh, God!"

There was another silence.

"Has he been taken to the hospital?"

"No. He is upstairs in his room."

Peter turned his head slowly toward the wall where the orderlies were standing.

"And how many of you are missing?"

Vedres answered for them:

"Three have joined the Reds; two have escaped. Somoggi, the fisherman, is dead."

Comrade came in, wagging his tail. He went up to Peter, laid his head on his knees, and raised his eyes to look at him.

"You are here too!" said Peter, rubbing his ear.

Then he turned to Mezei.

"And what's become of the guards?"

"Three of them are still here. You remember the gorilla?"

"Yurovski?"

"Yes. Nicolai, who is still here, came to me one morning and told me we must be on our guard because Yurovski was trying to persuade them to kill us."

"What did you do to him?"

"Vedres wanted to attack him with a knife—"

Vedres modestly examined the tips of his shoes.

"But I sent for him, reasoned with him, and even gave him some money."

"Is he still here?"

"He went long ago. Someone told us lately that it was he who had murdered the Tsar!"

Soon after they went in to dinner. There was something in the expression of Peter's face and in his long silences that weighed oppressively upon them all. These eighteen months of exhausting travel, of hospital, and prison life had worn him out.

Neteneczky, who was sitting beside him, laid his hand on Peter's shoulder.

"Don't despair, brother! Believe me, we're still the luckiest of the lot. We can wait here for the end of all this, and at least we won't die like dogs."

Before going to bed, Peter went in to see Bartha. He all but recoiled on the threshold. Bartha lay in bed, gaunt as a skeleton, his yellow face covered by a beard of several weeks' growth. His orderly, who was sitting on a chair beside him, got up as Peter entered and stood at attention.

Peter walked to the bed. The sick man fixed his fever-glazed eyes upon him as upon a stranger. But after a moment he recognized Peter.

"You have come back?" he whispered.

"Yes! I couldn't make it. And you—how do you feel?"

"I feel a little better just now—"

He turned his eyes from Peter and raised them toward the ceiling. Gently, cautiously, he tried to cough.

It was easy to see that the meager vitality left in him was a burden. He closed his eyes again and asked Peter no more questions.

Peter felt a lump in his throat and soon went back to his room.

When he saw the familiar walls around him once more, the stove, and the corner of the window upon which his unmoving eyes had so often rested, he felt he had returned to a friendly old dwelling. Thinking of Bartha, he suddenly decided that, if he had to die, it would be better to die here. During these five long years their lives had grown to be part of these walls. His spirit was so weary now that he wanted neither to think nor to feel. He made up his mind never to stir from the yard of Misery Hotel, never to see Zinatchka again. Hardly had he touched the bed when he fell into a deep heavy sleep.

But next morning the thought of Zinatchka recurred, and in the afternoon he started out for town and made his way toward Petrovka Street. He had not seen her for a year and a half.

When he laid his hand on the door latch, the thought suddenly crossed his mind that perhaps another man was sitting in Zinatchka's room—there in the corner of the shabby green couch where he used to sit. He didn't know why, but the thought terrified him.

The tac-tac of a sewing machine could be heard coming from the room.

When he went in, Zinatchka looked at him for a moment, uncomprehendingly, then jumped up with a cry and flung herself upon his neck.

From that day they resumed their former life. Once Zinatchka leaned her cheek against Peter's hand and said: "It is God who sent you to me!"

She always regarded Peter as one in whom some unearthly spirit dwelt, a creature purified and transfigured by suffering. To her he was a mortal, kind yet possessed of a demonic power, whom destiny had placed in her path.

Bartha's days were numbered. Csaba never left his bedside. He would slip his palm gently behind the man's wasted neck, raise his head a little and say, "Come, dear Stefan—take a little milk."

They were at lunch one day when Bartha's orderly came down, pale-faced, tiptoed to Mezei and whispered: "Please—the lieutenant is dead—"

They all rose and, following Mezei, entered Bartha's room. All seven of them were there, and one by one the orderlies appeared, holding their ragged caps in their hands, and ranged themselves along the wall. The little room was hardly big enough to hold them all.

Mezei was nearest the bed. He gazed at the waxen face of the dead man, wondering what he ought to do now, what would be most fitting under the circumstances.

Neteneczky turned, as if to give the cue to the others, then joined his hands, bowed his head on his breast, and began praying aloud, "Our Father which art in heaven—"

Heads lowered, the others repeated after him, "Hallowed be Thy name—"

They all knelt.

The droning of the men's voices filled the little room and seemed to caress the dead man's face.

The funeral took place in the military cemetery the following afternoon. The Russian priest performed the ceremony coldly and rapidly, like a man in a great hurry. At the edge of the grave, the Calvinists chanted the psalm, "Strive, Eternal, against those who strive against me—"

When they returned from the cemetery, Mezei had the black flag raised and for many weeks it floated above the entrance of Misery Hotel.

X

Miette was sitting in Dr. Varga's waiting room. To her left an elderly woman in mourning, who had brought her granddaughter for an examination, was sunk in an arm-chair. The child, about ten years old, was gravely turning the leaves of one of those summer-resort albums intended to relieve the tedium of patients while they waited.

Miette was pale and depressed.

When Bolshevism had broken out, the Csereys had been able to escape to Vienna in time, and had taken Miette with them. Those had been frantic moments. Miette had been obliged to come to a decision, make her arrangements, and pack her trunks, all within half an hour.

A few weeks later Golgonszky had arrived, unshaven, in muddy riding boots, and without a trace of luggage, having been compelled to ford the river Lajta, at the frontier, by night.

Still those few months in Vienna had been pleasant ones. It was true that the city had been filled with Hungarians whom they knew, but they were living at a time when no one thought of wondering why Miette and

Golgonszky were seen together everywhere with the Csereys. Who bothered about things like that now?

So they lived in Vienna for almost six months, where conditions were such as to permit their love, grown lately more and more wild and agonized, a happy period of serenity.

They were able to manage so that the Csereys suspected nothing of their relationship. Golgonszky lived in another hotel, but spent almost every hour of the day with Miette and the Csereys.

Miette and Golgonszky always avoided each other at Hungarian gatherings. They behaved with the utmost prudence, and were completely on their guard. For days and days they would find no opportunity of being alone together for even a few minutes, but when by chance such an opportunity did present itself, those few stolen moments gave an incomparable savor to their love. It was then that they would make swift, agitated plans as to where and when they would meet.

Golgonszky had chosen a small hotel in Schönbrunn for their meeting place, where Miette, harried by her fear of detection and her thirst for love, always arrived promptly at the hour set. But sometimes a fortnight would elapse before they could flee to the little hotel room, filled with the resinous odor of pines.

Meantime they met in public, under the mask of a friendly relationship, yet revealing no special interest in each other—which lent their love a strange, new charm. The muffled ring of the doctor's bell roused Miette from her reveries; after the woman in mourning, it was Miette's turn.

Varga eyed her in amazement as she entered and, taking her arm, drew her into the office.

"Well?" he said, tenderness and anxiety in his tone.

Miette didn't answer. Pale as death, she closed her eyes and leaned against the door, looking as if she were on the point of swooning.

Varga took her hand into his, holding it as if to weigh this little hand that yielded itself so lifelessly.

Meantime his eyes studied Miette closely and his knowledge of the situation made it easy for him to guess, after a moment's reflection, that she was pregnant.

"Something's wrong?" he asked in a low voice, his meaning clear.

Miette didn't even open her eyes, but simply bowed her head helplessly.

He went to the window and, looking out into the garden put a few questions to her, without turning, as if asking these questions of the trees.

Then he turned back to Miette and when he saw that she was still standing, leaning against the wall, her eyes half closed, apparently ready to faint, he took her nose tenderly, playfully, between his fingers in that paternal gesture that physicians use to hearten patients who are going through a bad time.

"Never mind—everything will be all right."

Then he went to the table, took something from it, and said, "You must undress."

He seated himself on a chair, placed Miette in front of him, and helped her unfasten her clothes, for her fingers were powerless. He undressed her as tenderly, as impersonally, as if she were a child.

Miette stood there, in her short little chemise that revealed her round knees; and shivering, looked uneasily in the direction of the door, though she knew it to be closed.

The doctor motioned her to the operating table. That padded table, covered with white oilcloth, sent an icy shock through her whole body as she took her place upon it. At the chill contact of the oilcloth her teeth began chattering, though more from fear than cold.

Varga had his back turned to her and was making a noiseless search through his surgical cupboard. It was as gruesome as if he were preparing for a murder.

Then he lit an alcohol lamp, opened a drawer, and offered Miette an Egyptian cigarette. There fell a strange silence about them, in which the faint rustling of the tinfoil over the cigarette could be heard. Miette stretched out a trembling hand to take one.

The cigarette served no purpose at that moment except to divert her attention.

Varga returned to the table and held something that Miette couldn't see to the flame of the lamp.

"And Tomi—what's become of him? Is he still alive?"

"Yes!" she murmured.

A few minutes passed during which her cigarette went out in her fingers.

Then the doctor, completely preoccupied, approached her and began the operation.

The whole thing lasted a few seconds; after which, with quiet, methodical movements he replaced his instruments.

While she resumed her clothes, he stood in front of the washstand and, making a thick lather of the soap, washed his hands slowly and carefully.

When everything was finished, he went to Miette, took her chin in his hand, and looked long and affectionately into her eyes.

"Shall I have a cab called, little Miette?"

"No, thanks," Miette answered in a low voice, then bade him goodbye and left the office.

She stopped for a minute in the darkening street, swept by a wave of sickening self-disgust. She saw Varga before her—with his long white smock and grizzled beard—in the meticulously clean office that smelt of carbolic and glittered with the chaste white reflections of glass and nickel. She heard the hissing of the alcohol lamp, and the whole thing seemed to her so revolting that she feared she might go suddenly mad. She felt this frightful, unspeakable nausea that had just overwhelmed her clinging to her palate, she felt her soul stripped bare of every feeling, and in her empty, shuddering soul she began to hate Golgonszky himself.

She hailed a passing cab and had herself driven home. At the slightest jolt of the vehicle she was pierced by a sharp pain, a sickening reminder of the experience she had just undergone.

Once home, she passed through the dining room and

paused in the living room, in the empty place where her piano had formerly stood. She didn't turn on the lights but remained standing in the dark room, a prey to horror. Twilight, blended with the glow of the street lamps, came in at the window. In that feeble light she could scarcely distinguish the features of her mother's portrait—her mother who, like some fantastic living fragment torn from the beyond, seemed from her large dark frame to be listening to and watching Miette.

For a long time she stood motionless on the same spot, in the darkness, looking herself like a piece of furniture or some other inanimate object, listening to the weird silence as to the murmur of her own soul.

Then she looked around the room. The floor gleamed duskily, for she had sold the two large living-room rugs. She looked about her as if she were seeing the room for the first time, and with an intensity that pierced her heart to the core, she realized for the first time the desolation surrounding her. It was an experience that showed her the fearful face of reality and imbued her at the same time with the idea of complete extinction. She wasn't aware of its precise significance, for it was an experience hitherto unknown to her. She felt vaguely that she had been despoiled of everything and now must die.

She lay down on the couch and folded her hands over her breast. Her mind strove desperately against the darkness that was invading her soul. She looked for God in that darkness, but didn't find him.

Confused, disconnected images were entangled in her memory. Golgonszky's room, certain episodes in their love, the bed, Golgonszky's eyes, the design woven into the tapestry hanging on the wall. She could see her little slippers trailing across the floor and her chemise thrown over the arm of a chair. She was seized by such loathing that in her agony she turned on the couch with a sudden brusque movement and, grinding her teeth, bit into the silk cushion, feeling again as she flung herself wildly, hysterically about, that strange, dull pain she had brought from the doctor's office. Then she lay still to ponder in dismay that curious twinge, hardly perceptible, yet so terrifying.

She remembered having felt a somewhat similar twinge down in Florence in the gray dawn when, lying in a disordered bed and listening to the masses of invisible waters roaring outside, she had not known where she was. Well—the girl in her had been killed then. Now it was something altogether different—an indescribable agony gushing up from the depths. And this time it was the mother in her that had been killed. Clearly, distinctly she saw at that moment the two bodies of herself, those two dead figures, those two corpses of a murdered woman. They were radiant, white, terrible in their nakedness. And both those corpses were Miette; they had her face, her hands, her legs, her breasts. One of them was a girl of twenty-one with a heavy braid of tawny hair, with the gracious lines of slenderness, with the thousand charms of virginity in her tender little breasts. That was Miette, untouched. And the other was a young woman of twenty-eight, mysterious shadows under her eyes, the braid perceptibly thinner, the divine burden of motherhood in her womb, like that woman from Linz.

Yes, both were dead within her!

She took the cushion to draw it out from under her head, and the cushion eyed her, too. It eyed her like a deeply furrowed, melancholy face, absorbed in a knotty problem, and she saw it again as it had looked that August evening on her return from the station, crumpled by Peter's hand where he had seized it during their last embrace. And she felt the atmosphere of that spring evening hovering about her when, in the mysterious shadows, as darkness gathered in the room, she had given herself as an offering to Johnny.

She strained her ears toward Father's room, enfolded in a deep, impressive silence.

What would happen if she, too, should die?

It seemed to her just then a simple and beautiful thing, and she saw nothing terrible in the idea. She would write two letters, one to Peter, the other to Golgonszky. She pondered these letters and saw the long, purple hand-writing on the note paper. To Peter she would write only: "Peter darling, why did you leave me alone?" Those few words would hold all the secrets of her life, her plea for forgiveness, her love, her abasement, her expiation—while to Golgonszky she would say: "What have you been to me?" Nothing except those few words, yet they would pose the terrifying question: "What have you been to me?—the most beautiful gift of life, the divine voluptuousness of love?—or the angel of death?"

She rose from the couch to go to the desk and write these lines. But she was so weak she could hardly drag herself to the table. When she had lit the lamp that shed a yellow radiance about her, she had the feeling that the words she had just meditated were vanishing within the radiance.

She left the lamp burning and returned to the couch.

After all, why should she write? If she died, they would know without that why she was dead.

Mili entered the dining room, switched on the lights, and began to set the table.

The idea of getting up, sitting at the table, dining alone seemed to her senseless and horrible.

The loathing she felt for herself blended with the sharp pain that stabbed her at the memory of her father, and it was all mixed up with the maddening uncertainty about Peter and with this passion that tortured and burned her, with this consuming love that Golgonszky had kindled in her. She began to weep aloud. Then, abruptly, she fell silent. She fell silent like a tearful child whose attention is suddenly caught by a voice or a strange vision. Something in her nervous system had snapped, and now, as through a broken dam, the thought of death was flooding her soul. And this flood filled her being with wondrous serenity, as the high tides, overflowing with dread, majestic serenity the brown ploughed fields, the pale stubble, the black ditches, the blossoming lanes, the willows planted in long rows—as these waters, reflecting the heavens, cover the whole countryside with the mirror of the infinite. In the same way all her memories and the meaning of her life were engulfed in the thought of death.

Like a translucid, shimmering wave of silver, like buoyant water, the idea began to enfold her, dimming her eyes till all the objects surrounding her grew shadowy to the point of unreality—the desk, the paperweight, the couch upon which she lay, everything that fell within the range of her clouded, distraught gaze. She felt a passionate, an irresistible eagerness to put an end to the fearful source of these rending agonies—to put an end to her life; and already she saw herself beyond death, safe in the shelter of an exquisite peace, transfigured in the imagination of all who had known her. She saw herself stretched on her bier, in the same room where her father had lain, in the night of black draperies, beneath the watchful candles and the delicate touch of flowers and veils. And, beside her head, the invisible angel of forgiveness.

Her mind dwelt on this picture; this last, dark vision took possession of her anguished soul and all her pain seemed at an end.

She opened the lower drawer of the desk where Peter's revolver lay among the few yellow, cylindrical cartridges of a hunting gun. For long minutes she labored over it, fingering and pressing it feverishly in an effort to discover the secret of its mechanism, while some dreadful canker gnawed at her heart, for she wanted to be finished with this final torment as swiftly as possible. She was seized by an uncontrollable nervousness, a wild impatience, and, failing to fathom the workings of the revolver, she flung it from her.

Then she rushed to the next room, paused for a moment but, encountering no obstacle, ran out to the landing. Her flight took her from there to the service stairway, and she raced up, two or three steps at a time till, swept along by some silent power beyond her control, she reached the top floor.

Grasping the iron railing that ran around the upper corridor, she leaned far out over the void. Her fingers clutched the rusty iron convulsively, and as her body swung somewhere in midair she uttered a piercing scream.

The street door was closed, and that long-drawn-out shriek pierced the silence of the court well like the hoot of a siren sounding an alarm. The terror-stricken faces of servants appeared at lighted kitchen doors and the pound of precipitate footsteps could be heard dashing up the stairs.

She was floating over emptiness when a hand fiercely grasped her shoulders and with a single movement drew her back.

When, a long time after, she opened her eyes, she found herself lying in a poor little bedroom, on an old sofa, one of whose broken legs was propped up by a pile of books. It was Mr. Sinka's room, the room of that gentle, taciturn Mr. Sinka of whom Rose had once spoken and who warmed his bed with a hot brick during the harsh days of winter. Mr. Sinka, his neck fastened tight into a celluloid collar with pale blue lights, his freckled face white with emotion, bent over Miette and asked anxiously, pityingly, "Dear Madame—do you feel better now?"

Miette turned her eyes, infinitely weary, toward him, gently murmured, "Yes," and closed them again.

After a moment she felt a hand stroke her own, a damp, rough hand that touched her with humble, sorrowful tenderness and that must have been the hand of some servant in the house.

XI

During that long winter the inmates of Misery Hotel hardly stirred from their rooms, rarely venturing even into the yard, lest they attract the notice of some local Soviet agent passing that way.

Though Doroviev, the former staff captain, had turned Red, at heart he remained the son of the aristocratic landowner of Novgorod, who in pre-war days had even traveled in Europe and spent some glorious days at Vienna. Their only hope lay in Doroviev.

Only very early in the morning, while it was still dark, they would slip out into the yard to stretch their numbed legs a little. And when their food supply was low, they went at night to fish beneath the ice of the Irtysh. Vedres often skated in the inky blackness of night.

Zinatchka had gone with old Dmitri to live at the Deers' Ranch, the name given to the little farm her mother had bought when she had become a widow. There was a pretty little whitewashed house with an orchard and a few acres of arable land. It was situated on the slope of a hill, near the Irtysh, several miles from Tobolsk.

Peter had seen Zinatchka only twice since she had gone there to live. The trip was exhausting and dangerous, entailing a walk of hours through darkness and snow.

For them these were the most terrible months. History blew like a tornado over the vast Russian steppes, sweeping away whole villages. And everywhere famine raged. Women of apparently gentle breeding sat on the steps of churches, stretching out their emaciated hands, begging for bread. In villages, in the depths of the infinite Russian steppes, in pelt-covered *yurtas*, millions of men were living on the same plane of civilization as at the time of the Tatar invasions. Now they came swarming out of their lairs.

Sometimes a rapid volley of gunfire ringing out through the city could be heard even at Misery Hotel. Igor Krukov, the fat proprietor of Laskutnaya Restaurant, where the prisoners had first taken their meals, and Licharov, the pharmacist, were among the dead. The corpses, bound together by twine, hard as stone under the frost, lay for days in the snow near the wall.

It was during this time that Peter received a letter from his sister, telling him that their mother had died of kidney trouble after a few days' illness. She had been buried at Brassó.

This letter was no blow to him. It was as if everything that was happening to him and about him had lost all relation to reality. And he felt his previous life so far away, so completely engulfed in time, that it seemed to him it must have vanished forever, never to be revived.

Soon after, there came a letter from Miette. These letters had been brought not by the Russian mail service but by the Red Cross. Miette's letter came by way of China, and it seemed to him that the soul of the Miette of other days had been lost somewhere over the seas.

". . . And would it not be better (she wrote) if we never saw each other again? Your eyes would always be searching mine, to find if I had remained faithful, and my eyes would ask the same question of you. We would never tell, but we would hate each other; we would hate those secrets in each other which exist because we believe in their existence. Could our spirits ever draw close again . . .?"

With a desolate heart Peter put this letter aside.

Little by little, spring came.

Fragrant breezes, bearing the perfume of the young birch forests, rose along the banks of the Irtysh. And the springtime of that year—1920—was troubling as perhaps the spring had never been before.

The young shoots of the vernal fields saved the men from famine. There were so many hares in the forests and the grassy meadows that they could be hunted with sticks. The woods along the Irtysh were black with the nests of crows who settled there by millions and whose nestlings were already hatched. One had only to take them.

The fury of the revolution abated somewhat during these days of Nature's luxuriant burgeoning. The city took on an almost human aspect, and though the Soviets had strictly forbidden trading, the dealers resumed their places at the vegetable market. At the approach of the People's Commissar, they would snatch up their baskets and run away.

The shops were closed, but for five hundred rubles one could buy a half pound of veal. The Tatar women went from house to house, selling a kind of clove cake. Only clothes and boots could be found nowhere. A woman was seen walking along the main street, one foot shod in a yellow slipper, the other in nothing but a piece of bark tied beneath the sole.

The prisoners were beginning to venture once more into the city streets. The windows of the Licharov Pharmacy were broken; the interior of the shop was an indescribable mass of bricks and mortar, with human excrement everywhere. The Kashanski Sobor, with its graceful, drowsy cupola—on whose tiles Peter had first seen Zinatchka— now lifted its four ravaged walls toward the skies. Its blue dome, lying among the soot-blackened walls, looked like a fallen fragment of heaven.

The prisoners began to reckon what was left of their captivity by months instead of years. The first Japanese ship had weighed anchor in the port of Vladivostok and was awaiting the war prisoners who were to be repatriated.

Peter felt no emotion at the thought of returning.

At the end of April an important event took place at Misery Hotel. Csaba announced that he was going to marry Tatiana, the daughter of Fedor Gutchkov, the furrier. He invited his friends to the betrothal ceremony.

Mezei proposed that the festival be celebrated outdoors, in some forest clearing. They were all delighted with the suggestion.

Szentesi struck the table, and after a moment's thought cried, "Boys, what do you think of this? Suppose each of us brings the lady of his heart?"

Vedres burst out laughing and slapped him on the shoulder.

"After all, we're one family, aren't we?"

The others moved somewhat uneasily in their chairs and grew thoughtful. "For the moment, I'm a widower!" Neteneczky sighed.

Mezei twisted his mustache in embarrassment at the sudden vision he conjured up of the rather fat and no longer youthful figure of Mme. Isaac Kashinov, whom he would have preferred not to exhibit to his young companions.

Hirsch must have been occupied with the same thoughts, yet he was the first to say, "Szentesi is right; but I want to tell you right now that my girl is no Venus de Milo—"

Szentesi burst into loud laughter.

"But, my dear Zoltán, Papa Hirsch didn't make an Apollo of you, either!"

Hirsch's nose seemed to have grown longer than ever during captivity and his head balder.

Mezei, too, in an effort to prepare them for Isaac Kashinov's widow, put in, "We took whatever we could find—"

They agreed to arrange a picnic.

When Peter told Zinatchka of their plan next day, her face lit up. "Come to the Deers' Ranch. The ramblers are in bloom!"

"I'll ask my friends," Peter said.

Of course they accepted the invitation enthusiastically.

The betrothal was celebrated in the garden of the Deers' Ranch on Sunday night. Old Dmitri had given the house a fresh coat of whitewash for the occasion. The walls, standing out against the dark green background of the trees, beckoned a welcome from afar.

The house was situated on the slope of the hill, a few hundred feet from the crossroads. To the left the road disappeared behind another hill in the direction of Tobolsk. To the right it led through the birch woods to the village of Osov.

The front of the Deers' Ranch was covered with rambler roses.

The company began to gather toward seven in the evening. They came in three carriages. Papa and Mama Gutchkov and their daughter Tatiana were seated in the last. Csaba sat beside the coachman and drove the horses. Mezei, Vedres, and Altmayer were in the second carriage; Neteneczky, Szentesi, and Hirsch in the first. Each had his girl friend, and the carriages could hardly hold them all. Netene alone had no one.

Comrade raced behind the last carriage, with Szentesi whistling and shouting to him incessantly.

Peter and Zinatchka, who had gone on ahead, received the guests at the door of the house.

After the introductions had been made, a moment's awkwardness descended upon them, but gradually the atmosphere grew friendly. A certain nervousness, a little embarrassment, hampered Zinatchka in her role of hostess. She ran to help Dmitri carry the chairs into the yard. But Tatiana stopped her.

"Don't bother about chairs, Zinaida Ignatovna! We're going to sit on this beautiful lawn!"

They all settled themselves on the grass. The women's spreading skirts checkered the lawn with patches of blue and yellow and red. They had brought food and drink with them in little baskets.

The sun had not yet set, but its disc was already grazing the contours of distant hills and touching the fields about them with gold.

Papa Gutchkov laid his hat on the grass beside him.

"How beautiful it is!" he said, crossing his arms over his chest.

Below, on the other side of the road, the white trunks of the young birch trees gleamed against the apple-green background of the foliage. They seemed to be laughing softly, showing their white teeth softly and silently.

Papa Gutchkov's head was bald, but his chin was adorned by a charming little cherry-colored goatee, thick and silky as fur. Mama Gutchkov, snub-nosed and round-chinned, followed the movements of the company with soft, eager eyes—especially those of her daughter, anxious to discover whether Tatiana pleased these strangers.

In her tulle dress Tatiana looked like a big wild butterfly. There was something in her face, too, that suggested a cindery butterfly with rust-brown wings and ebony eyes. Her face was covered with a thick layer of rice powder, reminiscent of a butterfly's silken belly. She was ugly, yet there was a certain beauty in her ugliness.

They grew more and more hilarious. They built a fire in the middle of the yard and Szentesi began cutting spits of wood with expert hands, exactly as if he had been at

home, in the vineyards of Györ. And the air was soon
filled with a faint, agreeable crackling and with the
pungent odor of broiling bacon.

A woman of about thirty was seated next to Hirsch.
When she laughed one saw that two front teeth were
missing. Her freckled face was of a pronounced Jewish
cast, and her eyebrows, the color of baked bread, came
so close together as almost to meet. But she must have
been a good soul, for she lavished upon Hirsch a thousand
marks of tenderness, cutting a piece of bread before
passing it to him.

A young woman with Tatar features, a short neck, and
inquisitive eyes sparkling with vitality sat beside Szentesi.
Her thick calves threatened to burst her black stockings.

Anna Rocker was the prettiest of the girls. She never
left Vedres' side for a single moment. Her younger sister,
who had come with Altmayer, looked very like her but
was not so pretty. She created an effect of sickliness and
chilliness. Altmayer was always trying to put a shawl
around her shoulders, but she would reject it in a nervous,
whining voice.

Anna was altogether different. Laughing incessantly,
she moved gaily about among them, with her luxuriant
knot of ash-blond hair and her magnificent, graciously
swaying breasts.

The Rocker family had been interned at Tobolsk since
the beginning of the war.

Isaac Kashinov's widow was over forty. She was a thin-
lipped, staid-looking woman, who wore a dress with a
bustle and, perched on top of her head, a ridiculous little
old-fashioned hat. She had probably been obliged to sell
all her dresses in turn during the famine, and these clothes,
inherited from her grandmother, had come out of some
old closet. She felt ill at ease in this gathering. One idea—
it seemed—kept trembling from the tip of her nose—
regret at having come to make a public spectacle of her
respectable female virtue. She would cast a glance at
Mezei now and then, as if to reproach him for having
brought her here.

She wouldn't have laughed for anything in the world but when, in the midst of a chance silence, Neteneczky sneezed so violently that his old silver watch leaped from the upper pocket of his blouse, she bent her head and smiled broadly.

Zinatchka, too, had made herself as pretty as possible for the occasion. She wore white cotton stockings, patent-leather slippers with buckles, and her knitted sweater of a beautiful vermilion went very well with her black hair. Excitement had made her beautiful, and her eyes shone with childlike joy. She had her guitar with her.

Comrade sat close to the fire, greatly disturbed by the smell of the broiling bacon. He was constantly shifting his position. Finally he settled down beside Vedres and kept nuzzling his arm, making Vedres drop grease all over his trousers.

Darkness fell slowly.

Szentesi flung some heavy logs on the fire, whose red and yellow lights danced over the faces of the people grouped about it. In the light of the flames, Papa Gutchkov's beard took on the color of the gilded nuts that are hung on Christmas trees.

The crescent moon rose above the hills, coquettish, bewitching, like a naked girl. In the birch woods she had let her silver chemise glide noiselessly to the ground.

Zinatchka laid her guitar across her knees and began plucking the strings. The sounds drifted softly about the fire. Then she began to sing:

"On the Volga's blue waters,
    Floats a little boat—"

Those who could sing drew around her. The men's deep voices were content to hum an accompaniment to the song, but Tatiana's flute-like notes leaped and soared like a turtle dove's.

Zinatchka let Tatiana's voice dominate her own, and followed it a third below. And now they both sang;

"Loose thy storms upon him,
    Upon the lover who hath betrayed his faith—"

The sounds drifted through the spring night, and

the melancholy of the Little Russian air pierced their hearts.

The moon was shining its brightest when Tatiana suggested a walk. They all rose, moving in pairs toward the river bank.

The yellow waters of the Irtysh flowed lazily beneath the moonlight, and the black willows along the shore looked like crouching satyrs, holding their breath as they watched the graceful, voluptuous play of the waves and the moonbeams.

Zinatchka and Peter paused at the bank. Papa Gutchkov's voice could be heard behind the foliage, explaining something to Neteneczky. And a little farther away, from under the hanging willow boughs, came the clear laughter of Anna Rocker.

Zinatchka leaned her head against Peter's shoulder. Then she clasped her arms about his neck and raised her shining eyes to his. Peter stood there, unmoving, yet he was near to bursting into sobs.

XII

During a tennis match in Buda Miette took advantage of an opportune moment to murmur to Golgonszky, "Tomorrow afternoon, at five—"

Recently, whole weeks had passed without their seeing each other; yet it had been those very separations that gave their meetings special zest. Now their love was shot through by a kind of undefined, searing pain, for they both felt that they would soon have to part.

They were infinitely tender with each other, their hearts wrung, as they sat together in silence, by the thought of separation. Their eyes and the touch of their hands were often instinct with the almost physical anguish of farewell. But never by so much as a single word did they broach the subject, as if their love were there between them, like a third person, and they wanted to hide from it the fact that its days were numbered, that it was doomed to death.

Whenever Miette appeared on Golgonszky's threshold he would turn pale, and a question would smolder in his eyes, for he was in constant torture lest she should tell him she had come that day for the last time.

During the winter months Miette went out a great deal and attended all the Csereys' parties. She formed new acquaintances, made friends with young women, went to formal balls, and little by little began to be recognized as one of the most beautiful and interesting women in Budapest society. There was something mysterious about her. Her beauty, that was barely beginning to lose its first freshness—or that reflected rather the shadows of all the agonies of a harrowed soul —had a singular power of attraction for men, and her independent position kindled in each of them the hope that he might perhaps conquer this slender, golden-haired woman with the superb carriage, mistress at once of a cool reserve and a charming friendliness, beneath whose low laughter some secret sorrow was discernible, whose shapely body, whose perfect hands and feet were the subject of conversation in every fashionable ménage.

Men flocked about her. They knew that her husband had been a prisoner for six years, and they sought feverishly to discover who her lover might be. Miette felt the excitement of the chase surrounding her. This new game amused her, and she took pleasure in putting her pursuers on the wrong track. She would leave faint little clues behind her here and there—clues that would be pounced upon by these gentlemen who had fallen in love with her, or by women who were beginning to eye her enviously, as the atmosphere in which she moved grew ever more mysterious and interesting. These clues led of course to blind alleys, and the pursuit would be renewed with fresh ardor.

Only two people knew of her love for Golgonszky— his valet who waited on them, and Dr. Varga. But the secret was buried more surely in them than in a grave, and Miette knew she had nothing to dread from either.

The only person who caused her any alarm was that strange woman who still leaned against the window frame of the house opposite, and whose eyes followed her until she had disappeared through Golgonszky's door.

With Mathilde, she didn't know what to believe. She often had the impression that Mathilde knew everything or, thanks to her unfailing instinct, at least suspected it. But she knew also that Mathilde loved her too well and too deeply ever to betray her.

Some of her suitors were consumed by their tragic passion. A colonel of hussars, well along in years, developed neurasthenia as a result of this belated blaze, and everyone knew that the wild orgies into which a certain young nobleman had plunged were caused by his hopeless love for Miette. It was said, too—though it would have been difficult in that case to establish the exact truth—that the young writer whose novels and plays had met with such tremendous success in the last two years had committed suicide because of Miette.

She had never trifled with these serious passions, but neither had she tried to check them. It was possible that, without herself being aware of it, her body and all her being exuded the lure of surrender—a mere fragrance that hovered about her, mingling with the warm breath of her hair and shoulders. But she drew back coldly from any attempt at a more dangerous intimacy. And her attitude served only to fan the blaze in the hearts of her adorers.

Her telephone rang all day long. She would lounge for hours among the cushions of the couch, the center of a conflagration of avowals that reached her by that route, never burning herself, but warming her life at the pleasant flame.

She permitted no one to visit her, though her suitors besieged her with pleas more or less frank.

Even if she had wished to entertain, it would have been quite impossible, for her apartment was completely denuded. Little by little, she had sold all the rugs, all the valuable pictures, all the fine furniture. Two rooms were absolutely empty, stripped; her jewels and all the beautiful silver service had passed into the hands of the money lenders.

She would have needed to say only a word and Golgonszky would have put at her disposal as much money as she wanted. He was a very wealthy man. But she had never asked even the Csereys for the slightest assistance.

In her barren, pillaged apartment, she felt somehow stronger and cleaner, and sometimes when there was so little money left that Mili could hardly get together the most frugal of cold meals for them both, she had a feeling that, thanks to her privations, she was walking a little way along the path of repentance.

She told herself that it would not be difficult to explain to Peter why the apartment was so empty. She admitted to herself that it would be a sickening lie, but her one desire now was not to rob Peter of his illusions. She was ready to begin a new life with him when he returned— a straitened, arduous life. He would have no position, but that didn't frighten her much, for among her admirers there were many whose words carried enormous weight. And as for herself, she had no doubt that she would eventually adjust herself to the situation. She pictured her future existence with Peter as simple and modest— a complete renunciation; and the thought that the existence would atone for everything restored equanimity to her soul.

The innumerable visits, the balls, the innocent flirtations —all this was a deliberate, sorrowful farewell to her present life.

One morning she found a message on her desk, asking her to present herself that afternoon at the office of the Association for War Prisoners, where she had been a frequent visitor of late. The message was urgent and said that the president wished to speak with her.

She knew what it meant. Her face was pale as she entered the president's office.

He was an old man—seventy perhaps—who treated everyone like a child.

He grasped Miette's hands and held them in silence for a long time. Then he said: "I might have sent you an official message, but I wanted to tell you the news myself. Yesterday I received word from our Riga representative that a boat would be leaving Vladivostok some time next week. Seven years, good God, seven years! . . . In two months your husband will be back!"

Closing her eyes, Miette clung to a chair, as the tears flowed from beneath her lowered lids.

The president, overcome by emotion, too, remained standing in front of her. Presently she dried her tears and took leave of him.

She went straight to Golgonszky, who was waiting for her. He noticed nothing in her face as she entered the room; but when they were seated side by side on the couch and he was about to take her into his arms, with a gentle, indescribably mournful gesture she pushed his arm away.

Pallid, whispering the words as if she were afraid they would rend Golgonszky's heart, she said, "I am with you today for the last time—"

Having said them, she looked down at the floor; she couldn't bear to watch his face.

He rose and went to the window. He stood there for a long time, silent and motionless. His back was turned to Miette and he was staring out; the effect as he stood there was of a man desolated by grief.

Several times Miette raised her eyes to him.

He came back from the window, sat down beside her, and took her hand into his. For a moment he caressed and stroked her fingers silently with his own that seemed to have grown stiff. Then, in a very low voice, in a voice transformed, he said, "You have been the dearest blessing of my life!"

He paused abruptly, pulled Miette savagely toward him, folded her in his arms, and buried his face in her hair. She felt that he was weeping, and a strange sensation, at once beautiful and terrible, pervaded all her being at the thought. Yet she did not weep. Her soul was in the grip of an icy calm.

After a long interval, Golgonszky released her from this awkward embrace, and she saw that he was white as death.

Then she whispered, "And you—what will become of you?"

He didn't answer for a long while. From the expression of his face it seemed to Miette that he wanted to speak but couldn't.

At last he began, in a very low voice that was curiously calm: "You see, Miette, I have thought and thought about all this—I must do something, else I shan't be able to endure it! I can't stay alone; that would be suicide for me. I am absolutely certain I should kill myself if I did. I have never loved—I shall never love—anyone but you."

"Marry—" she whispered.

He didn't answer at once.

"Yes—that is my only salvation!"

"Whom have you in mind?" she asked gently.

"Jeanne—She is an intelligent girl, and I know she loves me. She's not very young any more, past thirty. What do you think?"

"You're right. That's what you must do!"

After a moment she added: "But—still—we shall see each other again?—later?—among people?"

He seized her hand and pressed it against his cheek.

She rose as if she were ready to go; with a ghostly smile, in a voice that was hardly more than a breath, she said, "Well—now—I will go—"

There was a curious little note of unnatural gaiety in her voice.

He didn't release her hand, but cried in anguish, "No—stay a little longer . . ."

She dropped helplessly to the couch again.

They sat silent for a long time; suddenly Miette's hand began to tremble violently in Golgonszky's.

With a wild cry she burst into tears. She threw herself down on the couch and, pressing her hand against her mouth, began sobbing convulsively.

In vain he tried to quiet her. Miette jumped up and began tearing at her clothes and lamenting like a madwoman. She screamed so loudly that Golgonszky rushed to the door to draw the tapestry that served as a portière.

"I will not endure it—it will kill me! Do something! I don't care what—anything! Why is he coming back? Why is he coming back?"

She pressed her fist against her mouth and shrieked incoherent imprecations.

"Why is he coming back? How dare he come back?

Then, suddenly, she was silent. Her staring eyes sought the words she had just uttered, her horrified eyes followed them as if they had remained suspended in midair.

She sank into a chair, drew on her gloves, and began slowly to button them. Then she walked to the mirror and arranged her hair and her hat. With a suddenly arrested movement of shock she scrutinized her transfigured face.

Then she turned to Golgonszky, gave him her hand and said, as if she were in a great hurry: "Goodbye—"

Golgonszky took her in his arms and they exchanged a long last kiss.

He hardly realized that she had slipped from his arms and disappeared behind the tapestry at the door.

He sat, bewildered, for a long time.

Then he began pacing up and down the room. He stopped at last in front of the closet and opened one of its doors, scarcely knowing why. There were Miette's belongings—her apricot negligee, filling the closet with a soft mysterious perfume; and beneath it, the two little red mules, standing side by side—like the two scarlet flowers of passion and of sin.

Quickly, abruptly, Golgonszky closed the door again and covered his face with his hands as if he had seen something dreadful. Bowing his forehead against the closed door, he remained thus, his body racked with sobs.

XIII

In the yard of Misery Hotel, the most varied collection of articles was spread on the ground. Beds, tables, straw mattresses, cloudy mirrors, striped pillows, old coats, sealskin boots—all the things that had been part and parcel of the prisoners' lives and were now about to change hands.

The sharp-faced second-hand dealers walked slowly about among these sorry-looking odds and ends.

Vedres, holding a large iron pot in his hand, was arguing with an old Jew who wore on his head a moth-eaten cap of fox fur.

"You don't want to give more than a hundred thousand rubles for this? For this?"

He looked around and, catching sight of an orderly, cried, "Come here, Emeric, and throw this pot into the river for me."

The old junkman touched Vedres' arm: "A hundred and fifty—"

Vedres put the pot back on the table.

"I won't give it to you for less than three hundred!"

The old man meditated, then laid two hundred thousand paper rubles on the table, signifying that that was his last word.

This was at the time when the value of the ruble was shrinking hourly.

Vedres eyed the old man from head to foot, surveyed the pot, and said, "Take it!"

Neteneczky was standing under the birch in the middle of the yard, holding a heavy coat in his hands. He was turning it over and over, displaying its points to a young dealer.

"Examine it, my friend—you won't find a single flaw!"

The dealer's hand vanished into the fur and he fingered the seams thoughtfully.

Someone was haggling at every table. Csaba was selling the spades and hoes; Szentesi was taking care of the fishing nets, to prevent the orderlies from being swindled. Altmayer had ranged his pictures along the wall and was waiting for buyers. Hirsch was standing in front of the table on which the inkstands, hammers, and saws were laid out.

It was the end of March, about ten in the morning. The sun shed its light, still weak and heatless, over the yard. The weather was unusually mild. The snow had already melted.

Old Dmitri thrust his head in at the gate, but ventured no farther.

Szentesi called him.

"What have you brought us, little brother?"

"I came for the dog."

They had decided to present Comrade to Zinatchka. The dog seemed to sense that they were talking about him, for he ran to the bottom of the garden and crouched close to the hedge, hoping thus to avoid notice. But he was dragged out and Dmitri tied a cord around his neck.

They all gathered about the dog. Vedres squatted in front of him and held out his hand for the animal's paw.

"God keep you, Comrade!"

Mezei bent and stroked him behind the ears.

"You've been a fine dog!" he said.

The orderlies stroked him and patted him affectionately on the back.

Comrade felt that something of importance to himself was happening and he turned his head quickly from side to side, then jumped from one to the next. But Dmitri took the cord and began pulling him away. The dog was reluctant to follow, and as they passed the gate a sudden movement on his part flung the old man into the hedge.

One by one the junk dealers left the yard. The orderlies

picked up the remaining articles, turning them over and over in their hands, trying to decide whether they were worth taking on so long a journey.

They were to leave at five that afternoon. The little steamer *Ratıslav*, carrying civilian passengers, too, was waiting for them in the harbor.

Mezei looked around.

"Where's Peter?"

"Upstairs in his room; he doesn't feel well," Csaba answered.

"What's the matter with him?"

"I don't know. A cold, maybe. I went up a moment ago."

Mezei and Neteneczky, anxious-eyed, started for Peter's room.

He lay in the bare room on a broken bench, one of whose legs was propped up by a brick; his hands were crossed behind his neck, and his brown beard made a somber frame for his face.

Everything had been removed from the room. Only his luggage—all ready to go—lay on the floor: a large knapsack crammed full, and a little black trunk.

"What's wrong with you?" asked Mezei.

"I don't know. I think I have fever. I feel so weak—"

"Look here—you're not going to do anything foolish now—at the last minute!"

He went over and laid his hand on Peter's forehead. Finding nothing suspicious there, he unbuttoned his blouse and opened his shirt, as if in search of the fever that Peter thought he had.

Neteneczky peered over Mezei's shoulder through the opening of the shirt.

Mezei spoke affectionately, "You must have caught cold. I'll send for the doctor!"

When he turned, Neteneczky was no longer behind him, but he found him in the passage, leaning his head, held between his hands, against the wall. He was livid.

"What's the matter with you?" Mezei asked in consternation.

Neteneczky didn't stir but whispered in horror, "Did you see those little red spots on his chest?"

"What spots?"

"It's spotted typhus!"

"Don't talk nonsense!"

But as he walked downstairs Neteneczky was still holding his head between his hands and whispering to himself, "It's spotted typhus!"

They stopped in the yard and began deliberating in low voices. Szentesi approached them and asked nervously, "What's the matter? What's happened?"

They told him that Peter was ill. Then the others gathered about—even the orderlies. And for a long time they debated as to what should be done.

Finally Vedres and Mezei went to town to fetch the doctor, while the others sat around on their luggage, silent for the most part.

"Netene—you'll see that you were wrong," said Szentesi, "and that it's nothing serious."

Neteneczky didn't answer.

Toward noon Mezei and Vedres returned with the doctor.

While he was in Peter's room upstairs, the others stayed down in the yard, their eyes averted from one another.

Vedres, his hands clasped behind his back, walked back and forth on his long legs beside the wall, a sign with him of extreme nervousness.

Mezei went to meet the doctor as he came down, and the others crowded about him.

"You were right," said the doctor. "I'll have him taken to the hospital for contagious diseases this afternoon."

The words burst like an abomination into their faces.

Observing their agitation, the doctor added a little lamely, "Yes—but—after all, everyone doesn't die of it!"

At the gate he turned once more to say, "He won't die! He has a sound constitution."

They stood motionless. After a moment Szentesi said, "What are we going to do?"

No one answered.

"Let's take him along!" said Vedres in a low voice.

Mezei shook his head slowly. "We would be endangering not only ourselves but him, too. Would you put him on a boat in that condition?"

"That's true! At least he'll be in the hospital here," said Kirsch.

Szentesi walked to the wall and returned. "Someone will have to stay with him, my lads!"

He didn't say so, but they all knew, and his face made it clear, that he was thinking of himself.

There was a long silence. Then Mezei said, "I thought of that, too—but what good would it do him?"

"Don't be so hopeless," said Csaba eagerly. "Remete had it too, and wasn't even put to bed. Besides, Zinatchka will certainly not desert him."

Mezei nodded approvingly.

"In a fortnight, when the worst is over, he will be able to follow us. He can easily overtake us at Khabarovsk. I'll go up and speak to him—"

He started for Peter's room, but no one followed him. They scattered about the yard, as if they hadn't the strength to climb the stairs.

Mezei entered the room and took Peter's hand.

"Dear Peter, the doctor says that you have caught a severe cold. You have a kind of grippe. Now it is for you to say whether you will come with us or stay here. If you stay here, you'll be taken to the hospital this afternoon and follow us in a few days. You can catch up with us at Khabarovsk."

"I'll stay here," Peter whispered.

"What would you like me to send you for lunch?"

"Don't send me anything. I'm not hungry."

"A little soup—"

Peter shook his head.

When Mezei had left the room he closed his eyes. His confused thoughts lay shattered about him, like incorporeal entities. What had he been thinking of just then? Oh yes—the letter—the anonymous letter that he had

received ten days ago. A woman's handwriting, disguised
—from Budapest. He had wanted to tear it up immediately, but he hadn't the courage. He had read it a
hundred times since then, and even now it was there,
in his wallet, like some hideous object—like a severed
human finger or some other horrible thing.

The letter was stupid, sickening, cruel, replete with
ready-made phrases.

"You are suffering a holy martyrdom for your country,
while here, your wife—Perhaps you think I am accusing
her unjustly? I am enclosing a series of memoranda
where you will find noted at exactly what hours, as
exactly what minutes in the last four years your wife has
entered the door of this house, and at what time of the
night or morning she has secretly left it. Chance has put
these dates into my hands. I am not giving you the man's
name, because it is not the man but the woman who is to
blame."

Who could have written this terrible letter? Whose
curse was it, whose hatred, whose fiendish idea? In vain
did he ransack his memories. He found no one whom he
could suspect.

His thoughts fell wearily away from him.

He saw a door, an unfamiliar door, its shape and color
like those seen in a dream. A woman's slender figure
slipped furtively through it.

"Miette!" he spoke voicelessly to himself.

Like a slow, melancholy murmur he felt Miette's name
all about him in the room.

Yes! That was how it was doomed to end—how could
he have imagined that from here, from this distance, he
could keep Miette for himself for seven years? Her
memory no longer made him suffer. Miette was dead
within him, surrounded by tender thoughts of forgiveness.

"Yes! That was how it was doomed to end!" he
repeated to himself.

The years go by—and time drives each human life
into other channels.

He thought of Zinatchka. What would happen if he

said to her, "Listen—I give my weary life into your hands.
Do with it as you will. If you like, we will die; if you like
we will go on living—"

Zinatchka would be happy. They would live out there,
at the Deers' Ranch. Old Dmitri would live with them,
and Comrade would mount guard over the black stump
of the old pear tree. Below, where the roads branched,
one toward Tobolsk, the other toward Osov, a Tatar cart
would go jogging along. In the spring the kitchen garden
would be filled with the blue and lavender heads of
kohlrabi, and with green, dewy cabbages. They could
spread their nets beneath the willows of the Irtysh, and
the nets would be filled with pike, with carp, and with
eels. They would have children, too, and life would pass
over them in its flight like the sweet sound of Zinatchka's
guitar.

They would take him to the hospital that afternoon. It
would certainly be the hospital for contagious illnesses.
How easy it would be to escape life now! He need only
change the chart above his bed some night with the chart
of a dead man. Who would pay any attention to that?

How stupid, how feeble, how confused were his
thoughts! Perhaps he would die, too. Yes, that would be
best! Yet was it possible that life might still be beautiful?
The fresh mornings, the golden afternoons, the sweet,
dusky evenings of a new life! Still, it would be better to
die! No, no, he must live!

At three in the afternoon steps sounded in the passage,
and the next moment the men, all very pale, were standing
at the door.

Mezei entered first, and held out his arms to embrace
Peter.

Peter sat up on the bench and pushed him gently away.

"Don't come too near! You can never tell—the
contagion—"

Vedres went to him and kissed him. Tears were rolling
down Szentesi's face. "We'll see each other again in
Budapest," said Csaba hoarsely.

"At Khabarovsk," whispered Hirsch.

Neteneczky didn't go into the room at all; he stood in the passage outside, leaning his head against the wall and sobbing quietly.

"Now stay here quietly, dear Peter," said Mezei. "In half an hour they'll come for you from the hospital."

After which they all left.

Peter went to the window and leaned against it.

He saw the orderlies, dragging the heavy luggage, go out first.

Then, one by one, they disappeared—Mezei, Altmayer, Csaba, Szentesi, Vedres, and last of all Neteneczky.

They didn't see Peter watching them from the window. Neteneczky stopped at the door for a moment, leaned his head against one of the pillars as if he were dizzy, and seemed to be weeping.

Peter turned his face away.

Now he was utterly alone.

The yard seemed dead, plunged in inscrutable silence. Scattered upon the ground beneath the birch trees lay a pile of junk that had been left behind—a dented blue basin, a pair of torn shoes, a rusty jug, and some overturned chairs; a board, warped by heat and cold, where the rain-dimmed inscription "Hungarian Home" was still legible. Farther off, the shaft of the well was visible, rising toward the sky, for they had sold the bucket and the pulley. The leaves of the birch trees were motionless.

As he leaned against the window, looking down into the yard, the sense of the flight of all things, the sense of annihilation, welled up in his heart.

And once more, coming whence he knew not, the beautiful, terrible thought drew near—to take the name of a dead man and by Zinatchka's side to escape again into life. He could see his grave in the military cemetery of Tobolsk. The simple wooden cross—with the words "Peter Takács."

Beneath the cross would rest a nameless dead man— the body of some *moujik*, perhaps—but still that grave would be his—the grave of his former life.

And he would live with Zinatchka at the Deers' Ranch.

But would he live?

He unbuttoned his shirt and stared for a long time at those mysterious little red spots, as if he would have sought in them an answer to the most fearful question in human life.

An hour later a hoarse horn sounded invitingly before the gate of Misery Hotel. It was the ambulance from the contagious diseases hospital.

XIV

It was only seven in the morning, but Miette was already sitting at breakfast in the dining room.

The table was laid for luncheon, exquisitely, bountifully laid, for a unique and solemn occasion—the coming of the guest. A bottle of good wine, clear and sparkling, stood on the table, lifting its tinfoil-wrapped neck proudly above the glasses and plates. There was carefully sliced cold meat on little platters, veal cutlets, ham, a roast duck; there was salad, decorated with the green stars of gherkins and the ovals of hard-boiled eggs. Miette had laid the roasted liver of the duck, in its brown gravy, on a glass plate, for she knew that, served with hot toast, it was one of Peter's favorite dishes. Everything produced the effect of a first-class grocer's window display, yet it was obviously arranged with the utmost care and affection. In order not to disturb the attractive arrangement, Miette had settled herself carefully at one end of the table to drink her tea. The sleepless night was still shadowed in her eyes. Her very movements were languid, as if she had just left her bed after a long illness.

She was wearing a brown dress so dark that it looked almost black, with narrow sleeves that clung to her arms, making her seem slenderer than she was. Above its high collar her face was white as a flower, and her rich russet hair that had gleamed with brilliant tones of gold and bronze by sun and lamplight was lusterless now and dull like brown autumn leaves, and in her face, that had grown a little thinner, her eyes seemed larger, deeper, and darker.

It was gray and gloomy outside, and the room itself was still half dark. In the dim light of that cold, rainy morning, the apartment, stripped of its furniture and rugs, seemed more desolate than ever. One empty corner, where the wallpaper showed the marks left by the vanished furniture, was like a scar on a mutilated limb.

Mili crossed the room, the corner of her apron thrust through her belt, her feet in their shapeless slippers trailing over the floor.

As she passed Miette, she stopped for a moment.

"What time is the train due?" she asked in a low voice.

"At ten," Miette answered. Eyeing the old woman in her hideous felt slippers and thick, grease-stained apron, Miette spoke nervously and querulously, "Fix yourself up a little, Mili!" "Of course, of course!" she answered, a little hurt that Miette should have thought she would welcome Peter in this garb.

Miette went into the other room, sat in an armchair, threw her head back and closed her eyes. She grasped the two arms of the chair, as if it threatened to fly away with her. A mask of pain descended over her tired face.

She rose and walked nervously up and down the room and then sat in the armchair again, feeling more and more desperately that these few hours of waiting would never end.

It seemed to her incredible that she was going to see Peter again; yet with each passing moment he was drawing nearer. In a few months it would be seven years since she had seen him. Once again she went over in her mind the tiniest details of their last moments together; obliterated in spots, still they returned with painful intensity and fantastic accuracy to her memory. It was nine in the evening and they were at the Kelenföld station. The bugle was sounding the tattoo at the end of the long military train. She heard again the men's voices each group singing a different song, the confused roar muffled by seven years of time. She felt Peter crush her once more—for the last time—in his arms as they kissed, their mouths melting into each other.

As she ran with the train, raising her hand to grasp his, she heard him say again, "Look out! You might stumble."

Those had been Peter's last words.

The train was gone and she was alone. She had been twenty-one and married for four months. Peter had been part of her life for only one short year. Before him there had been twenty years, the snow-white fields of memory losing themselves in the infinite distances of her childhood; and after him, these seven years filled with the burning fevers of her youth, during which she had dwelt in the mysterious, shadowy labyrinth of her secret thoughts where the air was heavy with tropical vegetation—in dark green lagoons, whence rose the thick vapor of her desires and the sweet, decaying odor of sensuality.

Yes, seven years had slipped by since then, and now she was sitting here in this ravaged room—ravaged like her life—waiting, her soul vacant, for the moment when she would go to the same station to meet Peter.

He had been twenty-seven when he left, slender and lithe; there had still been something childish about his neck when you looked at him from the back. Now he was over thirty-four; perhaps he was a little bald, or fat, his body heavier—perhaps he had a thick mustache that changed the expression of his face—perhaps the long, unfathomable years were reflected in his face, in his rough hands, in his unkempt nails—perhaps his appearance and his clothes would retain traces of Misery Hotel. And perhaps he had forgotten those little laws of physical cleanliness to which she had grown accustomed with Golgonszky, who carried them indeed to extremes.

What alien world was he bringing back with him—after seven years? The physical life has its own laws, apart from the life of the soul. Poor Peter, sunk to the animal level of mere physical existence—where had he sought, where had he found deliverance for his body in the fearful depths of prison camps, in the human puddles of dirty little cities in Siberia, through the blind alleyways of his long imprisonment? She remembered the newspaper articles she had read, describing the ghastly diseases bred by prison camps. The thought of all this chilled her with horror.

She conjured up the long winter afternoons when Peter had begun calling on her and the room was lighted only by the reflection of the snow and the stove; the overwhelming, boundless excitement of that first kiss as they had stood beside the stove, and she had leaned her forehead against its warm, apple-green tiles; she remembered her wedding night, and the mysterious roar through the small hotel's window at dawn; the golden brown Arno River under the blackish stone bridge; the cab drivers of Florence with their medieval oilcloth top hats; then their sojourn on the shore of Balaton—the swaying of the *Neptune* on the limpid waters, in the light breeze and sunshine. She was trying to rekindle the dead flame of those bygone days—a blaze that was crumbled to ashes—in order to fortify her soul for the moment of meeting, in order to release, beneath the petrified layers of seven years, the spring of gushing tears and ardent cries with which she was preparing to fall into Peter's arms when he jumped from the running board of the train.

She sat there in the chair, clutching its arms convulsively, her head thrown back, her eyes closed, knocking at the door of old memories with fierce, impassioned intensity to create a link between the past and the imminent future. It was as if she were tearing with her nails at the dead fibers, to make them sensitive again, to make them bleed again, so that this blood might restore circulation to her benumbed heart. She tormented herself, she shook and clawed at herself, so as to be able to stir some feeling within her, to be happy, to tremble when they met, so as to be able to carry with her to the station, throbbing, flaming, bleeding, that old love that she had felt seven years before.

But all her self-torment was in vain. She was wounding a corpse; the sluggish blood merely trickled from its open wounds.

She opened her eyes and looked in dismay at the clock.

It was nine already. Hastily she picked up her coat and went to the kitchen.

"Mili," she said, almost shivering, "I'm going to the station; be sure that everything is in order."

Mili, clad in chemise and petticoat, stood in the middle of the kitchen in the process of dressing. The slack, wrinkled skin of her arms and shoulders and her withered old body made a shocking impression upon Miette just then.

Once in the street, she took a cab. On the way to the station she began wondering whether upstairs, in her closet or boxes, there didn't remain some tiny trace of her love for Golgonszky that might by chance betray her some day. She made a careful mental inventory of every nook and corner of the apartment, of the most insignificant objects in her secret drawers and boxes. She had a little tortoise-shell cigarette case and an ivory penholder that he had given her, and from which she had not had the courage to part. She had two explanations ready for these things; one had been given her as a souvenir by the woman from Linz; the other she had bought herself. Now that she was in the cab, nearing the station, she was prey to a devouring anxiety; she regretted with all her heart that she had kept them. She had a feeling that her voice would tremble when she gave Peter those lying explanations, though she had practiced them over and over to herself.

It was a quarter of ten when she left the cab at the East Station. She was surprised and disturbed to find the station ceremoniously decorated to welcome the returning war prisoners. There were policemen, silver helmets on their heads, and an inspector who asked her courteously for her pass, since only members of the prisoners' families were being admitted to that part of the station.

Having shown her pass, she entered the huge glassed-in hall, empty, deserted, filled with a kind of solemn dreariness. The doors of one room that had been turned over to the Association for War Prisoners were draped with the national colors.

A small group stood in front of the door—several

officials, an old general, and an elderly, bearded gentleman in a top hat, whom she recognized as the president of the association. Mme. Brezovits was there, too, with her little boy. When she saw Miette she hurried to meet her.

The little lady was flushed with excitement, and her eyes shone with the consciousness of her own importance in having a leading part to play among these high officials, and a share, as secretary of the association, in organizing the reception.

"Good morning, Madame. Is your husband coming in today?"

"Yes!" Miette's voice was faint as she answered the little woman, whose acquaintance she had made through the association.

She glanced nervously about. A few steps behind her stood a large group composed of members of the returning prisoners' families.

"My husband is coming on the twentieth!" said Mme. Brezovits brightly; then, turning to her son; "Say good morning nicely, Pityu."

Miette had just enough strength to give the child a faint, wan smile.

Mechanically Mme. Brezovits straightened the hat on the child's head, then turned again to Miette; lowering her voice as if to tell her something in confidence, she said, "You remember Mme. Fabian?" And without waiting for an answer, she continued: "That big, blond woman? Don't you remember? She was always coming to the association with her two children. Well! The thing that happened to her last week!"

She drew a step nearer Miette without looking directly at her and began talking quickly, casting uneasy glances about for fear of being interrupted in the midst of her recital.

"The poor woman—she was a quarrelsome person, very unhappy with her marriage—now she didn't know that her husband had married again out there! Of course the rest of us knew it because the prisoners who had already

arrived had told us. But who would have the heart to
break such news? Isn't that so? And then, we didn't
know that his wife would come to the station to meet him.
It was a week ago, and she was here with her two children,
the boy eleven and little Elise nine. The children were
carrying bouquets of flowers in their arms. Oh God, it
breaks my heart to think of it!"

She heaved a profound sigh and was silent, looking
about at the family groups, in whose midst were squeezed
children in holiday attire, carrying flowers. Then she
whispered to Miette: "Who knows, poor people, what the
day has in store for them! Have you heard of the ravages
caused by spotted typhus among the prisoners? Good
Lord, if only they were all back!"

She took the little boy's hand and bade Miette a smiling
goodbye.

Miette's eyes followed her thoughtfully. Now her heart
was pierced anew by the thought she had had once
before, when she had met Mme. Brezovits and her child
for the first time at the association. If she had had a child
she would not be here with her soul torn, her mind
desolate, bearing within her the tomblike silence of a
ruined life. If she were holding the hand of a little
daughter, if she could have put on her little dress that
morning and her little shoes, and could have said to her,
"Do you know what? We're going to meet dear Papa—"
And she actually felt the cool little feet in her hand as she
slipped them feverishly into their snowy socks—she felt
the child's slim little gloved hand in her own right hand—
they would be waiting here at the station—and it was as
if she actually saw the child's face, in which her own
features and Peter's were fused.

Yes, if she had had a child she would now be a clear-
eyed, clean-souled woman, like this pleasant, garrulous
Mme. Brezovits. She, too, would be filled with the
blessed joy of the coming reunion. All the agitation, the
thousand clamors of her body that so often in the course
of these seven years had driven her precipitately from her
bed to the telephone, had compelled her to write fervent

letters to Golgonszky—the ardent murmur of youth, of the blood, of her woman's body that had led her like a sleepwalker that night at St. Hilben to Golgonszky's room—the smothered fires smoldering beneath the ashes —all that devouring blaze would have been transformed by the child into passionate maternal love!

She drew closer to the wall and her distracted eyes strayed among the family groups. There were a hundred to a hundred and twenty people there, men and women, children and graybeards—people who looked like laborers and others whose appearance stamped them as people of quality; a few officers; fathers, mothers, wives, brothers, children. Some of the women wore mourning. Miette heard one of them, turning to an acquaintance, say, "Poor fellow, he doesn't know yet—"

One old woman was being supported under both arms to keep her from swooning. A tall, gray-haired man was twisting his mustache nervously. The people in that group were silent and deeply affected. When they spoke, it was in a murmur of low voices; children gazed about, pale and bright-eyed; great emotion, deep emotion, was apparent on each separate countenance.

A military band marched in and drew up against the wall. Some of the musicians were blowing cautiously, tentatively, into their big pot-bellied horns, and the dim, high, silent glass vault gave back the echoes of those alien little sounds that nested among the steel girders above like strange birds flown from their cages.

The black hand of the huge station clock drew slowly— its jerking plainly visible—toward the hour.

Next moment, one of the upper station employees passed along the platform and, adjusting his arm badge with the easy, mechanical movement of long habit, spoke to the old gentleman in the top hat in a voice loud enough for everyone to hear.

"Mr. President, the train is coming in."

The effect of those words was indescribable. The family groups were suddenly galvanized into motion, a wave of fearful excitement broke over the crowd, and there was a general forward movement. Blanching faces, wide-open, staring eyes turned toward the great crystal dome where the train would pull in, and on whose damply glistening rails a gentle drizzle was now falling.

The policeman and a number of officials wearing arm bands were holding back the thronging crowd with soothing, sympathetic words.

"Stand back a little, please! A little patience, if you please."

The bandmaster took his place in front of the musicians and raised his baton, and slowly, solemnly the music of the national hymn rang out, the notes of the bugles and, clarinets filling the glass dome with their echoes. At the sound of the music that seemed to unnerve them completely, a strange frenzy seized upon the crowd. Women's cries could be heard, long-drawn-out words pronounced as if in a trance, piercing the music; great, strangling sobs, the hysterical screams of weak childish voices, across which the music tried vainly to spread the golden, sonorous veil of the hymn. They pierced it as the blood of a man covered with wounds, writhing in agony, soaks the sheet covering him.

A few hours earlier, sitting like a ghost in an armchair in her lonely bedroom, in the gray light of a misty morning, Miette had striven in vain to revive her feelings and her memories; but now that she was here, in the midst of the vibrating music and the heartrending cries of these people, her heart opened of itself and all her memories of Peter flooded her soul.

She leaned against the wall, as if some force from without had flung her there; she bit her brown glove and, swept away by the terrific storm of emotion surrounding her, she, too, sobbed aloud.

A moment later the huge black breast of the noisily puffing locomotive turned the curve, as if dead with fatigue, it seemed to be making a final dragging effort to jerk the train, like some frightful, fantastic burden, into the hall behind it.

Then the train stopped. On the running boards and at

the windows the returning prisoners stared out, all shockingly pale, enveloped in an air of remoteness. In many faces the corners of the mouths drooped and tears flowed from the staring eyes. The waiting groups had broken through the guard. The band was still playing, but the roar of the crowd, multiplied by the glass roof, swept away and prevailed over everything. Men and women milled on the running boards of the train and a mad racing began, hither and yon, from one car to another. They shouted to one another, waving their arms toward the carriage windows, and in the midst of the tumult a young woman's piercing cry could be heard distinctly: "Franci! Franci! I'm here!"

Miette was dragged along by the hurtling crowd, unaware in its passionate frenzy of what it was doing. The prisoners jumped from the train, one after another, dragging their tattered knapsacks and their little trunks, as if fleeing a fire that had suddenly broken out in the compartments. One after another Vedres, Mezei, Hirsch, and Csaba jumped down from the train. Altmayer had got out at Vienna; Neteneczky and Szentesi had stopped at Győr.

Csaba held Tatiana by the arm; pale and moved, she gazed at these people who passed her as if borne along by a whirlwind. They all disappeared in the crowd. Not one of them suspected that the pretty woman in the dark brown suit was the wife of Peter Takács.

Miette was standing by the train, wringing her hands and weeping aloud. Terrified, her eyes darted swiftly from the face of one prisoner to the next, seeking to recognize Peter in each. Beside her, the old woman whom two people were supporting had both her arms clasped about someone whose head alone was visible, and that head, grotesquely shaken by sobs, was being stroked by another hand. A few steps farther away, near a column, a woman in mourning was telling a prisoner something. He was a young man with a thin, blond little mustache, his face overcast by an almost greenish pallor. He flung himself against the column, beating his forehead with heavy, resounding strokes of the palm, all but screaming in his grief.

"Why didn't you write me? And I thought all the time she would meet me at the station—"

An official rushed to him and took him by the arm. He staggered as he was led away, and his head drooped on his breast.

The band stopped playing. The crowd was gradually dispersing; Miette ran, stumbling over the luggage piled up on the platform, from one car to the next. Tripping against a trunk, she fell to one knee, and had barely enough strength to pick herself up. Breathless, she began running again, calling toward the windows of the empty train.

"Peter! Peter!"

She ran thus along the whole length of the train, and when she retraced her steps the platform was already deserted. But still she ran about, calling beneath all the empty windows.

Just then a captain approached her, saluted, and said gently, "I am Captain Szilvássy. Are you waiting for someone, Madame?"

"My husband," Miette answered, her lips trembling.

"May I ask his name?"

"Peter Takács."

"What rank?"

"Lieutenant."

"Will you wait a moment?"

He went back to the officers' group and said something to them. They looked over their shoulders at Miette, then turned round again and consulted together. Miette knew they were speaking of her.

The captain returned a moment later. He smiled and spoke very gently.

"Please—will you be kind enough to come to the office?"

He drew back to let her pass and walked behind her, half stretching his arm toward her so that he seemed to be supporting her without really touching her.

Meantime the officials had returned to the office. When Miette entered with the captain they all rose. The president was there, too, standing near the wall, turning his top hat nervously between his hands.

Miette looked with aversion at the people and the objects in the room. The manner of her entry, her expression as she stopped in front of the table, the captain behind her, her appearance, and indeed the whole situation produced somehow the effect of a woman before a tribunal that was about to pass judgment upon her. All eyes were focused upon her.

A colonel was standing behind the table, leaning on his two fists, his body inclined courteously forward.

"Have you received no notice, Madame?"

"What notice?" Miette asked, a shudder of apprehension in her voice.

The colonel didn't answer. The others exchanged furtive glances.

"We received a telegram from Russia last night." The colonel spoke hesitantly, and again fell silent. Miette looked about, her eyes suspicious, their expression shockingly changed. A silence so deep reigned in the room that the asthmatic old general's breathing could be heard. When the silence had grown insupportable and, to Miette, maddening, the colonel took a few steps toward her and, resting the hand that held his plumed cap lightly on the table, he said in a very low voice, "Madame, your husband is dead—"

A moment's deathlike silence settled upon the room; then Miette uttered a bloodcurdling shriek, as if a knife had been plunged into her heart. With that shriek she collapsed, striking her head sharply against the flat edge of the table as she fell, and dragging Captain Szilvássy, who had seized her to hold her up, down on one knee beside her.

They put her on a couch and sent for a doctor. She soon recovered consciousness. The president and the colonel took her back to the apartment, and the doctor stayed with her for a while.

She sat in an armchair in the living room. Her neck was thrust forward in a curious, unnatural pose, and she stared into space with unblinking eyes. She didn't answer when she was addressed. The doctor tiptoed out of the room and told Mili that there was no danger—that all she needed was rest.

Mili sat in the dining room near the stove and wept softly, noiselessly, pressing her gnarled fingers to her trembling, toothless mouth. Now and then she would glance warily into the next room. Miette was still there, unmoving, in the armchair.

In the dining room the table stood untouched, with the bottle of wine in the center, its fastidiously arranged meats, its carefully laid silver—a living thought clinging to each object. That untouched, masterless table was itself like a dead man. It produced the effect of a strange catafalque.

Toward one o'clock Mili entered the living room and touched the armchair tenderly.

"Shall I bring your soup in here?"

Miette didn't answer. She only shook her head slowly to tell Mili that she needed nothing.

The hours passed and still Miette sat in the armchair, speechless, motionless, shattered by grief.

XV

Five years had passed since that rainy May morning when the train carrying the war prisoners had arrived at the East Station.

And now it was springtime again—a beautiful, radiant May.

An automobile stood waiting before Golgonszky's house. The huge English car was amply provided with spare tires and heavy trunks, and the seats were heaped with handsome lap robes and dusters. It was evident that the car had been made ready for a long journey.

It was eight in the morning. The May sun, piercing the

foliage of the Indian chestnut trees, scattered in flecks of green and gold on the ground

A valet and a maid emerged from the house and placed some small traveling bags in the car. Then they took their stand beside it, to see it off.

Finally Miette and Golgonszky appeared. Miette's body had grown a little fuller in the course of the past five years. She was wearing a long traveling coat, and a mauve veil was fastened to her hat.

A nurse came out of the house with two children. She held little Ivan, who was three, by the hand, and carried little Mari on her arm. Ivan looked like his father, and Mari, with large green eyes and dark golden hair, like Miette. Before getting into the car, Miette and Golgonszky kissed the children once more. There were traces of deep emotion on Miette's face.

The valet gave a last look at the luggage, and said to the chauffeur, "Is His Excellency's bag there?"

Golgonszky was now minister plenipotentiary.

A second valet whom they were taking with them was seated beside the chauffeur. When they had all taken their places in the car, little Mari, who was not quite a year old, stretched her tiny arms toward them. Her diminutive cherry-red mouth puckered into a little pout and a big tear slipped from beneath her eyelid. She began to cry and her crying was like the frail note of a whistle softly blown.

They waved goodbye to the children and the servants, then the big car leaped lightly forward and rolled through the gate.

Miette had been urging this journey upon Golgonszky for two years. When she had become a widow—and knew that Golgonszky would marry her—she felt there were two things she must do.

One of them was to reconstruct Johnny's life. She made inquiries and learned the name of the girl who had nursed him in the hospital and with whom he was in love.

Her name was Helen, and she was the daughter of a postal official. Miette easily found an opportunity to make her acquaintance. Then she invited her to her home several times and little by little made a friend of her. Helen was a simple, friendly creature who was flattered by her admission into so brilliant a circle.

Miette never mentioned Johnny's name to her. She knew that Helen would speak of him one day herself. Didn't they sit together for whole afternoons over their embroidery, reviving memories of other days?

Helen told her, as if it were a long-forgotten, unimportant story, that during the war she had become acquainted at the hospital with a wounded lieutenant to whom she had more or less engaged herself. But when the dressing on the young man's face had been removed and she saw that one side was disfigured forever, she had broken the engagement.

Miette dropped her work on her lap, gave Helen a long look, and said, "That was a frightful thing to do!"

And from then on it was not difficult to turn the girl's heart toward Johnny.

It was Miette, too, who found a position for Johnny, though he never knew it. Helen had been Johnny's wife for two years now but Miette had not seen him again.

Her other gnawing, melancholy desire was to visit Peter's grave. She wanted only to walk through the streets of Tobolsk, to see the old Siberian city that her imagination had so often assailed in vain, where Peter's life had vanished into nothingness.

She wanted only to stand for a moment at Peter's grave and leave some flowers there.

Golgonszky understood this wish of Miette's. He had spent some years in Russia before the war, and he had influential connections; but the journey would have been hazardous even for him in those first years, and he had tried to dissuade Miette from the idea.

But now that German scholars, French journalists, and English businessmen had, one after the other, penetrated flaming Russia, Miette would no longer postpone the trip.

"This year we will go not to Nice but to Tobolsk!" she said to her husband.

Golgonszky offered no further objections. He made various applications, procured the necessary papers and passports, and they started out.

They had been traveling for six days now. Miette bore uncomplainingly with the wretchedness of provincial hotels, first in Poland, then in Russia, feeling all the while a kind of melancholy happiness in the experience.

They decided to visit Alexander Petrovitch Ilyin on the way, the engineer at whose brother-in-law's house Peter and his companions had stopped on their journey toward Asia.

After the peace had been signed, he had succeeded in reentering Russia, and at long intervals he and Miette had exchanged letters. Those of the Russian engineer, overflowing with gratitude, always referred to Miette as the greatest benefactress of his life.

They reached Serjebinsk one afternoon, weary from the constant shaking on the bad roads. They immediately discovered the house of Dr. Nicolai Krylov opposite the church, with its two black poplars in front of the wrought-iron gate that bore a copper plate with the words: Zemski Vratch.

Katerina Ilyina was at the window and, seeing the travelers, thought they had come to fetch her brother to the bedside of some patient. So she didn't go to meet them, merely peeping out from behind the curtains to watch the doctor receive them. But when she heard them asking for her husband, she ran out, terror-stricken.

"Ilyin? Ilyin has been in Moscow for a fortnight. What do you want to see him about?"

Miette introduced herself.

Katerina Ilyina clapped her hands together, her eyes filled with tears, and she began kissing Miette's shoulder and her clothes.

"Oh, my God! Oh, my God!" she kept saying, as she stroked first Miette's arm, then Golgonszky's.

"You come from Hungary! Oh, Hungary!"

She led them into the living room, so overwhelmed with joy that she had difficulty in regaining her composure.

"If Ilyin knew this! Oh, if he only knew!"

She disappeared and shortly thereafter the table in the adjoining room was laid with a meal of tea and cream, of cold fowl and honeycakes, exactly as it had been eleven years before when the Hungarian officers had stopped there for a brief hour on their journey eastward.

Meantime the doctor was talking with his guests in broken German, telling them that his brother-in-law had gone to look for work in Moscow; he had been able to find nothing to do since his return.

They sat down at the table and began talking of Hungary. The conversation was interrupted by frequent emotional outbursts, when Nicolai Ivanovitch Krylov would gaze at the center of his plate exactly as he had done eleven years before.

He and Golgonszky remained at the table while Katerina Ilyina took Miette into the living room and gave her a detailed description of the scene that had taken place between her and Peter when he had told her of his plan to escape. She stretched out her arm, seeking to revive those long-dead moments.

"He stood right there, by the piano—I shall never forget the expression on his face . . ."

Miette crushed her handkerchief to her eyes, and they both wept in silence.

Katerina Ilyina wanted them to spend the night, but Miette could not be persuaded to remain.

A half hour later they were on their way again.

They passed through wretched little Russian villages, leaving behind them, one by one, Tjebinsk, Gurgan, Vetjous, Kavlovsk, Izram, and countless others. Golgonszky was always deep in the road maps spread on his knees, while Miette, her eyes closed, abandoned herself to her thoughts.

Two days later they crossed the Volga and reached the ferry house at the Chivaga River, and next day they were ascending the Irtysh.

It was nearly six in the evening when, slowly folding up

the map on his knees, Golgonszky said in a low voice, "We are nearing Tobolsk now—"

Miette was white.

The car slowed down and stopped uncertainly at the crossroads. One road led up along the slope of the hill, while the other went down through the birch woods. The chauffeur turned. "Right or left, sir?"

Golgonszky consulted the map but couldn't quite get his bearings. He left the car to look for someone who could direct him, since the chauffeur spoke no Russian.

A little whitewashed house with a peaked wooden roof and small windows stood a hundred feet from the road. In front of it rose an old pear tree, its dark trunk rosy in the afternoon sunlight. The front of the house was covered with crimson ramblers.

It was the Deers' Ranch.

Zinatchka, a bucket in her hand, was about to enter the house when she caught sight of the car. She stopped on the threshold and, turning, looked down over her shoulder.

In the yard a little boy, scarcely able to walk, was toddling unsteadily about. He was amusing himself by digging both hands into the hair of a large white dog that he was trying with all his might to push forward. Comrade would cast an occasional backward glance of reproach at the child, and plump himself down on the ground. But soon he would be up again, submitting once more to the exigencies of the game.

Old Dmitri sat by the wall, weaving a little reed mat with shaking, awkward fingers.

Golgonszky walked toward the house.

Leaning against the hedge of the yard stood a booted man who must have been the owner of the little place. His face was framed in a dark brown beard, and he wore the light blue blouse of the Little Russians.

Golgonszky halted a few steps away and asked: "Can you tell me which is the road to Tobolsk?"

The man pointed.

"To the left for Tobolsk; to the right for Osov."

"And where is the military cemetery?"

"Here—behind the hill!"

Golgonszky raised his cap and turned away.

The man saw the woman in the car on the road below, her face hidden by a mauve veil, bow her head a number of times in acknowledgment of his courteous information. His eyes followed them up the hill. He supposed they were distinguished travelers from Kasan or from the vicinity of Baikal, since the gentleman spoke Russian with the accent of another part of the country.

The car climbed the little hill and disappeared over the crest.

Only a cloud of golden dust was left behind them, flooded with the soft light of the setting sun.

The cloud of dust hung motionless for a moment in the sun's rays—then, yielding to the light breeze, disappeared over the bare, limitless Siberian plains.

THE END